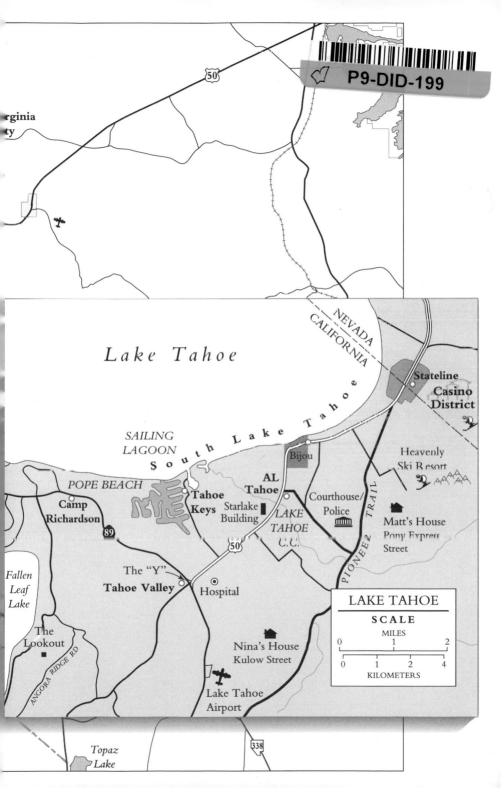

P9-DID-199

Lake Tahoe

NEVADA
CALIFORNIA

South Lake Tahoe

Stateline
Casino
District

SAILING
LAGOON

Bijou

Heavenly
Ski Resort

POPE BEACH

Tahoe
Keys

AL
Tahoe

Starlake
Building

Courthouse/
Police

Matt's House
Pony Express
Street

Camp
Richardson

89

LAKE
TAHOE
C.C.

50

Fallen
Leaf
Lake

The "Y"
Tahoe Valley

Hospital

LAKE TAHOE

SCALE

MILES

0   1   2

0   1   2   4
KILOMETERS

The
Lookout

Nina's House
Kulow Street

Lake Tahoe
Airport

Topaz
Lake

NV
338

WRIT OF EXECUTION

ALSO BY PERRI O'SHAUGHNESSY

Motion to Suppress
Invasion of Privacy
Obstruction of Justice
Breach of Promise
Acts of Malice
Move to Strike

PERRI O'SHAUGHNESSY

WRIT
OF
EXECUTION

DELACORTE PRESS

Published by
DELACORTE PRESS
Random House, Inc.
1540 Broadway
New York, New York 10036

This novel is a work of fiction. Names, characters, places, and incidents
either are the product of the author's imagination or are used
fictitiously. Any resemblance to actual persons, living or dead, events,
or locales is entirely coincidental.

ISBN 0-385-33483-4

Book design by Glen M. Edelstein

Manufactured in the United States of America

DEDICATION

To Our Teachers:

Lucille Garrard, HJH; Miss Balsam, CES; Paul Ruud, Bertha Sheets, Mr. Ney, and Mr. Aranguren, CHS; Alan Dershowitz, Diane Lund, and Lawrence Tribe, HLS.

Maureen Linder and Edna Rappaport, RUHS; Helen Chuvarsky, Carolyn Copenhaver, Gerhard Koehn, Ray Pharr, Mr. Locke and Mr. Shook, VHS; Kenneth Rexroth, UCSB.

A special tip o' the hat to Mrs. Dora Polk and Mr. Ctvrtlik, LBSU, who taught both of us Writing and Russian.

And to all the other teachers along the way: thank you.

It's a strange thing, I haven't won yet, but I feel and think like a rich man and can't imagine being anything else.

Dostoyevsky, *The Gambler*

Yet the ear distinctly tells,
In the jangling,
And the wrangling,
How the danger sinks and swells,
By the sinking or the swelling in the anger of the bells—
Of the bells—
Of the bells, bells, bells, bells,
Bells, bells, bells—
In the clamor and the clanging of the bells!

Edgar Allan Poe, "The Bells"

ACKNOWLEDGMENTS

We gratefully acknowledge the no-nonsense, very capable editing of Danielle Perez, Senior Editor at Bantam Dell. Irwyn Applebaum, our hardworking publisher at Bantam Dell, has given us much-appreciated encouragement as well as strong support. We also very much appreciate the support and assistance of Nita Taublib, Deputy Publisher of Bantam Dell. We have benefited greatly from our association with these fine people.

Also at Bantam Dell, we appreciate the support and help of the talented people in the Design, Publicity, and Marketing Departments. We especially thank Glen Edelstein of Bantam Dell and Fred Haynes of Hadel Studio Incorporated, who helped design the Tahoe map in this book.

Grateful thanks as always to Nancy Yost, our agent at Lowenstein Associates, Inc., for her vision, conscientiousness, intelligence, and sense of humor.

Thanks to our brother Patrick O'Shaughnessy, Esq., of Rucka O'Boyle Lombardo and McKenna in Salinas, California, for help with the plot and characters.

We would like to acknowledge the Washoe tribe of Nevada and California and the fine people of Tahoe for providing ongoing inspiration for our books.

We thank Auston Stewart for his help with arcane computer lore, and Ann Walker for help with research.

For help with one of the characters, we read *The Psychology of Gambling* by Edmund Bergler, M.D., International Universities Press, copyright 1958, 1970. Fyodor Dostoyevsky's *The Gambler* also had a thing or two to teach us.

For Tahoe news we read the *Nevada Appeal, Tahoe Daily Tribune, The Record-Courier,* and *North Lake Tahoe Bonanza* online. We especially thank Geoff Dornan, a reporter for the *Nevada Appeal,* for his reporting on the gaming industry. For medical research we went online to various articles in the *New England Journal of Medicine.*

We appreciate so much the love and support of Brad, Andy, June, Connor, and Corianna. And thanks to Peter, for sending the first e-mail.

WRIT OF
EXECUTION

1

KENNY DUMPED THE LEASED BLACK Lexus in the parking lot at Prize's Lake Tahoe casino at precisely ten P.M. on July fifteenth. Sunday night, Milky Way spilling over the black mountain ridge in a sixty-degree arc, no sleep for thirty hours.

He had driven into the Sierra from Silicon Valley, festering in hundred-degree heat, without stopping. At an altitude of over six thousand feet, South Lake Tahoe had a different microclimate, much cooler and drier. He could see the ghostly reflections of old snow pockets on the mountains looming over the casino district. As he climbed out of the car, stuffing his pockets with the few things he intended to take with him, he began to shiver.

Pulling nonessentials from his wallet and leaving them on the seat, he slid the worthless credit cards and the two thousand in cash into the pocket of his black silk sport coat.

He opened the glove compartment. The Glock gleamed in there.

He pushed his specs up on his nose and stashed the gun in the inner pocket of his jacket. Money and a gun. So all-American.

Prize's would be his last stop. This had not been his original intention, but a decision had hardened in his mind as he drove up to the mountains. That morning, before his courage fled, he thought, I will tell them, and then I will spend the rest of my life making it up to them. I will be a kitchen boy. I will hire myself out for road construction. Anything. Somehow I will save them from what I did.

But as he drove alongside the surging American River, the idea of going to his parents with the news of his colossal failure began to seem pointless. He couldn't save them, and he didn't have the guts to face them.

They would find out soon enough.

The Five Happinesses restaurant would be sold first. He had worked at his family's Tahoe restaurant from the time he was eight years old, chopping vegetables and packing rice into small porcelain bowls, doing his homework in the back room with the Taiwanese news on the TV.

Then the frame house where his mother swept the porch each morning before going to the restaurant to cook, where he and his brother and sister had grown up, would have to go. He had ruined them all with his—his overconfidence! his cockiness! The big visionary with the big ideas! If only he had died at birth and saved his parents the misery of his life. His brother, Tan-Mo, stoic, solid, and destined for all the traditional successes, was in his second year at Stanford Med. Now Kenny had destroyed his life, too.

"I saved for thirty years, Tan-Kwo," Kenny's father had told him, using his Chinese name. "All consolidated. Savings, pension money, a loan against the restaurant fixtures." He had waved the check at Kenny while his mother watched, eyes watery, face perspiring above a boiling pot at the restaurant. Colleen, younger than her brothers by several years, had clicked away on her Nikon. "One, two, three, smile," she said. It was his parents' twenty-ninth anniversary.

Mr. Know-It-All, Mr. Brilliant Future, a shit-eating grin on his face, held out one hand for the check, shaking his father's hand with the other, a moment immortalized on Kodak paper in a steamy haze of bright colors that would never fade.

Four hundred fifty-seven thousand dollars. Years of hot summer days spent sweltering in the kitchen at the Five Happinesses, years of holidays skipped, luxuries scrimped, and birthdays ignored. He had taken away their past and their future. He had squandered it all.

"Your father believes in you, Tan-Kwo. I know how much that means to you. But . . . what is this thing? This cityofgolddotcom?" his mother had asked him later that night.

"Just the City of Gold, Mom. The dotcom is only an address." In a fever of excitement about the check, his mind darting like a cursor around a thousand new possibilities now open to him, he had tried to explain.

"Sounds like dreams," she said when he finished.

She was so right.

But he had been convinced the money would roll in. The City of Gold was the next step for the Net—the step into beauty and poetry, like putting modern art up in a concrete bunker to make it livable and gladden the spirit. He should have known. The techies who ran the Net were too used to the industrial, minimalist look. The City of Gold was too lush a paradigm, too lyrical . . . too beautiful. . . .

Yesterday, for the first time since that day in the restaurant kitchen with his family, he had awakened from his dream. There was no more money. The venture capitalists he approached on Sand Hill Road talked to their experts, who said he was overreaching. Eyes fixated on his Palm Pilot, Jerry Casper of Wildt Ventures had said, "It's not like it was, where all you had to do was stumble over a sprinkler in this neighborhood to get your funding. We need to see a definite path, a rapid advance toward profitability."

The City of Gold would attract lawsuits, Casper claimed. And besides, Bill Gates and Steve Jobs had the basic platforms sewed up for the next century. They were sexing up Windows and OS X, but the files and the drop downs would stay. And the rebel companies using Linux weren't going to risk good money for a radical paradigm shift that would have to be marketed intensely because it was so novel.

Kenny leaned his head back and looked up at the brightly lit twenty-story hotel and casino. He could smell the tang of the deep mysterious lake somewhere out there in the darkness.

Like a man under water who finally gives in and floods his lungs, he took a deep, ragged breath and pushed open the glass door to the casino.

Inside, flashing lights, gleaming metal, a low roar of voices punctuated by short blasts of ringing, and a feeling of entering a different universe where there are no clocks and no one ever sleeps. Slot machines squatted in long rows, and tourists cruised up and down the aisles or sat on stools pushing buttons. He joined the flow of people, looking for a dollar slot machine. It was important to him to pick the right one. Three reels only, a classic. Dollars, because he knew that by putting three in at a time he would be broke within two hours and in the right frame of mind to use his credit card one last time to check into a room.

And then—finis!

He had a mathematical vision of bracketed sets folding inward from infinity down to a single point. Himself, no longer quantifiable.

The casino would clean up after him. Hotel rooms were popular places to die. Broke tourists did it up here on a regular basis. Even though the windows in the rooms probably didn't open wide enough to allow impetuous jumps, there were options everywhere—the terry cloth bathrobe belts, the glass from a broken coffeemaker. . . .

The Glock would be easy and fast. He would think of a way to minimize the splatter of the brains which were the cause of this entire intolerable situation.

Kenny passed a group of blackjack tables and the craps table, where a crowd had gathered around and the stickman was hooking the dice. He could lose it faster there, but he wanted two more hours to acclimate himself to the notion of death and to prepare himself for his ignoble end. Let a slot machine decide how close his estimate came.

Ah. He spotted a bank of dollar slots called the Greed Machines. He walked closer, observing their rhythms. The Greed Machines spoke to him. Win, lose, die—very simple.

The logos on the reels of the Greed Machine were gold bars and dollar signs and little brown banks. He found an empty seat between a girl in a wheelchair on the left end of the aisle and a white-haired man wearing a denim shirt whose skinny rear was planted firmly on his stool on the right. Kenny pulled out the stool and crowded in with them. He liked being wedged between two human beings. Utter strangers, they still comforted him with their bodies, their single-minded joint pursuit. Piglets and puppies rooting together at the mother's teats must feel that same primitive comfort. Udder strangers! It reminded him of nights long ago when he and his brother slept together in the same bed.

He cast sidelong glances at his neighbors, fixing them in his mind— her asthmatic breathing, the sour odor of house drinks he emitted. They were important people, among the last he would ever see.

He inserted a hundred-dollar bill into the slot and the credit window blinked back "100 credits." He jabbed the Play Max Credits button and the reels began to fly.

In two minutes he blew the first hundred without registering a single gold bar, much less a bank.

Another hundred-dollar bill. He pressed, watched the reels blur, and saw that he had lost. He pressed again. He fell into a rhythm of steady losing, broken now and again by a cherry which gave him back six credits or a set of mismatched bars which gave him fifteen. The trend was rapidly downward, about one hit per twelve to fourteen plays. He'd expected that. Prize's was reputed to have the tightest slots at Tahoe.

His company had lost money in a similarly jerky but inexorable fashion over the past nine months. Heady days, when he and his temps sent out prospectuses and brochures and labored over the GUI, morphed into jittery all-nighters, when he fed himself on the illusion that all he had to do was work his hardest and success would come. He lived and breathed in the City of Gold those nights until, incoherent with exhaustion, he slept, a cool blue screen saver his night-light.

He was losing fast. He put in another hundred while he stepped up the self-flagellation. He was stalling. If he wasn't such a coward he'd go upstairs right now and . . .

He didn't. The Glock pressed against his chest under the jacket. The stifling casino air smelled as rank as his freezer back at the condo in Mountain View, and the place was hot, but he couldn't take off his jacket, so he sweated.

The girl next to him talked to her machine, coaxing it. She lost faster than he did, but never lost the hopeful upward curve of her lips. Three small silver rings looped through each ear. Her dark hair was pulled sternly back from a wide, pale forehead. Every few minutes a biker-type Kenny took to be her boyfriend arrived to pass her a few twenties. She paid him with bright eyes and a big smile, like, Isn't this grand? And he'd pat her hand and wander off again to wherever he had chosen to unload his share.

She seemed to be fine above the waist, nothing wrong with her arms or her neck, but the legs beneath a long cotton print skirt never moved. She couldn't ski or hike, but she could gamble and be part of something, until the money was gone, anyway.

She would have loved the City of Gold. Kenny's software had been made for her. She couldn't walk, but she could have flown.

At this thought, which reminded him of how much he loved the City of Gold, Kenny's throat closed up and his eyes got so watery he had to take off the gold-rimmed specs and rub them on his sleeve.

He couldn't live without the City of Gold to work on, to play with, to believe in. For three years he had built it, slaved over it like Ramses' architect, every moment since he had graduated from M.I.T.'s master's program in computer science. The City would never exist. He would never have a better idea, never again have the passion and strength he had put into the City.

"Having a good time?" the girl said to him.

"Uh."

She gave him a sympathetic look. "It's just for fun."

"Fun. Yeah."

The cocktail waitress came around again and gave Kenny his Budweiser. The girl in the wheelchair was such a nice girl, a quiet girl, with a friendly mouth that would never say the cruel things he deserved. He felt a sudden urgent desire to spill his guts to this girl who unwittingly represented all humanity to him at this moment, but she was at it again, eyes stapled to her machine, so he slurped down some of the Bud instead. No sense ruining her night.

He was on beer three, and while successive beers did not taste better, the alcohol tingled through his arms and legs. Because he gave her five dollars each time she appeared with a fresh glass, the waitress kept him sharp on her radar. She hovered nearby, off to the right, ready to dip toward him at a nod. He angled his peripheral vision to include her black stockings.

He had hoped drinking copious amounts would dull the fear that lanced his stomach every time he thought about what he was going to do, but it had the opposite effect. His senses became hyperacute. Sounds shrilled. The fabric of his jacket scratched. The colored lights pierced his optic nerves. The alley of shiny machines he sat in resonated with deep meanings, alluring and significant, all heaven and hell present in its seated figures.

The guy with the white hair on his right hit something, not a big hit, but the light above his machine flashed and twirled. Three gold bars—thirty credits with three dollars in.

"All right!" Kenny said, desperate for distraction.

The man showed no sign of pleasure. He hadn't even looked at the Credits Won display. He was watching the numbers gyrate on the marquee above them as people in four states pumped dollar tokens into Greed Machines. Kenny saw that he had whipped out a notepad in which he wrote with a freckled hand. He tucked it back into his shirt, snarling, "What are you lookin' at?"

Kenny felt a stupid smile form. He tried to stop it, but he had the habit of being inoffensive. He turned away, back to the business of rocketing toward oblivion. The man would be as flat as he was soon enough. The odds of winning on a slot machine were ridiculously low, especially on a progressive.

Suicidal odds.

Time passed and Kenny's world compressed. He was immune to the seductions that had been built into the slot machine, the bright logos flashing by, the ringing on occasional hits. His whole body vibrated with a fierce, growing fright as he punched the button, watched the reels spin much too quickly, saw them slam to a stop on—nothing, over and over. He tried not to calculate the speed at which he was losing, the percentage of the return, but he had the calculation habit, and the numbers marched through his head.

He ignored his watch. The machine would let him live as long as his destiny allowed. Then, one moment soon, he would reach into his pocket and find it empty. It would be time to go upstairs.

He considered burial arrangements. He would leave a note with instructions. His father was a Presbyterian, his mother a Buddhist. Go with the Buddhists, he decided. Better chance postmortem with them.

No nonsense about hell, just another rebirth. Maybe he would come back as a roach. A large, insensitive, unkillable, hard-carapaced cockroach like the ones in his dorm in Cambridge, scuttling at midnight around his PC, ignorant that the warm machine was imagining a new universe . . .

At least he would not experience again the humiliation of being a Chinese-American whiz kid flunking out of Silicon Valley.

Yeah, go with the Buddhists. He already felt like a cockroach anyway.

Kenny gulped down another Bud and motioned to the waitress. He wasn't a good drinker. The room swirled slightly, but the lights and the numbers sharpened as the acuity of his vision steadily improved. His neighbor on the right was also drinking beer, playing mechanically, cheekbones jutting like Ping-Pong balls above the long angular slope of jaw, big white flipper-fingers jabbing at the button. His eyelashes were colorless, as if they had been attacked by some toxic plant mold. When he won a small payout, instead of seeming pleased, he waited impatiently until he could push the button again. He was a character out of an Ingmar Bergman film, emaciated and driven.

The girl on Kenny's left drank bourbon and soda, laughing to herself as her bell jangled. Thirty credits! When she saw Kenny had noticed, she gave him a wink and a thumbs-up.

At least they all had a buzz on. He liked her attitude. Too bad he couldn't be like her, playing for fun, without a care in the world. . . .

The absurdity of that thought hit him hard. She couldn't walk. And then a bruising thump of fear brought him back to his own situation as he took out a bill and his hand registered the sinister thinness of his bankroll.

He was spending the last two thousand of his parents' life savings. His failure had to be absolute.

The biker boyfriend came back. The smiles back and forth were tentative now, a little ritualized. Like, we *are* having a good time, aren't we? This time he didn't seem to have any money to give the girl. They consulted, heads together, his goateed chin bent over her.

She nodded and pressed the cashout button, but nothing clanked into the bin. Her friend appeared much older than she was, from what Kenny could discern under the baseball cap, and had to be sweating in the zipped leather motorcycle jacket.

Kenny groped around in his pocket. He had two of the hundred-dollar bills left.

The biker got behind her wheelchair and started pushing the girl away, but he looked back one more time, toward Flipper-fingers, who had just hit bar bar bar, giving him two hundred thirty dollars' credit.

"I'll be watching you," he said to Flipper-fingers.

"Good-bye," Kenny said, but the girl was rolled away before she could answer. Kenny watched her go, and now he felt an overarching drunken Buddhist compassion for all of them, all the dreamers and schemers and six-time losers on a wheel of life that crushed so many and took so few to the heights.

"Hey, mate," Flipper-fingers said suddenly. "Wanna make some fast money?"

2

NEAR MIDNIGHT, INSIDE HIS SHADOWY sixteenth-floor hotel room at Caesars, Nina dropped her coat onto the rug and stood in front of Paul, naked.

Mountain silhouettes and a crescent moon filled the window. The remains of Paul's dinner littered the table under it. The rumpled bed told her that he had jumped out of it to answer the door.

She had come late. She wanted to surprise him.

Paul stared at her breasts, which caused her to pull back her shoulders, which made them stick out just a little bit more. She pulled in her stomach, raised her chin. Let him stare.

He swallowed.

A Mexican standoff. They were both pointed at each other, so to speak.

Nina said not a word. Many months had passed since she had been with Paul, and she wanted to make this memorable. She owed Paul her life, her son's life, even her love, at least for tonight. A grateful, mindless impulse had driven her here. She wanted to be with him and only him.

The bedside light barely touched them as they stood by the table and her empty glass. Her chest was warm with the whiskey. Her cheeks flamed. She felt reckless and brave. Sexy.

A few moments passed. Nina wet her lips.

Without taking his eyes off her, Paul put his drink on the table. He squinted as though the view was too much.

She put her hands on her hips and grinned at him. When even that didn't jolt Paul out of his paralysis, she stuck her tongue out at him, widened her eyes, and made a face.

"Why, you wanton little minx," Paul said. He bounded over like a lion and seized her by the shoulders. She looked into his eyes and knew he was off balance. She liked that. She wanted him unsure and hot as hell.

Then he pulled her to him hard and she felt his whole strong length against her, the hardness and the heat.

They fell back onto the bed, she on top, lips locked to his. Paul's kisses were devouring, overwhelming. He was much larger and stronger than she remembered, a physical animal now hugely aroused.

She reached for the waistband of his shorts and his right hand moved down her back and began caressing her rear. Now she had the shorts halfway down and she let her fingers move in on him. No underwear, he hadn't had time. . . .

"Ah," he said, his eyes closing as she touched him.

He rolled her over onto her back, jumped off the bed, and dropped the shorts. He was hairy for a blond man, muscular. His haunches were hollowed at the hip joints. His skin glowed like gold. He breathed hard, as if he had been chasing something for a long, long time. . . .

"You are going to get it good for surprising me like that," he said. "Right now."

She bit her lip. "That's the plan."

He sat down beside her and ran his hand along her body, stopping here and there to squeeze or rub. He smoothed his fingers over the curve of her hip. She reached for him.

"No," he said, putting her arm down by her side. "You wait."

She reached again and he held her arm.

"No," he said again. "You're mine now. You came to me. I do what I want with you."

Then he was kissing her neck, her shoulders, her breasts, her belly, and Nina started to moan in pleasure, and she put her hands in his hair and ruffled it and slid her hands to his biceps. No thinking, no complications, just pleasure . . . *luxe, calme, et volupté* . . . she repeated the phrase over and over in her mind as all the shivering tangled fibers in her body unwound, easing into complete surrender. . . .

3

BUT KENNY WAS BUSY NOW, hurtling toward his own death. The reels spun and he rushed closer, closer, fascinated. . . .

"I'm talking to you." A finger jabbed Kenny. He registered the strong English accent.

"Bite me," Kenny said. To hell with propriety, to hell with your big fist, my friend, for tonight, I die. It matters not whether I die drunk, sober, physically intact, or beaten to a pulp.

He waited to get knocked off his stool, but nothing happened. He was being reevaluated.

"I have to go to the loo. Do me a bloody favor here." The tone was slightly more civil.

Kenny just looked at him. The long peremptory finger came up and poked his shoulder, hard.

"You shitfaced?"

"Trying."

"Listen. Don't let anybody sit here. Nobody, nohow. Got that?" He pressed the cashout button and the light flashed and the bell rang so everybody would think he'd hit it big. He glared at his machine until the noises stopped, then swept the tokens into his white plastic bucket. "You got that?" he said again.

"Hold the seat?"

"Hold my bloody seat."

"I can't promise to do that."

"Huh? You're sitting here. How hard can it be?"

"I may not be here long. I have a prior commitment."

"Your commitment is on hold until I get back. Understand? You go anywhere, I find you and break your legs."

"Oh. Is that so."

The pale-eyelashed man sat back, surprised at Kenny's shrug. His menacing attitude mutated into a grimace of brotherly goodwill. "Look, friend, this is my machine. I've just lost almost three thousand bucks in it. You know how that feels?"

Kenny nodded.

"I'm gonna piss all over this stool if I don't go right now. So, you'll help me out, won't you?"

Kenny folded his arms and thought about this.

"Two minutes," the man said. "Two friggin' minutes." He fidgeted on the stool. "I'll give you a hundred bucks when I get back."

Kenny's mind went through rapid-fire computations. Maybe ten more minutes, landing like a bar bar bar. "First say the magic word."

The man stared at him, a palpable, pupilless, uncomprehending stare. Then he raised his hand to grab Kenny's jacket. Kenny moved his eyes upward to the Eye in the Sky, the one-way security mirrors in the ceiling through which guards always watched the action on the floor.

"Fuck!"

"No. That's not it. Good try. Try again. The magic word."

The man cleared his throat. "Please."

"I didn't quite catch that."

"Please! Bloody hell!"

"Well. In that case."

"So?"

"Okay."

The man slid off his stool and jogged away, looking back over his shoulder once and almost colliding with Kenny's friendly waitress. She had a smile and a fresh Bud for him. Kenny chugged it.

Hardly a half minute later, he watched his first two reels hit bank bank, and the third bank hesitated for a millisecond on the middle line, then slithered right past it and stopped just below. In spite of everything Kenny was analyzing the play. Intriguing how the machines pandered to your hopes like that, advanced programming stuff, although come to think of it, weren't these things supposed to be random? Still, the psychology behind a close miss, how it made him reach so eagerly for the next tokens, well, that was interesting.

A woman slid onto the man's seat. She flicked a cigarette butt from the coin bin onto the floor, took out a paper roll of silver dollar tokens, and broke it on the edge of the bin. She had three tokens in before Kenny could open his mouth.

"Excuse me," Kenny said.

She turned a face like the moon to him, all trembling lower lip and radiant black eyes, her skin poreless and burnished, and whatever he had been thinking of saying died like a sloppy theorem under the elegant proof of her beauty.

He froze, staring at her.

He knew her. She was one of his avatars, a woman he had created to live in the City of Gold in his computer, the same soft brown skin and black shining bangs hanging over limitless eyes.

Joya. He had designed her and clothed her and made her move. Sometimes, in fact, he had made Joya move in ways that now, remembering, fired up a heat flash in him that caused sweat to break out on his forehead.

After swiveling quickly on her stool, giving the room a once-over, she turned, head bent so that all he could see was her profile, the straight nose and chiseled lips. She was healthy and athletic, with strong shoulders. Her machine began to whir, and Kenny remembered the man with the big fists, who would be right back.

"I'm afraid that—that someone wants this seat," he said. It sounded lame and halfhearted. "A British guy asked me to hold his seat."

"Tough," she said. "I like this seat."

If she liked it so much, Kenny wondered, why did she hunch over like that? Why did she turn her face away when people walked nearby?

"He had a lot of money in."

"His problem," she said. She huddled herself over the machine and dropped a few more coins, then looked around again, her lips twisting with what looked like worry to Kenny, who was an expert.

Kenny shifted around on his stool and pressed the button again. His hip brushed her hip, scorching him like a mouthful of pepper oil meeting a capsaicin receptor in the brain. She was wearing a black sweater and jeans and scuffed cowboy boots. He could smell soap, Ivory or something else plain and clean.

For a minute or so they both played with self-conscious concentration. He knew that she knew that he was watching her from the corner of his eye. He knew he made her uncomfortable. In a second she would get up and stomp away, as numerous women of his acquaintance had done throughout his life.

But for some reason she didn't leave, just drew up her shoulders and leaned forward as if she were trying to meld with the machine, her back to the aisle and her elbows held high, hiding the glorious breasts of which he had had only a glimpse.

"My name is Kenneth Leung. I live in Mountain View," Kenny

ventured. The extra hundred bucks were not to be. *C'est la vie,* he thought, or should it be *le mort?*

She played Max Credits and hit a cherry. Three dollars lost, only two back, but the ringer went off in a short burst as though she'd won.

He opened his mouth again. "Although I'm from Tahoe originally. I'm a virtual architect," he said.

Only a slight tensing of the shoulders indicated that she might have heard him.

"I developed a GUI—that's a user interface—based around the metaphor of a beautiful city, in contrast to the tedious desktop metaphor we have all been stuck with. You know, folders and files and pages. Windows. The whole life-sucking business office metaphor. Do you use a computer?"

She looked around again, stopped at his face, and frowned.

"You boot up the hard drive, and my City of Gold comes up on the monitor with towers and turrets and marble columns and houses on cliffs. You have a home in this City, what you call a home page now. But this home and this City, they're 3-D. Your home is furnished however you want, grand or simple. And you can be whoever you choose. You design your own avatar, sort of an alter ego, with this nifty sub-program I developed. You can be a goddess, a gnome, an animal, a changeling. . . ." He took a Bud from the waitress and she faded away. "What about you? Are you up from the Bay Area? You use a PC? A Mac?"

She had gone back to her machine, but this time she shook her head. She really didn't want to talk. But she was the last person who would ever hear about the City of Gold. He needed her to listen.

"I made it work with both platforms, and also with Linux. But it's so much more than the usual graphic eye fodder—it's more of an alternate universe. It's full of avatars who are really help programs and who take your avatar to the different markets and neighborhoods. You can fly overhead, looking down at the Bazaar."

She appeared to grit her teeth.

"It's like ancient Rome. There's the Temple of Archives where a wise old avatar locates your document files. And the Amusement Coliseum where the games are kept, and the Factory where the applications and control panels are kept. Oh, and there's the Library, and the Art Museum, but that's only the beginning. All around, there're the Net-bookmarked locations to fly to. . . ."

"You're attracting attention. Stop," the girl who looked like Joya said.

"I just want to tell you this one thing, but it's complicated. See, the bookmarked locations are all freed from the Windows metaphor and become underwater cities and planets and wonderful cities on vast plains. I was already designing some of these permanent locations. Imagine the eBay marketplace, the camels bringing in their loads, the avatars jostling up against each other and bidding—and it would have been cheap for users—that was the real beauty of it."

"I said, leave me alone," she said, and for the first time, he realized she was frightened. Of him? Or someone else?

He looked around, blinking. "I'm sorry," he said.

"Forget it. Just—"

"My company went bankrupt."

She played like the hounds were behind her and would eat her up if she didn't play, play, and play some more.

"I lost everything. I'm a complete and total failure."

"You're drunk." The frown deepened. She looked around nervously, then turned to face him long enough to say, "Why don't you go home and sober up?"

"It's just that—and I will definitely not bother you after this—I just had to tell you—you look just like someone I am in love with, someone who isn't even real—isn't that stupid! Actually, it's one of the avatars I was explaining to you about!" He couldn't stop himself now, he started roaring with laughter and dropped his glass and watched the foaming liquid pour out of it while the glass bounced harmlessly onto the red carpet, soaked into the rug like blood, his blood, so soon to come.

She straightened her shoulder strap and started to slide off the stool.

"No, really, don't go, I'll shut up. I'm done. I am really, well and truly done." He stopped, which left his mouth just hanging there. He reached into his pocket and found it empty

He had no more money. There was no reprieve.

He felt for the Glock. Still there. Cold, hard, not a dream. His punishment. A final spiraling out and away, away from his contemptible downfall, the pain of his parents, the destruction of his family.

He looked up but his glasses needed another rub. The girl was still sitting there.

She made a sound, a mewing sort of sound. She was staring at her screen bug-eyed, absolutely motionless.

Then he watched as she spread her arms and fell backward, and if he hadn't been there to catch her she would have fallen right off the stool and maybe cracked a vertebra. Was she having a heart attack? He wasn't too sure about his CPR, how many breaths per minute was it? But fortunately, her eyes were wide open. She was conscious and breathing. Lifting her hand limply, she pointed up at the video screen of her slot machine.

Kenny's blurry eyes followed her hand—

And saw the three banks.

Three banks, lined up precisely right across the pay line. Right down the middle. Little brown banks with little white pillars.

They were in a frozen universe. She was trying to draw a breath— he could see the tendons in her closed throat, and he made the observation in a sludgelike way. He held her like that, right arm supporting her warm back so she didn't fall off the stool, left hand trying to push up his specs and look again.

Three banks. Three credits in.

The thought formed at last.

She had hit the jackpot.

At that moment, a light on top of the machine began to twirl and emit shattering yelps, irritating and mind-numbingly piercing like a fire alarm.

He pushed the girl back up on the chair.

"Oh, my God!" she said. Then she said it again. He recognized something in her voice. Fear.

The world descended into chaos as the first people came running.

"Jackpot! Jackpot!" he heard as he was poked and crowded from behind. The bells rang and rang, attacking his ears and shredding his sanity. He was still supporting her back, his fingers sticky against her sweater. She steadied herself and stood up. He looked at the machine again. The three banks were still there. None of them had slipped off the line.

Somebody had a flash camera and the screech of many voices formed into one mighty roar in the stale air. There were shrieking notes and bellowing notes, and he had to stand up too or be suffocated by the people who were goggling at the monitor with its three banks like the Israelites goggling at Moses' tablets. All the while the machine caterwauled as if it were crying for help.

Kenny looked up at the numbers which a moment before had been streaming by on the display board above the bank of machines. They had stopped moving. She had stopped the great machine. It seemed impossible, but she had won whatever number was up there.

Yes, it had stopped. Stopped at a long series of numbers which he struggled to comprehend. Seven-seven-six-seven-three-three-nine-point-six-four.

Seven million, seven hundred sixty-seven thousand, three hundred thirty-nine dollars and sixty-four cents.

She had won that.

"You hit!" Kenny yelled.

She raised a hand to her forehead and closed her eyes. "I've got to go," she said. "I can't do this." She shouldered away a man leering close to her and wedged herself into the crowd. She pushed hard. In a moment she would be gone forever.

She was leaving! Without thinking, Kenny grabbed her.

"Let go!" She tried to wriggle away but many hands touched her now, wanting to commune with her magic. Her eyes hunted back and forth through the crowd.

Two men materialized beside her, accompanied by Kenny's waitress. Behind these people, two more men in Prize's security uniforms. Behind them, pushing and shoving, tourists and change people and locals. The wheelchair girl was back. She studied Joya, the boyfriend's hand on her shoulder. The suited guys in front were grunting from the effort of getting through the crowd, which was now celebrating like the millennium was happening all over again. The whole casino was trying to jam into their aisle.

The casino officials stood next to Joya, muttering with each other and scrutinizing the numerical display. The security men in their blue uniforms were busy clearing the aisle now but didn't bother Kenny, who worked at remaining upright on his stool.

Finally a very big man with a gray crew cut, who was wiping his forehead with a handkerchief, turned to her and smiled. His smile was notable in itself, Kenny decided, sharky, jealous, staggered. "Let me be the first to congratulate you!" he shouted.

Joya looked from one side to the other, as if searching for a pathway out. The crew cut lost it. Turning to the crowd, he shouted, "Jackpot!" The crowd screamed back

The cocktail waitress was beaming and the other man in the suit continued to look at the machine and shake his head. He couldn't take it in. None of them could.

They were all looking at Joya, or whatever her name was, who had in this instant transformed into an uncanny being who could strike them dumb right now with the merest twitch of her finger, that terrifying finger which had pressed the button at the inconceivably right time.

Joya, a goddess! He half expected her to unfold a set of wings and take off.

"How much?" came the mighty roar. "How much—how much—how much!"

A familiar face pushed its way through the crowd. Kenny's ex-neighbor had returned at last.

"What the hell!" he screamed, first at Kenny, then at the girl. The gush of harsh obscenities that flew off his tongue blended into the cacophony of the crowd. No one was listening. He got to within two feet of Joya, his big fists balled, his body poised to attack, before a security guard stepped efficiently behind him, pulling his right arm into a half nelson. The guard marched the ranting man away from the girl, while another guard made a way for them through the crowd.

"You're dead meat!" he shouted back at them. "Fucking dead!" His eyes roved between Kenny and the girl.

Then he was gone and the remaining guard, looking very determined, was standing in front of her, his hand on his belt holster.

Someone from the casino came up and started taking pictures. Joya backed away, hiding her face. Kenny reached for his beer and didn't find it. He saw the empty glass still on the carpet.

"Aw, now," said his waitress to Joya. "Give 'em that winner's smile, honey. You're a winner!" A slot mechanic pushed through and started sealing off the machine, and the security guard finished bulling the crowd out of the aisle. They could hear again.

"Leave her alone," Kenny said as the photographer angled closer.

"Hey, this is big news," said the excited guy with the crew cut.

Kenny blocked the photographer's view. He shoved Kenny. Kenny shoved him back.

"Can't you people take me out of here?" Joya said.

"Sure, in just a second we'll go upstairs to the office," said the big man. "We just need some photos down here. We can set up the press conference later."

"No pictures!"

"You're a multimillionaire, honey. It's our casino and we're gonna take pictures." He draped an arm around her and smirked, saying, "Shoot," to the photographer. "What's your name, honey?" he said to Joya. She bent her head down until her hair hung down in her eyes. The camera flashed. The photographer danced around trying to get a better angle.

"She's not feeling well," Kenny said. "It's a shock."

"We'll bring her anything she wants. Sit back down, honey."

"Get me out of here." Joya held her hand over her face. "Right now."

Kenny heard the steely warning in her voice. Under these circumstances, he imagined many people, he included, would break down, weep, clutch at someone for support. Not Joya.

Her warning was not lost on the big man. "Okay. All right, we'll go upstairs. Come on, Derrick, Chris, you go in front. Give the lady some room. Show's over, folks. Read the papers tomorrow. So what's your name, honey? What do we call you?"

Kenny couldn't see her anymore. The suits had interposed themselves between him and her.

She was going upstairs to her future, like Vargas, the Brazilian dictator, whose suicide note read: "I leave life to enter history."

With a jolt, he remembered that he was going upstairs too. He had a duty to shoot himself, also like Vargas, though it seemed to him in his drunken and fevered state that he was in love with Joya and had just lived through an eternity with her. Furthermore, even if—just as a hypothesis—he decided to live awhile longer, she had just been snatched forever from his penniless reach. Kenny gripped his slot machine to steady the room.

She, who had no gun in her pocket, had won, and he, as usual, had not. If he had been eighteen inches to the right in the space-time continuum, he would have won. With that money, triumphant, he could have saved his company, his honor, and his family, taken Joya out to the movies—

Not to mention saved his life. Epic irony. Pitiless fate.

Game Over. He'd leave the last of his beer money on the dresser as a sort of apology.

The terror came back. He wouldn't be able to do it if he didn't hurry. He looked for a way through the crowd at the end of the slot machine alley.

And heard his mother's name.

Was he that drunk? He listened, and heard it again, this time distinctly.

"I said, call me Mrs. Leung."

It was Joya. What was this outlandish mockery?

"I'm not going anywhere without him." The broad back in front of him stepped away and they were face-to-face with each other again. "My husband, Ken. You're coming, aren't you?" she asked Kenny. She gave him a forceful, almost commanding look.

Kenny's eyebrows went up, and the specs went down. The Glock pressed against his chest under the jacket. He was confused. He had a prior commitment.

"Kenny?"

"Yes?"

"You coming?"

"I'm coming, Joya," he said.

4

THE PHONE RANG.

They both jumped. Paul stopped for a moment, then continued his minute explorations along the terrain of Nina's skin. But the phone didn't stop. It rang and rang. Nina thought, What if Bob has an emergency? She had left Paul's number on the kitchen table. Bob needed to be able to reach her. He was only thirteen. Story at ten: house on fire. Kid calling in panic. Mom and lover don't answer due to sex game in hotel room.

Mom and lover! Ugh! "Paul," she said, starting up on her elbows. Ring . . . ring . . . ring . . .

"No." He pushed her down.

"I have to."

"Don't even think about it!"

"It might be Bob."

This potent thought dislodged him. Still, he would not allow her to answer. He reached over and grunted into the phone. Hormone-soaked silence filled the room. Nina's senses were heightened, maybe from the blood racing around in her body, and she could swear she recognized the metallic sounds going into Paul's ear.

It couldn't be! She wouldn't dare!

But it was and she had. Paul passed her the phone. "It's Sandy."

"I know. I know," her secretary told her. "But it's urgent."

"Bob?"

"He's fine. He was watching an old action flick when I called a minute ago. Oh, I know. *Gone in 60 Seconds.* Said his friend scored a copy on the Web. Said it's majorly full of chase scenes and way better than the remake."

"Sandy!"

"He gave me your number. Paul's number."

"It's Sunday night!" Nina's mind ran through her cases—the clients in jail, the clients in custody disputes, the clients who might have just been arrested. A frightening thought struck her. "My dad? Or Matt?"

"Relax. It's a client."

Paul went into the bathroom, walking slightly bowlegged, shaking his head. He looked like a swimmer from behind, his shoulders and back making a V, his butt white and indignant as it disappeared through the bathroom door.

"Grr," Nina said.

"You're gonna love this."

"You may, I won't." As soon as she said it, she knew that this display of ill temper would cost her.

After a short silence which was like the silence of the sea just before the hurricane blows in, Sandy said, "Hey. We were playing checkers and eating nachos, and now Joseph has gone down to his workshop and I won't see him again until tomorrow."

"Well, I'm sorry."

"You don't sound sorry."

"I am sorry."

"Not as sorry as me."

"Look, Sandy, I'm sorry, I really am—"

"I'm not supposed to care about being disturbed; I'm just the secretary. Socially inferior. Never should have given us the vote. Try to do the right thing, get in touch with you. I'm the sorry one."

"Sandy, tell me right now what—"

"He'll probably spend all night downstairs now. We were snug as a bug in a rug, but now he got away. He's making a cupboard for the bedroom—"

"—or I'm going to hang up." Paul came back out, buttoning a shirt. He sat down on the edge of the bed and started putting on his shoes.

Nina took a deep breath and exhaled slowly while Sandy said a few more things about the cupboard and the nachos and the checkers and the status of Native American pink-collar workers in American society. Sandy had been slightly offended by Nina's peremptory tone, and Nina was now paying the price, and there was no way out of it.

When Sandy finally took a breather herself, Nina said in a very calm voice, "So what is it?"

"What is what?"

"You know darn well."

"You mean the legal matter?"

Nina gave no response to this. She was becoming enraged. She thought she heard a muffled dry chuckle on the other end of the phone. She wondered why she hadn't fired Sandy a long time ago. She opened her mouth to fire her.

Sandy said, "New client. Has to see you right now. Happened to know I was a legal secretary and called me here in Markleeville. She's over at the office right now with some guy, waiting for you out in the parking lot."

"She knows you?"

"I didn't say that. Anyway, she's got to get back to Prize's soon. They're waiting for her. She told them she was feeling sick and had to get some medicine from her car, then she drove down the highway to the Starlake Building."

"What'd she do? Get caught cheating? Assault somebody?"

"No. She just won a slot machine jackpot. A whole lot of money. Something like seven million bucks. You still there?"

"Wow!" Nina said slowly.

"Uh huh."

"Does she have a cell phone? Good. Sandy, call her back and tell her to go back and smile and sign the forms and collect the check and come by in the morning. About ten."

"That's the thing. She says she can't sign the forms. But she does want the check."

"I don't blame her for being nervous but I'm busy!" This came out sounding somewhat plaintive. Paul was sliding his wallet into his hip pocket. He was fully dressed and there was no longer even a whiff of sex in the air. The party was ruined.

Sandy went on, "But, see, she says she can't tell them her name. And she's got this guy with her and she says she can use his name, only she doesn't even know him, so she wants a lawyer to make an agreement between them before she goes in and does that—"

"What? The IRS won't let her get away with that. How much did you say she won?"

"Over seven million dollars, like I said. Except she says she's going to leave town without the check if she has to use her name."

As the hormonal tide subsided, Nina's brain began clicking again. "Maybe there's a warrant out on her. This is interesting."

"I told you you'd love it."

"Maybe." Nina had the phone crooked between chin and neck, and she was finally pulling on her coat, which Paul had just handed her, looking away.

"So what should I tell her?"

"Tell her fifteen minutes."

"I'll come," Sandy said. Now Nina recollected one reason why she didn't fire Sandy, in spite of her obstreperousness. Sandy was devoted in her way.

"Thanks, but don't worry about it. It's a long drive for you, and it's late. I'll bring Paul. If there's paperwork, I'll rev up the computer myself."

"You sure? If you want I'll call Bob and tell him where to call in the next hour."

"Do that. I'll be all right. Bye." Nina hung up. "I'd really like another shot of whiskey," she said. "And I really would like a shot of you. But I have to go."

Paul stuck his keys in his pocket. "Not without me. Let's get it over with, then," he said. "Just remember not to take off the coat."

Nina laughed. "I brought clothes. They're out in the car. I took them off before I came in. Because—you know—I couldn't leave home like that. What if I had an accident on the way?"

"Very sensible." He took her in his arms. "Very sensual."

"I'll have to go home afterwards. I guess I should take the Bronco, since the office is on the way."

"You're not coming back?" He let go of her.

"I only gave myself until one A.M. Bob's home. It's the first time I've left him so late. I'm really sorry, Paul." She lowered her eyes. She felt ridiculous.

Paul had the grace to crack a smile. "It was a great performance, I had no idea you'd show up I thought never mind what I thought. And then, the coat. I'm gonna have a coat fetish after this."

"Something always goes wrong," Nina said.

"The lawyer's creed."

She grabbed her purse and Paul followed her out, pulling the door shut with an energy that reminded her of just what she was missing.

She bumped out of the big parking lot onto the highway. The valets at Caesars were keeping busy in the height of a midsummer rush. As she passed Bill's, which along with the Lakeside Inn was the locals' club of choice, she saw two men reel out toward the street from the open entryway, but the Tahoe police had erected a fence so they couldn't teeter into the traffic.

As she crossed back over the state line into California, the casinos blinked out and the motels began. The night had cooled. Cold clouds rushed across a windy sky. In the driver's mirror she saw Paul following in his new shiny red Mustang. She passed the Embassy Suites at Ski Run Boulevard and took the curve where the lake can finally be seen from the road and the forest comes up on the other side and the businesses regress to frankly funky.

She looked for it. She always looked for it. But Lake Tahoe was just an enormous lightless pull of gravity on her right, lacking enough moon to dent the water with its reflection.

A couple of miles farther she pulled into her own parking lot next to the Starlake Building, Paul right on her rear . . . if only . . . and only one car sitting right in the middle of the lot, an old Honda Civic with the salt rust along its flanks that made it a local car. As she swung down from the Bronco, wishing for the thousandth time that she was taller, the Civic disgorged a man and a woman. Paul came up, and they all shook hands.

"The witching hour," the girl said, not smiling. "Thank you so much for doing this."

"Let's go in." Nina unlocked the main door and they traipsed down the darkened hall to her office by the stairs. She opened up and turned on the lights. Paul pulled in an extra chair from the reception area as they passed through, and they all sat down in Nina's office, Nina behind her desk. She switched on her desk lamp but it didn't do much to dispel the third-degree atmosphere of bright overhead fluorescents in dark night.

"Make yourselves at home," she said. "I'll get some coffee." She went into the law library, which was also the conference room, pulled the French roast out of the bar refrigerator she kept in there, and got the espresso maker going. She could hear Paul making small talk in her office as she pulled out the mugs and poured the milk into the foamer. She pumped up a lot of aerated milk, poured it into the thick brown liquid in the cups, and went into her office with the tray.

She would classify this wiry girl as Native American. In her early twenties, she had short black hair cut with long straight bangs and a sculpted face with exceptionally big, long-lashed, watchful eyes. She sat up straight and still, hands on her knees, cowboy boots firmly planted on the floor.

Her companion, lagging behind, even sitting slightly behind her as if wondering what he was doing there, didn't fit with her. He was shorter, a rather round young man with gold-rimmed glasses and pointed tufted eyebrows. A mop of coarse black hair spiked to one side, like hair blown by severe wind and frozen in place. He wore a disheveled but expensive silk sport coat, his tie pulled loose. An office worker, Nina decided, his glossy eyes showing that he'd had a few too many.

The next thing Nina noticed was how close to the edge the girl was. She appeared to be hyperventilating. Her face, which should have been a soft brown, had faded to putty. Her eyes had a stricken look.

Neither of the two visitors paid any attention to the surroundings, which was a shame, because the office was finally starting to look good. The healthy fiddle-leaf fig in the corner scraped the ceiling, the certificates sported new matching frames, and a Francis Picabia print hung on the wall. Modest, orderly, upstanding, reflecting, Nina hoped, that a respectable lawyer practiced therein.

Maybe a room at the Mustang Ranch would have caught their attention. This room didn't.

Paul sat near the window with its white blinds, surveying the scene through heavy-lidded eyes. He had forgotten to comb his hair. Nina suddenly wondered if she'd gotten her clothes on right side out in the dark, and looked down. The buttons on her red cardigan were duly buttoned.

"They're waiting for me," the girl said in a rush. "At Prize's. I won, and then it got really insane. They took us into an office and a man, he said he was the vice president for operations, said we would wait for the—the—I can't remember—"

"The Global Gaming representative and the IRS officer in charge of gaming taxation in this region," said the young man.

"And you are?" Nina said.

"Ken Leung. You can call me Kenny." His voice was soft.

Paul interrupted, "I note that you're carrying a concealed weapon. Are you licensed?" All eyes turned to Kenny Leung's right hand, which had jumped to an area of his jacket near the left armpit.

"Oh, that," Leung said. "It's not loaded."

"That's good. But we do have a policy—no guns in the law office. Okay? You can set it outside on the secretary's desk." The young man got up without a word and went out the door, leaving Paul sitting up, vigilant. A second later he reappeared, opening his coat so they all could see the gun was gone.

"It's not anything bad," Leung said. Paul went back into his slouch but his eyes remained on patrol. The girl's mouth had firmed while she watched Leung take his seat. She rubbed her forehead.

"Just my luck," she muttered.

"You're all getting the wrong idea," Leung said. "I'm a businessman. Look. I have business cards. Embossed and everything." He opened a soft leather wallet and pulled out several. Paul examined each one carefully.

"So let's get back to the situation which has us sitting here at midnight," Nina said to the girl. "I understand that you won a jackpot."

"On the Greed Machine. A progressive slot machine. I never heard of it before. I just played some dollars. I had been there less than five minutes."

"More like three," Leung said.

"With him yakking nonstop the whole time," the girl said. "I had about twenty dollars left when the banks lined up. I was just about to leave. I was actually getting off the stool when I saw them stop—kachung kachung kachung—in a perfect row. I didn't know what it meant. But then the bell went nuts. Everything went nuts."

"Seven million, seven hundred sixty-seven thousand, three hundred thirty-nine dollars and sixty-four cents," Leung said, and he wasn't consulting any notes.

Silence rang like bells in the small room. What a stunning amount of money. Nina thought, This can't be true. People actually won that kind of money on slots? The girl, hand pressed to her jaw, appeared thunderstruck, but Leung recited the amount calmly.

Of course, he wasn't the winner.

"I can't believe this!" the girl said to Kenny. "Did it really happen?" She combed a hand through her hair. "Why me? I can't even imagine—what if it's really true?"

"Might as well be struck by lightning," Nina said.

"I—I just don't believe it's true," the girl went on. "How can I jump up and down? People like me don't have this kind of luck."

Paul said to the girl, "That's a lot of silver dollars. It is going to change your life. Unless you're already rich?"

She answered him with a short laugh. "I have two hundred sixty dollars left in my checking account. I'm staying with my aunt because I can't afford my own place. I need to buy food. I need to pitch in on the rent. I've got a part-time job that pays peanuts, no future at all that I could see, in fact, until just this moment."

"Why were you gambling?" Paul asked. "I mean, you say you were practically broke."

All three of the other people in the room stared at him.

"Okay, dumb question."

"There actually was a reason," she said. "I thought someone might be following me. I ducked into the casino to hide. I wasn't planning to stay long. You know, it does bring up another question, though. Why did I throw my money away down that machine? And the answer is—

because there's something so hopeful about gambling, showing you have . . . faith in the future."

"Or just believe in good luck or a benign universe," Kenny said. "Not that I actually do."

"It's a dream, one of those dreams that come around sometimes where you live out your wishes. I just don't want to give my name and I don't want anyone to know about this."

"I'm sure the casino will demand a photograph and a name," Nina said.

"They took a picture already, which I ducked. I don't think they got much," the girl said.

"You didn't give them your name?" Nina asked.

The girl looked embarrassed, then evasive. "I'm afraid I won't get the money after all, but I do need it. I need it! So I thought a lawyer could think of something and I called Sandy"— Nina noted this use of Sandy's first name—"and she said she'd call you. I know it was lousy timing."

"The way it was described to me, I wouldn't have missed coming here for anything," Nina said. "I'm not going to insist that you tell me your identity right now. It's plain that you have some reason you don't want it known, and there's no confidentiality privilege at this moment because Paul and Mr. Leung are here also. You understand that? We can talk alone in a few minutes."

"Okay."

"What happened when you refused to give your name?"

"They said, 'You have to.' This was while we were still on the casino floor. I couldn't answer. But then I got an idea."

"She told them to call her Mrs. Leung," Leung said, leaning forward. "She used my name."

"Are you married to Mr. Leung?" Nina asked.

"No, ma'am! I don't even know him! He was just sitting on the stool next to me jabbering at me and he had told me his name and that he didn't have any money. I didn't know what to do. They were pressing me and pressing me. So I thought, Well, I'll pay him to use his name."

"You have agreed to pay Mr. Leung—Kenny—some money?"

"A million dollars," the girl said.

5

"STOP RIGHT THERE," NINA SAID. She looked at Kenny Leung. He was trying to look nonchalant.

"Here's my plan," the girl said. "We go back to the casino. I say I can't find my ID, that I don't have my driver's license because my husband drove us up here from the Bay Area. And I'll tell them to cut the check in my husband's name. We'll use his Social Security number since you need one.

"But then I have to be protected since it's not my name on the check. Kenny has to sign a paper that says the jackpot isn't really his. And we need an agreement between us that he will be paid when I get my check. That's where you come in."

Nina said, "That's your plan?"

"Right."

"Some plan," Paul said.

"And what do you think about this, Mr. Leung?" Nina asked.

"Don't look at me like that. It was her idea. I'm helping her. It's fair compensation for losing my virginity," Leung said, pushing his glasses up on his nose. "That's a joke."

"You're not even close to losing your virginity, trust me," the girl said.

"Well, anyway, it's only about twelve point eight percent of the winnings. That's a fair percentage, if she can't collect without me. Besides, why not? One final futile gesture in the face of an indifferent universe. Indifferent to me, anyway."

He was waving his arms and blinking rapidly as he spoke, and he looked more and more like a Dilbert who had escaped his cubicle, not the type to rush into a wild scheme like this so enthusiastically. How drunk was he? And what was he doing with a gun? Still, for that amount of money, anybody would feel adventurous.

"And you think I can write up an agreement tonight between you and Kenny that will ensure that Kenny turns that money over to you when the check clears?" Nina asked the girl.

"What do you mean, when the check clears?"

"Well," Nina said, "the bank is going to want a week to ten days to process it. Minimum. I'm talking about the first check. It'll be paid in installments over twenty years. I have no idea how much the initial pay-out will be. But it certainly will be a week or two before you have any cash in hand."

"No," the girl said. She looked over at Kenny Leung, who nodded. "The casino said that they were having a special promotion on the Greed Machines and the jackpot was an instant payout."

"That's right," Kenny said. "They said it would all be paid tonight, if we make it back there to collect it, that is."

A silence fell over them. Nina was having trouble imagining a seven-million-dollar check. "That's very unusual," she said at last. "But you're still going to be signing at least one document under penalty of perjury that certifies that you're married and that this is your name. Giving a false name will certainly be looked at as some sort of attempt to avoid paying taxes."

"You're saying there's nothing I can do?" She sagged back into her chair, overwhelmed with disappointment.

"I'm not saying that. Don't tell me your name and please don't tell me if you're wanted for a crime. But I need a general overview. Why can't you give your name?"

"Publicity."

Nina nodded. "Someone will know you won?"

"Someone will be able to find me. He'll find me, and then . . ." Her voice had risen.

"And then what?"

"He'll come after me. Maybe kill me."

"Is this the man you thought you saw following you?" Paul asked.

She nodded. "No one should know I'm here or who I am. I don't have anywhere else I can run. I've been safe here, but now—unless I can think of something—can't you help me? Can't anybody help me? There must be a way." She rocked the chair closer to Nina's desk and leaned forward. "I didn't have the money two hours ago—I should just leave, but—but—I need it, you understand? I have to take the risk, I need that money! I had no life before, just fear."

They sat around and thought.

"Why can't it just be simple?" the girl said, calming down. "Why are there always strings? Why can't it be—"

"Unalloyed," Kenny Leung said, eyebrows drawn together as if he were reevaluating the adventure. Some of the strings on the money were starting to look more like steel cables.

Nina checked her watch. She felt a headache leaking from the left side of her head to the right. She was not at her sharpest after midnight. "Is this someone you are afraid of connected with law enforcement?" she asked.

"Oh, no."

"Someone's trying to kill you. That's what you said, right?"

"He wants to take me down. But he's not going to. If I have to kill him first, I will. I'm trained in weaponry and self-defense. It has to stop here." She squared her jaw. Nina suspected that a buff physique was in hiding underneath the jeans and sweater.

"I see." Nina gave Paul a sideways glance. He didn't look like he had any bright ideas, and he didn't look happy.

"You think I'm crazy or paranoid," the girl said. "I'm not."

"Then your safety has to come first," Nina said.

Paul jumped in. "Then this is really your lucky day. I have quite a bit of security experience, up to and including securing the safety of a United States senator. I'll go with you and stay with you until other arrangements can be made. You won't be harmed. You won't have to defend yourself."

The girl said, "You have to accept that if he finds out where I am, there will be nothing anyone can do to stop him."

"Your name's going to be splattered across the pages of newspapers all over the U.S.," Paul said, "whether you like it or not. This is not like the lottery, where you have some control, at least right at first."

Nina said, "If you do claim the jackpot, the casino may require you to sign paperwork agreeing to have your name and picture used for publicity purposes. Do you have a restraining order against this man that is after you? You've tried to stop him? There is a strong stalking statute in this state."

"The law. Sure," she said. "Forget it."

"Why? Why haven't you gone to the police?" Paul asked.

"I tried that already, before I came here. Somehow, there's never any evidence."

Paul started to ask another question, and Nina understood his curiosity, but they had already gone too far. She shook her head once, sharply, and he sat back in his chair.

"Can't you do anything to help me?" the girl said, turning back to Nina. "Tell me what to do! Is it hopeless? Do I have to just blow the money off?" She leaned back, as if exhausted with the effort of explaining.

"I could put it in my trust account," Nina said. "But I can't just go in as your agent without you and keep you anonymous. It's the IRS. They'll insist on something from you. We could demand that your name not be provided to the press, but—"

"Get real," Paul interrupted.

"What about my idea? Telling them I'm married? Giving them a name?" the girl said.

"You're saying, Kenny gets handed the check and he hands it over to me, right there at the casino. That would keep it safe and gain us time. But you'd still be lying about your name. It could void the jackpot. I'm sure that there will be some sort of rule providing that. They are just not going to let you get away with using a false name."

"Then I guess I can't go back."

Kenny Leung's alarm lifted him out of his slump. Paul looked exasperated.

"Listen," Nina said sharply to the girl. "Do you realize what you're saying? You stand to lose a fortune simply by refusing to give your name. Give your name, take the money, hire lawyers and bodyguards, and live behind an electrified gate."

"He'll find me within twenty-four hours. He'll do worse than kill me."

Her chilling words ratcheted up the tension in the room. What could be worse than death? Nina asked herself. Was this person a sexual predator?

"What's that supposed to mean?" Paul said, his voice crisp, professional. Nina had watched the way his body hardened before her eyes, tensing at the first whiff of violence. That was the trouble with both of them, Nina thought. They were always trying to fix everybody's problems, even the impossible ones. Paul's methods were very different from hers, though. She chased away that uncomfortable thought.

The girl shook her head and closed her eyes. Against tears? When she opened them again, she looked dry-eyed and resolved. "It's our only hope, pretending we're married. Him getting the money and me getting it from him."

"No," Nina said. "You're not married and you can't get away with pretending." What had just occurred to her was too far out to say out loud, and certainly went beyond her charter as a legal adviser. Why, here they were smack in the middle of the land of easy marriage and di-

vorce. . . . Just a few miles from an instant, prepackaged, lifetime commitment. "Pretending will just get you in trouble. Too bad you aren't
really married. That would make things easier." She crossed her leg and
examined her shoe, wondering who in the room would be first to reveal a mind as twisted as hers.

A pause, while the words sank in. The girl picked up on it first.
"What if—what if we don't pretend. What if we actually got married?"
She turned to face Kenny, who was shaking his head violently.

"The normal world of love, marriage, and children is mine only in
fantasy. There's a church in the City of Gold, and a synagogue, and a
mosque, and a Buddhist temple. Sanctuaries and celebrations everywhere . . . but not for me. I can't marry you like this. I am not worthy. I
can perpetrate a fraud, yes, certainly, I can die for you—would you like
me to die for you? Just say the word—and my mother would be furious
with me, how could I do it to her, Tan-Mo is never going to get married, I was supposed to carry on the family name . . ."

They all stared at him. Was he still drunk? He went on in this vein
for some time, spouting irrelevancies.

"Well, that's real useful," said Paul. "But I am impressed that you're
turning down the money. As well you should."

"I didn't mean that. Just not—not a real marriage. Use of my once-
proud name, that's what I signed up for—"

"Got any more coffee around here?" the girl said, rising. Nina
pointed toward the empty pot.

The girl went into the next room and ground coffee, interrupting
Kenny's filibuster with the noise. "Look," she said when she came back
in. "Show some courage, Kenny. At least show some greed. I'm not
paying you otherwise. I've decided. It's our only chance. We could go
right away. It's only forty-five minutes to Reno."

"Are you proposing to me, Joya?" Kenny said, finally focusing. He
stood up. "But your timing is so bad. I can't get married now. I'm a
dead man! And anyway, my mother would want to be there. . . ."

"Not a real marriage," the girl soothed him. "Just a formality,
Kenny, a kind of fantasy. Like—like the City of Gold. Something beautiful but—temporary."

"Marry you right now? A virtual marriage?"

"In name only, just until we get the money." She lost patience.
"You know, I'm offering to pay you extremely well. You haven't earned
anything yet, buddy."

Kenny folded his arms in front of him. "I don't know. This is not as
simple and direct as it first appeared. If it's a sign, it should go down easy.

Smoothly. It should interrupt the fatal flow and provide a convenient bend, not a lot of twists and turns."

"A million dollars," the girl said.

Kenny appeared to be computing something in his head. "It's too neat. It's very suspicious. It's like a folktale, and you are the princess come to rescue me, but I don't really believe—"

"Oh, for Pete's sake," Paul interrupted. "Nina, how can we do this without him?"

"No, no. I'll do it. I always do it in the end. Lunge for that brass ring. Fall off the horse. I'll do it."

He earned a brilliant smile. "I won't let you back out."

"Now, listen here," Paul said.

The girl said, "Deal."

Kenny shuffled over to her and bent over her hand, planting a semi-sober, wet kiss. The Cary Grant effect he must have intended fell slightly short due to the pungency of his breath, which reached all the way to Nina several feet away.

Paul gave a lopsided smile, the one that said, This is complete and total bullshit; what loony bin have I landed in?

But Nina couldn't resist. "Are you married now?" she asked the girl.

"No."

Paul said. "Nina? Isn't this illegal?"

"Do I have this straight? Are you paying him to marry you?" she asked the girl.

"You're the lawyer. You tell me what to call it, if it's illegal for him to marry me for the money. Isn't there something called a prenuptial agreement?"

"It certainly wouldn't be the first time that's been done," Paul said.

Nina shook her head. "Kenny, what about you? Are you married?"

"Never been married. I've been saving myself for Joya." He raised his eyebrow to the girl. He reminded Nina of Mike Myers trying to be debonair, the smile that was a little too wide, the too-bright eyes.

"Let me see your driver's license." Kenny reached into his jacket pocket and pulled out a wallet. He handed Nina his license. Nina passed it on to Paul. Kenneth Leung, aka Tan-Kwo Leung, street address in Mountain View, California. Born in 1972. Sixty-eight inches tall, one hundred eighty-four pounds. Must wear corrective lenses. The license was current. The photo had caught Leung with his eyes at half-mast.

"I am not a crook," Kenny said in a gruff voice, raising his hands and making V-signs with his fingers. He laughed. Nobody else did.

"Could have fooled me," Paul said. "What's with the alternate name?"

"I felt I needed an easier name for business," he said. "A Caucasian one. It's perfectly innocent and legal. Turns out I was wrong. Half the people I deal with speak Chinese or Japanese."

Paul went into the front office and photocopied Kenny's license, then handed it back.

"Nina . . ." he said.

"Just a minute, Paul. The good news is, marriage wouldn't give Kenny any legal claim on the money, because the marriage took place after the jackpot."

"I just want my share," Kenny offered.

"That's what I'm worried about," Paul said. "It's too much money."

"I'm not dishonest. She's pulling me into this. I don't have to live— I mean, do it."

"You don't seem to be kicking and screaming," Paul said, "which I seem to be the only one here to find surprising." He pointed his eyes at Nina, then turned back to Kenny. "Marriage is not entirely a business decision, or haven't any of you people thought about that? Holy matrimony ring a bell? And if that doesn't give you pause, there's the less morally questionable but vexing issue of logistics. License. Blood test. Ceremony."

Nina was probably the only one to appreciate the bafflement in Paul's voice. He had tried marriage twice and failed at it both times. He clearly didn't like what he took to be their cavalier approach to an old-fashioned institution.

"This is not like picking up a ninety-nine-cent burger, you know," he went on.

"Speaking of which, have you got any snacks around?" Kenny said.

"I think we have some Snickers bars from last Hallowe'en still in the freezer of the bar fridge in the conference room," Nina said. Kenny got up and checked it out, finally pulling a candy bar out of the ice it was embedded in. He started pulling shreds of wrapper off, bit by bit, making a stack of trash on the table.

Nina saw Paul's mouth tighten.

Tonight had been so frustrating for both of them. It was the first time they had been together as a couple in nearly a year, and along came these two young strangers, talking about getting married as if marriage were only a bizarre business deal. She and Paul had wobbled around with the marriage idea for ages, right up until she had married another man. She didn't blame Paul for his mood, which had to be due at least in part to their own rocky history.

But there was an irresistible simplicity to the notion. "They could go to Reno and do it in a couple of hours," she said, wandering into the murky moral terrain, just following the logic of the thing, having to admire the legal possibilities. "The registry's open twenty-four hours a day and so are the wedding chapels in the big casinos. Your casino could wait a few hours. We could think up some excuse. Of course, this is all theory."

Kenny and the girl stood beside each other without touching. Kenny looked over at the girl, offering a chopper-filled grin. Chocolate smears around his mouth detracted from the smile. The girl, having struck her deal, put her hands in her pockets and ignored his gaze.

"It's a terrible idea," Paul said, his eyes stony. "Are you all nuts?"

But the girl interrupted the sermon he was gearing up to deliver. "Let's do it," she said. "But this is just business, not a personal relationship. That has to be crystal clear."

Kenny winced as he absorbed that, and Nina thought, So he is interested in this young lady. She factored in that complication.

She finished off the last of her latte, leaving enough solid precipitate at the bottom to tell a fortune. Staring at it, knowing that it was late at night and that she should think twice, she said, "This idea has aspects that might be called fraudulent by unfriendly parties. It's a voidable marriage, because you don't intend to live together as husband and wife. But it might get the check into our possession and we could straighten it out later and make sure the IRS got its due, and no one could claim any damages, so I don't see who would bother to complain."

"Possession," Kenny said. "Always get possession."

"Name changes are actually quite simple. You change your name by starting to use another name. No formalities are required. The sole requirements that I know of are that you must be older than eighteen and that you don't do it to defraud anyone. You could change your name without Kenny—wait"—Nina raised her hand to prevent Kenny from interrupting—"but then you would still have the problem of having no ID to show these people. And even if you married Kenny and flashed his driver's license at the casino, they may surprise you and still not pay out the money until they see your own ID."

"I'll do it if he will," the girl repeated.

"With pleasure," Kenny said.

"Just a minute, pal," Paul said.

Leung folded his arms, a vision of obstinacy. He faced Paul, the supercilious look fading and his bleary eyes narrowed.

"What's your story?" Paul went on. "Let's hear it now rather than later, when it might come as a rude shock."

"Anyone would do it for that kind of money."

"Maybe so. But you make me nervous. Packing a Glock, maybe that has something to do with it. Humor me."

"The money is for my parents. Payback on a loan. Business reverses."

Paul seemed to understand that—Nina knew he supported his parents in San Francisco—but the dubious look in his eye remained.

Leung glanced toward the outer office where the gun was, and Nina thought, Holy smokes, was he thinking of using that thing on himself?

"I'm also doing it for Joya," Leung went on, as if that ought to clear the matter up.

Paul turned to the girl. "Is that your name?"

She shook her head.

"Joya is all that's left of beauty and love in this world," Leung said with a lachrymose catch to his voice.

"Oh, he'll make a fine husband," Paul told the girl. "You're both chock full of secrets. The two of you belong together. Listen. Go back to Prize's and tell them who you are. These kinds of complications, you never know where they may end."

"He's right," Nina said to the girl. "I know you're afraid right now. But I believe, no matter what the problem is, that Paul and I could protect you."

"No. I can't take a chance. I'm sorry."

"Paul, would you take Kenny into the outer office for a minute?" Nina asked.

Paul got up and the two men went out, shutting the door. The girl squeezed her eyes shut again, as if she were experiencing severe emotional pain.

The almost playful philosophical exercise had suddenly strayed into the realm of substantial possibility and Nina felt the need to backtrack. It was one thing to answer questions and offer legal information, but how could she, in good conscience, encourage such dealings? "I'm concerned and uneasy about this marriage idea," Nina said as soon as the door closed. "It made sense to consider marriage as an option among other options, but Paul's right. It could have unpleasant, unpredictable consequences."

Such as Kenny Leung deciding to make trouble about a divorce or pushing for more money at a later date. Such as the casino people finding out and withholding the jackpot indefinitely. Such as Kenny really being married to someone else, or even this girl really being married to someone else. "Let's shelve this idea. You don't know this young man. You could find yourself in bigger trouble than you are already in."

"Isn't it better than just lying and saying we're married?"

Nina considered her answer. "Maybe. It's technically better. If those are the only choices you have. But we can think some more about this. It's shady."

"I'm trying to save my life! It's not going to hurt anyone. This is my only chance. I'm going to do it, and I really need you. Will you help me? Will you meet me at Prize's afterwards to get the check so that turkey in the outside office can't just walk off with my money?"

Nina heaved a sigh. She thought about it. Shady, but the intent wasn't fraudulent. She could fix the problem in a few days, when the girl calmed down. Then she thought about logistics. Bob, home in bed, all alone. She'd have to draft up some sort of agreement to protect the money from Kenny and it would be three or four o'clock in the morning before Kenny and the girl could get back from Reno.

She could roust her brother, Matt, and ask him to go get Bob. She looked at her watch. It was almost one A.M. She made her mind veer away from what she and Paul could have been doing.

"I'll pay you twenty-five thousand dollars out of the check for your help tonight," the girl said.

"Don't throw away money you don't have yet," Nina said. "I charge two hundred an hour plus expenses and"—she rummaged in the top desk drawer for a retainer agreement—"and I'll ask for a five-thousand-dollar retainer when and if the check clears, because part of this is that I'm going to try to help you with the other problem you have. And I'll charge you for travel time tonight. Is that fair?"

"More than fair. I may not be able to pay you all that if—if this is all for nothing."

"I'll take that chance."

"Thank you. Thank God Sandy knew you. What about—the blond man out there? The bodyguard?"

"Paul van Wagoner's my investigator. You hire me, you get him too."

Nina filled out the top portion of the retainer agreement and passed it on to the girl. She read it and signed it. "I'll give you a copy at Prize's," Nina said. "And now I want your name. I can't read this signature."

"But . . ."

"I won't tell anyone," Nina said. "It's privileged now, because we are alone and you're my client. But I have to know who my clients are. Who are you?"

"No one? Because if you do—it won't just be me . . ."

"I promise."

"My name is Jessie. Jessie Potter." She whispered it.

Nina had half expected the name to be infamous. My name is Lizzie Borden, nice to meet ya. "Okay, Jessie Potter. Nice to meet you. Now, how do I reach you?"

"Sandy. I don't know my aunt's number."

"Is she listed?"

"Sandy will be able to reach me."

"You're a member of the Washoe tribe?" Nina said then, because Sandy was a Washoe, a small tribe of Native Americans based around Tahoe and Northern Nevada.

"Yes."

"Is there a family member you could call for advice about this? Your aunt?"

"No one with any better judgment than I have, including my aunt. She's eighty and living in about nineteen fifty these days."

Nina's headache was getting worse. She gave up. "All right, Jessie. Let's go get that check," she said.

The girl stood up. "Now, where is the registry office? How do we get there?"

They went out to Paul and Kenny Leung. Leung was drinking thirstily out of a paper cup.

"She still wants to do it," Nina said. "What about you, Kenny? If I were you, I'd want to talk to a lawyer first. About the marriage idea, and the agreement I'm about to draw up. I advise you to do that."

"Not necessary," Kenny said. "I waive legal counsel. Voluntarily. And with full appreciation of the potential adverse consequences of failing to be represented by counsel when this much money and my pristine bachelor status are involved. Because, you see, I just don't care. Because this is my final challenge to the gods—"

Nina interrupted, "Are you intoxicated?" He had to say no and walk without staggering, or she wouldn't be able to go ahead.

"Not since I visited the head just now. Want me to prove it? Calculate your income to within, say, five grand?" He was coherent when he wanted to be.

"No need," Nina said hurriedly. "Okay, then. We'll meet in the parking lot at Prize's as soon as you can get back."

"I'm going to Reno with them. I'll drive," Paul said.

Nina nodded. "Call me when it's over," she said to Jessie. Jessie and Kenny went out into the hall.

Paul lingered. As soon as the door shut, he said, "You have to be kidding."

"You have a better idea?"

"I do. The phone rings in my hotel room. We're busy. We don't answer."

"You wouldn't miss this for the world, Paul. And neither would I. I wonder if they can pull it off."

"I don't trust either one of them. Or you. You're being reckless. I know that look in your eye. You think this is a big adventure."

"Don't be patronizing."

"Don't be a fool."

She sidled up to him and put an arm around his waist. "Look at it as a gamble, Paul. She needs us to help her get that check safely. Let's go for it."

"What about the f-word?"

"This is no time to talk about—about the coat!"

"I meant fraud. What did you think I meant?" He gave her a wolfish grin. Then he patted the pocket where he had put Kenny's gun, and Nina noticed he didn't give it back before they left.

6

BY FOUR A.M., WITH ANOTHER jolt of French roast helping the ibupro-
fen tablets eat away at her stomach and an agreement that she hoped was
ironclad drafted, printed out, copied, and resting uneasily in her briefcase in back, Nina lay in the Bronco—the driver's seat, pushed back—in
that tortured state known to red-eye flyers in which you can't sleep and
you can't stay awake.

She was parked in the middle of an acre of parking lot behind
Prize's and even the moon had gone to bed, leaving the stars glimmer-
ing down, far from the madding crowd still doing their thing in the
predawn.

She had called Matt to go get Bob, then called Prize's and made au-
thoritative sounds and said Mrs. Leung had asked her to come in at four
with her to make sure this momentous event went smoothly, no, no
problem, just with this astounding jackpot, naturally she and her husband wanted support. John Jovanic, the vice president of operations,
wanted to know if they would have to wait all night and sounded like
he was having a struggle being polite, and Nina moved to soothing
sounds about how young the winners were and how this had really
knocked them off balance. Et cetera.

Now her mind skipped around like water on a griddle. It seemed to
her suddenly that they were all making a big mistake, she most of all,
because she was the lawyer and supposed to knock sense into everyone
else. Was there any real alternative to this cockeyed scheme?

The time pressure was real, and Nina believed that her new client
was frightened and resolute enough to walk away from all that money if

she had to. Who was this stalker? Why was she so sure her life was in danger?

Well, nutty or not, here came the newlyweds, roaring up in Paul's Mustang. Jessie was sitting up front with Paul, who wore a grim line where his mouth should be.

"They did it," he reported through the driver's window. Jessie waved a piece of paper at Nina. She looked grim too. Leung was already getting out and pulling the knot of his tie tight. He looked sick, but quite sober, and had an excited look in his eye. Why, he's having fun, Nina thought. Well, why not? He had nothing to lose but shut-eye, and a million reasons to celebrate.

They came together like the co-conspirators they were, in a tight little group, though the only other cars were a long way away. In the peculiar stillness of the hour Nina could feel, beyond the casinos, the heavy pull of the mountains and the mammoth lake less than a mile away. Examining the marriage certificate, she said to Jessie, "Still up for this?"

"I have to be."

"They won't like you not having any identification. Women aren't adjuncts of their husbands anymore."

"If they insist I'll just walk away. Turn my back and leave."

"Don't worry, Joya," Kenny said. At Nina's quizzical look, he went on, "Well, I have to call her something. Consider it a pet name."

"I am not your pet."

"Ow!" was Kenny's response. The girl had given him a neat kick in the shin.

Nina pulled out the agreement she had drafted, which provided that Kenny was authorized to accept a check for Mrs. Kenneth Leung from Prize's for the sole purpose of delivering it to her attorney for placement in said attorney's trust account, and furthermore that Kenneth Leung acknowledged and averred that he had no claim of right, title, or interest in any funds obtained as a result of Mrs. Leung's gambling winnings, with one sole exception, which was that in consideration for certain services rendered in connection with collection of the said funds, Mrs. Leung agreed to pay to Mr. Leung the sum of one million dollars within ten days of the clearing of the cashier's check.

And a lot more legalese.

Kenny read it and signed it without comment. Nina took Jessie aside and made sure she understood the various impacts of the agreement. She signed it, and then Nina signed it as Jessie's attorney who had prepared the agreement, and then Paul signed it as a witness and general factotum. She had both of them sign a conflict of interest waiver. Nina tucked it all back into her briefcase with the marriage certificate and locked it in the Bronco.

It was done. Now all they had to do was go in and face a lot of people who had been waiting a long time, including the media, which had had several hours to assemble en masse.

Paul said, "Ready?"

Nina gave Jessie a scarf and dark glasses, the best she could do on short notice. Jessie wrapped her hair in the scarf à la a forties movie star. Enough of her face showed so that Nina could observe her fright, but it was Jessie who led them to the big double glass doors that led to the casino floor. Paul stopped her and forged ahead, indicating that Nina and Kenny should flank her from behind.

Their entry created a sensation. Everyone in the whole place had been waiting and seemed to know instantly that the big winner had arrived. All activity halted. Whatever they were doing, winning, losing, hoping, despairing, they paused to watch the procession winding around the blackjack tables and toward the elevators. Several security men caught up with them, adding bulk and gravity to the small group.

People clapped, slowly at first, then gathering energy. Boozy late-night faces came up, beaming. By the time they neared the elevators, they made a parade. A group of reporters poured out of the bar and started snapping pictures, and the security people made no effort to stop them. A dreadlocked kid with a distorted face darted forward—what had he meant to do?—but he was caught and bundled none too kindly back into the crowd before Jessie even saw him.

So this was how it felt to walk with royalty; the pleasure of the spotlight, the fear of the bullet.

The Palace At Four A.M., Nina thought, flashing to Giacometti's surrealistic art construction. Anything could happen at four A.M. They were participants in a surreal happening. How was she supposed to know what to do? Security had sent several uniformed men to walk in front and keep the way clear, and here was a large grinning crew-cut man beside Jessie, taking her arm.

Volts of anxiety shot through her. She noticed something else behind all the glitz that she had never noticed before, a faint odor, corrupt and metallic and inhuman like the smell of a corpse in a rusty coffin. She had smelled it on her own hands many times after playing the slots, but now it seemed to pervade the floor. It was the smell of silver tokens. She wondered about those legions of hardworking people whose labor had won them a few minutes on the Greed Machine.

Shaking herself, she stretched her neck toward the ceiling, and followed like a dignified lady-in-waiting.

Or like a rat dancing after the Pied Piper.

Or like a member of a funeral cortege in New Orleans, following the band up ahead, the horns swaying in rhythm, the music half joyful, half a dirge . . .

At the twentieth floor, in a large glamorous suite, a group of men in dark suits awaited them. They descended on Jessie. Nina just had time to glimpse a mahogany bar laden with bottles and hors d'oeuvres, and another contingent of voracious eyes held back by invisible lines in the background, the reporters, who must be under orders not to take pictures yet. It wasn't the food they were voracious about. If Jessie could keep her Grace Kelly thing going with the shades and her hair covered, she might be unrecognizable in tomorrow's papers.

Introductions were made, accompanied by bone-crushing handshakes all around. In rapid succession, Nina met seven smiling men, all masking various degrees of fatigue and discomfiture. She forced herself to concentrate, to get the names and faces straight.

John Jovanic, vice president of hotel operations for Prize's, was the crew-cut man, jowly and jolly, in his forties, fingering his wide tie, radiating goodwill. But his eyes were too small and his heartiness wasn't quite convincing. When he looked at Jessie, Nina thought she saw envy or worse.

Thomas Munzinger of the Global Gaming Corporation jackpot response team came next, tanned and seamed like the Nevada rancher he probably was, straight out of an old Marlboro ad. There was a hard direct challenge in the eyes above the smile. He said, "So she brought a lawyer."

Nina smiled too. "Just along to enjoy the show."

"What is she so worried about?" Munzinger asked.

"She's not worried. She's excited. Wouldn't you be, Mr. Munzinger?"

Munzinger didn't answer. His blue eyes stayed blank. Yikes, Nina thought, but she kept on smiling.

Prize's director of communications, Andy Miguel Doig, had a head full of auburn curls and a patient smile. He seemed to be the one appointed to keep the reporters in check.

Gary Gray, the aging slots director for Prize's, still wide-eyed, shook his head in amazement as he greeted them, though four hours had passed since Jessie's win and he should be adjusted to the concept by now. He held Jessie's hand for a long time, staring at her as if he couldn't get enough of her. He wore a red rose in his lapel.

Ully Miller, an electronics engineer with the Nevada Gaming Control Board, which Nina knew was the state agency regulating the gaming industry, was a quiet, close-shaven, middle-aged man. When he shook her hand she noticed he was wearing soft kid gloves. When he smiled, Nina saw that he had a gap between his front teeth, like Alfred E. Neuman or David Letterman. It gave him a slightly goofy appearance.

"Sorry about the delay," Nina said.

"Oh, there would have been a delay anyway. We had to check the machine very thoroughly. It takes a couple of hours. And for this size jackpot, naturally we checked even more thoroughly."

"And—I assume there was no problem?"

Miller said, "No problem at all. Bet that's the best news the little lady ever had. She sure is skittish. A win like this, I can understand, though. She still has that stunned look. She okay?"

"It's the amount. She just can't believe it."

"It's one of the biggest wins in Nevada history. Incredible. What will she do with it?"

"We haven't even talked about that."

And last but definitely not least, Nina shook hands with the one she worried most about, a short, gingery man straight out of South Boston wearing green suspenders under his suit. He was P. K. Maloney, supervising agent for the fourth district of Nevada, United States Internal Revenue Service. She had heard of him. He was part of the audit process, an awe-inspiring figure. She had not wanted to meet him.

An ornate, curved-legged desk sat under the window. While Paul chatted with the others, Nina, Jessie, Kenny Leung, and Maloney adjourned to the desk. Jessie had an inch-thick stack of forms to sign, and not one of them was easy. Nina sat down beside her and read through each form, talking to her in a low voice, trying to keep it all straight. Kenny readily produced his driver's license when Maloney asked for Jessie's, and the trouble roared out of the tunnel.

"We'll need yours, Mrs. Leung," Maloney told her. "You're the winnah."

Nina took his measure. A long Irish lip. A fleshy Irish face. He looked like her dad. Tired eyes, the eyelids drooping. A cleft in the chin. The expression of one who endures. Rough skin and a small curvy mouth. And a pair of ears at a ninety-degree angle to his jaw.

She smiled and said, "We'll be glad to provide that in a day or two. The Leungs are from Mountain View. Mrs. Leung forgot to bring her wallet up here. But, after all, Mr. Leung has his ID."

"But my dear lady. His ID is not her ID."

"What's the problem, Mr. Maloney? We all want Mrs. Leung to get her check tonight, don't we? That's what these folks from the press are waiting for, aren't they? And we all want to get some sleep. Mrs. Leung is exhausted."

"It's a regulation, Mrs. Reilly," Maloney said, not stiff but not bending either. "You understand." There was no Mr. Reilly, but this was no time to get picky. Nina nodded.

"I'm aware of that." She had looked it up just before she left.

"You see my problem," Maloney said. "I don't have the authority."

"But you're the one here in the field tonight and you have to have some discretion in handling these things," Nina said. "You must get winners who are drunk, unable to speak English, with all sorts of problems."

"They've all had driver's licenses up to now," Maloney said. "And Mr. Jovanic has probably told you, this is a major jackpot. The club has to be able to establish that she's over twenty-one, for another thing, even if I could . . ."

"She'll sign an affidavit to that effect, which will protect everyone. I took the liberty of preparing one," Nina said, pulling it out and handing it to him. "You'll note that in that document Mrs. Leung also declares under penalty of perjury that she is in fact Mrs. Kenneth Leung and currently married. It includes her address and Social Security number, and my own acknowledgment. You're in substantial compliance with that reg."

"Maybe we should all sleep on this," Maloney said. "I could call my office."

"Mr. and Mrs. Leung need to get back home to the Bay Area," Nina said. "There's nothing in the regs that allows you to compel them to stay here. She has to sign your form W 2G as required for all big winners. She is prepared to do that."

"Why, goodness me, I'd be the last to compel anyone. But surely you're not going to go out in the dark of the night when the casino wants to comp you into this fabulous suite?" Maloney said to Jessie. He spread an arm. "Why not stay?"

"I have important business to take care of at home," Kenny Leung said, speaking for the first time.

Maloney looked him over. He didn't seem impressed.

"I am the executive vice president and chief operating officer of City of Gold, Incorporated, an Internet firm with its primary offices in San Jose," Kenny went on. He handed Maloney one of his company cards. "Unfortunately, I have to get back."

Maloney raised his eyebrows. He took the card, read it carefully, turned it over. He seemed to be wavering. He read Nina's affidavit. "What's the hurry? Look at all these good people gathered here to celebrate with you. And tomorrow, why, you'll be treated like the King of Siam."

"I have important—I may say crucially important—conferences tomorrow," Kenny said firmly. "And my wife's not feeling too well, as you can imagine. She has a stress-related condition. She'll have excellent security in our home. Therefore, we'll be going home as soon as we have the ch—uh, completed the formalities." Jessie was looking at Kenny with astonishment. Kenny seemed to have mustered up a new persona, and he was pulling it off. There was some Dogbert in his Dilbert.

"It's very, very unusual," Maloney said, frowning, but his ears being what they were, his solemnity still had a comic edge, like Ross Perot pondering the success of Jesse Ventura.

Nina took her turn. "Mr. Maloney, what exactly is the problem? The Internal Revenue Service isn't going to prevent this nice young couple from collecting their prize tonight, I hope? Look at all those photographers and reporters waiting over there. I know they've been waiting for hours."

"We've all been waiting for hours."

"Well, then," she said briskly. She looked at her watch. "I'm sure none of us want to tell them the casino, or the U.S. government, refuses to give my clients their winnings. Particularly since Mr. Miller has certified the win as legitimate. That would be such a black eye for all concerned. I hate to think of it—instead of the papers saying, 'Woman Wins Jackpot,' they'll say, 'Woman Wins Jackpot, Casino Keeps the Cash.'"

"Well, we do have her Social Security number," Maloney said. "That, plus your ID and the affidavit, might be enough for now."

"I don't want that number leaking to anyone," Nina said. "By the way."

"Thomas will need it. For Global Gaming. That's the outfit that cuts the check," Maloney said, nodding toward Munzinger. "But he won't give the number out." He was vacillating. There were powerful pressures on him from both directions.

"Ah, Mr. Maloney, Mr. Maloney," Nina said. She cocked her head and looked him in the eye. "If there's one thing known to an Irishman, it's that the most sensible course isn't always strictly the one in the regs." She gave him a melting smile, then noticed Paul, watching from across the room, pretending to gag.

"It's true that every jackpot is different," Maloney said. "I suppose we have plenty of documentation. Certainly, we can get additional information later if necessary."

"Let's talk it all out tomorrow," Nina said. "I'll be at my office just waiting for your call. Now, how about the check?"

Through all of this, Jessie maintained a poker face. The gaming officials sneaked looks at her, trying to see behind the dark glasses. Maloney started folding up the paperwork, still not quite convinced.

"Why does the company that made the machine pay the jackpot?" Nina asked, to keep him from thinking any more about the documents.

"Global Gaming owns the Greed Machines," Maloney said. "I forget that most people think the casinos make the payouts on progressive slots. Global Gaming has a control room at their factory in Reno where they keep the progressive slots running all over this country and the world. It sells the machines, keeps them repaired, and makes the payout when somebody wins. Thomas Munzinger, there, he's the money man. Of course, the State Gaming Control Board watches over the operation. That's Ully Miller. Been with them twenty-two years, longer than I've been with the service. Well, let's get this stuff signed and sealed."

Thomas Munzinger came over and checked his share of the papers. The dour expression on his tanned face contrasted sharply with John Jovanic's laugh as he swapped stories on the other side of the room with Paul. Perhaps that was because Prize's was getting a sizable publicity boost, while Global Gaming was getting an enormous mark in red ink. Kenny's earlier second wind was showing signs of blowing out. His face wore a fixed smile, ghastly in its rigor. He faded from the group at the desk and Paul rescued him, whispering into Nina's ear.

"Time to go, unless you want a startling show and tell from this front. His veneer's cracking."

"I think that's all of it," Nina said rapidly to the room. "I wonder if I could have copies of the signed papers. Tomorrow would be fine." More cards were exchanged.

"Well?" Jovanic boomed. "All set?"

"So it seems," Munzinger said.

"Then come on over here, honey, it's time to make the payout. Andy, pop the corks. Thomas, you ready?" Munzinger left the room. Jovanic came over and put an arm around Jessie, saying to Kenny, "I'm sure you won't mind if I do this. It's the biggest jackpot any of us will ever see."

Then they all drank Dom Perignon from crystal glasses as the press settled into their task of taking pictures and running videocams. The champagne worked its usual magic, making Nina want to lie down on the floor and slip into a lovely pastel-colored dreamland. But the lateness of the hour was working to their advantage, as what might have been an endless party was going to have to be abbreviated before they all keeled over.

Munzinger held up a hand and the place quieted instantly except for the reporters shifting around trying to get a good view. He walked over to Jessie, whose face, what was visible of it, looked pinched, and said, "Ma'am, in a minute I'm going to give you a real check. But first, I want to present this to you." He unwrapped a brown-paper-covered poster of a giant check with the full amount of seven million and quite a few hundred thousand change written on the pay line in thick black marker ink. He held it up for photos and handed it to Jessie.

They all applauded vigorously amid a blizzard of flashes. He shook her hand. "Thanks for being such a good sport!" he said, inspiring scattered laughter. More flashes. Munzinger's smile was perfect, but the eyes stayed cold. Nina looked at the other officials. The glamour and magic of their business seemed not to affect any of them. The Prize's people, Jovanic, Andy Doig, and Gary Gray, stood together and clapped along with the rest. Gray kept staring at Jessie. Ully Miller had stepped into the background. A shadow man, tough and competent, Nina imagined.

Jessie didn't seem inclined to hold it up herself at first, but she finally held it up in a way that covered most of her face.

The cameras went nuts. Nina could hear several reporters making live transmissions. "Congratulations," voices babbled all around. Jessie continued to smile valiantly. Nina hoped she wouldn't collapse. Fatigue swept through her, bringing visions of her down comforter and thick pillow. She couldn't wait to pour herself a glass of water, brush her teeth, and climb into her own bed.

"Come on, Thomas," Jovanic said loudly. "Now give her the real thing!" Lots of laughing and bonhomie.

This time the check was regulation-sized. Munzinger drew it out of his wallet—it seemed an extraordinarily ordinary place to keep it—and handed it to Jessie in a gesture so offhanded it was almost an anticlimax.

"Global Gaming congratulates you," he said. He gave another cold smile for the cameras, which faded as he stepped back.

Much more applause. General backslapping. Then John Jovanic was back for another photo op with Jessie, shaking her hand and congratulating her. Doig and Gray, both looking happy for Jessie, were next. Ully Miller came last. He shook hands nicely, saying, "It's an incredible win," with a perhaps unconscious stress on "incredible." Nina thought, I'll bet they tore that machine apart as soon as Jessie left, trying to find a malfunction so they could void it out. He still didn't seem to believe it.

Jessie's jackpot had cast an unsettling spell over the room full of men in suits, rattling their imperturbability. They looked like people struck by a semi, disheveled and surprised to be there.

Nina hoped there wouldn't be trouble, knew there would be, and looked again at Jessie, who stood alone in the middle of the circle of interest, an aura around her, mysterious and aloof, scared and triumphant.

It took another fifteen minutes, but the four of them finally made it to the parking lot, this time accompanied by an entourage.

"Whew!" Jessie said. Her smile widened into a grin. Her white teeth gleamed. "I won! I've never had such luck. Until the moment he handed over that check, it didn't seem real."

"We did it!" Kenny said. He held out a palm and Jessie slapped it.

"What now?" Nina said. "Kenny, where's your car?"

"Over there." A black Lexus sat in the far corner of the lot, splendid in its solitude. "But I don't want . . ." He didn't finish, but it seemed to Nina that he didn't want the show to end, that he was afraid to have it end and to separate himself from them.

"They can't drive off in separate cars," Paul said, eying a few lingering press people at the edge of the lot. "Wouldn't look good."

"I'll come with you," Kenny said eagerly.

"We'll all go in the Mustang," Paul said. "Nina, you can leave the Bronco here and we'll pick it up in the morning. Okay? Joya, your wheels are back at the Starlake Building. . . ."

"I just want to get in my car and get out of town," Jessie said.

"And go where?" Nina said.

"Close. I'll come to your office on Tuesday if you need me to."

"Why not later today?" Nina said.

"I'm so tired. I'll call you when I wake up. We'll see." She yawned. This set them all off on a mass yawning fit. Nina didn't want to let her go, but she had to.

They all climbed into Paul's Mustang, which sagged so low to the ground Nina was afraid they'd scrape the asphalt. He took the California exit out of the lot. There were several cars behind them.

"They got their pictures. What else do they want?" Jessie said.

"To talk to you," Nina said.

"Yeah, well, I don't want to talk to them," she said.

"We have the check. The hard part is over. Everybody have their seat belts on?" Paul said. They took a screaming left behind a gas station and headed off into the forest on a side road. They took the second right and went up a short dark gravel path that seemed to head right into the mountain behind the casino. Paul cut the motor.

Distant engines, getting more distant.

"It was so easy," Paul said. Just then they saw a Ford Explorer turn onto the road.

"Damn!" They U-turned and roared down a residential street. Turning here and there, they finally came out on Pioneer Trail. The first pale streaks of dawn were coming over the mountains.

"The Starlake parking lot will be staked out," Paul said. "I don't see how she can just get into her car and drive off."

"But I have to have a car," Jessie said. "How can I get home? How can I get back to see you?"

Nina said, "Paul will drive you home tonight. Okay, Paul?" Paul rubbed his eyes, but nodded. "And can you pick her up when she's ready to come back?" She turned back to Jessie. "We can get you home without company, but we can't do it if you're in the Honda. Paul, you drive us to the Starlake Building lot. Give me the scarf and glasses."

Paul groaned. "That trick is older than Sue the dinosaur. It'll never work," he said.

"Well, I've always wanted to try it," Nina said. She was already pulling off her coat, and Jessie, getting into the spirit, traded her jacket. Nina wrapped herself up and adjusted the sunglasses on her nose.

"You're about six inches shorter, Greta baby," Paul said. "They're gonna notice."

"I'll just stand tall. Here's a pen," she went on, talking to Jessie. "It's time to endorse the back of the check. I'll keep it in my home safe and take it to the bank first thing in the morning."

"Here," Jessie said. She handed Nina the check, which felt as heavy as if it had been all in one-dollar bills, and Nina care-fully folded it and tucked it into the zipper compartment inside her bag.

"And your car keys," Nina said. "I'll get the check into my trust account as soon as I can tomorrow."

"What about me?" Kenny said. "The Lexus is back at Prize's."

"I don't want him knowing where I am," Jessie protested. "He's not coming to my home."

"What town do you live in?" Paul asked. "Give me a clue. I may not know your name or your game, but looks like you're going to have to spring that information, or I can't get you home."

"Near Markleeville." The town of Markleeville was in Alpine County, over the seven thousand foot Luther Pass, forty-five minutes away. "But do we have to take him?"

Paul sighed. "Okay. Okay, let me think. Okay. I know. We'll just drive all over this doggone town 'til either they or we fall down dead from exhaustion, how's that? The Lexus is in the opposite direction from Markleeville. I just don't think I can make it back to Stateline, then all the way across town yet another time to get us on the road out."

"But I don't know him!"

"You don't know me," Paul said.

"But I trust you."

Kenny said, "Wrap a cloth around my eyes so I can't see." Even Jessie smiled at that, and he went on, "I promise I will tell no one. They can pull out my fingernails starting with the pinkie."

"Isn't there something else we can do?" Jessie said. She looked around, but the mental processes were shutting down one by one. Jessie's face fell. She had realized she had no choice. Kenny would have to know, or she would be bringing home a train of reporters.

"If you tell anyone, I mean anyone, not only will you get no money, but I'll—I'll—"

"You'll divorce me," said Kenny.

They pulled into Nina's office parking lot. Jessie's battered Civic had company. Two vans with TV station logos, six people. Another car was just roaring up.

"It's just showbiz," Nina said. She got out with Jessie. They embraced. Nina got into the Civic, carrying the jumbo poster of the check, and after some difficulty started up. She pretended to be fumbling with her seat belt. She could hardly see with the shades on. She couldn't drive that way. She wrapped the scarf tighter, pulled them off, and at last clasped the buckle. The two vans that had been waiting started up too.

Paul and Jessie and Kenny left without haste, a Mustang with nothing to hide. Nobody paid any attention to them. Nina snapped the seat belt shut and took off in the opposite direction. The Civic was chaos, full of clothes and books. Jessie could have split at a moment's notice with all this stuff.

Nina drove home to Kulow Street in the Honda. She pulled down the short driveway and got out, removing the glasses and scarf. After marching up to the lead car idling outside the house, she handed the surprised reporter her card. "She's long gone. Sorry," she said. "So we can all go to bed."

Vigilant yellow-headed blackbirds sputtered in the tree next to her house, and a long low ray of sun caught her as she pushed open the front door, weary as Methuselah must have been during his nine-hundred-and-sixty-ninth year. Her briefcase was clutched to her chest, and the check reposed within.

Morning had broken, Blackbird had spoken. It was the end of the first day.

7

"I HAVE TO HAND IT to you," Paul said when he called Nina eight hours later, but in spite of this encouraging conversation opener, he sounded disturbed.

She had slept into Monday afternoon. Sandy had called and woken her a half hour before Bob had busted in, back from the tennis camp she had put him in for the summer.

She was ministering to her caffeine habit out on the deck, her eyes crusty as though she'd gone through a sandstorm, the portable phone in its usual arthritis-provoking position between neck and chin. The check had been reverently placed in a small safe in a hole behind the bathroom mirror upstairs.

She could just see Bob, half-hidden in the limbs of a gnarly giant in the backyard, the only oak for blocks among the firs and pines. He sat there eating a baloney sandwich, his legs swinging, and she hadn't had breakfast yet. Hitchcock, their black malamute, rushed around in disorderly circles under the tree, barking thunderously.

"You would have thought of it," she said. Paul-style, he was starting with something easy to talk about. He would get around to whatever he would get around to soon enough. In preparation for that moment, she treated herself to an extralarge slug of coffee.

"The scarf and the sunglasses—yeah, I see now that you had a couple of things in mind, not just helping her avoid the reporters. You manipulated the situation so I had to drive her home," he said.

"Guilty," Nina said. "But thanks, Paul."

"Even so, she got out at the entrance to the neighborhood, so I still don't know exactly which house she lives in. Man, she is paranoid. And then I still had to park Kenny someplace and get back myself. So I just put Kenny up at Caesars where I am. On your credit card. He claimed he was broke."

"That's fine," Nina said. "I'll check with Jes—uh, Joya about the expense item, but I imagine she saw that coming. At least we can keep an eye on him there. She told me she was a Washoe, Paul, but I hadn't had a chance to tell you. Sandy lives out that way. There's a loose-knit colony there, although most of the tribe members live in Dresslerville out in the Carson Valley."

"Why don't they just call it 'the rez,' like other tribes?" Paul said.

"I don't know. Maybe because there's not a typical reservation."

"Why not?"

"To make a long and tragic story short, so many of them had died off by 1880 that the government figured the Washoe were too close to extinction to bother even acknowledging. They weren't officially recognized as a tribe until the twentieth century. But they survived, although there are only about fifteen hundred of them."

"If Sandy and Jes-Joya are examples, I'm not surprised they made it," Paul said.

Damn the man's steel-trap mind. "Oh, they're doing pretty well these days. They finally got some land back at Tahoe, and they're about to develop some acreage along the highway near Dresslerville."

"A casino, no doubt," Paul said.

"That has been suggested. Sandy tells me that there's a company which has brought in some limited partners to try to convince the tribe to build a casino. But so far most of the tribal council seem to be leaning toward putting in an office complex instead."

"Why not gambling? Moral qualms?"

"You'd have to ask Sandy," Nina said. "Anyway, we know where she lives. Sort of."

"Seen the *Chronicle*?"

"I'm reading it now." *The San Francisco Chronicle* had somehow gotten news of Jessie's jackpot into its Monday morning paper. Her photo was on the front page of the Datebook section, a photo from the conference room at Prize's, being hugged by John Jovanic, lost in his bulk and Nina's scarf. The photo and accompanying story wouldn't give the man she was afraid of many clues. "They must have held the presses on this one," she said. "Didn't make the Tahoe paper yet."

"I watched a news program on CNN at noon," Paul said. "There she was, shrouded in glamour and your blue scarf."

"Don't use that word, Paul."

"What word?"

"Shrouded."

"Do you believe all this stuff she said? About the stalker?"

"I can tell she's scared. She was pretty convincing. Look what she went through to avoid having her name come out."

"Well, something's come up. Along those lines."

Nina stiffened.

"We have a problem," Paul said. "The gun—Leung's Glock—I had it in my pocket after we left the office at one A.M. In all the excitement, I didn't lock it in the glove compartment like I should have. I left it in my pocket. I remembered it when I woke up this morning, and I checked for it. It's not there anymore. The only good thing I can say is, it wasn't loaded."

"Kenny? Maybe he—it belonged to him, after all."

"I already called him. He's two floors down. Woke him up. He says no. So let's go through my movements. I picked up the gun off Sandy's desk and went out with Leung and the girl and drove them to Reno. The girl sat up front with me. I waited in the car while they got the license downtown. Then we drove to the Reno Hilton and went down to the wedding chapel. I stuck close to them throughout. The minister and his helpers never came within fifteen feet of me. Then I drove them to the parking lot at Prize's where you met us. Then we went through the casino and up to the second floor and sweated out the victory party. Then we made the switch with the scarf and I drove her to Markleeville, came back to Caesars, and hit the rack."

"You've searched the Mustang?"

"Yeah. The gun was lifted. I didn't lose it. There's a flap on my jacket pocket. The flap was down." He paused to let this sink in. "I was careless sticking it in my jacket pocket like that. It made a shape, if you knew guns."

"It was late."

"I was careless. No excuses."

"You know the word that comes to my mind?" Nina said. "Ominous."

"From the root 'omen,' a threatening portent. In other words, disaster coming. Anticipate it or bail now."

"She sat right next to you in the car."

"She was closest, longest," Paul agreed. "I was in a crowd as we walked through the casino, though, and upstairs."

"How would anyone else know you had a gun?"

"Exactly. Unless it was opportunistic, which is always possible where there are people who are losing money left and right."

"What's that girl going to do with a gun, Paul?" Nina asked. "We have to get it back."

"When you talk to her, why not ask her to bring it in?" Paul said. "Never know. Maybe she will. I don't have a phone number and I don't know just where she is. I can't waltz in there and search the neighborhood."

"If she has it, I'll get it."

"Hope you're right. She said she'd call you this afternoon."

"We obviously have a few things to talk about." Nina felt alarmed and disappointed. She harbored some vestiges of idealism about her clients, and it hurt when they persisted in acting like clients, namely, people in trouble.

"Okay. Brand-new subject. Let me get to the final reason for my call. I know how to take away that ominous feeling. It appears that we have the afternoon and evening off, and I have plans for you. This time there will be no phone for miles."

Nina said, "I'm sorry."

Silence at the other end.

"I have to deposit that check right away. Sandy has a couple of late appointments lined up for me at the office. The day's shot, and I have to work late. And I've got to do the laundry tonight. Bob's down to one pair of skivvies. And I have to hit the grocery store. I can't leave Bob again tonight. He's spending half his life at Matt and Andrea's as it is." Bob, in his tree, hung from one arm like a monkey. "Careful," she called to him. "Use two hands!"

That was all she needed, a kid with a broken leg. Paul had just gotten over a broken leg himself. They were both getting over things, and maybe she had knocked them both askew, running off to his room. In the shadow of night obscure motives had seized her, and they were unimaginable to her now.

"I can hardly believe my ears. You can't see me because you have laundry to do. Do I have that right? Is that what you want to tell me?"

She didn't know what to tell him. She had had time to think; the mood had passed and the memory of her appearance at his door wearing nothing but a coat embarrassed her. "No," she said. "Yes."

"Was last night—I mean when you came to my room—a dream? Or some kind of impulsive thing that came over you and will never be repeated?" Paul said, reading her mind.

"I'm not sure, Paul."

"You're not sure. Woman, do you know what you did to me? You're an underground seismic movement and I'm—I'm magma. I'm a great big flow of disturbed magma, and the channel out just closed up. I can't stand this, Nina. We need to spend some time together. When are you going to be free for a few hours in the evening?"

"You were so wonderful last night. Lighten up. We have so much going on. . . ."

"Nothing's going on," Paul muttered, "and that's the problem."

Apparently, lightening up wasn't in his daily planner for today. "I can't talk about this right now," Nina said. "I can't even think about it. Come in to the office first thing tomorrow morning. Where are you on the Brink divorce investigation? We have to finish that. The new client's going to need a lot of my time." Nina made it sound casual.

"Sure. Is your young nameless client going to need any of mine? Because otherwise, I'm done here. I'm still putting the business back together in Carmel. I've got a home there that I need to tend to. I'm not going to stand around in front of Caesars baaing whenever you walk by."

"I'm sorry! Okay? I've got to work and take care of Bobby, those are the first priorities. . . ."

"Don't give me that," Paul said. "Don't give me that, Nina. You're backing off. That's you all the way. Make a move from the heart, then get scared and backtrack. And use Bob as the excuse."

"Don't. I try. . . ."

"Try harder."

"I can't try any harder! I—"

"Aw, shit," he interrupted. "We've been through all this before. You know what? I hate repeating myself. It offends me. You've offended me. So screw it."

"Then make your report and go home. Because—"

He wasn't on the line anymore, so she didn't have to finish that thought. Just as well. The heat had escalated moment by moment, and a flush composed of frustration, self-pity, desire, and fatigue burned through her cheeks. She had wanted to scream at him, really let loose.

Tears came up. She had lost a certain amount of emotional control in the past year. All feelings, not just those connected with her husband's death, were stronger. She was going to have to get that control back or forget about courtroom work.

Forget about Paul. Take a shower and go to work.

She put the mug to her lips for another swallow of her milky brew, but only dregs dribbled out. "Bob!" she called. "Five more minutes." She wanted him out of that damn tree, reading a book, eating, unloading dishes, doing anything at all inside where he couldn't break his neck and his mother's heart. She went through the sliding glass door into the kitchen to fry some eggs and to refill Hitchcock's water bowl, keeping a nervous eye on Bob as he made like a chimp.

The phone rang again. She sighed, put it against her ear, and turned the eggs in the pan with a spatula.

"It's me. Jessie."

"Hi! How are you?"

"Everybody here knows about it. But they're pretty cool. I haven't seen any reporters around and I asked everyone not to tell."

"I'm glad you're in Markleeville. Your neighborhood seems like a good place to be left alone, since that's what you want."

"Oh. So Mr. van Wagoner—Paul—told you."

"You said you were staying with an aunt?"

"Yes. I was raised here. I'm very hard to find. I feel safe." She didn't add any more.

Nina really didn't feel like getting into the gun question yet. She needed to eat, settle down. She couldn't face another confrontation this soon. Maybe, before the accusations started, Jessie would mention it herself.

"So what's up?" Nina said. "Other than that it's your first day as a wealthy young woman?"

"I wanted to thank you again for last night. No matter what happens, I'm so glad you were there."

"You're very welcome. I wouldn't have missed it."

"And I—I feel like if I don't talk to someone, I'm going to explode. Are you—I realize I'm taking up so much of your time. . . ."

"Well, I'll let you take up another hour of it. How's that?"

"Thank you. Uh, I was thinking about Mr. van Wagoner. Paul."

Nina turned off the fire and slid two of the eggs, salted and peppered and curry-powdered, onto a paper plate.

"Would he be willing to go to Hawaii for me?"

The curiosity this aroused in Nina overcame her hunger. Story coming, she thought, sitting down at the table, her heart beating faster. She put the forkful of egg down and said, "Is that where this problem of yours started?"

"It's where I was posted, with Combat Service Support Group Three at the Marine Corps base, Hawaii, at Kaneohe."

"You were in the Marines?"

"I joined right after high school. For two years. I thought the Corps would be my career." Little things about Jessie began to add up. Her physical fitness, the stalwart way she had gotten through the night, her confident negotiation with Kenny Leung.

"I fell in love," Jessie said. "It was the first time I'd ever been in love. I fell in love and I got married. He died in an accident."

"Oh. I'm sorry. I lost my husband too, very suddenly."

"Then you know. It's like the future is here, you know who will be in it, you finally have a center to your life. You relax. Then it's gone. You fly apart. You're not like before. It's like being shot in the gut. You're weak in the one place where you had been so strong. It's very hard to go on."

"Yes. I know." Nina looked down at her left hand, at the rings she still wore, and flashed through her brief marriage, the anguish of losing the one she had loved more than herself.

"When I met Dan, he was a Punahou boy who was a junior at the University of Hawaii," Jessie said at last.

"What's a Punahou boy?"

"Punahou is the school where all the rich, smart kids go in Hawaii, the kids who are going to grow up and run the companies and be big shots in the government. His name was Dan Potter. Danforth Atchison Potter. His father is a partner in a law firm in Honolulu."

Jessie's voice changed in a very definite and significant way, turning thick and anxious as she mentioned the father. What was coming was obvious. Nina made a face as the story re-contoured itself around the unsettling information that a well-connected lawyer was after her client. The feeling this evoked was alarm, as if Nina had been snorkeling along a reef and suddenly found herself staring down the razor-tooth-guarded maw of a mo-ray eel.

"What kind of law does he practice? Dan's father?"

"Uh. I think Dan told me once it was insurance defense."

The most dangerous species of them all, powerful, secretive, wily, impervious to the spear gun.

Jessie rushed ahead. "Dan grew up in a big *kama'aina* house in Manoa Valley. But Dan wasn't a snob at all. I met him one evening running on the beach. He was a runner too.

"We started seeing each other. It got so we wanted to live together, but that wouldn't have been good for me in the Corps.

"Anyway, he asked me to meet his father. We didn't even go to the house, Mr. Potter said he'd take us out to the Sunset Grill in Waikiki. I knew the minute I met Mr. Potter that we were going to have some trouble, but I never could have guessed how bad it would be. I didn't pass the test. Mr. Potter didn't like me at all. He told Dan that he would be an idiot to get married. He had plenty of excuses—that Dan was too young, that he should get his degree first—everything but the real reason."

"How old was Dan?"

"Nineteen. But he wasn't a boy anymore."

"And how old were you?"

"Nineteen."

"Is Dan's father the man you're running from?"

Jessie didn't answer.

"Guess that's my answer right there," Nina said.

8

"I THOUGHT IF I LET Mr. Potter run me out of Hawaii he might forget about me," Jessie said.

"Your husband's father?"

"Yeah."

"What's his full name?"

"Atchison Potter."

"How old is he?"

"I would say—fifty to fifty-five. He looks younger."

Nina realized that she was in the middle of a client interview. She should have done it earlier. She pulled a legal pad out of the kitchen drawer and found a pen. She wrote the date at the top and her initials, and "Jessie Potter" at the top. Then she started scribbling.

"Go on," she said.

"It's hard. Give me a minute."

Nina had time to get the basics down on paper, have a bite of her breakfast, and drink some grapefruit juice. Hitchcock let out a yip at the back door. She pushed back her chair and went over and let him in, the phone still at her ear, and he raced for the kibble.

Jessie's voice again, resolute. "You there?"

"Right here," Nina said. She sat back down.

"Okay. This is pretty painful for me to talk about. We had been married eight months. Dan's father didn't come to the wedding, which was a civil ceremony in Honolulu. Just my friend Bonita and Dan's friend Byron came. I told my superior officer that I needed to go off-base and he helped me fill out the forms. Dan and I rented a condo in Kaneohe. His father was still sending him money until he finished school, but Mr. Potter was—he just seemed to despise me. He was like granite. Dan couldn't change his mind, so they stopped talking. I know that hurt both of them, but there was nothing I could do."

"What did he have against you?" Nina said.

"It's not easy to explain. Let's see. Mr. Potter—Dan tried to explain this to me—Mr. Potter had some major insecurities. He was adopted as a baby into one of the old missionary families. His adoptive parents couldn't have kids of their own, or something. They were hard on him. Whenever Mr. Potter did anything his mother didn't like she would remind him about how they had adopted him out of Christian charity and he could be on the street. He didn't look like them—he's dark, but not like a Hawaiian—Dan told me they acted ashamed of him. So he never felt like he belonged, but he had the name, and, when they died, the property."

"They never should have adopted," Nina said.

"I suppose he could have become a lot of things with that background. What he became—it's peculiar—he became a snob. A fanatical snob. Do you know what I mean?"

"I'm starting to."

"Dan's mother passed away when Dan was ten, so Dan was all Mr. Potter had. He wanted Dan to be someone, and to marry into the right family—you know, it still means something in some families in Hawaii. Social standing was everything to him. And then I came along and spoiled everything. I was"—she gave that short laugh again, the painful one—"way too dark."

"An outsider," Nina said.

"No. Might as well be specific. I'm too dark. Dan didn't look as dark as his father, you see—didn't look dark. But I'm darker than Mr. Potter. I know that's what the real problem is. Mr. Potter hates his own skin color. He isn't even that dark. He has no idea what his background is, Filipino maybe. I always thought he looked more like an Arab than a Filipino. But it's so bizarre, in Hawaii of all places, where everybody, practically, is a different shade of brown, he wants to out-*haole* the *haoles*."

"*Haole*?"

"The way I'm using the word right now, it means Caucasians. I won't bother trying to explain Hawaii's racial differences, because it's much too complicated. Anyway, to be plain, Dan's father wanted Dan to marry a Caucasian. I was a big slap in the face. He even winced when he first met me. I knew right away."

"How do you know a thing like that?" Nina said.

"You know. It's in the first split second. You just know. And later

Dan talked to me about it. Nobody else knows Mr. Potter feels this way. I suppose he's just fine with his colleagues and his clients. It's a sort of personal, limited racism."

"Can there really be such a thing?" Nina said, and realized how naive she was about the thing that Jessie was trying to explain. The shapes of racism were inexhaustible, and this was Potter's. That was all she really needed to know. "Okay," she said. "What was Dan's reaction to all this?"

"Dan loved me a lot. But he was close to his father. He felt a lot of guilt that his father was so unhappy and had cut himself off from us. He kept trying to talk to him about it, but—it's a funny thing about racism. To Dan the problem was as clear as can be, but Mr. Potter never once admitted it. He acted very angry that Dan would think such a thing about him.

"But we were happy. At night Dan had to study, so we stayed home a lot. I think Dan felt under a lot of pressure between school and worrying about his father. But we were doing all right.

"Then a strange thing happened. Dan started getting these abdominal pains every once in a while. They got pretty bad and he had it all checked out twice but Dr. Jun couldn't find anything wrong. He had Dan take an MRI and everything. Finally Dr. Jun decided it must be anxiety over the—the marriage and his father, and Dan went on Xanax. But it didn't help. The pain would still come on pretty suddenly, he never knew when, about once every two weeks or so. All of a sudden he would be in this agonizing pain, doubled up on the couch, moaning. It was difficult for me not to be able to help. I felt so sorry for him. He started just suffering through it at home, because he had realized that in a day or two the pain would go away and he'd be absolutely fine again."

Nina scribbled furiously.

"It was—it was February seventh of last year. Dan and I were out in our kayak, over by Chinaman's Hat. Do you know Oahu?"

"Not that well."

"It's on the Windward side, past Kaneohe, heading toward North Shore."

Nina formed a hazy impression. She had visited Oahu briefly and remembered some parts of the Windward side of the island very well, over the mountains from Honolulu.

"It's a tiny island not far offshore, a bird preserve. The morning was very hot and muggy, but you could see the mountain ridge on the island of Molokai to the south. I remember Dan talking about Molokai, how the light was hitting the mountain so it seemed to be floating. . . ." Jessie stopped again.

Bob threw open the kitchen door and came in, dropping pine needles all over the just-swept floor. Nina scowled and pointed down, and he said, "Oops!" and tossed his hat on the couch and kicked off his shoes, which landed in two different corners of the living room. Hitchcock, ever game, skidded after the shoes, pushing the Swedish rug askew, and in a moment appeared at Nina's side, his jaws full of sneaker. His paws had something slimy on them. In an instant the neat living room had been reduced to rubble.

Nina mouthed severe words. Bob was trying to get his shoe away from Hitchcock. His hands were filthy. Hitchcock danced around him in circles.

"Jessie—I'm sorry—just a minute." Hand over the receiver, she said, "Wash 'em."

"Trees aren't dirty! He's got my shoe!"

"Wash 'em!" He went to the sink. As he passed Nina she smelled the scent of the trees on him, the sap and the fresh needles. She reached out and tickled his waist under the baggy sweatshirt.

"Okay," she said to Jessie. Hitchcock lost interest and set the saliva-shiny shoe carefully on the seat of the easy chair. Nina anchored the phone against her ear with her left shoulder, bent over to hug the dog's barrel chest from behind with both arms, and pitched the dog back out the kitchen door.

"Dan had an attack in the boat," Jessie said. "It came on—one minute he was fine, the next—I started rowing us in to shore, but he was writhing, that's how bad it was, and it was choppy, a lot of whitewater—we went over. We were alone out there. It was overcast and the water wasn't clear. I saw him struggling and I crashed through the water to him but he wasn't there anymore. He had gone under that quickly.

"I went after him right away and I dove and I dove until I—it was deeper than I thought. I couldn't see and the waves were crashing over the rocks about thirty feet away. Dan was—he was gone in the first few seconds. I think he swallowed water right away. I don't know if he even knew he was in the water, he was in so much pain. I never saw him, never touched him." Her voice broke. "He wasn't even twenty-one years old. It was shattering."

Nina saw them in the water, the boy sinking, the girl searching blindly, thrashing to the surface for breath, diving for him, reaching for him.

"I stayed out there and I kept diving. About ten minutes later another kayak came by and they called for help. They made me come in. I was completely worn out by then. Some guys fishing off the sandbar in Kaneohe Bay found him the next morning. I went there. My friend Bonita came and helped me. I wasn't in very good shape."

"It must have been unbearable."

"Dan was a wonderful person."

"I'm sure he was."

"We never should have gone out in the kayak, not until we knew what was wrong with him."

So Jessie was playing that destructive game called second-guessing. Nina played that game, too.

"There was an autopsy?"

"Yes, an autopsy and an inquest. It was at the inquest that I realized Mr. Potter blamed me for Dan's death. What a sickening shock that was. He came up to me, his voice shaking, his face really red, and he said, 'You can fool them, but you can't fool me.'"

"What was the finding at the inquest?"

"Accidental death. But the police talked to me several times. I was under suspicion of—killing Dan."

"That's what Mr. Potter told them?" Nina said.

"Yes. Because there was no sign of anything wrong with Dan that would make him fall out of the boat. They just didn't want to believe what I told them. The autopsy report didn't find anything wrong with him."

"But he'd been having these attacks—"

"Dr. Jun—we had gone to him twice, did I mention that?—testified. He had his records. But all he could say was that he hadn't been able to make a diagnosis. He said that all the tests were negative and he thought Dan's pain must be psychological. The medical examiner wanted to know if Dan might even have been poisoned. He was a friend of Mr. Potter's. You see what Mr. Potter was doing? But even so, the medical examiner ruled it an accident. I was there and I told what happened and that was that, I thought.

"Dr. Jun didn't know Dan had kept on having the attacks, because Dan had stopped going to him. One of the officers asked me why I was telling all these lies about Dan having an attack if it was really an accident. I felt like saying, Make up your minds! Did I poison him so he was sick, or did I lie about him being sick and kill him some other way? I felt like because I was a Marine, it actually hurt me. Like I was some kind of freak, a woman Marine, who might do something like kill her husband. I think I almost was arrested, but the police finally decided there wasn't enough evidence.

"But they had dragged me into this nightmare, with Mr. Potter pressing them to arrest me, and my superior officer started looking at me in this funny way. I'd walk into a room and they'd all be talking about me. Some of the guys complained to my superior officer that they didn't trust me. I think Mr. Potter spread the word that I had something to do with Dan's death. Mr. Potter wrote letters to the newspapers saying the police weren't doing their job. He hired a lawyer. But the police closed the case. All this happened in about a two-month period between February and April.

"Mr. Potter was doing things to me that whole time." Jessie's voice changed again as though her throat were constricting.

"My landlord asked me to leave and wouldn't give a reason. I found out later that Mr. Potter and he both belonged to the Honolulu Club. My credit card was canceled. I started getting phone calls, hangups. I couldn't sleep. I changed my number and it kept on. I reported the harassment. No more calls, but then I woke up one morning and someone had been in the condo while I was sleeping. Somehow he had gotten a key."

"And how did you know that?"

"It's disgusting. I haven't told anyone else this. I should have called the police, but I—"

"Don't worry. I've heard it all," Nina said.

"I had a photo of myself dancing in costume at a powwow in Carson City a few years ago. It was in a frame, next to the TV."

"And?"

"I walked into the living room and the photo was in the middle of the floor. And someone had—there was feces on it."

"And you didn't call the police?"

"No! I mean, I was afraid. What if they thought"—her voice got small—"that I was trying to deflect suspicion and did it myself? What if it was reported in the paper? What would they think on base? My life was harsh enough."

"Still, you should have." Nina was thinking, there is a sexual component to this, and a mighty sick one. "Wait," she said. "Just a minute. I just can't follow this. Why in the world was Dan's father so positive you killed his son?"

"Because he's crazy with resentment that I took his son away," Jessie said. Her voice caught on the last word. "That his son died on my watch. He has a lot of money and power and there's nothing I can do. He's been careful, so I can't catch him directly at anything."

"But what motive could he possibly think you have?" Nina insisted.

"I don't know!"

"So what did you do?" Nina said.

"I went to talk to Mr. Potter."

"That was brave."

"A security guard met me at the gate. He called the house and said Mr. Potter wouldn't talk to me unless I had come to confess. Mr. Potter called the police and said I was stalking him, coming to his house. It was hopeless!"

"Then what happened?"

"I was lucky about one thing. My tour of duty finished in April. I didn't reenlist. I had no future in the Marine Corps."

"They should have rallied around you."

"Yes. The fact that my buddies didn't quite believe me hurt the most. Bonita was the only friend I had left. I decided to leave Hawaii and come home. Here. I made some zigzags in case he was still following me. I think maybe he was, but when I came back to the Sierra last April, I didn't notice anything. But I watched for him, expected him, any day."

So she had been hiding for fifteen months, a long time to maintain such a high level of emotional intensity.

"Mr. Potter never asked Dan anything about me. He knew I was Native, and he knew I was poor and came from the mainland but that's all he knew. My aunt—she's not really senile or anything, just confused sometimes—anyway, she arranged for me to work part-time at the Smoke Shop—you know, on the highway right outside Minden. . . ."

"Sure. I've stopped in there. Jewelry and souvenirs. I bought a beaded barrette there once."

"And cheap cartons of cigarettes. The ranchers come from miles around. Anyway, I—I took the long way home from work on Sunday night. I was, well, you could say I was upset about my life, or you could say I was crawling out of my skin from never doing anything but hiding and working. I just wanted to forget everything."

"All alone?"

"Yes. But as soon as I hit Tahoe I started feeling very anxious. This was the first time I'd been out in such a public place in months. I thought I saw Mr. Potter pulling up outside Prize's. I panicked and went down the aisles and sat down at a dollar slot. The Greed Machine. I would have been dead broke in another five minutes."

Nina put down her pen and transferred the portable phone to the other ear. Bob trotted down the hall to his room and a fingers-on-the-chalkboard scratching started up at the door.

"Well? What do you think?"

"It's a hell of a story," Nina said.

"And now this. Is it really true? Am I—that is, is it—"

"Well, I've got the check. I'd say you have quite a history ahead of you," Nina said. She laughed.

"So—do you see why I was thinking that Paul might help me? He can go to Hawaii and prove I didn't kill Dan. It's the only way. I have to face Mr. Potter, but with some facts."

Oh, sure, Nina thought, two people in a boat, no medical findings, nobody's ever going to prove anything. But all she said was "I'll call Paul. Ten A.M. tomorrow, okay?"

"Uh oh."

"Problem?"

"Someone's at the door! I think he may have peeked in the window a second ago."

"Don't answer," Nina said.

"Okay, I'll just sit here until he goes away."

"Hello?" Nina could hear faintly over the phone. "Meter man."

"It's just the guy who reads the meters," Jessie said.

"Saying it doesn't make it so."

"You're right. I won't answer, then."

"I just need a signature," Nina heard.

"He's wearing a uniform and everything," Jessie said. "I don't want to cause any trouble for my auntie."

"Ask him to slip whatever he wants signed under the door," Nina said. She heard Jessie's phone clank against something, then Jessie telling her visitor just that.

"Sure," the voice said. "No problem. You're Mrs. Potter, right?"

Suddenly Nina was afraid for Jessie. She had just heard a hair-raising story and now Jessie was standing in a line of fire talking to someone who might have a gun. "Jessie!" she yelled into the phone.

"Jessie!" No answer, but she didn't hear anything alarming either. A few moments later Jessie got back on the line.

"He wasn't a meter reader."

"I was afraid of that. What was he?"

"I don't know. They're legal papers. There are numbers on the sides of each sheet, and a stamp on the one on top." Jessie was silent, reading. Then she said, "I don't understand. 'Application for Entry of Judgment Based on Sister-State Judgment.' What's that mean?"

"I don't know yet."

"There's a whole sheaf of papers. What could it be? My name's on the front. It's some kind of legal notice and they call me a Judgment Debtor."

Bob came out with his backpack on his back. The neck of his new electric bass stuck out of it. It would probably fall into the road on the first bump. "Bye," he announced. "Going to Nikki's."

"When will you be home?" Nina said, putting her hand over the phone.

"Before dark."

"Home by dinner."

"It's summer!"

"You heard me." She said to Jessie, "I think he was a process server, Jessie. This could be too important to wait until tomorrow."

"I just can't get up to your office today. Tomorrow is okay, but not today."

"Then fax me the papers."

"There are fifty pages at least. I don't have a fax. I'd have to go to a Mailboxes Etc. somewhere. It would be expensive."

"You can afford it. Go and fax me the papers. Here's my fax number at the office."

"Look. I can't get away, okay?"

"Why not?"

Silence. Nina couldn't shake the feeling that Jessie still hadn't told her everything. "This is important," she said. "How do you think he found you? I have to see those papers right away."

"Okay. I'll fax them."

"Right away. Can you get into town by ten A.M. tomorrow morning?"

"Yes."

"Good. And Jessie?"

"What?"

"When you come, bring Kenny's gun."

"Huh?"

"The gun. Paul told me it was taken from his pocket last night."

"Oh, no. Who would know it was there? He must have dropped it."

"You knew it was there."

Jessie protested. She said she hadn't touched the Glock, hadn't even noticed Paul picking it up off Sandy's desk. She asked a lot of questions herself. She seemed to be startled, seemed to have no idea what had happened to the gun.

Ominous.

Nina hung up and rubbed her sore shoulder. She couldn't take the urgent scratching anymore. She let Hitchcock in. Let's see, purse, briefcase, contact lens case—leave Bob a note—

Hitchcock divined her purpose instantly and ran to the door, casting urgent looks back.

"I have to go to work, boy," she said. "Bob'll take you out later." She looked at Hitchcock and Hitchcock let her have it, his heart on display in his brown Raisinet eyes. He was still shedding his winter coat in July and as he wiggled his body and wagged his tail, hair floated off his coat and glistened in the sunlight as it fell to the floor.

"You stay," she told him. He understood this and his grin drooped. The brightness faded from his eye.

But when she gave up and pulled on her running shoes, the dog forgave and forgot, prancing around her, nudging with his head.

"You're a nag," she said. "G'boy. G'boy. Okay, walk." She had uttered the magic word and his whole body thrilled with it. "A short walk," she said. "No! Don't slobber!" They went outside. She wrestled the dog onto his leash and walked up Kulow Street toward the Jicarilla Meadow. It was about eighty degrees. The forest of pines was all around her, the one her cabin sheltered in, and she looked at the trees gratefully. She knew she was safe for the first time in a long time, and she only wished Jessie Potter could feel the same way.

Jessie's refuge had turned public. Where a process server had gone, others would follow. What was in those legal papers?

9

NINA SAT WITH HER BARE feet up on the desk, dictating a will for a young man with leukemia. Her watch, a thin-banded Gucci that her mother had worn, told her that it was four-thirty in the afternoon. It was still Monday. Time had stretched thin and long over the last couple of days.

The fax machine, stocked with a new roll of paper, hadn't shuddered under the opening salvo of whatever pirates were after Jessie's win yet. Nina had been checking it every ten minutes.

Sandy was filing a complaint at the County Clerk's office on Johnson Boulevard, trying to beat a five o'clock deadline, and the town seemed to be in the grip of a midsummer afternoon snooze.

She put her notes down and stretched her arms behind her head, looking around. She had moved in two years before, after being downsized from a respectable appellate-law job in San Francisco. Her office might be just a modest suite on the first floor of a two-story redwood building on the highway, but it was her modest suite, where she was the boss. It consisted of Sandy's office where clients waited, the inner office where she was now sitting with its big windows with their views of Mt. Tallac, a sliver of the lake, and the boulevard, and the conference-room-slash-library.

The suite had one major problem. Sandy constituted the only boundary between Nina and whoever came through the outer door. If she was down the street at lunch or in the conference room, Nina had to leave the inner office door open a crack in case someone came into the reception area. Now and then the visitors were disgruntled, unwilling to wait, or spooky. The office needed a partition with one of those

glass windows that slide open. Maybe next January, the only time of
year when no business was conducted at Tahoe, because everybody was
out of money and too tired to quarrel. Meantime, her office door was
wide open so that she could see the corner of the outer door.

The wide-open door had admitted several murder cases in the past
year, and one or two big civil cases. Nina was developing a rep as a last-
resort, pull-it-out-of-the-hat litigator, rash but effective. But there were
also the quiet, nonadversarial legal tasks, the timeless ones like drawing
up deeds and drafting wills. This client, a very sick boy of nineteen,
wanted to give specific bequests to friends and family—his tennis racket
to his brother, his high school ring to his sister, his bowling shoes—
bowling shoes!—to his best friend.

She gave away the bowling shoes in a choked-up monotone that
Sandy would have to decipher tomorrow. He was a brave boy. His
name was Alex, and he would be coming in in the morning.

She finished that tape and turned to the other pressing cases, the
contract matter and the custody battle and the marijuana bust and the
fender bender, jumping up like a jackrabbit to check the fax whenever
her anxiety got the best of her.

The trick was to take one small solid step forward on each case, dic-
tate a letter, return a phone call, rev up Lexis and look up a legal point.
The court cases moved jerkily forward in a back-and-forth with opposing counsel, the speed contingent on many things out of her control. All
she could do was take the next step on her side as soon as possible.

The afternoon passed and the sun went down in a flight of gray and
purple clouds over the mountains. No fax.

One last check of the daily calendar. Jessie's check was safely
deposited. At eight-fifteen the next morning Nina would be in court
on another matter. Jessie at ten. Alex and his mother sometime
before lunch. A hearing on a custody case in the afternoon. Nina
stretched, hands folded together behind her head, pushed her chair
back, put her socks and Nikes back on, packed up, and pulled open the
outer door.

The fax! It began to produce Jessie's paperwork with excruciating
slowness. She was due home and her eyes were shot. She stuffed the papers in her case to read later and ran out the door and into the parking
lot.

A man waited by the Bronco, a platinum-haired hooligan inadequately disguised by a broad smile.

"I recognized your car," he said. "You're the lawyer."

The accent was English. Nina didn't beep the truck, but she kept
her hand on the beeper, which with the right press of the finger would

set off the alarm in the truck and bring somebody running. The man's bleached-white hair had been buzzed practically to the scalp, but with long close-cut sideburns. He had an anciently busted nose and deep creases around the eyes. Heavy-duty black jeans, black T-shirt, and muddy thick-soled boots with chains on them . . . he was a skinhead from a foreign clime, exotic even in this town full of travelers.

They were alone in a darkening lot, with distant yellow pools from the streetlights across the street the only illumination.

"I'm a lawyer, yes," Nina said. "But I don't have time to talk right now."

"It's a rush," the man said. She heard mockery in his tone and didn't like it. He wore a buck knife in a pouch hanging from his waist. She didn't like that either.

"I've lost something very important and it's urgent that I get it back," he went on.

She pulled out a card and gave it to him, saying, "Call me tomorrow. I can't talk to you right now."

A couple of fast steps forward and he was blocking the driver's-side door. "Millions of dollars," he said. "Now, don't you think that's worth chatting about? I had that seat saved, and that was my machine. Your young lady took my seat without my permission and now she's stolen my jackpot. It's that simple."

"I don't know what you're talking about."

"Balls. Jessie Leung. Should I talk to her instead of you?"

That was an alarming idea. "No," Nina said. "You can discuss your problem with me. You had the seat before Mrs. Leung sat down?"

"Dead right, and that husband of hers promised to save the seat. I was gone less than five minutes. See the problem?"

"I see that you're very upset. It's a lot of money. If you want to talk to me about it, though, it has to be during regular business hours."

"Leave me the fuck alone," he said in an exaggerated falsetto, mocking her again. "Oh, I know you'd like me to. But this can't wait."

"What is it you want, Mr.—"

"I want half of it. Just half. A private deal, no publicity, and I go away. Simple, easy, everybody happy. Sale price, today only, since the bitch—I mean, since the young lady managed to slip it over on everyone and she gets something for that."

"You want half the jackpot," Nina said.

"That's right."

"Or?"

"Or what?"

"What's the alternative?"

"The fucking alternative is too drastic for me to elaborate on at this fucking time. Get me?"

"I'll tell my client what you said," Nina said. She wished she was a black belt. She wished she carried a machine gun. She wished she wasn't afraid, but she was in this deserted parking lot and all she wanted was a way out in one piece. "I can't make any promises."

"Tell her now. You got a mobile. All lawyers do."

"I don't know where she is."

"She's hidin' over in Alpine County with a bunch of Indians," the man said. "The husband is nowhere around. I know just where she is, but I'm trying to be nice, talk to her mouthpiece, make a reasonable offer."

"I don't know how to reach her," Nina repeated. "It's going to have to wait."

He pursed his lips, pretended to think about that. "Okay," he said. "I'll call you about eleven tonight and you give me an answer. Don't worry, I got your home number."

"And just how did you get that?"

"Your number? How hard do you think that is?"

"Who are you?"

"Charlie Kemp," he said. "The pleasure's mine." A sarcastic smile.

"Mr. Kemp, with this size claim, you need a lawyer. You need to know what your rights are and whether your claim is likely to prevail— I need to talk to my client, and I can't get hold of her by eleven."

"I will call you at eleven, sharp. Drive down there and talk to her. You got time." When she didn't move and he didn't move, he made an elaborate show of stepping away from the Bronco. "Oh, pardon me. So sorry. I seem to be in the way."

"Good-bye, Mr. Kemp."

"Don't blow it, love," Kemp said. He reached out and chucked her on the chin, and Nina stood there, face burning, knowing she could get a lot worse if she fought back. He moved off jauntily toward the sidewalk. Nina waited until he was fifty feet away, then beeped the Bronco, threw open the door, jumped in, and locked herself inside.

Then, soaked in cold sweat, she breathed. All that was left was the sick taste of her humiliation, her physical helplessness, the fact that she had been forced to talk her way out instead of telling him what she really was thinking and pushing her way by him. She thought, I have to do something. I have had it with this physical menace from men.

But as soon as she got home, she called Paul.

• • •

Paul arrived at Nina's house at ten. Scouting the neighborhood, he walked around the yard with Hitchcock and looked under the house. He was thorough and he was armed. Bob, oblivious, played ear-splitting music in his bedroom.

Nina made a fire in the orange Swedish stove in the living room. "Thank you for doing this," she said as he stamped back in. "I'm going to wire the house." He took off his brown bomber jacket and hung it on the banister.

"Good idea, but it won't help tonight. I guess we wait," he said. "I'll take the call. He won't bother you with me around."

"It really got me that he knows where Jessie is, and that he has my home number. I have no doubt he knows where I live." She had told Paul Jessie's first name.

"Relax. The Man is here."

"Would The Man like a beer?"

"Might take the edge off. So I'll pass. Coffee, if you don't mind."

Nina couldn't sit, so she loaded dishes into the dishwasher. Paul seemed to have gotten over his anger at her, or maybe he was just being professional? She wondered if she really was stringing him along, keeping him in Tahoe, because she needed him so much.

"Kenny said he did promise he'd hold the stool for him. I asked him tonight before I came over," Paul called to her from the living room. "So aside from his bad attitude, what kind of case would Kemp have if he went after Jessie legally?"

"He has no legal right to one cent of that money," Nina said. "He knows it. That's why he's trying to extort it, but he hasn't said quite enough yet for me to go to the police. The one who pulls the handle wins the jackpot. He had no right to ask Kenny to hold the seat."

"But Kenny said he would, and said he'd take a hundred bucks for it."

"But Kenny didn't have the power to hold the seat, so that agreement was invalid from the start."

"Can't blame him from one point of view," Paul said. "I myself might behave badly under the circumstances."

"Not this badly. I suppose I should have expected something like him to wriggle out from under the pine needles, but I've never had a case like this. I think he's only the first."

"We could tape him."

"Inadmissible in court since he didn't give permission. I could even be charged criminally like Linda Tripp."

"The police could get a wiretap order. Or we could try to put him off again."

"Give it a shot," Nina said. "But I suspect he's going to take it as a no, and then I don't know what he's going to do." Paul had stretched out on the couch and turned on the TV with the sound muted and somehow found ESPN, which she had long ago deprogrammed. There was a golf match on. The players were standing around in their pastel shirts, staring at another player who was getting ready to putt.

"Well, at least she has a gun," Paul said. "Maybe."

"Paul?"

"Uh huh."

"I really ought to talk to this jerk myself. My self-respect is suffering, thinking of how easily he leaned on me in the parking lot of my own building."

"Why? I'm here, aren't I?"

"Because I'm disgusted with myself. I do criminal law, the people get rough sometimes, and I have to run and hide the minute there's even a hint of a physical altercation. I'm telling you, I'm sick of it!"

"Take a class in self-defense," Paul said. "You could be a real Tasmanian devil."

"Maybe I should. You really think I could ever get confident enough to take on a guy a foot taller than I am? I was thinking mace, or even—"

"No," Paul said. "Forget guns, Nina. You wouldn't kill him, and he'd get it from you. Mace? You've still got to have that physical confidence to get it out and hurt somebody."

"I can imagine doing it but I'm not sure I *could* do it."

"So you keep me by your side. On the couch, at the office, in the bed."

"Too expensive," Nina said. Paul laughed, and gave no sign of irritation. He was there on business, the business of protection.

"How's it going with the cocktail waitresses?" Paul asked. Nina had just associated in with a Nevada attorney named Marlis Djina in an employment discrimination case against all four of the big gambling clubs at Tahoe.

"Cocktail servers," Nina said, correcting him.

"As if there ever was a male cocktail waitress," Paul said. He laughed again. He was actually in a good mood, because he was getting ready to out-muscle somebody, and this now began to irritate Nina. "That's why it isn't discrimination, that they have to wear high heels. All 'cocktail servers' do, so where's the discrimination?" he went on.

"You think the Kiss My Foot campaign is pretty funny, don't you?"

"Well, when they all got together and burned their spike heels on a mock fire for the press—that made them look silly," Paul said. "Like the bra-burning."

"That never happened. Some guys' wishful thinking. And these women didn't really burn high heels. They staged a symbolic protest. Some of them have to carry heavy drink trays in three-inch heels," Nina said. "It's torture."

"I'd do that before I'd work in a coal mine, or weld heavy machinery, or be a sewer worker," Paul said.

"Have you ever tried it?" Nina said. She went upstairs and found a pair of Manolo Blahnik spike-heel sandals with Roman lacing. "Put them on," she commanded.

"I'm not looking for the prince," Paul said. "Like you women. Besides, you are a world-class spike-heel wearer. What hypocrisy."

"The difference is that I don't *have* to wear them. I never wear them if I'll be standing up for very long. Those women walk miles and miles each shift. Sometimes they go home with blood in their shoes. Why should they have to suffer physically for men's visual pleasure? The job is to deliver drinks and take orders."

"The job is to get the men in and keep them in," Paul said. "The men still have more money to blow." His smile had faded.

"The clubs don't need it," Nina said. "Gambling is a big enough draw. They don't need the sex."

"They need to use sex along with everything else to draw the suckers in. Anything to take the men's minds off how badly the gambling is going," Paul said. "Topless dancers, free booze, shiny cars as special prizes, sports bars, prostitutes . . . so the waitresses have to wear high heels and smile and look sexy. Big deal."

"Women in physical pain aren't sexy no matter what they're wearing."

"Okay, Counselor," Paul said. "You win." He turned up the sound on the television. The hushed voice of the golf announcer noted that Tiger Woods had missed his birdie putt and was going for par. "Sorry," Paul said. "I have two hundred bucks riding on this tournament. I'm betting that Tiger Woods will win by more than ten strokes. It's only the first round."

"You're betting on a *golf* game?"

"Look, Nina. Let's start over. Come here and sit down. Take it easy." He watched the tall, broad-shouldered young player putt from six feet. The crowd sighed as the ball rolled just past the cup to the right.

"Well, I'll be. He's going to bogey. There goes that bet," Paul said, and after Tiger did just that, he went back outside for another of what he called his "perimeter surveys."

Nina went to organize Bob into bed.

Eleven o'clock came. They sat there with the phone in Paul's lap and waited. Eleven fifteen. Midnight.

"I can't believe this," Nina said. "I have court tomorrow at eight-fifteen."

"What do you want to do?"

"Go to bed," Nina said. "I still have some legal papers to go over before I'll be able to get to sleep." In answer Paul pinched the phone cord and pulled it out of the phone.

"Let's call it a night," he said. "You have to pace yourself. You're supposed to show up in the morning ready for anything. What's the worst thing that could happen?"

"Kemp could come here."

"That's covered. I'll stay."

"What if he goes to Jessie's? The process server found her. I know Sandy warned her, but . . ."

"Trust me, he's bluffing. Kemp doesn't know exactly where she is in that neighborhood, unless he's Washoe himself. And somehow I doubt, from your description, he'll pass for a neighbor and get lots of information out of the locals."

Nina thought of the bleached hair and Brit accent and said, "Not unless he's a very peculiar Washoe." She yawned.

"Now the sole remaining question," Paul said, "is—where do I sleep?"

"Oh, Paul. We can't. Bob wouldn't—it wouldn't be right." She looked at the couch. "I'll bring you some bedding." Bob came out at that moment in his oversized T-shirt and baggy shorts, collected a Fruit Roll-Up from the basket on the counter, took a sharp look into the living room and surveyed the situation, then said, "'Night, all."

"He'll take good care of you in a few years," Paul said after Bob had gone down the hall. "What is he now, fourteen?"

"Thirteen."

"Seeing much of his dad?"

"I doubt Kurt will ever leave Germany. I heard he was engaged, but I don't know anything about her." Nina had three or four major regrets in life, and Kurt Scott was one of the biggest. She didn't regret her first precious love affair, and she sure didn't regret the son that had resulted, but she had handled things badly, denying both Kurt and Bob a relationship they deserved for many years.

"What does Bob think about getting a stepmother?"

"He pretends it's nothing but I know he's nervous. He doesn't want to be number two." Anxiety came up in her. "What kind of game is this jerk Kemp playing with me, Paul? Why doesn't he make the call? What could he have to gain by putting me and Jessie through all this anxiety for nothing?"

"Not enough information to tell," Paul told her. "Run along to bed, now." She bent over him and kissed his mouth. He held her close and made her do it again, until the kiss took on a life of its own and threatened to drown them both. She pulled away.

"Hurry," Paul told her. "Or I won't be responsible."

Jessie's faxed papers lay on the bed. Nina, however, had come to the end of her personal marathon. She picked them up and made her eyes move mechanically around on the top sheet, but her brain refused to follow. Sleep rolled under her and bore her away.

She dreamed that she was in a department store looking at a marvelous sleeping bag for professional women who had to spend the night on the job, very neat and official-looking with various compartments. When you pulled on the string, the bag opened out like a chifforobe into a hinged apartment. On one side, which was as big as a room wall, there were drawers for an office, bunk beds, and hanging stairs leading to a complete hanging bathroom, all decorated in Danish Modern.

Finally! How she wanted to move in, but she was out of time, she had to get to court. Her clothes lay in a heap on the floor. She saw an iron and ironing board. She picked up the iron and started furiously ironing her skirt, trying to get those wrinkles out.

10

"WELL, WELL," SAID JEFFREY RIESNER as Nina walked into the law and motion session on Tuesday morning. "What a charming surprise."

She hadn't had coffee yet. Her skirt was wrinkled in spite of the dream and her hair was flipping into anarchy. Jessie's papers were still sitting unread in her briefcase. Her client, Hector Molina, wasn't needed and she was expecting a quick impersonal in and out. They were in the upstairs Superior Court and Judge Amagosian hadn't arrived yet. Three or four male lawyers, all of whom Nina knew, clustered around Riesner.

He came right over and took her arm like he owned it. She shook it off. Dominating body language was his specialty. He smelled like a Parisian hair salon and his tie was Hermès. Infuriatingly tall, the hair ever thinner above permanently raised eyebrows, he was extremely successful at his work, which was representing insurance companies and well-heeled defendants in criminal cases. Today his face bore a rancid, mocking look she knew well. "Now, don't be coy, Nina," he said. "We need to talk. Or haven't you seen the papers?"

"I'm busy right now."

"You seem to have a problem using my name," Riesner said. "It's Jeff." When she said nothing he said, "Can't we just get along? Why do you hate me?"

Because you're a phony, Nina thought. Because you are loathsome and deceitful. Because you will do anything in pursuit of fame and money. Because you've got the morals of primordial ooze.

She was not in a good mood.

She let him lead her to the back of the courtroom. The bailiff was filling out forms at his desk and she was ten minutes early, so she had time to talk and he knew it. "All right," she said. "What do you wish to subject me to this morning?"

"So she didn't give them to you yet. Maybe I ought to let you read them first. But no, that would be too courteous." He had the exhilarated look of a man about to land a solid punch. "It's your new client, Mrs. Leung."

Jessie? What did Riesner have to do with Jessie? She didn't react. She didn't want him to see her surprised or ruffled or angry, not ever. Any sign of emotion was like the smell of steak to a man like him, an invitation to feast hearty. "Court's starting. What is it?"

"My client has a money judgment from Hawaii against your client. We filed the judgment with the clerk yesterday and the clerk entered the judgment."

"Go on."

"Mrs. Potter was served yesterday with the Notice of Entry of the Judgment. So was your bank. Oh, by the way. I'm serving you too." He handed her a number of documents, which looked like replicas of Jessie's documents, and which she took because she didn't think there was anything else she could do. "After all, it's your trust account," he said. "Just following the rules."

She held the papers at her side. She wasn't about to look at them.

"Naturally, my client was concerned that with your record an attempt might be made to withdraw the money before the writ could issue," Riesner went on. "We couldn't allow that. We have obtained an ex parte order placing a lien upon the funds until the writ can issue. So don't even think about it. The funds are frozen."

"The writ?" Nina said. "What writ?"

"A Writ of Execution. Against your client. To seize the funds to satisfy my client's judgment. Unfortunately, we have to wait thirty days for that."

He gave her only a second to register all this. After a plaintiff obtained a judgment in a civil case, the plaintiff could seize the defendant's nonexempt assets up to the amount of the judgment. The legal pleading which authorized seizure of the assets was called a Writ of Execution.

"I'm listening," Nina said. "You're requesting a Writ of Execution based on a money judgment your client has obtained against her?"

"Right. In Hawaii's First Circuit Court. Honolulu."

"This is the first I've heard of it."

"Really? You should start talking to your clients. As I said, she was served yesterday."

"Who is your client?"

"His name is Atchison Potter. She tell you about him?"

Nina bit her nail, noticed what she was doing, and put her hand firmly into her pocket. The ugly surprises had begun, and they were excruciatingly, almost brilliantly, ugly. She thought, Here we go.

"He sued her? For what?"

Riesner said, "Wrongful death."

"Whose death?" But she knew what was coming.

"Her husband's. Mr. Potter's son. Danforth Potter. The police wouldn't act. He had to do something. So he sued her in civil court."

"She had a lawyer? She defended herself?"

"She didn't wait around. She split."

"She was served with the complaint in the case?"

"She left Hawaii just in front of the process server. They had to serve her by publication. The notice was published four times, as the law demands."

"Ah. In the Hawaii newspapers," Nina said. "After she left. Naturally."

"That was her legal domicile. He made diligent efforts to find her. She didn't choose to make herself amenable to process."

"She didn't know she was sued, she therefore didn't have a lawyer. And your client picked up a default judgment, do I have this straight? My client never appeared in the action?"

"Mr. Potter presented his evidence at the default hearing, and a circuit court judge granted the judgment. It's all quite impeccable."

"It's all quite easy to vacate," Nina said. "We'll file a Motion to Vacate the Judgment. You'll have the papers in the next day or two."

"Alas. It's been more than six months. It's as final as a lethal injection."

"Not quite. She just heard about it for the first time yesterday," Nina said. "There's an exception to the final judgment rule. The whole case can be reviewed when you try to enforce it in another state."

"Naturally the State of California will give full faith and credit to the Hawaii judgment."

"Don't be so sure."

Riesner chuckled. "You haven't even read the paperwork yet."

"It comes from you, doesn't it?"

He barely winced. He readied another punch.

"Oh. I almost forgot. The court has also granted an ex parte Order for Examination of Judgment Debtor. That's in the paperwork too. We don't have to wait thirty days on that. So less than ten days from today I plan to sit down with Mrs. Potter and have a nice chat with her about her assets and debts. And other pertinent information."

"That's premature," Nina said. "Before it is even determined whether a writ will issue? There's no need for that."

"Wouldn't want her running around wasting her assets."

Nina thought about asking him to do the right thing—to put off the examination until after the hearing she was going to request. But what was the point of asking? All she had to do was look at him to see how much pleasure he was taking in stomping on her toes and sticking bamboo slivers under her fingernails. The cattle prod to the genitalia he hadn't managed yet, though.

She said, "It's too soon. I'm sure she'll want to contest the motion for a writ. You won't be sitting her down to quiz her about her assets for a—"

"On the contrary," Riesner said. "You don't have a ground in the world for protest. I don't have to wait for the writ. I'm going to sit her down, without you present, as is my client's right and privilege, and I'm going to take her through every shoddy financial event in her life. She's not going to get lost again."

"Your client is a harasser," Nina said. "What he really wants is to know her address and any other personal details he can glean that will allow him to harass her further. This isn't about money at all. He hates her. He's wrong to blame her for his son's death. She was never charged with . . ."

"Thank goodness, the civil courts of Hawaii stood ready to redress the failings of law enforcement," Riesner said in that officious slimy tone that always made her want to scream and lower her head and butt him in the stomach, which was about as high as her head would reach on him.

She squared her shoulders. Enough of being pushed around. "Don't interrupt me again, Riesner," she said. "Or your head will be even further up your ass than it is now."

"You're so cute when you try to play with the big boys. Listen, he's got the judgment. There's nothing you can do. That's the beauty of it," Riesner said, chuckling, enjoying himself.

The court clerk and the stenographer had come in and sat down, signs that Judge Amagosian was ready.

"All rise," said the bailiff.

Simeon Amagosian appeared on the bench up front, his white hair and shaven cheeks looking as fresh as sheets of fabric softener, and said, "Well, what have we got today?" Riesner was still standing next to Nina in back, and he was waiting for the question she did not want to ask but had to ask. So she gritted her teeth and whispered it.

"How much?"

Riesner came in close, dousing her in the sickly sweet odor of his aftershave. "The judgment? It's for eight million dollars," he whispered back. "Everything she won, plus he can garnish her pay for the rest of her life. I thought you'd never ask."

Back to the office on Lake Tahoe Boulevard she went, finally set free from Riesner's presence. The mountain god had ordained a perfect mountain morning. No wind, no haze, no cloud, a filmy blue sky. Transparent wavelets brushed innocently against the shore. A man with calves like small hairy tree trunks jogged in the bike lane, pushing a stroller with big wheels.

She wondered what a vacation felt like.

Leisurely breakfasters jammed the parking lot at the Red Waffle Hut. The town was filled up for the summer season. A kid rocketing by on his skateboard had the stunned, joyful look of Wen Ho Lee the day the Feds gave up.

Nina pushed open the office door with her free hand, the briefcase weighing down her shoulder in the other. Notwithstanding her discussion with Paul about shoes, she was wearing three-inch heels today and could feel exactly where the bunions would erupt in a few years.

"Good morning, everyone," she said. Her will client, Alex, and his mother had the chairs near the door, and Jessie was already there too, reading one of the Sherman Alexie books Sandy kept at the side table. The gentle samba of Carlos Botelho played in the background, hopefully soothing any savage breast that might wander in. Up against the far wall, behind her desk, Sandy was on the phone. Giving Nina a significant look, she inclined her head very slightly toward Nina's office. Translation: don't talk to anybody until I get in there.

"Be right with you," Nina said, and passed through the door into the relative privacy of her office. The pink slips she had disposed of the afternoon before had reappeared and proliferated on her desk.

Pushing them aside, she pulled the faxed sheets from Jessie from the briefcase and began comparing them to the pleadings Riesner had just laid on her. Riesner had spoken truly. Somehow Atchison Potter had managed to convince a judge for the First Circuit Court of Hawaii to give him an astonishingly large judgment against Jessie. Or maybe that was the going rate for a man's life.

The legal papers gave a thumbnail sketch of the story.

The Complaint for Wrongful Death and several other causes of action alleged that on or about June first, 1999, Jessie Jo Kiyan, born on

September 11, 1979, and Danforth Atchison Potter, born June 27, 1979, had become husband and wife.

The complaint told how the couple established their joint domicile at Kaneohe, Island of Oahu, State of Hawaii, and how Jessie immediately and on numerous occasions thereafter showed great and unusual interest in a trust account established by Plaintiff Atchison Potter in the name of and for the benefit of Plaintiff's son.

You can allege anything, Nina thought, but she didn't like hearing this.

Then came the kicker, in the unemotional language of the law: a few paragraphs down, the complaint alleged that on or about February 7, 2000, Jessie had caused her husband to drown in a negligent and/or deliberate manner hereinafter to be shown.

No details, except the bald statement that Dan Potter was in excellent health at the time of his death. There must have been evidence taken at the hearing. The marriage had lasted barely eight months. Dan Potter had been not quite twenty-one years old when he died. It was a tragedy no matter how it had occurred.

As Riesner had said, the summons had been published four times in the newspaper. The Hawaiian Petition To Serve By Publication alleged that Jessie had thereupon left Oahu on or about April 3, 2000, and that diligent attempts to locate her thereafter, which were set forth in detail in the accompanying Declarations, had failed to find her.

Nina looked at the "due diligence" Potter had used to find Jessie. No forwarding address. Military records confidential. Attempts to find local family members. His lawyer had made it look like Potter had moved heaven and earth to find her.

When he hadn't, the court had allowed him to have the hearing without her. Under the law, she had been "constructively" served.

An eight-million-dollar default judgment against a Marine! They could only have been thinking that the money amount just didn't matter, since Jessie couldn't pay any amount.

Talk about luck! Potter must have danced a jig when he finally found Jessie. It must have been the photos. The Honolulu papers might even have reported Jessie's amazing jackpot. Or could he have somehow learned about Jessie's Social Security number on the IRS forms?

Or could he have known Jessie was living near Tahoe, found her the night of the jackpot, watched her enter Prize's, watched her try to hide in the aisle of Greed Machines, watched the win, as she had feared? There would have been just enough time to hire Riesner and get the papers on file.

The date-stamp on the complaint indicated that it had been filed on

July 10, 2000, just three months after Jessie's disappearance and five months after Danforth Potter's death. Atchison Potter had wasted no time suing her.

Nina went on to the Judgment after Default. The Hawaii lawyer seemed to have done all she should have for Potter. After a hearing on the evidence, the court had, on November 12, 2000, issued its judgment against Defendant In Pro Per Jessie Kiyan Potter in the amount of Eight Million Dollars, plus costs of suit, with interest to run from the date of issuance of the judgment.

That was the value Atchison Potter had persuaded the judge to place on his son's lost life. The closeness of the judgment amount to the jackpot was a stunning coincidence.

Nina thought it was no more than that. No one could have predicted the amount of the jackpot. Fate itself had decided to play a game with them.

She looked at the July desk calendar. The judgment had certainly been issued and entered more than six months before.

If Jessie had stayed in Hawaii that judgment would have clamped on to her life and never let go. No one would have expected her to pay it. But for ten years, renewable for another ten, the judgment debtor could be hounded, questioned repeatedly, lose a large portion of her wages, lose any inheritance. Jessie would become an indentured servant to her father-in-law.

All the judgment debtor could do was run far away, get lost, and stay lost. Jessie had done that for other reasons, and because of it, now that she was in California, the Hawaii judgment could be reexamined on a limited basis by the California court before a Writ of Execution could issue.

Nina set the papers down. She had wondered where the trouble would come from. She hadn't imagined the trouble would be this big.

Sandy filled the door. Today she wore a full blue cotton skirt, new leather sandals, and a purple blouse with fringe along the pockets. Her functional but carefully selected clothes struck Nina the same way a strand of lights on a Christmas tree struck her, as a superfluous enhancement to one of nature's grand creations.

"News," Sandy said, taking a step in and closing the door behind her. "From Paul."

"Paul? What's he up to so early in the morning?"

"You're gonna want to be lying down with a wet washrag on your forehead after I tell you this."

A blood pressure jump. "You're making it worse, Sandy. This withholding thing you do—you have to stop doing it. Just tell me."

"I guess I'll just lay it out."

"Please!"

"He said to tell you that gun is nowhere. And Kemp seems to have disappeared. Paul wants you to ask her again, does she have the gun."

Nina groaned. "How does she seem this morning?"

"She's toughened up some. She got knocked for a loop but she's going to handle it."

"I guess I better get her in here."

"First, you have to see Alex. He's not doing so well." Sandy handed her Alex's blue-backed will.

"Keep Jessie out there, Sandy. You already knew her, didn't you? That's why she called you."

"You took good care of her. I knew I could count on you."

"Is Jessie—is she a relation?"

"She's Joseph's grandniece on her mother's side." Joseph was Sandy's husband.

"Why didn't you tell me right away? That she was a relation?"

"I thought it was up to her. She wasn't even sure she was going to tell you she was Washoe. She wasn't sure about you. You better get to work. I'm gonna make some coffee."

"Thanks."

She didn't leave. "And you gotta have foamed milk?"

"It makes better coffee, you know."

"One hundred strokes. Up down on the pusher thing." She set a finger next to her mouth, waiting for further useful information.

"I need foamed milk, and by God, I deserve foamed milk. I'll make it myself, Sandy. Don't bother."

"I'll do it," Sandy said, holding up a hand, showing her generous nature would expand to include even this zany proclivity.

Nina, aware that a point was being made at her expense, appreciated the gesture anyway. Sandy's problem with the foamed milk was that it was such a WASP-y cultural artifact. Requiring foamed milk was putting on airs. She had never made it for Nina before.

"One more thing, Sandy."

"Yeah? I got to get out there, you can't leave clients on their own."

"I'll give you details later, but these papers—Jessie's got another legal problem."

"Jessie told me a few things."

"So you know about the opposing counsel. . . ."

"Rosemary's baby, all grown up into Satan in a suit."

"Yeah. Riesner."

"This time, let's get him good."

"Sandy? What happened between you and Riesner?"

Sandy swayed in the doorway for a moment, and then, as if dislodged by a sudden wind, sat down in one of Nina's orange client chairs. "You want to know after all this time."

"Yes." When Sandy didn't speak, just sat there drumming her fingers on her legs, Nina said, "He can't stay away from me. He delights in insulting me in and out of court. I think he's spreading rumors about me to other attorneys."

"No wonder. He's after you."

"Ugh. You don't mean—please. Take that back."

Sandy pursed her lips. "I told you once, it's dog-eat-dog up here. Well, he's the rottweiler. That makes you the chihuahua."

"I know he's out to get me. When you came to work for me, I called him and asked him for a recommendation. And he said not to hire you. Remember?"

"Sure. I remember. But you hired me anyhow."

"Well, why *did* he fire you?"

"You sure you want to know this?"

"Whatever you can tell me."

"You can't tell anybody else."

"Whatever you say."

Sandy said, "I guess it's time you know what you're dealing with. He's a deep one, deeper than you know. Well, he had a client. A woman in her eighties. We handled the will. He'd come out and greet her with this big smile and get her into his office and shut the door. And I don't know what all he would tell her then."

"Uh huh."

"Yeah, she was a smart bird but he was smarter. She was lonely. That man was sending her flowers, practically standing on his head for her."

"Because she had money?"

Sandy nodded her head emphatically.

"But the lawyer who draws up a will shouldn't be a beneficiary," Nina said. "Not in this situation."

"Not in his own name. But he has so many corporate shells, he could string a necklace. I filed the corporate papers, I ought to know. And I saw one of the names again. Rose Crown Enterprises. As primary beneficiary under the will. No fingerprints of that man on those papers either. Or his wife. Used the name of some crony he planned to split with, I guess."

"The old lady died?"

"He was at her bedside at Boulder Hospital. A week later, I'm filing his stuff and here's her estate going into probate. That man was the executor. Rose Crown was the beneficiary. I think I was the only one at the firm who knew what he was up to. He has a personal secretary who does his typing, but she's a dingbat."

"What did you do?"

"Hey, no job is worth putting up with a crook for a boss. I went in and told him I knew what he was up to. Gave him a chance to straighten up. Next day I was demoted. New status. Disgruntled, powerless soon-to-be-former employee."

Nina waited.

"So I stole the will," Sandy said. "And the copies. I knew where they all were. File clerks know where the bodies are."

"You did *what?*"

"I still had my key and they hadn't had time to change the locks. I drove over there about ten at night and went in and took the will and all the copies. I went to work for you. And that was that."

"Where is the will now, Sandy?"

"Around."

Nina thought about this. "You shouldn't have done it."

Sandy's expression didn't waver.

"You could have filed a complaint with the State Bar on the estate's behalf."

"The governor had cut the State Bar's funding so bad they wouldn't have gotten around to it this century. You know that."

"You could have told his partners."

"Then the papers would disappear and I wouldn't have any proof."

"He couldn't probate the estate without the will," Nina said thoughtfully.

"You got that right. Her money eventually passed intestate. To her grandnephew in Arkansas," Sandy said. "Heard that boy had a whale of a party when he heard the news." She tapped her lip. "Yep, whale of a party."

"One thing I don't understand, Sandy," Nina said. "Why did you keep the will? Why didn't you destroy it?"

"So he won't sleep good. He knows I have it."

Nina said slowly, "That's actually a pretty good reason."

"Some of 'em, you have to keep a club handy so they don't uncoil and sink a fang into you a long time later. So. You asked me what his problem is with you. Maybe part of it is, he thinks I told you."

"Why didn't you tell me before this? I've asked you enough times."

"Hey. It takes a while to get to know a person."

Nina took that as the high compliment it was.

"Well, he's got the judgment," she said. "I'd give us one chance in ten of stopping him."

Sandy opened the door. "Where's your gumption today? Did he put something in your cereal?"

She went out.

Alex and his mother came. Visibly paler and thinner than two weeks before when he'd asked her to make the will, Alex sat down immediately. His mother was a blond soccer mom, a Tipper Gore of the 'burbs, the bubbly kind who takes the team out for pizza after the game. She pulled her chair in close to her son's. She was making the best of things. Nina felt her own resolve coming back.

Alex read the will and said it was cool. Nina went down the hall, passing Jessie, who was still reading, shanghaied the real estate ladies who worked in the office by the rest room, and brought them back with her. They stood by soberly and witnessed Alex signing his will, and then they signed. Alex thanked them and they left.

"All done," Nina said. "If you'd like, I'll keep the original in my files and you can take a copy."

"Might as well," Alex said. He shook hands and went outside. His mother stayed with Nina.

"Don't give up hope," Nina said. "You never know."

"We're down to praying for miracles," she said. "He's so calm. It helps me. I didn't want him to make his will, to even think about what's coming. He was right, though. He wants his leaving us to be as easy as possible." She brushed away a tear.

Nina hugged her. "Let me know if I can do anything else."

"Can you keep him from dying? I'm sorry. Sorry. Thanks."

Ten-thirty. Sandy came in. "Can you see Jessie now?"

"Send her in. Anything else from Paul?"

"Not a thing."

"Hi," Jessie said. "I thought the earlier I got here the better. Did the Englishman call last night?"

"No." Nina paused. It seemed implausible that this neat, trim young woman in her cotton windbreaker could be the center of such a whirlwind. It was hard to see the girl with the millions of dollars swirling around her.

"I called Kenny this morning. My husband," she said with a nervous laugh.

Nina had forgotten about Kenny Leung. She sipped her latte, which was mostly hot milk, and which she considered a medicine, not a food—caffeine for energy, calcium for calm. Calm alertness, that was the ideal state, and she didn't have time to get there via meditation. Chemicals would have to do.

"He just can't wait to get his hands on his share," Jessie went on. "Anyway, he deserves it if this works out. Yesterday was great, really peaceful. I got some rest."

"That's good."

"I feel much better with you helping me, and it's all coming together." She smiled.

"Like a couple of seven-forty-sevens heading for each other above San Francisco Airport," Nina said. She drew a couple of planes smashing into each other, wings flying everywhere, on her legal pad as she spoke.

"Excuse me?"

"That's how it's coming together. You're an important figure in this town all of a sudden, Jessie. I warned you about that, but I don't think anyone could be prepared for the storm that is blowing up."

"What do you mean? Is it the papers? I couldn't stand to look at them. I had too much else on my mind."

"I'll try to summarize," Nina said. "Then we'll talk. We now have the following situation going on on this beautiful morning. One. There's the jackpot and your marriage of convenience and those fellows in suits in that hospitality suite on Sunday night or actually Monday morning. And the media.

"Two. There's Atchison Potter. You have been found, Jessie. Those papers you were served with yesterday came from him."

"I see," Jessie said, her voice small. "I saw that some of them were about Hawaii. I was afraid to read them."

"I'm going to be blunt. Brace yourself." Nina watched the spine straighten, the face go impassive, the eyes focus on Nina's face like parallel-track laser beams. This girl is not helpless, she thought.

"Go ahead," Jessie said.

"Mr. Potter sued you after you left Hawaii. He obtained something called a default judgment. He claimed, just as you said he would, that you were the cause of your husband's death."

"Yes, ma'am. I knew he wouldn't quit. I knew it deep down."

"The judgment is for an enormous amount of money. He wants your winnings. All of it."

"No, he doesn't. He just wants to destroy me."

Nina drank some more coffee. Calm alertness. Alert calm.

Jessie suddenly banged the desk with her hand, with enough force that the desktop actually shook and Nina's carefully balanced coffee went over.

"This is how you protect me? How did he find me?"

"Be right back," Nina said.

She marched down the hall to the bathroom, took off her blouse, which luckily was not silk or rayon today, and rinsed it under cold water for a while. The coffee spot darkened, widened, and melted into the rest of the fabric until it disappeared. She held it under the hot-air hand-dryer for a couple of minutes until it reached an acceptable state of clamminess.

Always the sticky strings, she thought. A vision came into her mind, of Jessie all wrapped up in a cocoon of slimy legal maneuvers like a colonist in an Alien movie, only her face exposed. Pleading, "Kill me."

It better not come to that. She buttoned her blouse and went back to work.

11

THERE IS ONLY ONE ACTIVITY in life in which the reality principle has no advantage over the pleasure principle.

Gambling.

When we're very young children, we think we are the pint-sized lords of the universe, that we can command the clouds to move, and they will. But time passes and after many humiliations we learn that we cannot have all we want simply by wishing for it. We learn to give up our craving for absolute selfish pleasure, to delay gratification. We accept that we are not gods and that we have to work. We learn that actions have corresponding consequences and that there is no free lunch.

That is maturity. Accepting the reality principle relieves much frustration and suffering.

Gambling, however, revives these infantile fantasies of omnipotence. The gambler wins or loses without relation to any rule or reason. He feels godlike if he wins. He has commanded the clouds, and they have moved for him. The pleasure is the pleasure of the infant, deep within and ordinarily well suppressed.

And the sooner Red got his infantile fixation stuffed deep down again, the sooner he could stop compulsively betting everything he owned.

A psychologist had told Red all this the year before, when Donna made him seek counseling. And it was all true, just the conclusion was dead wrong.

"Seek counseling." How he loved that phrase, which encapsulated the whole bourgeois schtick. Melt into the mainstream. Submit to the authority of some dimwit who couldn't make it through medical school. Admit he was powerless over his addiction and surrender and get humble and hold hands in a circle and drink coffee in a roomful of losers. Give up the only thing in life that was truly his, private, thrilling, and more important than anything else.

Gambling was even more than that. The scare when he was watching the roulette ball about to sink into the slot was the only time he felt truly alive. During those moments he connected to the flow of fortune through the universe. Intuitions and portents moved through him like currents. Sometimes he knew for sure he would win.

And when Red was fortune's child, when fortune smiled on him, he knew it. He could do no wrong. He could hit on an eighteen at blackjack, bet the double zero on the roulette table, throw chips onto the inner crap lines where nobody wins, bet in a daze. His hands would tremble and the sweat would break out all over, and he would be gripped by that uncanny certainty—he just knew! And he would win. That moment was everything. He rode the real power and it was ghostly, ghastly, indifferent, like white lightning.

When he lost, of course, that was bad. Then there was anguish, the feeling that he was no longer fortune's favorite. But that was when he felt the urge to gamble the most. Because all that mattered then was to get it back.

That was how Red had started out two years before, winning. What started the gambling off was a longer story, which he didn't mind telling to the psychologist because he didn't want her sifting through nasty Freudian junk in her mind when she looked at him.

He had it figured out. It was his mother. The "precipitating event," as the psychologist put it, was that his mother died before he had a chance to tell her what he really thought of her. She knew, though. She didn't leave him a dime. It all went to the old folks' home where she'd spent the last five years.

She was a German Russian. Her folks had emigrated from the Volga region to Kansas in the twenties to get away from Stalin and the gulags, just as their ancestors had emigrated from Germany to Russia when Catherine the Great invited them to come visit in the seventeen hundreds. Over and over they started, with nothing but their Bibles and their backs. After all these centuries of wandering and persecution and poverty and making something out of nothing, all Red's people wanted was to build square houses and stay put and live rigid, safe, controlled lives.

All they knew was the reality principle. No pleasure for them. Red's grandparents had worked his mother almost to death before she ran away to Nevada. And had him eight years later, by some long-gone cowboy sonofabitch whose picture Red had never seen, since she tore them all up.

"Bose Junge," she used to call him in her Volga German dialect. No umlaut. Bad boy. And she had started working *him* to death.

In her mind, she would always live on the Volga, in a dirt cave dug into the banks, only a potato to eat here and there, freezing. She always refused him anything to make his life easier, always made him pay with chores for every bit of clothing, every school fee, made him work himself through a crummy college because she said she didn't want him spoiled, when he was smart enough to go to Yale. No comfort ever came from that downturned mouth. He ate baloney sandwiches for fifteen years for his school lunches.

Her crowning achievement had been the guilt. She treated him like shit and then made him feel like it was all his fault. The guilt was like a sickness she passed on to him from her dementedly hard-working ancestors.

He explained all this to the psychologist. The psychologist wanted him to be sympathetic, rise above. Forgive her! "It was hard for you. You weren't sure of her love."

"She didn't love me. You don't love your slave." Red was picking his teeth with a mint toothpick. He saw the psychologist make a note about that.

"There was something in my teeth," Red said. "Do you have to turn everything I do into a symptom?"

"You do that a lot. You clean things. Remember those dreams you told me about, where your teeth are falling out?"

"So what? This is not a dream, this is something from lunch in my teeth."

"Okay. Let's leave it at that for now." The jerk stole a glance at the gloves Red wore, because of the germs everywhere.

"Let's leave it at that forever," Red said. "I'm having a slight upthrust of aggression and hostility."

"All right. Let's get back to your feelings. She wasn't able to nurture you. She made you feel lost and lonely."

That was the last time he saw the shrink.

Red was not lost and lonely!

His mother gave Donna and him a casserole dish for a wedding gift, while her Cisco stock was zooming. She got rich in her old age scrimping and working and investing. Salt of the earth, her neighbors would say when they saw her sweeping up every last dust molecule from the rickety steps outside the cottage in Reno where she lived even after she could have bought the whole block and never missed the money.

She never bought herself anything. She just swept the steps, wiped the lid on the ketchup bottle, scrubbed the walls, bleached the clothes, wiped the doorknobs with Lysol. That was her pleasure. It was like she had to wash things for the rest of her life to make up for the ancestral mud of Russia. She swept the steppes!

He used to lie awake at night thinking about burglarizing her place, maybe even killing her somehow. But then she went into the home and it was too hard. And then she died peacefully in her fucking sleep before he even had a chance to tell her off. She escaped and he was left twisting impotently . . . no. He wasn't impotent.

This Bose Junge could still get it up. He could even make the clouds move sometimes.

Red had worked around casinos all his life, starting in security. He knew more than anybody about gambling. Up until then, he had never gambled himself.

But after she died, he started. He started dropping quarters into the slots at the Sparks Nugget, where nobody knew him. After a while, quarters bored him and he moved to the dollar slots. He learned black-jack. He was good at it. The jump from two-dollar to five-dollar tables took about three months. The roulette came later.

It was the kind of pleasure he understood, fear-pleasure, the plea-sure and the dread all mixed up together. Once he got used to it, he couldn't live without it. It was the vice he had been made for.

So he gambled, and he won at first. He won much more than he lost. For the first time in his life he really enjoyed himself, stealing silver from the sky, cheating the odds, doing it all on the sly.

Donna figured it out early. At first, when he was winning, when he came home with bouquets and nightgowns and electronic equipment, she was right there with him. Then when he went into the losing streak she started looking at him and checking the accounts and noticing things.

She didn't talk until one night she had screwed up her courage with a couple of gin and tonics and said, "You're going to lose your job. You have to stop. If your boss finds out . . ."

Having just popped a few pills which hadn't kicked in yet, he had been getting ready to go out and hit the blackjack tables at Circus Circus in downtown Reno. Combing his hair in front of the mirror, he said, "He won't find out."

He could see her behind him in the mirror. Donna, she of the open emotions, had a closed-up look that made him afraid somehow. He turned. Putting his hand on her cheek, he said, "Not now, sweetmeat. I have such a good feeling about tonight. It's going to change everything. Don't bring me down. I might lose the feeling."

"But you've lost over twenty thousand dollars in the last two months!"

"So? Before that I was winning. I still had some things to figure out. I learned a lot about how to ride the streaks. It was a lesson, babe. Watch how I do tonight."

"Please. Please don't go."

"This is the last time. You'll see."

He went out and played smart, played good, but she had ruined his confident mood, inserting doubt like a cold rectal thermometer. He knew he couldn't win. Even so, as the sweat dripped off him, he wrote more checks, knowing he couldn't cover them. That night, the dealers were on fire and his cards were ice. He had left, swearing never to go to Circus Circus again.

Then came a long spell when nothing he did brought him luck. It seemed to him that he needed to bet more, play more, get through it. He lost their savings, the whole thing, the cashed-out 401K plan, the mutual funds, the savings account. Then Donna really started in on him. She couldn't understand that he had to keep on, get through the bad spell, and for that he had to have a stake.

He forged her name and refinanced the house. He played smart, downtown where the club take wasn't as high, pacing himself, following the rules, helping fate.

But he lost it all one night. He had broken one of his rules, which was not to drink. He had been winning and he had decided to reward himself at the bar before he went home, and then the idea got into him to go back and play a few hands at the $25 minimum blackjack tables.

He blew through the rest of their life savings in ten lousy minutes.

He stopped for several months. Donna made him stop by threatening to leave him, and what was worse, she swore through her tears she would tell his boss that he was gambling. That would cost him his job.

Because he was one of only a few people in Nevada who wasn't allowed to gamble. He couldn't gamble because of his job. It was unthinkable, which was, as even the psychologist might have eventually concluded, one of the reasons he had to do it. He was showing them all up, thumbing his nose at the eight-to-fivers, showing what he was really, an adventurer, a rebel, an iconoclast who played the daily game so well he had them all fooled into thinking he was one of them.

Of course, by now he had developed a disguise, only it wasn't really a disguise, the suit and tie he wore to work was the disguise. He had gotten the idea from his wife's uncle, a card counter named Al Otis. Uncle Al had been 86'd out of every casino in Nevada, so he had started wearing women's clothes when he went gambling. It worked. Red had followed the lead, taken on a secret name and secret persona.

The new personality, which he kept in the trunk of the Porsche Boxster he leased, was his other self, his real self, expressed in a fake ponytail and goatee, a baseball hat, leather jacket, and Harley pins. He didn't get rid of his outfit even after he promised Donna he would stop gambling. She didn't know about the outfit. He had the only key to the trunk.

So for a few months he didn't gamble, and it wasn't too hard because things got hairy at work. He clocked in right on time every morning, good boy, and he did his job very well, analyzing the slot action all day long to see if any were paying out too much, watching the security tapes on the jackpot winners, making sure nobody got anything if he could help it.

A big problem cropped up when a tourist lined up three eights on a Quarterinsania slot machine, which would have given this clod almost two million dollars, but the eights weren't evenly lined up even if they were all touching the center line. The bells didn't even ring.

So a couple of techies went in, and they ran through the code on the EPROM chip top to bottom until they managed to pinpoint the problem, which turned out not to be the chip at all. It was a malfunction in peripheral equipment. A coin box drawer on the inside of the machine had opened and crashed the chip. It wasn't a scam, it was a machine failure.

This was not related in any way to the jackpot, said the tourist. The result was right there for all to see, and the machine said, three eights on the payline, you win

Which wasn't true, hadn't been true for years. The EPROM chip source code on the inside was all that mattered. If it showed a different result than the payline the tourists saw, the payline didn't matter.

The jackpot was disallowed. Global Gaming, the Gaming Control Board, the casino, they all agreed on that.

And the stung player took them to court, which resulted in an embarrassing few months because the whole thing about how the Erasable Programmable Read-Only-Memory chips worked wasn't really in the public awareness.

Of course when it all came down, the Nevada court ruled for Nevada.

Once they had the court case out of the way, there were some newspaper articles written with more insight into "random" gaming technology than Global Gaming liked to see, and more outraged citizens to placate. He worked with the other casino PR guys to bury the case. As the Nevada Supreme Court had said, "The good will of the state of Nevada is at stake in a situation like this."

People needed to believe in luck, so the noise died down fairly quickly. But Red was very busy for a while, and his other self stayed stuffed in the trunk.

Then one night in June, he stopped off for a drink at the Sparks Nugget on the way home, still in his suit and tie, and he started talking to this English guy who had just won a bundle. He was buying the whole place drinks, celebrating, young good-looking girls on both arms. It resurrected the longing in Red. He started thinking, Why can't I do the one thing in my life that's fun, that I want to do, that makes life worth living?

He couldn't, though. He had no money except his next paycheck, and they had to eat. They had to cover the lease payments on the cars or else his boss would find out for sure and fire him, and he'd be humiliated, divorced, and homeless. He knew that happened to other guys. He had seen it more than a few times in his business. He didn't expect it to happen to him. He was different, clued-in.

But he couldn't risk losing Donna. He needed Donna. He wouldn't be able to stand it if she left him.

He just had to be smart. He thought a lot about it. He needed a gigantic stake so that he could gamble all he wanted.

And he thought up a way to make it happen.

He got the Englishman's room number upstairs and he called him about a week later. This time the guy was on a losing streak and not friendly and not forthcoming, but he told Red he'd meet him.

The roughneck's name was Charlie Kemp, and he was from East London by way of the oil fields in Seal Beach. He was a complete stranger with absolutely no connection to Red.

Perfect. Red made him the offer. Kemp didn't believe anything he said at first. Red had to show him his ID, talk to him a long time. But when he finally got it he said sure, he'd do it, and he called Red "mate" and put his arm around him. Red thought, Yeah, we're going to do it, mate, but don't screw up, because you may look tough, but I'm smart.

That had been two weeks before, the beginning of July.

So now it was Tuesday morning and he was lying on the bed with the curtains closed. Donna had called his office for him.

He was too sick to work today. He was sick with humiliation.

Kemp had called him against all orders for a couple minutes just after it happened on Sunday night, told him how he had gone to take a whiz just for a second, mate, thinking he still had some time left on the schedule. That fucking asshole had screwed up in such an unbelievably stupid way, Red could hardly take it in.

He had been right there at the Greed Machine aisle! Five minutes before! Told Kemp he'd be watching! But then Amanda, whom he had brought along for window dressing and who didn't know what was going on, used up all his money, and they couldn't just sit there at a progressive and not play. So they moved over to some quarter slots and eked out a little play and then the bells were ringing.

"Jackpot!" Amanda said, and he pushed her back there, knowing just where to go.

But a girl was sitting on Kemp's stool!

And he, Red, then had to go away and take the cell phone call and change back into his suit. He came back and sat with the whole crew, casino people, Global Gaming people, Gaming Control Board people, while the tech guys spent two hours verifying the fucking code on the machine, and, funny thing, it looked absolutely legitimate, but Red called his boss, Prince Hatfield, about postponing the check ceremony anyway. He needed time to think of some way to salvage the fucking situation. But Hatfield, still smarting from the bad press on the triple-eight incident, told him the big guns had decided Global Gaming should pay off.

It was rich. Really rich. He felt like the old woman was back on earth, pushing him away all over again.

Then, to add to the whole thing, the big screwup by the screwup, the loss of all that money he had lined up, on top of all that, *he had to watch the girl with the scarf take his fucking check,* some nobody who never had fifty cents to her name in her whole life before, along with her husband who looked like a reject for a comedy show, who had told Kemp he would hold the seat!

What a night. He had gotten up on Monday, painfully, and taken three Motrin. Then he shaved, dressed, and went to work to see if there was anything he could do. There wasn't. When he got home he took a long shower and went to bed.

He didn't feel well.

So now it was Tuesday. The first day of the rest of his lost and lonely—shut up! Donna was still at work. His watch told him it was past three in the afternoon. He had another shower, washed his hair a few times, and flossed hard. Then he felt better.

Later, after a freezing dinner with Donna, who he really didn't feel like talking to right now, who had just gotten the bank statements and wished to inform him that they were overdrawn, who looked at him with mistrust in her eye—he said he had to go out. And she said, "Don't you dare."

"I'm not going to gamble."

"You're lying."

"I give you a reason not to to trust me lately?"

"It's building up. You're so tense. Don't pretend it isn't."

"Well, I'm not going to gamble. Look. No money." He actually turned out his pockets for her. She didn't care. She just sat at the dining-room table and didn't even take her head out of her hands.

Which only made it build up more.

That was how bad things were between them. But he had to go, he had a problem named Kemp. He changed into his outfit in his car and drove to the corner 7-Eleven and called Kemp, who didn't answer.

Red got back into the gold Boxster that cost a fortune every month and that he was three months behind on the payments for, and drove over to the Reno Nugget, which was just powering up for the evening. Passing by the happy laughing tourists on their way over to the black-jack tables he struggled with a powerful emotion that combined violent jealousy with a choked-up distressed feeling.

He tried to picture the two of them, him and Donna, as one of those simple, vapid couples out there nuzzling each other, nothing to worry about, spending the evening at the tables, looking forward to getting back to the room later and more satisfying moments to come. He couldn't. Fortune had abandoned him. Donna—she would leave him if they lost the house.

He felt like a little lost child.

At Kemp's room on the third floor, he knocked on the door. He was holding things back, things that wanted to overwhelm him, but he had to be cool right now, make sure there were no loose ends.

An eye through the spyhole, then Kemp opened up in a cloud of marijuana.

"Great. Get yourself arrested," Red said. Kemp's room was a jumble, clothes and leftover room service all over, and Red felt even worse. He saw very clearly now that he had squandered his jewel of a plan on a loser.

Which made them both losers.

He sat down in the chair Kemp indicated and said, "Open a window."

"They're welded shut. I opened the vent, not that it helps." Kemp didn't seem upset. He almost seemed to be enjoying himself. Stubbing out the spliff he was smoking, he put the whole works, ashtray, lighter, Baggie, and roach, into a drawer. He turned a straight chair so its back was to Red, sat down in it with his elbows on the back of the chair, legs in the blue jeans spread, unwashed narrow white feet resting on the rungs, and said earnestly, "Hard luck, man."

"That's an understatement."

"I never would of effing believed the machine would go off in just a few seconds like that."

"You were supposed to stay there."

"Yeah." Kemp shook his head and blew out his lips in what was supposed to be sympathy. "Can we try again?"

This guy was unbelievable. "No way. Not for a year, anyway." And within a year, if he was lucky, he would be living out of his suitcase in a cheap hotel room on the slippery slope, just like Kemp was now.

"I didn't expect you to show up, especially with a girlie in a chair," Kemp said. "That was a surprise. Might have thrown me off a bit. Who's she?"

"An old friend. I thought I'd make sure you were all right. You waited until I left to fuck up."

"It was nerves. I was excited and me bladder was going to explode all over the casino if I didn't do something." The way he said it, it sounded like "somefing." His speech and his manner were making it harder for Red to stay cool. He was a moron. Red couldn't believe he'd made him a partner.

"Well, the way it worked out, I had a potentially very dangerous problem Sunday night," Red said. "The husband saw me in these clothes and later I was in the room when the payout was made to his wife. He looked at me pretty hard. I don't think he recognized me, though. He was half dead with excitement thinking of all the ways he was gonna spend his wife's money."

"You're kidding, mate. You had to watch her taking the money?" Kemp threw back his head and started to guffaw.

Red pulled out the gun he had taken out of the detective's pocket two nights before and said, "Shut up," very quietly. Just "Shut up," no particular affect to the words, the gun providing the affect.

Kemp stopped mid-laugh. A loud silence filled the room. His face had gone slack.

"You stupid cocksucker," Red said. "You think this is some kind of joke? You think I'm afraid of you? You think I'm a loser like you? I'm fifty-two years old, and I only had this one chance here and now. I made a major mistake with you, but I'm going to give you your cut—a cut of the contempt I feel for myself right now. Because you hurt me when you blew this chance."

"Hey now, hey now."

"Open your big fat mouth. I'm going to put a bullet down your fucking throat. And if you don't, I'm going to shoot you through the jaw. You might live longer, and you won't want to."

"W-wait, mate. Lemme j-just say one thing."

"Yeah. Your prayers," Red said, his humiliation hot in him, feeling a strong need to squeeze the trigger.

"I'm fixing it," Kemp said, speaking very fast. "I talked to the lawyer for the girl."

"You did what?"

Red was starting to feel even worse, like something had started that he was losing control over. He stood up, gun pointed at Kemp, and Kemp put up his hands and said, "Please."

Red didn't say anything. "I offered them half," Kemp said. "I told the lawyer lady it was my jackpot."

"You did what?"

"I scared her, told her I'd call her last night and then I didn't. I'm making them sweat. They'll come through. They won't want trouble. The husband—he knows that was my spot!"

"Did you tell her about me?"

"No, never in a thousand years." Red breathed again.

"You stupid . . ." He told Kemp what he thought of him, and Kemp took it because Red had made him believe he was going to be dead sooner rather than later if he didn't. When he was finished, Red forced Kemp to open his mouth. He put the barrel of the Glock right in there until Kemp gagged.

"They are going to wonder if it was a con," Red said, moving the gun around to make his point more vivid. "The husband—he might remember me." He was thinking aloud now. Kemp was in no position to chime in. "Have to do something. But what? What?"

The thought, when it came, was such sweet relief that Red took the gun out of Kemp's mouth. Kemp spat on the floor and the smell of stale marijuana filled the room. Red said, "Don't move. I'm thinking." Kemp froze and Red started walking around the room, kicking crap out of his way.

Until he took the gun, he had never once broken the law in his whole life. He thought about that. The reality principle, the emperor with no clothes, the scared little professor behind the curtain in Oz. You had to buy in to it.

Anyone could make the clouds move if they wanted it bad enough, like he did. All you had to do was see through the reality principle. And then there was the pleasure of doing exactly what you wanted.

"We have to force the win," he said. "We could. Just make her pay us when the money comes in. How, you may well ask. By snagging the husband. Put him away somewhere and let her stew, then, you know, like in the movies, demand a ransom. A very private deal. You can talk now."

"Kidnap him?"

"He has to go anyway. You talking to the lawyer, the husband being at the awards ceremony. I have to get past this losing streak, have to hang in there. So get rid of the husband and collect the money," Red said. "Look. Let bygones be bygones. You ready to take this a step farther?"

Kemp swallowed. "You were just about to kill me, man. Now you want me to be your partner again. What, then you kill me? You're c-cra—"

"Don't ever think that thought," Red said. "I'm not crazy. I'm the smartest man you will ever know. Now. You bring the husband to a place I'll tell you about. I make the call to the girl. She passes on the money. Then we deal with the husband. We move fast. Two, three days max, it's over. No more loose ends."

"Except me. No offense."

"Look. You bragged about some of the jobs you did while you were working the oil rigs. You claimed you killed a guy one time and nobody knew. Was that real? Do you want another chance at half a million dollars? That's still your share." He shifted gears. "Yeah. Go on. Leave. I don't need you for this. I wasn't going to kill you. You are an irritating person and what you did was worth killing you over, but I wouldn't do that. Bad odds. I stay in control. So, you want to go, go. I'll take care of it myself, and fuck you." He sat down and set the gun in his lap. "You look like shit," he told Kemp.

Kemp went into the bathroom and washed his face and slicked back his hair in the mirror. Red watched him, keeping the Glock in his lap. He thought, Make a move, try me. He didn't know what he would do if Kemp tried to quit. You had to cut losses and liabilities to get what you need. The only question was, how do you make the clouds move?

He felt better. He had seized the situation and would not let go again.

When he came back, Kemp had recovered his swagger. He said,

"Let's talk this through, my friend. We are going to win this one. I can feel it."

"You gonna go get him?"

"Yeah, why not?"

"Then take this, but don't kill anybody." Red tossed him the gun.

Kemp gasped but caught it before it hit the floor. He pointed it at Red. "Gave me the gun, eh? Maybe I'll make you open your mouth to me," he said. "Eh?"

"Try," Red said.

Kemp let the hand with the gun fall to his side. "Let's have a drink," he said.

12

KENNY HAD SPENT THE REST of Sunday night in a hotel room at Caesars dead to the world. The good news was, he was not really dead, and in a way, that was also the bad news because going on was problematic.

He had basically no money. Within limits, he could charge things to the room, so he wasn't going hungry at least, but the sating of his body did little to fill the aching in his soul.

On Monday, eating salads and rice dishes from room service, he spent the whole day in the hotel room, staring gloomily out the window at the mountains, fending off despair. Nina's investigator, Paul, called him and told him his gun had disappeared, which gave him an eerie feeling. He couldn't even bring himself to rev up the laptop and play with the City of Gold.

The City of Gold was dead, and he was grieving.

He was grieving at being married, too. He really was a virgin, and he and his mother had imagined his wedding day many times. He couldn't quite convince himself that what he had done was only a desperate business ploy to save himself from bankruptcy. He had stood, blinking, in front of a man in a robe, in a chapel, even if it was a chapel in the basement of a casino, even if the woman beside him was a stranger. It was another slap in the face of his parents. He felt ashamed.

And what, really, were the chances that the promised money would materialize?

As for Joya, she obviously didn't like him.

He didn't even have his gun anymore.

By Tuesday afternoon, discovering that his theory was correct, that he couldn't open the window wide enough to jump, he was so bored with himself that he went downstairs and explored the casino.

He discovered theme restaurants, a plaster bust of the real Caesar, colors, and the incessant clamor of bells everywhere, reminding him of the jackpot, how it was not his, and how he had entered into yet another dream, this time one belonging to someone else, but just as nebulous.

After browsing the shops and looking at the paperbacks at the bookstore, he took the elevator down to the pool level. He showed his room key to the attendant and walked to the edge of the large, asymmetrical pool. Sun gleamed in from a skylight and the water shimmered. Three people were in the pool. A pixie of a woman, probably a dancer in one of the shows, stretched her legs against the sides. An elderly couple swam back and forth together, splitting at the cement island and rejoining as they got beyond it.

The scene had a Zen-like tranquillity. He felt better.

He would have liked to go back to the Greed Machines and play some more, but that was not an option. Gambling had been forbidden by Paul, who had ferreted certain facts out of Kenny while Kenny was the worse for wear. Paul had threatened to tear his eyeballs out if he gambled, particularly if he abused the privilege of credit at the hotel. Kenny's months of intimate relationship with a computer keyboard in a dark room had done his physical confidence very little good. He thought he would lie low for a while. He might be suicidal, but he was no longer drunk.

He decided to go for a swim. He knew he needed exercise. Unfortunately, he had no trunks. A quick check of the shops upstairs did not net him anything useful, so he decided to take a chance on the street. He knew there was a store that carried athletic clothing right on the state line, a short walk away. Maybe they would have something he could wear. Maybe they would be old-fashioned enough not to notice his credit card was only a reminder of better days.

Out on the street, high-altitude golden midsummer. Even here, on casino row, where the tall buildings formed a ridge of artifice in the midst of forest, the air filled with the sweet oxygen of the tall trees, sweeping away the exhaust fumes from the automobiles on the street.

He moseyed up the street, hands in the pockets of his khakis, in spite of himself enjoying the sunshine and pleasant communion with happy human beings. Then, crossing a short street directly in front of the store, he froze.

A dark-haired man who looked like his father passed briskly by without a glance.

He ran across the street and ducked into the store, puffing.

He shouldn't be out here.

What if Colleen should show up, or Tan-Mo? What if his father should suddenly appear, searching for the financial newspapers he used to buy at Cecil's, before they tore it down?

He should never have left the casino. His family did not gamble. They were too busy working hard, tucking money away for their worthless, useless, hopeless scum of a son. . . .

Now that he was here, he turned himself so that he could watch the door and flipped through the hangers of swimsuits, selecting a baggy pair of trunks. While the clerk rang up his purchase, he hovered near the door.

"Card's been canceled, dude," said the clerk suddenly. He picked up scissors and cut through the gold, watching the two halves fall on the glass counter with satisfaction.

Kenny riffled in his pockets. Rather than risk losing his other credit card, the one that still offered minimal possibilities, he used the money he had planned to leave for the maid, which turned out to be just enough.

He paid. The clerk took his money without further unpleasantness, then began to fold T-shirts and stack them on shelves behind the counter.

Kenny looked carefully around before leaving the store. What an idiot he was, buying swim trunks with the last of his cash! He was cleaning his pockets out down to the lint to serve some obscure need of his psyche. But knowing what he was doing didn't mean he didn't have to do it.

Outside once again, he felt nervous. The street was so open. He decided to duck down the alley between the Embassy Suites and Harrah's. He would meander toward Caesars through the parking lots where there were cars for cover.

The narrow, one-way alley didn't really offer a good place to walk, so he stuck close to the wall of the casino.

Of course, a car pulled in right behind him. Realizing his error, that he had chosen the side of the alley that allowed no exit, he pushed closer to the wall.

The car refused to pass.

Thinking that whoever was in that car must be afraid that they would hit him, Kenny waved the car on. He couldn't see inside. The sun visor was down in front, and the back windows were tinted. The car remained behind him, halted.

Kenny shrugged and decided that, in keeping with the work philosophy that had been at the heart of the City of Gold, the best policy was always a bold stroke. He stepped into the alley directly in front of the car, thinking he would cross over to the other side, into the valet parking area for the Embassy Suites.

The car lurched forward.

"Hey!" Kenny shouted. About eighty feet away, accelerating at an unknown speed. Not calculable. He jumped clear in less than a second.

He fell and his glasses flew but he did manage to avoid being knocked down. While the valet came running up and helped him get back to his feet and unbent his glasses for him, the car whizzed past, turning left before he thought to check out the license plate.

"He almost killed you!" the girl said, putting the glasses on Kenny's nose, adjusting them. "Want some water or something? There's a restaurant inside. I bet you're shook up."

"No, thanks," Kenny said. If anything, he was shaken at his own instincts. That survival thing kicked in, and you could do nothing except bow to its superior power. Dusting his clothes off, he thought, Maybe I should face it. Maybe I could move on. The City of Gold dead, hundreds of thousands of dollars of debt.

"I'll treat," the girl added, smiling at him.

"Sadly," Kenny said, "I'm a married man." He flashed the dime-store ring Joya had bought for the ceremony.

She tipped her head to the side. "Watch out for cars, then, honey."

Waving good-bye, feeling a smile on his face that was not stupid for a change but the earned result of a moment in the sun of this girl's interest, not to mention the fact that he had not been killed, he walked over to the parking lot behind Harrah's. Apparently, he was supposed to live a while and see if this latest gamble would pay off. As he made his way he suddenly felt the altitude and found himself puffing again, so he slowed down.

So much money here on the border of California and Nevada, so many beautiful cars. Gleaming metal, stacked in rows as primly as the Hot Wheels he had played with as a boy, stretched for what looked like miles. He spotted a new Jaguar and a Land-Rover and even a Hummer in one row. Sell them and support a small third world community for a year. . . .

He heard a sound behind him. When he turned around to look, he saw nothing, no sign of the silver car. In the distance, two men argued by the trash cans behind the hotel. Two young men in hotel uniform helped an elderly couple take their luggage out of their car. The only person nearby wore a dark hooded sweatshirt and appeared stooped and old through Kenny's now scratched glasses.

He started to walk again, faster, his pulse quickening. He saw the hooded person dashing rapidly between vehicles nearby, as noiseless and fast as an earwig.

Like a man who feels himself to be in the crosshairs of a weapon, Kenny shifted direction and shifted it again after making rapid progress past a couple of rows. No need to panic, he told himself, dodging into a small passage between two cars. Don't be thinking there's a reason on earth for anyone to be after you.

He ran through the list of people and companies on his bankruptcy petition. His creditors had no idea where he was. And even if they did, he couldn't think of any who would decide to kill him.

Just to convince himself that what he was experiencing was the paranoia of a person who played too many violent video games in his off hours, he glanced behind. No one . . .

And then, suddenly, very close, no more than a hundred feet away, someone moved.

The hood.

His astonishment at the realization that he was, in fact, being stalked rooted him momentarily to the spot, just long enough for his stalker to start running right at him. He had a gun . . . a nine-millimeter Glock!

Kenny ran.

He ran until the blood from his heart pushed through his veins like wildfire, and ran some more. He was terrified, utterly and abjectly frightened beyond belief.

Someone was trying to hurt him. Take him out!

Gasping for air, hands balled into fists, he tore along a line of cars, zigging to and fro like the heroes in Dark Avengers, aware that he was not in a Play Station II now.

Other people in the lot melted away, and he knew himself to be a lone target in a low field, with nothing but the blank back wall of the enormous casinos and a distant guard as witnesses.

Then, like a miracle, the fast steps behind him stopped. A tour bus full of Japanese tourists had just pulled up in front of Kenny.

But he didn't stop running. He ran all the way through the side door to Caesars, up one flight of stairs, and then, panting, into the sports betting area, where he found a corner of the room where he could collapse.

The bettors were far too absorbed with following the slightly out-of-focus progress of the horses on the wall above to give a moment's thought to a man dripping sweat on the table in front of him, shaking and moaning. Besides, they had seen it all before.

Back in his room, Kenny shot the bolt and had a few handfuls of Fritos to calm himself down, sitting on the edge of the bed. Then he called Paul van Wagoner on the hotel phone, but he had to leave a message. Should he call the police?

He had no description except that the person in the hood seemed to have his Glock. How could that be? Leaving town about now would be more prudent than offering useless information to the cops and sticking around for more target practice. After he felt better he hooked his laptop up to the hotel jack, got onto Netscape, and began to roam until he found what he was looking for. He didn't know the numbered plate on the silver car, but he had found Joya's California plate number using a special software program.

Numbers stayed with him. According to his mother, when he was three, he would count light posts as they drove past them, then calculate how many there were per mile. His mother found this nonsensical, even humorous, while his father narrowed his eyes, seemingly full of the same sorts of calculations when he looked at Kenny.

Secure Web sites were bubble gum to Kenny. He chewed them up, spit them out, and found all the sugar he needed in ten different places. Joya's car was registered to an address in Markleeville. A hit! Unfortunately, he could locate no phone number at the address.

He wanted to warn Joya before blowing town. Had she lifted his gun? She said she was trained in weaponry. She was already on the watch for that guy who was after her, so what good would Kenny's warning do? Maybe no good, but he wanted to see her. He would have wanted to see her even if nothing had been wrong.

Shoving his computer into the plastic sack his trunks had come in, he made for the door.

Downstairs, he stopped at the concierge desk for directions to Markleeville and to drop off a note for Paul.

"Why do you want to go to that address?" the concierge asked with unusual indiscretion, giving him the once-over.

"Why wouldn't I?"

"Well, it's an Indian neighborhood," she said. "My sister lives not far from there. You don't look Indian."

"So what?" he said. He got awfully tired of assumptions made about him, that because he was Asian and worked in Silicon Valley at a dotcom startup, he was some kind of business wizard, born to succeed. He was living proof that the stereotypes were hilariously faulty.

"Sorry I asked."

"No problem. Actually, I'm going out there to talk to my wife." He enjoyed saying that.

She grunted in disbelief and turned to the waiting couple on his left.

He walked across the street to the Prize's lot and found the Lexus. The concierge's map didn't help much, other than with major roads. He took Luther Pass just past the Agricultural Station over the mountains. Things got tricky at Hope Valley. He had worried he might not be able to find the house, since his map was an overview that didn't identify individual streets in the rural neighborhood, but he shouldn't have. There were only about a dozen streets, most of them very short.

Cruising the compact neighborhood, he noticed that the houses were neat, some of them; small, most of them; and messy, some of them. The same array of houses could be found in the homes and yards in his neighborhood in Mountain View, in fact. Unlike his neighborhood, however, people were not piled on top of each other into condos, blocking the desert sunset. Low frame houses, mostly one story with porches, and a few garages dotted the sparse landscape.

Kids riding around on bikes and trikes pulled over to the side of the street to watch him pass. He felt out of place, although not necessarily unwelcome. A few smiles greeted him, and a few glares. Just like home, he thought.

He found the right number, pulled his car in front of a small cabin that looked more like someplace in Tahoe than the other houses, and got out. He walked up a dusty path to the door and knocked.

No answer.

He knocked again. Again, no one came.

He circled the house, peering into the windows, but they were shaded. Still, through one he saw the yellow of a lamp burning. "Joya?" he called. "It's me, Kenny!"

He heard footsteps. The back door opened.

"What do you want?"

Joya stood in the doorway, facing the sunset. She wore a red tank top that Kenny couldn't take his eyes off, and a pair of jeans-shorts that began somewhere below her exposed navel. She stood very still. Only her hair moved, shivering in a hot gust of wind off the mountains.

Kenny searched for his voice. She wasn't wearing a bra. She made a face, but he didn't think she minded him looking at her.

"Well?"

"I need to talk to you." He came around to the back to face her. "Can I come in?"

"No."

"It's an emergency."

She looked behind her furtively.

So she had someone inside waiting for her. Well, of course she did, a beauty like her! He was horribly disappointed.

Her voice softened. "What's the problem, Kenny?"

He really felt exposed out here. A few children had come alongside the house and were now amusing themselves by watching him. "It's private."

Again, the sidelong glance behind. "Okay," she said. "But this is a bad time. You can't stay but a minute."

He came into a kitchen about ten feet by six feet painted a deep azure with print curtains at the window. Old white-and-black linoleum tiles on the floor, eight inches square. He saw plants everywhere. She had been potting a plant on the counter.

"Sit," she said, reaching into the refrigerator. "Lemonade okay?"

He nodded, and sat at the table. While she rinsed her hands in the sink, then added ice to two glasses, he tried to see past her into the hallway beyond, but it was getting late and any rooms were shaded, unlit. The only light came from a stained-glass lamp that hung over the table. He could hear no other person around. He guessed that a single bath, two small bedrooms, and a living room pretty much completed the rest of the house. The boyfriend could be anywhere, sprawled in front of the stereo with headphones on; asleep, post-terrific sex on her sheets . . . it hurt to think about it.

She put two full glasses on the table and sat down, again blocking his view into the hall.

"Someone tried to kill me today," he said.

"Yeah, sure."

"It's the truth!" He told her about the car in the alley.

"Everyone almost gets hit by a car every day, Kenny! Geez, you're jumpy."

Then he told her about the man with the gun that looked like his Glock running after him, but before he could finish, she leaped out of her chair, upsetting it. "Get out of here. Now."

When he didn't move, she grabbed him by the arm and pulled until he stood, too, then tried to push him toward the door.

"Wait," he said. "Just a second!" She kept pushing until he was inches from being completely ousted. "Ouch, Joya. Stop! What's that sound?"

It was loud and it was lusty. Kenny knew that sound.

"What's going on?" Kenny said.

At the sound of the cry, Joya had stopped pushing and listened, obviously vacillating between her immediate problem of getting him out the door and placating what was beginning to sound like an enraged animal.

"You woke him up," she said. "Damn." Apparently giving up on her plan to remove Kenny for the moment, she left the room. She returned a few seconds later with a big boy baby on her shoulder, wrapped in a yellow blanket.

"He's hungry," Kenny said, after one look at a scowl that took up most of the baby's face. He was elated. No boyfriend, she had just been baby-sitting somebody's kid. "Loudmouth," he said with a laugh.

Joya went to the microwave and pulled a bottle out. The baby settled down into her lap. He looked almost big enough to brawl, with lots of fuzzy black hair and large brown eyes which regarded Kenny calmly now that he was sucking away. The eyes looked familiar.

"He's yours!" Kenny said, shocked.

Joya stroked the baby's hair with her free hand. "Kenny, listen to me. You have to promise me you won't tell anyone."

"I won't."

"Remember that guy I told you was after me?"

"Yes."

"Atchison Potter. He's the grandfather. And if he knows this little guy exists, he'll take him away from me. I won't let that happen. I'll die first."

"Why does he hate you?"

"He thinks I killed his son."

"Wow! Did you?"

Joya looked like he'd stepped on her foot, so he said, "Sorry."

"You think I would do something like that?" she said.

"I don't know. You surprised me, the way you brought it up, Joya."

"Call me Jessie."

"Okay." Jessie. He liked it.

She fed the baby for a few minutes while the sun finished setting behind the mountains outside the house and Kenny finished his lemonade. He didn't really want to go, had no place to go in fact, and he wondered what he was supposed to do now.

The child, after a heavy burp, fell asleep on her shoulder. She left and put him back to bed.

"How old is he?"

"Gabe is nine months."

"He's big. I'm going to estimate nineteen pounds."

"You're right," Jessie said, surprised. "You're a walking computer. I think I'll call you Rain Man."

"But Rain Man won when he gambled," Kenny said, "unlike me. How did you end up here?"

"I left Hawaii after my husband died. Last April. I was in the Marine Corps."

"Huh," Kenny said, thinking.

"Right. Dan never saw Gabe. He would have loved Gabe so much."

"How did Dan die?"

"He drowned."

She sounded angry. Kenny had noticed this about her. She got angry when he would have been blue. He found it unsettling.

"Whoa. I had no idea," he said. He had—face it, he had envied Jessie her win. But she had a baby, and she had suffered a lot. Kenny kicked himself for his selfishness.

"What about this place?" He motioned with one hand.

"I live here. My auntie Anita lives in the house connected to this place. Look. You have to go. I can't have Gabe in danger because of some screwball business deal in your past."

"Yeah. Guess I'll be going. I'll call you when I know what I'm doing."

"Call Nina."

"Okay. Good luck." She seemed to think he had just come to say good-bye. Her lips separated and she came close and got up on her toes. He felt the soft lips press on his cheek. Her body brushed against him, tall and strong. "Thanks," she said. "Even if it doesn't work out." His hands held her at the waist.

He kept holding her, his heart reeling.

"Well, get moving." She took his hands away and opened the door. Her words were harsh, but she was smiling.

"I hate to tell you this," Kenny said. "Especially with the baby. But this has to involve you. I don't have any enemies, or at least they can't find me at the moment."

"You're a white-collar crook, aren't you?" Jessie said. "On the run, like me."

"No! I'm an entrepreneur!"

Her face hardened. "What's going on? Why did you come here anyway? You say someone tried to kill you, and you come here. I have enough problems."

"It's got to be the jackpot, Jessie. Someone wants the money."

"Wait. Could it be . . . it might be Mr. Potter." She pulled him back inside and closed the curtains and turned on the light. "Are you sure no one followed you?"

"There was nobody on that road with me. Not one car. Could it really be your father-in-law?"

"I don't know!" she cried. "What did the paper say? Did it have a picture of you, too?"

Kenny nodded. "I think so. To the world, we're married, aren't we? Maybe that made him mad." He sat back, arms folded. She shouldn't forget that. Maybe she was responsible for this attempt on his life after all. She would be a widow twice over at twenty-one if that happened. An unlucky sort of woman, but this made her poignant, and the baby was beautiful. She was soft with womanhood. He had felt her lips. She couldn't hide her essential nature from Kenny anymore.

I am in love, he thought giddily.

She said, "Stay here," and she went into the back room. He heard a suitcase clicking closed. The light in the kitchen was dazzling. He peeked through the curtain. Deep twilight out there, the shouts of kids.

She came back in carrying a Portacrib and a suitcase. "Maybe you could help me load up," she said, "I intend to stay alive and kicking until that check clears. I've gone through a lot for it. Gabe needs it."

"Rapid advancement toward profitability," Kenny murmured.

"What?"

"It's just a phrase that has stuck with me. We're rapidly advancing that way, wouldn't you say?"

"Not fast enough for me."

"Jessie. I've been wondering. You don't have to tell me, but the money isn't just something you need to raise Gabe, is it? You have something in mind."

"Maybe I do."

"What?"

"I don't want to talk about that."

"Why not?"

"I—don't think you'd understand."

"Try me."

"Some other time."

"I need it too. That money is going to help me so much, Jessie. You have no idea how close I came to . . ." He stopped, unwilling to go into that right now. He didn't want to be questioned on the subject. He reserved the right to reopen that path in the future, after he paid his parents back.

"If we can just get it."

She raised her shoulders. "We have a deal. You'll get your money if and when I get it. Meanwhile, Kenny, you do have to go. Whoever it was. And I don't want you coming back, either."

"We could go together."

"I'm sorry," Jessie said. "I wish I could trust you. But I don't know you, so how can I? You understand? I can't put my baby's life in your hands."

"You can trust me," Kenny whispered. "But I understand. You know, Jessie, I . . ." but she shook her head.

They both spotted the silver car parked down the street at the same time. He recognized the pattern of the grille, but it was too far away to get the numbers on the plate.

He slammed the door shut. "He's out there! The guy who attacked me! Get the baby!"

But Jessie was already in Gabe's room. Within seconds, she came out again on her stomach and wiggled toward him, holding the baby gently above the floor. "Get down," she said. "If he has the weapon . . ."

Kenny squatted down on the floor. Jessie handed him Gabe to hold, pushed him and the baby under a heavy oak table, and shimmied over to a locked gun cabinet against the back wall. She took a key ring out of her pocket, opened a knife on the ring, and popped the cabinet.

"What are you doing?" Kenny whispered, trying to rock the baby, frightened. Were there footsteps out there in that desert night, footsteps that would take them all away from this life he was so uncertain about?

Jessie didn't answer. Keeping low, she began a methodical search of the room, cursing quietly to herself. "They've got to keep shells for these guns here somewhere," she whispered back. "But where?"

"Try the freezer," Kenny hissed. "That's where my dad keeps his." They had found the handgun and the hidden bullets when he was about twelve and Tan-Mo was ten. They had loaded the gun, shooting until it was empty into a pie tin hammered to a tree in the backyard and marked like a target. Their father had never known.

Jessie scooted down the hallway and out of sight.

Kenny heard the crickets singing in rhythm outside, indifferent to the looming horror that lurked somewhere out there among them.

He heard something, the garbage can going over.

She flew back into the room, loading an old, long hunting rifle.

Making her way to the front window, she kneeled by it. She pushed a wooden blind slowly to one side with the rifle barrel and looked outside.

"What do you see?"

"One body. Stay down!" She began crawling on her stomach from window to window, checking. "It's too dark."

They waited. Gabe, apparently exhausted from his initial brutal wake-up call, had fallen asleep again.

"How is he?"

"Fine."

They heard an unmistakable sound on the porch. The Glock's safety catch.

Jessie yelled, "I'm armed, sucker! I'll shoot!" She cocked the rifle. In the stillness it made a very definite noise too.

Wild racketing, as whoever had made it up to the porch jumped off it again. Whoever was out there had not expected them to mount a defense. They listened tensely.

"This is our chance. We've got to leave!" Kenny said. "We've got to get out of here! This place is a trap. We can be surrounded. . . ."

"Don't get hysterical. We're safe here."

"He could set the house on fire!"

"He won't get close enough. I've got us covered. We're staying." She pulled one of the windows open just wide enough for the barrel, and shot at the sky. "That's for scaring me, you turkey!" she yelled to the door. They heard alarmed voices, neighbors maybe. Someone would be calling for help.

"Don't kill anyone," Kenny said. "Please don't. It's very bad karma to kill someone. Are those kids still out there by the fence?"

"No. The kids around here are smart enough to run when they hear gunfire! Now, shut up, Kenny. And keep Gabe safe or I'll kill you, too."

"What's out there?"

"I think just one guy." Moving to the front window, she pushed a curtain aside. "The car's gone."

"Let me see." It was gone, but maybe that was a ploy.

"I'll go outside and check," Jessie said.

"Wait for the police."

"I can take him if he's out there."

She clamped her jaw. The skin on her arms, as smooth as marble, stretched to carry the weight of the rifle in her hands. Compact muscles rippled along her body as she moved, all the way to the straining blue veins of her hands. Kenny had never seen anyone so beautiful and dangerous-looking. He could have made her immortal in the City of Gold.

But now he wanted her real. Her real lips. Everything real. "You're not a soldier anymore," he said. "The police will come. All we have to do is sit tight."

"He could've hurt Gabe." But she sat down on the floor with him. She took Gabe and hugged him.

Kenny heard sirens.

13

Noon the next day. Nina waited at the gas station in Meyers, watching the traffic on the highway, radio blasting, wipers going fast against slaps of rain. Gray sky hung low and threatening overhead. After a few minutes, Kenny and Jessie arrived together in Jessie's Honda.

"You drive a Bronco," Kenny said as Nina put her key into the door lock. "Great truck. They don't make 'em like that anymore."

"They don't make them, period," Nina said. "I'm really hoping this one lasts a long, long time." She had already totaled one Bronco and would hate to see this one undergo the same sad fate. "Listen, why don't you two take a seat in here for a minute."

They climbed into the seat beside her, Jessie in the middle. Nina turned the heat up slightly. Even in summer, Tahoe had sudden dips in temperature and the jarring cold made her want to shiver. "Now, what is this about you being attacked?"

Kenny started out with a wild and vague tale of someone trying to kill him in the Harrah's parking lot. His story took a long time and included vivid details about his state of mind, his worries about physical fitness, and his pleasure at discovering that he could still run fast when he had to.

"Not like I'll be trying out for the Olympics or anything, but it's good to find out I'm in fighting trim."

At this, Jessie laughed.

"Not funny," he said.

"You're right. It isn't," she said.

"You say it might be the Glock that Paul took with him the night of the jackpot," Nina said carefully. "How sure are you about that?"

"It looked like my Glock."

"But it could have been any nine-millimeter gun, really, couldn't it?"

"Not really. The shape is distinctive."

"But how do you know it's your Glock? The missing Glock?"

"I don't, but it's a Glock, and someone up here has it, and from what I saw he likes hooded sweatshirts."

"But how could a stranger get that gun?"

"In the casino," Kenny said. "Just lift it out of Paul's jacket. So anyway," he continued, "I found out where Jessie was staying. . . ."

"How?" Nina and Jessie asked.

"I remembered her license plate number and hacked into the California DMV."

"I thought that was supposed to be impossible."

"It is. It must be getting on toward lunch. Got any snacks in here?"

"No," Nina said. "Want to get lunch?"

"Yeah," he said.

"Don't you ever stop eating?" Jessie said.

Kenny looked hurt.

Nina drove down a main drag until she could find a place that suited him, which turned out to be anywhere that served hamburgers.

They took a booth near a window and ordered food, which arrived promptly.

His mouth full, Kenny said, "Mmm. Spicy brown mustard. My favorite."

"Finish your story," Nina said, surreptitiously checking her watch. She had squeezed Jessie in, arranging to meet in Meyers on her way back from a rushed deposition down in Placerville. Meyers made sense for Jessie too, who had to drive all the way from Markleeville.

"Let me finish," Jessie said. She had ordered salad, which she had already disposed of efficiently.

"Fine," Kenny said, and Nina got the impression he wasn't too happy to turn the storytelling over to Jessie but wasn't about to cross her. "Be my guest."

"Kenny showed up. Someone was out there trying to break into my place. So I broke out a rifle. We heard the hammer pulling back on a gun on the front porch. No question what it was, right, Kenny?"

"No question."

"Told the sucker I was armed and he heard it cock. He drove away and I fired one out the window to speed him on his way. The cops came and we made a report. One of the neighbors saw somebody in a hooded sweatshirt on my porch. That's it," she said, refreshingly succinct. "Kenny slept on the couch last night."

Kenny wiped his face with a napkin, nodding his head.

"Do you have something you want to add to that?" Nina asked, not because she wished to open the floodgates again, but because something in his face told her he found Jessie's story essentially uninformative.

Kenny looked at Jessie, who looked back at him.

"No," he said.

Nina didn't believe him, but she could see he wasn't going to talk. "You say it was a man? Did either of you get a clear look at the person?"

"I'm revising my previous statements. It could have been a female," Kenny said, directing his eyes at Jessie, "easily."

"Could have been," Jessie agreed, "but it wasn't."

"How can you be sure?" Nina asked.

"Because the person shooting at my house was Atchison Potter, that's why," Jessie said. "He knew my place. He had just sent a process server there. I should have taken off earlier. That's the reality."

"Why would he try to kill Kenny?"

"I didn't say he tried to kill Kenny."

"Preposterous," Kenny said, dipping a French fry into ketchup, "that there would be two such similar unrelated events in such close proximity, geographically and temporally, especially if you consider me and my gun as connecting threads."

"Maybe he did go after Kenny," Jessie said. "Maybe Kenny's right and he found out about the marriage. I keep telling you, Mr. Potter's not just mad at me. He's out of his mind. He'd do anything to hurt me. The last time I saw him, he screamed—accused me—I'm beginning to understand there is no escaping him."

"These are affiliated events, that I promise you," Kenny said.

"There is another possibility," Nina said. "Someone else who might have done this."

"Who?" they asked in unison.

"Charlie Kemp. The Englishman who thinks it's his jackpot."

"How could he get my gun? Not when he was sitting next to me. Not when he pushed toward Jessie after the jackpot. Because Paul took it later, at your office."

Nina told them about her conversation with Kemp. "But he never called," she finished. "We need to involve the police."

"We did involve the police. But we didn't see enough of him to recognize him."

"We could talk to them some more and provide some context, which I'll bet you didn't provide."

"What's the point?"

"Protection."

"I'm leaving Markleeville anyway," Jessie said.

"Me, too," Kenny said. "I'm going somewhere."

"Jessie," Nina said, "you have a court hearing on Monday. You can't go far. We talked about this. Potter's lawyer has obtained a court order that you appear for the Examination of Judgment Debtor."

"I know, I know. Will Potter be there?" She had asked this before. Her dread and the defiance she used to fight it were such disabling emotions that Nina decided to waffle. Potter had a right to be there, though he didn't have a right to sit in on the examination.

"Mr. Riesner doesn't seem to think so. Riesner gave me some excuse, said Mr. Potter isn't feeling well. I don't even know if he's in California."

"Do I have to go? What do I have to do? Can you prevent it?"

"I'm going to protest, but if I lose, you have to be there. Because of the judgment, Mr. Riesner has the right to ask you questions about your assets and liabilities. You have to bring your income tax returns."

"That'll be easy. Except—this time he can't find out where I'm staying?"

"He will want to know that. You see, he doesn't just have to take your word for it, that you rent for a certain amount of money, for instance. He can gather information from you that will allow him to make an independent inquiry about your finances."

"Why does he get to do this?"

"Because, you see, the judgment—according to the law, unless and until I can change the situation, you owe this enormous sum of money to Mr. Potter based on this judgment. That's why the legal papers you received called you a judgment debtor."

Jessie's shoulders slumped. She said, "Clever man."

"Monday morning," Nina said. "Come to the office by eight o'clock, so I can prepare you. And please call on Friday so that I know you are all right. Both of you. Oh. Where will each of you be?"

Kenny looked uncertain. Jessie looked stumped. "I have to be pretty close," she said. "But not findable. I don't know." They all sat there. Nina scratched her head.

"Well, I have a place about an hour and a half from here, and nobody knows it exists," she said. "It's a trailer out in the desert. A client gave it to me last year. I haven't even recorded the deed yet. There is room for both of you for a few days."

"Won't it be hot?" Kenny asked.

"It can be at this time of year in the middle of the day, but we're heading into a cool stretch, if today and the news are anything to go by. If it gets too hot, head into town. Go to the library in Minden or get an ice cream in Carson City."

"Him too?" Jessie said.

"He's in trouble, too," Nina said. "But you come first. You're my client. You decide."

Jessie took a deep breath. "I'll think about it."

Kenny and Jessie waved as Nina pulled out.

"This trailer out in the desert she offered—it sounds kind of primitive."

"Sure does," Kenny said. The minute Nina described the desolate, isolated trailer she owned in the desert, he wanted to go there. He would be with Jessie.

"Remote," Jessie said dubiously.

"You have a cell phone, remember. With a phone, you can be anywhere."

"She said it isn't totally reliable there."

"We'll be fine. Nobody will find us. She says there's electricity. I can use my laptop."

"If they do, I have the rifle. You know, this doesn't necessarily mean we should stick together. I told you . . ." Her eyes were troubled.

He talked fast, hoping to change her thinking before her ideas got set in concrete. "I won't be a pest. I won't talk much and I won't make a pass or anything, if that's what you're worried about."

"Ha! You'd be so sorry."

"I've got nowhere else to go. I need a place to run to as much as you. I'm not going back to Caesars."

"Why not? I bet it's nicer than some trailer."

"That guy knows I was there. And it's just for a week. Nina said there was a bed in back and that the dining area makes into a bed. I'll take that one. I'll help protect you."

"That's a good one!" But his wheedling made her smile.

"I can help with Gabe. We'll camp out. Barbecue."

"You cook?"

"My family runs a restaurant." He hoped his return smile looked as well-intentioned as he felt. "Pack the soy sauce along with the rifle, okay?"

"It's not that far from Markleeville. I can get Gabe over there if I need someone to watch him. Aunt Anita just loves him." She breathed deeply. "Okay. Let's go. Just get back to the cabin, pick up Gabe at my aunt's, and pick up your car. . . ."

"Why don't you tell Nina about Gabe?" Kenny asked, climbing into Jessie's Honda.

"Gabe's none of her business. Yours either, for that matter. Don't mention him to anyone if you want to keep those legs of yours."

People were threatening him left and right these days. He supposed it was a symptom of the times, this tough talk and gunplay. He preferred his clean, well-ordered universe, made of pixels, light, and color. Harmless.

He rolled his window down. The summer squall had cleared and the weather had warmed up. He really loved feeling the heat and cold together, the blasting of the air conditioner, and the hot summer air outside. Things you didn't get from a computer. The milky smell of Gabe's breath . . . she would let him stay. He felt outrageously happy.

"I wish I could leave," Jessie said. "I wish I could ignore the money and just go. We can go far away from Potter with that money. He'll never need to know about Gabe."

"It's kind of sad, though."

"Sad?"

"He'll never know about his grandson. I mean, that would kill my dad, never knowing about his grandson." A pang, as Kenny ignored the improbability of his father mourning a grandson he didn't know he had, and thought about his family. They would be wondering where he was, wondering at his silence. Well, better that than reading in the morning paper about his brains speckling the bathroom at Prize's.

"Don't feel sorry for Potter. He doesn't deserve it."

Back in Markleeville, they made a quick stop at the cabin, packing supplies into both of their cars. "What's it mean?" Kenny asked, lugging a final bag out of the kitchen. "The name on this house, Memdewee. Do you know?"

"Deer run," she said. "It's Washoe."

"Appropriate. That's what we're doing, running like deer."

"Kenny, you're what my auntie would call an odd duck."

"Where is the rest of your family?"

"Dead. Father and mother and younger brother dead in a car crash when I was six years old. Middle of winter, a logging truck on Spooner Pass. But I was real young. I hardly remember them. My Aunt Anita raised me. But I have a family of my own now. I have Gabe."

He thought, but didn't say, and you have me, too. He didn't want her to know about that yet. She might make fun of him. She would probably leave him. She barely tolerated him as it was. Kenny had thought of a way to win her. He wasn't good enough for her yet, but he could be.

He followed her to her aunt's part of the house, but didn't go inside while she collected Gabe and talked with her aunt. After stopping at the small general store in Markleeville, they caravaned back to Highway 88, made a right, and drove past the turnoff for the Washoe Indian Reservation and farther into Nevada. They traveled some distance north on 395, then turned onto a dirt road in the Carson Range west of Genoa and followed it for a long time, making more turns here and there.

They had been alone on the road for miles, under a hazy sky. They were not being followed. The desert wasn't flat: they seemed to be on a gradual slope bearing toward a mountain range to the north. They wound between rocky bluffs and scrub. Some old rusting mining equipment lay dumped by the roadside. They were in prospecting country.

He followed the Honda Civic without any worries. Jessie would not let them get lost.

In the shadow of the mountain's late afternoon light, as Kenny was watching the horizon, bumping along the sandy road, a green flash lit up the horizon. The sunset came after, magenta and gray, but that green—he had read about it in a book but never thought he would see it, some sort of rare visual effect of the sunset.

He thought, It's a sign. My luck has turned.

They pulled their cars up beside the trailer and got out.

It was very quiet. Nights in the high desert were often cool, even in summer, and tonight was no exception. He saw a dirt front yard with a row of prickly pear cacti guarding ripe orange fruit. A padlocked metal shed, a carport, even a small empty corral with an unused horse stall. A ranchito, the Mexicans would call it. All neat and orderly, as a lawyer's hideout should be.

What did Nina Reilly use it for? Nina had impressed Kenny as the sort of lawyer who would be rich if she had set up in Silicon Valley—intelligent and experienced, but with a crazy streak. He imagined various scenarios for Nina in this trailer, all of them involving intrigue and drama.

The sky a luminous blue, Venus on the horizon. Stillness.

Maybe she just came here to sit in the metal folding chair by the side of the trailer and watch the rattlesnakes and think up legal arguments.

"I don't know if I like it. It's very exposed. But that could work in our favor. No hidden approach." Jessie didn't waste time looking around, but got the door open and checked out the trailer. Books and more books stacked on the table, on the bed in back, next to the tiny stainless-steel sink. Books on psychology, medicine, law, books of poetry, mystery novels, courtroom dramas.

Kenny had his answer. Nina read.

"Dust everywhere," Kenny said. He picked up a Steve Martini novel lying open on the floor. "I'll clean up while you get Gabe settled in."

He wiped a wet cloth around and made beds while Jessie found a spot for Gabe's portable crib. The moment she set Gabe in his bed, he began to cry.

Kenny went outside and fiddled with the propane tank. After a while, he admitted to himself that he would blow them all up and was going to have to ask for Jessie's help if he didn't want this brief idyll to end with a bang.

He went back in and started cutting up vegetables, waiting for Jessie to get Gabe to sleep. "What's the matter?" Kenny asked finally, after watching her fuss over the baby for quite some time without result.

"I don't know," she said. "He cried nearly all the way here. He usually sleeps in the car. But—he gets this way sometimes lately. Irritable. He just cries. I think that's normal with kids, isn't it?"

Kenny picked Gabe up. "He seems kind of—warm, doesn't he?"

Gabe was burning hot.

This time Kemp wouldn't meet Red in his room. Unhappy memories, Red had no problem with that, but when Kemp wouldn't tell him over the phone if he had the husband, Red got an unpleasant tremor in his gut, which he knew well. He felt separated from the action, left out. No control. He couldn't stand that feeling except when the money was on a number. Even then he couldn't stand it, but the pleasure was there, the hope.

It was past ten o'clock when Red parked out in front of the Pizza Hut in Minden. Kemp was already inside, sitting at a table in the crowded place, with a pitcher of beer in front of him. Red got out of the Boxster and locked up, then took a walk around the place looking at the security. Video cam facing the cashier. That seemed to be the sum total of their security measures except for a simple burglar alarm setup on the doors and windows. No outside cams. Kemp's silver Chrysler was empty. No sign of the kidnappee.

Okay. It could still be okay. Hear Kemp's story. Stay smart. He went in, skirting around the edges of the monitor's visual field, pulling down on the baseball cap.

A kid brought a large pizza with canned pineapple strewn over it to the table as Red sat down with his back to the cam. More brats at the table in front of them, no sign of the parents, booths full of young jocks in nylon T-shirts that read "Pau Wa Lu," celebrating some athletic triumph. Nobody else in the place was over twenty-one.

"Well?" Red said, standing there.

"Relax, man. Tell you in a minute. I have to eat. I'm starving. Have a beer on me."

Red had no choice. He sat down. Kemp's hair reeked and his eyes bulged red. His glove compartment was probably full of grass. He was a walking disaster, not a committed, organized criminal.

"What the fuck happened?" he said. "Where is he?"

Kemp worked his way through his second piece of pizza. He waved a hand, his mouth full. "Been a long day," he said.

He drank some beer. Red considered him, considered the restaurant, wondered how it had all come down to a Pizza Hut. Big score, rapidly dwindling in the distance as the rest of the pack headed into the home stretch. He was getting a stomachache watching the Englishman.

A toddler tried to climb off his chair, fell against Red. He didn't move. The teenaged mother picked him up and put him back in his chair, ignoring Red. Some people were rude, no way around it.

"I suppose you have guessed," Kemp said. "Slight postponement, I fear. The dish ran away with the spoon."

"Meaning?"

"I went after our boy. Tried to knock him down so I could get him into the car, but he managed to run. I followed him out to some godforsaken village across the mountains. The girl was there. She came out on the porch. I could have done them both right then, but that wasn't the plan, was it? I was just going to wait and see if he came back out, and then I was going to grab our boy when he finally leaves. So I reconnoiter and what should I hear but this girl yelling that she's going to shoot me. I jump off the porch and she sends a blast after me that bloody well almost took my ears off. I went as deaf as Winston Churchill. I step back, not wanting to be picking bullets out of my ass for the next hundred years. The neighbors are peeking out their curtains, I'm nipping under the porch for a second of shelter. It's nasty under there, they must have a lot of dogs."

"And?"

"And, I decide it's time to bloody well move out and wait my chance. I get out just in time. Police cruiser, red light flashing, on me left as I left."

"He saw you?"

"Two of them. Paid absolutely no attention to me. So there's only one highway out of this place. Deep forest all round. I pull off the road behind a tree and wait. And wait. And wait all bloody night."

"Poor you," Red said.

"Yeah." Kemp ate some more, his face working industriously through each bite with the deprived look of someone who had grown up malnourished. He hadn't looked this way when he was on a winning streak. Red caught a glimpse of his own face in the window reflection. He thought, I look old. Using a paper napkin, he brushed some of Kemp's crumbs off the table onto the floor, which was already a lost cause.

"And when I woke up, they was gone," Kemp said.

"What do you mean, when you woke up?"

"A man's got to sleep, last I heard. I was up at the crack, no lie, but they didn't come, so finally I took a chance and cruised by the place. Cars gone. I felt like beating something up, I did. So I went back to Tahoe, looking for them everywhere. Checked the lawyer's office, but she was gone."

Red considered this.

"I'm sorry. It wasn't my fault, though. You wouldn't have had no better luck."

"Fuck," Red said. "Fuck, fuck, fuck." The mom at the next table turned and shot him a shocked look.

He turned to her and said, eyes glittering, "You have a fucking problem?"

"I'm telling the manager," she said, jumping like a little girl whose brother has just pinched her. She grabbed her kid and marched toward the cashier.

"Come on," Red said. He pulled the baseball cap lower, made sure the goatee was on straight.

"Oh, no. Not after last time in my room. I want lots of witnesses. Look, it's just a matter of time. I'll get him."

"That's fine," Red said. "I have no problem with that. But we have to go. The manager's going to come over and throw us out anyway."

"Right out front. That's how far we go, mate."

"Fine." They walked out through a field of dirty looks.

"Over here," Red said, pointing around to the side of the building. "They're watching us."

Kemp hesitated. When Red didn't stop, he shrugged and followed him. He was a follower, that was his nature, so he followed. "Okay, so what's the plan now?" Kemp said, leaning against the dumpster out back of the restaurant.

"I've got an idea," Red said.

"I'm all ears."

"It's kind of far-out."

"I'm with you. I'll make it right, you'll see."

"You still have the gun? We'll need it."

"Right here." Kemp got it out.

"Hand it over." Red waited, hands in his pockets, casual. A moment passed during which Red felt a confusion overwhelming him and blurring his vision. The gun was the line he had never crossed. But the gun was the only hope. The power the gun gave him was the power to keep gambling and to keep Donna too. The gun was the only chance to take back his jackpot.

He didn't know why his whole life depended on the gun. He didn't know what to do now if he got the gun. He was whirling around the wheel, inside a gamble: Kemp would give it to him or he wouldn't. If he didn't, Red was finished. If he did, it would mean that Red was lucky again.

Kemp handed it over. Clouds moved in Red's mind when he did that. Red let elation fill him. He couldn't speak, it was such a big win.

"So what now?" Kemp said.

"Well, I'll be damned. There's a dog in the dumpster."

Kemp turned around to see the fucking invisible dog in the dumpster, and Red shot him neatly in the back of the head. The sound was brief, loud, and sharp. Kemp jerked forward and banged the edge of the dumpster. The top of his skull sailed twenty feet into the air like a cap blowing off in the wind.

Red leaned down. Picking him up by the legs, he dumped Kemp into the dumpster.

He looked down, looked at the gun, stuck it in his waistband, closed his jacket. Looked at his hands. Not a speck of blood on him, though the area around was a mess. Looked around. No witnesses, and he already knew, no cameras.

Checking the hat again, he looked around. Time to move. He couldn't wait to wash his hands thoroughly. They felt like they were crawling with *E. coli*. And that damn pizza—he needed a good flossing. His hand went into his pocket and he fingered the small white plastic container of mint-flavored waxed dental floss.

He walked rapidly down the street to the unlit place he had left the car. He locked the seat belt into place, took a breath, then reached up and patted his right shoulder with his left hand. Good boy. He rubbed and patted himself even though he needed to leave. Good boy! Good boy!

A whole new logic had unfolded inside of him.

14

"AN ENVELOPE WITH A MILLION dollars in it and more to come," Nina said. "Imagine it sitting in the middle of a field. Just outside Kenny Leung's City of Gold."

Paul snickered.

"A tattered note says it's the property of this obscure peasant. Stay away. Along comes the army of the black knight, Atchison Potter, with his general, Jeff Riesner. They gallop up and look at the money, and Riesner turns to Potter and says—what does he say, Paul?"

Nina, Paul, and Sandy were sitting in Nina's library after hours. Paul nursed a Heineken. Nina and Sandy had cracked a cold bottle of Sancerre. They would all be drunkards before this case was over.

"Riesner says to Potter, 'If the little peasant comes around, I'll cut her head off and hang it on the village gate.' He picks the money up on the prong of his shining lance."

"Correct." Nina took off her shoes, pulled up another chair, and stretched her legs out on it. "But while the money is still fluttering on the tip of the lance, along comes the king of Nevada with a much bigger army. And the king says to himself, 'That money ought to be returned to me and my son, Global Gaming.'"

"So they get in a fight. They're jousting around," Sandy said, getting into it.

"Right. The Nevada Gaming Control Board is taking a peculiar interest in the writ case, along with Global Gaming. Even Prize's is watching this Potter court case carefully. They seem to be looking for a way to void the jackpot."

"On what theory?" Paul said.

"I can't imagine. But Thomas Munzinger called me this morning. He said that he is sending a couple of lawyers over to observe the court hearing on Monday."

"He was the one who looked like a cowboy," Paul said.

"Right. The rancher. He has cattle and horses, anyway."

"Was he the one who handed Jessie her check?"

"Yep. Global Gaming. They build and maintain the progressives and they make the payouts."

"But she won it! So how can they go after it now?"

"I don't know yet," Nina said. "I've asked Kenny to work with me on researching the gaming industry through the Net. I've already checked out the newspaper archives and the Global Gaming site, but Kenny has time to take a systematic look."

"Indian givers," Sandy said drily.

"If Global Gaming recovered the jackpot money, Atchison Potter wouldn't get it," Paul said. "Interesting."

"Meanwhile, what about that peasant?" Sandy said.

"Jessie is currently scheduled to be crushed under the hooves of the more powerful parties," Paul said. "Should you just try to get her out of this alive? Maybe they would throw her a bill or two if she retreated quickly."

"That would be the prudent course. But the whole thing makes me mad," Nina said. "I want to fight 'em for it. Jessie agrees."

"I'll drink to that," Paul said. He raised his bottle and said, "To blind chivalry," and Sandy and Nina touched their plastic tumblers to it.

"Except how do we get paid?" Sandy said.

"As usual," Nina said. "Just to let you know, Sandy, I'm charging the usual hourly rate. We're not going to be part of the gambling. Jessie will pay us one way or the other."

"You could get rich if you charge a twenty-five-percent contingency fee and you win," Paul said. "Jessie would go along."

"It wouldn't be fair. I have a strong feeling about this. I don't want to have my judgment affected by too big a personal stake. I didn't get into this business to gouge people. I don't want to join the vultures trying to fly off with a piece of Jessie."

She felt slightly quixotic saying this, but Paul and Sandy understood immediately. They were both nodding approvingly. She smiled at them, knowing how lucky she was to be working with them.

"Well, with the costs you're advancing, you're gonna be writing the rent check late," Sandy said. She got up and went out to her desk. When she came back, she had the calendar and a legal pad and pen.

"The first battle is tomorrow," she said. "One-thirty, Courtroom

Two, Judge Simeon Amagosian. Has a ranch near Markleeville. Quite a few peasants workin' his fields."

"He's always been fair to me in court," Nina said. "But I'll keep that in mind. There's no point to this Examination of Judgment Debtor except to hound her. Potter already knows she doesn't have any other assets. But there is something I'd rather he didn't know."

"Which is?"

"The date of her marriage to Kenny," Nina said. Her brow furrowed. "I can't get away with anything, Paul. Ever since I was a kid. I really don't want that to come out right now."

"Was it unethical?" Paul said. "In retrospect."

"We weren't trying to defraud anybody. We were trying to protect the client. But it's not going to look good in Riesner's hands, and he's bound to find out if the examination goes forward. I'm going to ask Amagosian to put this whole examination thing over for a few weeks. The next hearing after this is the big one, when Amagosian decides if the Writ of Execution should issue. We still have about two weeks before that hearing. Meantime, the money's frozen."

"What do you want me to do?" Paul said. Nina looked at him, at the sharp hazel eyes under the blond hair, the big hand holding the bottle. She felt a rush of gratitude toward him. He seemed to feel it; he smiled and raised his eyebrows.

"I want you to go to Hawaii for a few days," she said. "We've got to attack Atchison Potter's judgment, and I can only think of two ways at this late date. One, prove Jessie didn't kill her husband. If we can do that, no court will enforce that judgment. Two, prove that the judgment was procedurally defective. Show Potter knew Jessie was in California and should have put a notice in the California papers. You need to copy the court papers in Honolulu, check out the notice in the newspapers, see what you can find."

"I thought once you had a judgment, you can't go back and try to overturn it," Sandy said.

Nina nodded. "After six months, a judgment becomes final and no matter how wrong it may be, you can't attack it. That's true, Sandy. But there is at least one exception."

"Always," Paul said. "Once you figure out the cardinal rule that there is always an exception, you are free to graduate from law school. So what is the exception?"

"When you are trying to enforce a judgment from another state," Nina said. "Here we have a sister-state judgment from Hawaii. The California court can review it before issuing the writ. And that's the hearing in two weeks. So we have to work fast."

Paul didn't look happy.

"What is it?"

"Things are breaking here," Paul said. "I need to find the gun. Kenny says someone tried to kill him with the Glock. Finding the Glock gets even more important. And I can't find Kemp. I'm figuring he's the stalker. Now is not a good time."

"I know. I hate to send you away. But I believe it's absolutely necessary."

"You're the boss. I'll leave tonight," Paul said. "I can get a flight out of Sacramento." Sandy nodded and made a note.

"Thanks, Paul," Nina said. "I made you up a file with a lot of my thoughts on this jotted down." She handed it over.

"Want to get together for dinner?" Paul said, getting up. Sandy's eyes moved from him to Nina. Nina's head was shaking, and she was going to tell him all about her impossible schedule and her neglected home life, but Paul's expression stopped her. He raised a hand. "Never mind."

"I'll book you an e-ticket from Sac," Sandy said, "and fax your confirmation numbers to Caesars tonight. You'll probably need to be there by nine in the morning."

He was gone. Sandy drank down the rest of her glass, saying, "Guess I'll call the airline. Then I'm going home."

"Me, too."

"I have some advice you won't take."

Nina drank some more wine.

"You're gonna lose him."

Nina said, "That's my business."

"He's getting tired of putting up with you."

"You don't understand, Sandy."

"You ought to be careful not to lose anything now."

Nina exhaled, set her glass down, and took her feet off the chair. "And why is that?" she said.

"Because you don't have that much left."

"I've got Bob and my work," Nina said. "It's enough for now."

The king of Nevada himself, Ully Miller of the Gaming Control Board, arrived at court just before one-thirty the next day. Thomas Munzinger of Global Gaming was with him, deferring to him as a dutiful son should.

Outside the courtroom, through the high window, Nina saw pine trees and blue sky. Her soul rushed out there and took a deep breath and came back refreshed. Jessie was sitting on her left, right beside Nina, with her shadow Kenny behind them in the audience. Riesner sat at his table on the right.

When Munzinger and Miller came in, Nina watched their greetings from an anthropological perspective: the two men striding up to the lawyer, Riesner's attempt to take Miller's elbow and the shakeoff, Miller getting his hand out first for the shake as if they were dueling, the way Munzinger stood by. Miller obviously held the weight of power.

Other than them, Amagosian's clerk Debra, and Deputy Kimura, the bailiff for the courtroom, nobody else had come in yet, not even the press. The locals had all left town so the tourists had Tahoe to themselves, but it still seemed odd that the press wasn't around.

Maybe they always did this, reported the joyful news of the jackpots, but downplayed the consequences, which must sometimes include court cases against the winners. The tourists wouldn't want to hear about that. Let them keep their illusions.

Riesner got up with many a flirt and flutter and came over to Nina's table. He wore Armani. He always wore Armani. How she hated Armani.

"My, you look lovely today," he said. "Except for your unladylike scowl. I suppose you can't really do anything about that."

"Go away," Nina said. He brightened. However meager the reaction, she had reacted, which always excited him. She watched him fill with air in preparation for the next taunt but then he stopped suddenly. She caught a glimpse of a couple of suited men attached to attachés entering the room.

Polite introductions. It was one-thirty-five. Time wore lead shoes and dragged from second to second. Nina wished it was over.

The lawyers, Felicidad and Moorhead, represented the State of Nevada and Global Gaming. They were seasoned, quiet, colorless. Felicidad had a fleshy, broken-capillaried face; a lawyer of the old style, who had obviously never embraced running or working out at the gym for relaxation but stuck by the old tried and true tonic of drink. "We're just here to watch," he said, sitting down in the audience next to Munzinger and Miller.

Atchison Potter came in. The powers turned to assess this new power. Nina too couldn't keep from turning around.

Potter walked straight over to Riesner and pleasantries were exchanged. Then he approached Nina. Another expensive suit, this one very lightweight, a real summer suit, what she would expect from an executive from Hawaii. He was a short, stocky man, angular in feature, black-haired and brown-eyed, about fifty, wearing rimless glasses, but even with the glasses, the kind of guy who has hair on his back.

He didn't say anything at first, just cocked his head to the side and looked her up and down in a way she knew he meant to be insulting.

She was tired of being insulted and tired of being the only skirt in a room full of suits, and the hearing hadn't even started yet.

"What is it, Mr. Potter?" Nina said.

"I want her to understand that she can't get away with it," he said. "My son was the most important thing in my life."

"And I want you to understand. I'm not going to let you hurt her," Nina said.

"How will you stop me?" His mouth compressed into a straight, mean line.

"That's not the question," Nina said. "The question is, how will you stop *me*?"

He looked startled, then started to laugh.

And aloha to you too, Nina thought.

Deputy Kimura got off the phone. "All rise," he said. "The Court of the Honorable Judge Simeon Amagosian is in session."

Judge Amagosian appeared on the dais in his black robe. Well-fed and tanned like Munzinger, he had notorious mood swings, although he had won a reputation for fairness. First appointed back in the days of Jerry Brown's administration, he had been around long enough to feel secure in his calling. That left plenty of room for the occasional volcanic emotional eruptions which Nina knew at this very moment simmered in wait behind his smile. Today he had adopted a folksy manner.

The clerk, until then lounging back in her chair, began to move papers around on his desk. The stenographer flexed her fingers and poised for action.

"*Potter v. Potter.* This is the time set for the examination of the judgment debtor on this judgment." The judge looked out at the audience. Spying Felicidad and Moorhead, he raised his eyebrows, giving them a friendly nod.

Ominous.

"I have your opposing papers, Counsel," Amagosian said to Nina. "We are moving quickly, but not precipitately. Ten days' notice for this examination is all that is required."

Nina said, "But it's potentially unnecessary, Your Honor. Makes no sense to examine the judgment debtor now when we have a hearing scheduled for two weeks from now to determine whether my client *is* a judgment debtor. Why the unseemly hurry? The only asset my client has, which Mr. Riesner well knows, is already attached pending the hearing on the writ. The jackpot money isn't going anywhere."

"How do we know it's her only asset if I can't examine her, Judge? How do I preserve other assets?" Riesner said.

Nina said quickly, "I'll answer that in a minute, Your Honor. But first, let me say something about this type of proceeding in general. I will grant that the underlying rationale for allowing these examinations is well-intentioned . . ."

"Oh, my, that's big of you," Riesner interrupted.

". . . but the potential for abuse is also enormous, which is why I am here today, Your Honor. I will represent to the court that Ms. Potter is afraid of Atchison Potter, in fact believes that Mr. Potter has made an attempt on her life. It is our contention that the sole reason for this proceeding is to punish and persecute Ms. Potter and to elicit personal information to make it easier for Mr. Potter to persecute her further."

"Your papers are a bit short on facts, Counsel." A tip for you, Amagosian's face said. You're going to have to give me more.

"Enough to raise the point, Your Honor. And what is it I am requesting? Merely that this hearing be postponed until it is actually determined that California will extend sister-state reciprocity to this judgment. It's a more efficient use of judicial resources. Where is the harm?"

Amagosian's eyes turned to Riesner, who stood up, saying very deliberately, "'Where's the harm?' she says. Her client kills my client's son, and she strolls in here asking the court to protect her client from a proceeding that is duly noticed and appropriate. Knowing Mrs. or Ms. Reilly or whatever she calls herself . . ."

Nina started to get up, feeling heat flashing in her cheeks, but Amagosian made a motion downward with his hands at her and said to Riesner, "Let's show some respect, Counsel."

"Knowing Counsel, I can only say that it is probably she who is frightened, not her client, Judge. What are they trying to hide?"

"Professional courtesy would call for a continuance of this hearing, if Mr. Riesner had the slightest idea what professional courtesy was," Nina said. "In the regrettable absence of that, I am compelled to ask the court for assistance."

"But we won't agree to that, Judge," Riesner said. "We've given due notice. We have a right to examine her today. No purpose would be served by delay."

"You can't find it in your heart to give this lady a few more days to prepare for this exam?" Amagosian said to Riesner.

"I'm here today and I am proceeding," Riesner said.

"Well," Amagosian said, giving Nina a "Sorry, but it's his call" shrug.

"In that case, Your Honor," Nina said, jumping in to take advantage of whatever small sympathy he might have mustered on her behalf, "if the court is inclining that way, I'd like to propose something. I have here a Declaration by Jessie Potter under penalty of perjury which gives a clear and detailed statement of her assets and debts." Nina handed the single sheet of paper around. Jessie's assets consisted of the jackpot winnings and some exempt items such as her clothes and her old Honda. She had no debts. "We'll stipulate that this is what the oral examination would elicit and save a lot of time for everybody."

"Oh, no. I don't think so," Riesner said. "I'm entitled to ask questions to determine where she might conceal assets, to get addresses and specifics so I can follow up on these so-called assets. I'm entitled to find out where she's been so I can make an independent check as to the items here."

"She doesn't have anything but the jackpot, Your Honor," Nina said. "This is harassment. It's a personal vendetta. Look at the judgment. Mr. Potter wrongly believes that my client killed his son. He's just trying to use your court to make her life hell, Your Honor."

"Mr. Potter will not be with me during the examination," Riesner said. "Just Mrs. Potter and myself."

"But Mr. Riesner knows exactly how to pass on the hurt," Nina said. Even Riesner looked surprised to hear her say something so out of line. She was flexing, because she wanted all these jokers to know she was going to fight on even if she lost this round.

Chock full of bogus outrage, Riesner protested. Nina controlled herself. She had gone as far as she could.

Amagosian's shoulders stiffened, and Nina could see smoldering aggravation in his dark eyes. "I'm going to allow the examination," he said. "Mrs. Potter, will you please stand up." He had Jessie sworn in and said, "Any questions you are asked, you are to answer fully and truthfully. A false answer will be considered perjury, and I do not take lightly to perjury in my courtroom. All right, go with this gentleman here. Deputy Kimura will take you both to a room where the examination will take place. You understand that the law provides that you do not have the right to have counsel present?"

Jessie said, "But I won't know if he has the right to ask me certain questions."

"Has your attorney prepared you for this examination?"

"Yes, but—I want her with me."

"The idea is for the examination to be conducted efficiently and, frankly, fruitfully," Amagosian said. "That is why the legislature in its wisdom has decided to keep other attorneys out of the room." He was looking very closely at Jessie, and Nina wondered what he was thinking.

"We request that a definite time limit be placed on this examination," Nina said.

"We should be finished with the lady by five," Riesner said.

"An hour and a half should be ample," Nina said.

Amagosian looked down at the list of Jessie's assets. "An hour and a half."

"Thank you, Your Honor," Riesner said, allowing just the slightest note of triumph to creep into his voice.

"We'll adjourn for five minutes, then get the settlement conferences going," Amagosian said to his clerk. "Court is adjourned." He gave Jessie another long, curious look before he disappeared.

Jessie stood up and said to Nina, "I'll handle it."

"Don't lie about anything. I'll be waiting out in the hall. Remember, it's all out in the open now. No use hiding anything."

"Yeah, right."

"Be careful."

"Right."

Deputy Kimura motioned to her, and she went toward the jury rooms, tailed by Riesner.

Nina grabbed her papers and went quickly out into the hall, leaving the suits to their crummy victory.

Nina passed the next two hours with black coffee in a foam cup and a lot of phone calls to and from Sandy. She was propped on a bench outside the courthouse in the sun when Jessie finally ran out, breathless. "I was just about to go in and drag you out of there," Nina said. "Uh oh."

Jeff Riesner strode up with a look that Nina, in her own mind, called his hypocritical horror look.

"I'm astounded, Nina," he said. "To perpetrate such a fraud—well, it goes beyond anything you've ever done before. You encouraged Mrs. Potter to misrepresent herself as a legitimately married woman. This puts me in such an awkward position. Naturally, I'm obliged to bring it to the attention of the appropriate authorities. It's such a shame, since this news may void the jackpot, which neither of us wants."

"It wasn't her! I told you that!" Jessie said.

Nina's cheeks had reddened again. "She *is* legally married. I've already explained it all to Mr. Maloney of the IRS," she said. "There was no fraudulent intent."

"No intent! She lied about her identity! What won't she lie about?"

"She didn't lie. The date of her marriage was not asked on any of the forms."

"Her marriage. Yes, her marriage. She promised to pay Mr. Leung to marry her. That's a very big debt she tried to incur with my client's money."

"It's not your client's money."

"It will be shortly."

"You should think about this and think hard," Nina said. "You'd be making a stupid mistake to tell Munzinger about the marriage. Maybe they will manage to get the jackpot voided as a result. Then what does your client get? Know what he gets? A big legal malpractice settlement. From you, for acing him out of a crack at the jackpot money."

Riesner got a thoughtful expression. Evidently, he hadn't thought this far.

Nina said, "They're all much bigger players than you are and they'll strip you clean and leave you in the gutter in about twelve seconds if you don't watch out."

"And where does that leave you?" Riesner asked her. "You're giving me legal advice? Bah! I've wasted enough time on you two." He turned to go, but thought of something, and came back. "I almost forgot why I came out. Your client won't tell me her current address. Where she is now. I know she's not in Markleeville anymore. I have an absolute right to know where she lives."

"Why?" Nina said. "So you can run and tattle to Mr. Potter?"

"So I can independently confirm that she is renting and doesn't own the place. Hiding assets. And so on. As you know. I am being forbearing here. What is her address?"

"I didn't tell him," Jessie said. "It's true."

"I instructed my client not to answer that question due to the danger of imminent physical harm. I've explained all this to you several times. I won't go into it again."

"That's what she said. You coached her well. I asked her for copies of the police reports to verify her claims. We'll find her, don't worry."

"Tell your client to stay away from her," Nina said. "I'm holding you responsible."

Riesner looked down his nose at her, checked his Rolex, and said, "Well, no more time to put up with your empty posturing. I'm a busy man with far more serious business to attend to. Good day, Mrs. Potter."

Looking as vulnerable and nervous as someone who had barely survived a beating, Jessie didn't answer. Her eyes were rimmed in red.

Had Riesner managed to make her cry?

Nina was so irritated that she didn't allow herself to speak until she could calm down and keep her language clean and nonviolent. They both watched the tall figure get into his Jag and drive away, after some difficulty getting into gear.

"Those cars are mechanical nightmares," Nina said. "All appearance, no substance."

"Pretentious," Jessie said.

"Despicable. I'm sorry. I wish I could have protected you better."

"It's the way the law is set up," Jessie said. "If you're poor. Somebody gets a judgment against you, for the TV set you couldn't pay for or the unpaid rent, and then they have a right to make you sit in a room and make you tell them all sorts of personal things and you'll go to jail if you don't answer. Well, there's some things I didn't tell."

Nina squeezed her eyes shut, rubbed her forehead. "Like what?"

"Private things." She smiled slightly. "I may never see that money. But you know what? I've really enjoyed dreaming about it. After I lost my bearings—I mean, I always intended to have a long military career—after that failed, I started thinking about what I might want to do. And there is something—but I never even dared to hope there was a chance in hell. Then I won this jackpot. I lie awake at night sometimes dreaming. It's really not much different than dreaming you'll win the lottery, is it? I mean, what are my chances of getting that money really? There are all these forces aligning against me. I can feel them sneaking around behind us. They're bigger, stronger, better prepared, able to fight longer and harder."

"Are you thinking of quitting the fight?"

"Of course not. Give up? No way."

"So you have definite plans for the money?"

"Yep."

"Want to talk about that?"

She smiled a shaky smile. "I don't dare. Might jinx me. When we're closer to actual money in hand, and not still hanging around the slots, waiting for a hit."

"Let's get out of here. Let me take you over to Heidi's for a cup of coffee or a sandwich or something before you get back on the road. It's a long way back to the trailer."

"No, thanks. I have to get going right now. The trailer—it's been great. It's peaceful out there and not too far from Markleeville. Thank you for letting us stay."

"How's it going?"

"Not too bad. Kenny . . ." She smiled. "He's so funny."

"Just watch out for the coyotes. They sneak around at night and you could mistake them for people."

"Then they'd be dead coyotes."

Nina said carefully, "Kenny hasn't found his gun, has he?"

"No."

"And you? Are you armed?"

"Don't start grilling me too!"

"Okay." There wasn't much else Nina could say at the moment. She decided to talk to Kenny about what exactly they were doing to protect themselves.

"What happens next?" Jessie had put on a pair of dark glasses with lenses so tiny they couldn't do much to help with the afternoon sun, but which drew attention to the full mouth. She didn't need makeup. "Kenny's been up all night working on whatever it was you asked him to do."

"I asked him to look into the Greed Machines, find out more about progressive slots in general," Nina said. "Something's going on. I'm looking for a vulnerability."

"He's smart. Smarter than me, but no common sense. I've found that I can trust him. I think he has a crush on me, or not really me, that creature he made up. Joya. That part's strange. And if he tries to lay a hand on me I'll . . . Well, he knows that by now."

"You don't like him?" Nina said.

"He's sure not my type, let's put it that way. He lives in a fantasy world."

"Is it a problem staying with him?"

"No. He's a good cook and I wouldn't like to be alone. Also, he has an interest in all this. Potter is after him, too."

"We don't know that it was Mr. Potter."

"Who else? You know, come to think of it, now that the news that me and Kenny are really strangers is out, maybe Kenny will be out of danger."

"Maybe. Well, anyway, Paul left last night for Hawaii."

Jessie nodded. "I'm really hoping . . ."

Nina's phone vibrated again. She watched Jessie walk away as she put it to her ear.

Sandy said, "Still got that wet washcloth? Put it on again."

"What now, Sandy?" *Et tu, Brute?*

"I was playing the radio and the news came on. Guess what."

Nina sighed.

"The body of a man was found in Minden this morning in a dumpster behind the Pizza Hut. ID in the wallet. Shot in the head, execution-style."

Nina thought back to that eleven o'clock call that had never come.

"Charlie Kemp?"

"How'd you know?"

Nina headed back to the office, where the waiting room was full of clients. About six she finished up and headed home. She didn't think much about Charlie Kemp. She was already overloaded with information, and his murder was just another blip on the screen. He was dead. A man like that would have many enemies. He had been a threat to Jessie, might even have been the one who had tried to run Kenny down and followed him to her house. R.I.P. She didn't want to think further, speculate, or juggle any more balls of thought right now. There was too much she didn't know yet. And she was tired.

The sun showed no sign of setting yet. It still had a couple of hours to go, but the light was late, long, a soft gold very different from the radiant blasting sun of midday in the mountains.

She turned onto Kulow Street and immediately spotted Bob and Hitchcock. In the pine needles and dirt that constituted their tiny front yard, the two had a unique game of fetch going. Bob threw the stick, a hard job, because then he had to chase Hitchcock to get it back. They came to greet her as she parked in the driveway. She rolled down the driver's-side window and Bob stuck his head in and Hitchcock put his paws on the door and did likewise.

She looked at their eager faces, thinking, I am the luckiest woman alive.

"Let me out," she said, laughing. They went inside and she changed into shorts and did the quickie cleanup. The three of them then took off through the hazy shimmer of a summer evening to the Big Rock. On National Forest land not far from the house, the rock sat amid a group of warm granite boulders in a field of tall ponderosa pines.

Now the light was growing dimmer, softening. She wished she had a camera, but contented herself with letting the beauty of the moment imprint itself on her memory. Bob ran on ahead with Hitchcock.

The Big Rock had one angled side that they could scramble up easily, even Hitchcock, and a small ledge at the top where all three of them could sit, heads in the trees. Nina scratched Hitchcock's back as the dog lay beside her. Bob sat with his knees drawn up. Nina noticed with a small shock that he had very hairy legs in the space between the bottoms of his pants and the white socks.

"Mom?"

"Uh huh."

"How was your day today?"

"My day? Oh. Fine. Lots of court stuff."

"Did you win?"

"Not this time. How was your day?"

"Good."

"Uh huh. What did you do?"

"Not much."

"Like what?"

"Hung out on the computer with Taylor. After lunch we went on our bikes to town and we had snow cones."

"Was anybody else with you?"

"Not really. Oh, Nikki showed up." Nikki was a girl, too old and too wise for Bob. Nina waited, but heard no more.

Bob was galloping fast toward fourteen. He had shot up to about five-ten in the past year, but he was still a child, and when she looked at him she saw the whole parade of years in his changing face, the towheaded baby crying at nap time, wanting to play on right through his exhaustion; the toddler who grabbed her leg and clung like lichen, loving her madly through an entire circuit at the Kmart; the excited kid on the way to the Monterey Aquarium, swearing he felt okay, throwing up in the back seat of her new truck.

And now this, an odd phase of life, half innocent, half sophisticated. Nina put her arm around him. They sat peacefully for a minute. The birds had gone to bed and twilight had come.

"Hungry? Let's go fix supper," Nina said.

At three A.M. she woke up. She wrote the dream down in her journal: she was swimming a women's marathon down a long dark lake, a primeval lake, with night-brush along the side, swimming with wonderfully fast and powerful strokes. She couldn't see the other side. Other women were swimming too, and there was one beside her chatting.

They swam along the bank but Nina said, There are too many obstacles, we are constantly having to avoid hippos and debris—let's go out to the middle. She wasn't really racing, she just had to finish. She swam so smoothly and so strongly it was like a video game.

After a while she looked back and saw how the backwash—the waves produced by the women—pushed the boy children out toward the sea, where they could become independent.

15

GABE HAD A VERY LOUD voice which he deployed in the jackhammer range when he got frustrated, and naturally he did get frustrated being confined in a cage. However, Kenny was not about to let this roller-and-tumbler out anywhere near an electrical cord, a toilet, or a bug, so in the Portacrib he would stay for now. Jessie was in the back room getting ready to go out.

Gabe emitted a scream, a happy primate scream related to some private emotion occurring in connection with a white stuffed lamb he was trying to tear limb from limb. Hard to believe that only a few days ago, Jessie had rushed him to the Carson Valley Medical Clinic. Nobody could get that fever down, and then next day, like magic, Gabe had woken up fine.

He shouldn't be that strong at nine months, but then, Kenny thought, look at his mother, who had filled up some plastic gallon laundry jugs after breakfast and used them as weights so her arms wouldn't get stale.

Stale. Her word. She used slang Kenny hadn't heard outside of movies from the fifties, Marine Corps language. Like describing the experience as "outstanding," when she returned from a run through the scorpion-infested desert at sunset.

The sleeping thing had gone well, if you wanted to stay a virgin forever. Jessie slept in the back with the baby and Kenny curled up on the vinyl dinette bench that folded out into what Nina had optimistically called a bed. He rolled himself up in the blanket and lay awake for a long time thinking that someone else, the mythical man in the magazines that he was not, would have taken her in his arms long before bed and then the baby would be the one out here with the coyotes.

After lunch he called Nina, who told him that the pale-eyelashed man sitting on the stool next to him had been murdered.

"With a Glock?" he asked.

"My question exactly. They didn't find the gun. They have the bullet but the test results won't be in for a few days."

"Murder," Kenny said. "The man in the hooded sweatshirt." He felt cold fear.

"Man or woman, you said. There may not be a connection. We don't know that it was your gun."

"Well, I'm sure glad, Jessie and I and—that we're out here in the desert."

"Me too. You're being careful?"

"Absolutely."

Nina said, "Are you learning anything? Could Kemp have had a reason to think he would win the jackpot?"

"I'm on it. I'll call you right away if I have something."

"Kenny?"

He was looking at the baby, and he was afraid. "What?"

"Hurry."

He got the laptop booted up, though without a surge protector he could crash anytime, Nina's electrical system being what it was. Jessie came out wearing her jeans and sweater and they talked about Charlie Kemp.

"What does it mean?" Jessie said.

"The shooter is at large, but we don't know why Kemp was shot," Kenny said. "Maybe it has nothing to do with us."

"Come on. He came after us too."

"I know. I'm glad we got out."

"So what now?"

"Keep on doing what we're doing, I guess."

"Well, since there's no McDonald's on the corner, I still have to lay in food," she said. "What kind of tea do you want?"

"Lipton's. We're only thirty miles from Minden, where the body was found. Maybe we should go together. But I have this work I have to do for Nina."

"I won't be long. I'll go to Carson City."

"Take the rifle." He couldn't believe he was talking like this. "Take the rifle," like in an old Western.

"I don't like leaving, but we have to eat. You and Gabe are safe here. No one could find us here. Don't be afraid."

"I'm not afraid. Except for you and Gabe."

"You know something?"

"What?"

"Now that the worst has happened, Potter has come at me hard, people are getting killed, I feel better than I have in a long time. I feel relieved. Waiting for the war is so much harder than the war. I know what I'm doing now. I'll check the booby traps on my way out."

He heard the car start up and roar down the sandy road. She hadn't even mentioned the money. With her, Potter was still the focus.

He put the Portacrib right by the computer and explained a few things to Gabe, who seemed to enjoy watching the screen. When he jumped into the Net, Gabe was right there with him.

Kenny wanted to know all about Charlie Kemp. As to how Kemp had ended his life in a dumpster in a small Nevada town not half an hour from the trailer, there was too little information to form a hypothesis, so he abstained. The *Nevada Appeal* and the *Reno Gazette* reported the murder with few details. A shooting behind a pizza place. No witnesses to the shooting, but police had some leads they weren't talking about. Kenny learned that Kemp was a welder from Nottingham, England, age forty-two, on an unexpired work visa.

Kemp's nationality posed a problem. Kenny couldn't find anything on his background in England.

He put Kemp aside for the moment and started working on the list Nina had given him. Her logic made sense. On what basis could Global Gaming show the jackpot was invalid?

The only answer would be cheating. But Jessie hadn't cheated. She was many things, but technologically hip she was not. Slot machine cheating would involve hacking into the microchip that controlled the machine. She couldn't do that. Supposedly, nobody could do that.

The wins had to be random. It was all in the doctrine of fair play Nevada guaranteed.

However, thinking about it, he was quite interested in the psychology behind the spinning reels. The reels came so tantalizingly close to lining up on a perfect hit so often. Could they actually program the microchips to do that? Make two sevens stop and the third go by? And was that legal, anyway?

There was lots of news about past jackpots on the Global Gaming site. A California woman had won more than eight million at the Tahoe Hilton in Crystal Bay at a Megabucks machine, lining up four eagles. In Las Vegas, someone had won over twenty-seven million at the same kind of progressive slot machine. The casinos and gaming technologists were taking advantage of the big news to offer up some of their own, a new game called Super Megabucks which would average fifteen million dollars per win. Just this year, the payoff had already surged up to over twenty-nine million at Harrah's Lake Tahoe.

The slots were now the dominant revenue-producing devices in the gaming industry. This was news to Kenny. He would have thought the gaming tables were the big moneymakers.

He found a site that discussed the computer chip inside the big-payout slot machines, called an EPROM chip. These chips used a program called a "random number generator."

"Gabe, you won't believe this," he muttered. Gabe made inchoate noises and kicked the Portacrib. Kenny hadn't been around children much. Gabe was a budding King Kong. Right now he was shaking the bars, trying to tear down the walls of his prison. The effort was grand but the effect was comic.

Back to the screen. Unlike the old mechanical free-spinning reels, video reels used a stepper motor which allowed stops to be programmed based on a secret "source code."

Several of the Nevada clubs had asked the Gaming Control Board for permission to "set" some of their slots more "loosely" than the others, so their Red Carpet members would have better odds than the hoi polloi. How could anyone do that? In what way was this random?

He tried to think. The chips were set to stop and to consistently provide certain percentages, yet they did so in a way that could not be predicted. How?

Puzzled, Kenny went to the Web site on the Triple Eight court case. First of all, he admired the psychology of using eights as the winning numbers. In China eights were very lucky numbers. He himself would have wanted to play such a machine.

All right. Three eights, but they did not perfectly bisect the win line. Kenny examined a diagram of the positions of the eights on the reel. The eights all touched the central win line, but haphazardly. Then Kenny read that Global Gaming had proved it wasn't a true jackpot by examining the random number generator, which indicated the machine wasn't supposed to hit right then.

Jessie's Greed Machine—he saw the three brown banks again. Right across the middle line. No problem there. But what about the random number generator? Jessie's machine must have already passed that test too. The check only took a couple of hours.

Kenny scratched his head. What the heck was this thing they called a random number generator? Software, obviously, on a chip they could remove and examine. So far, so good. It generated random numbers. Uh huh.

The real question remained: what was this random number generator?

He read on. Nevada casinos were free to set their slot machines so
that they paid out only 75 percent. And casinos did set their machines
and changed the payouts whenever they wanted to. They weren't supposed to change the random number generator program, though. Not
supposed to?

The Nevada Gaming Control Board had six field inspectors for the
state. In 1996, Nevada had 185,610 slot machines.

Kenny did the calculation. Say they could check one hundred machines a day—it would take them five years to do a round of the machines!

He had a sinking feeling in his stomach. He wished he had a strong
cup of tea right now. Working at the computer was no joke without tea.
This sinking feeling was a somatic expression of the thought he was
having, that Jessie's chances had sunk.

He went to Nina's cupboard in another search for a tea bag tucked
in a corner. No tea, but he found three kinds of coffee. Two more sacks
of the stuff in the fridge. She ought to get hold of herself. He played
with Gabe for a few minutes, then went back to work.

Cheating was as traditional as winning and losing in gambling. As
weevils will always burrow into flour, the industry would never be able
to construct a machine that was completely impregnable from the
cheaters.

But a lot of the cheating seemed to be within the industry. He
learned that it was legal in Nevada to program the virtual reels on the
slots so that, for instance, three sevens would appear above or below
the pay line. But it wasn't legal to put two sevens *on* the payline and
drop one below. In other words, programming a "near-miss" on a payline was illegal, a near-miss above or below wasn't.

And since the player who saw too many blank blank blanks on the
payout line might lose heart and leave, many machines were now programmed to detect that such a line was about to appear, and to insert a
couple of encouraging winning symbols.

In other words, what the player saw on the machine wasn't necessarily the actual result of his playing. If he won, he did still win, but if he
lost, the programming tried to make the loss look like a near-win.

The old mechanical reels had been fixed in the traditional way.
Every player noticed eventually that the winning symbols showed up
much more on the first two reels. That was because the third reel only
contained one winning symbol. This carnival-style scam had always
been legal and universal.

But the new programming offered a new world of cheating possibilities.

Now Kenny was looking actively for slot machine cheating. Software microchips that were illegally modified were called "gaffed" chips. In 1989 a slot machine manufacturer called American Coin had been discovered to be fixing the chips in their video poker machines to reduce the number of royal flushes. The programmer who had programmed the gaffed chips had been shot to death at his house in Las Vegas just before he was due to give testimony in the case. Nevada had decided this kind of industry deception was illegal. But where was the line?

Kenny even found a case of a Gaming Control Board official who had reprogrammed the EPROMs in some slots so they would pay out when a certain combination of coins was inserted. He did the programming and handed the gaffed chips to the field inspectors, who unknowingly inserted the cheating program into the machines while trying to test them. He had been convicted of attempted theft by deception.

The interesting thing was, this guy had used co-conspirators, people who sat at the machines and actually won the jackpots.

He thought of Charlie Kemp again, and of the faceless men he had met the night of the jackpot who owned, maintained, and supervised the payouts on the slots. But Kemp didn't seem to have any connection to the gaming industry, other than being a gambler. And being dead like that witness.

Kenny felt even worse. He was actually starting to believe someone could have somehow changed the EPROM on Jessie's Greed Machine. The Gaming Control Board seemed to be thinking along the same lines. But they must not be sure, or Jessie would be arrested.

How could they not be sure? All they had to do, according to these articles, was run a test program on the chip. They would know right away if the program had been altered. Then they would nullify the win.

What was going on?

Then Gabe needed food, a graham cracker with jelly on it and a bottle, then Gabe's diaper had to be changed, then Gabe had to be put down for a nap in the back room. Jessie had left written instructions, which Kenny carried out to the letter. And the little tyke lay right down and put his thumb in his mouth and went to sleep. Just like clicking off AppleShare and the ISP connection and shutting down.

Kenny tiptoed back to the front room. The ceiling fan whirred. He moved back to Charlie Kemp. He searched Lake Tahoe newspaper police logs for a few years, and found nothing. That didn't surprise him. A police record would have been a red flag to the Gaming Control Board inspectors.

He sat back, arms behind his head, and focused on his memory of the night of the win.

Kemp had been taking notes, and consulting his watch. He had been nervous.

Provocative. Suspicious. But so many gamblers thought they had systems.

But Kemp had acted like he was supposed to win. Like the jackpot was *his*.

Kenny thought about Kemp's speech, his level of intelligence as extrapolated from his vocabulary. Kemp hack into Global Gaming's security systems? No way.

Had to be an inside job. But an inside job would have shown up.

Jessie's Greed Machine had been tested down to the binary code. Kenny didn't see how they could find anything now after taking the machine down to its binary code. Nina didn't need to worry.

He would call her and—Kenny had just remembered that someone had said something to Kemp while he sat on the stool. He remembered the girl in her wheelchair, gamely having a good time. Had she spoken a few words to him?

Or was it the boyfriend, the biker with the ponytail. And what had been said? Kenny couldn't remember. Intoxication had affected his memory.

Somebody had said something to Kemp! An old rock song had gone through Kenny's head when he heard it.

The boyfriend had worn Harley pins. Kenny went to motorcycle club sites' membership lists. Nevada was full of bikers. No photos of this particular biker popped up. He pushed up his glasses and took another break, during which he cleaned up the harrowing results of Gabe's play with the lamb.

Back to the dinette table.

He logged on to some casino sites. He had a strong subprogram for hacking into HR sites. He spent time examining payroll records for Tahoe casino employees.

He found no sign of Charlie Kemp. If a casino had employed him, he had managed to keep himself well hidden or was using an alias.

Then, just as Gabe began making small sounds in the back room that contained within them the implicit threat of high-decibel sounds to come, Kenny found something.

He had hacked into some employee newsletters. And there on the cover was a picture for an article on disabled employees. And smiling front and center he saw the girl in the wheelchair.

Her name was Amanda Lewis, and she was a cashier at the Horizon.

Gabe woke up and took over the proceedings. Another round of diapers and food. Gabe spoke intensely throughout of his feelings but Kenny couldn't understand any of it.

Jessie got back about five, her arms full of groceries.

"Any trouble?"

"Empty roads. No trouble. Anything happen here?"

"Only in my mind."

"You found something on the computer?"

"I don't think Nina needs to worry. If there had been cheating, Global Gaming would have caught it right away and never made the payout."

"Great! How's the boy?"

"Rowdy. I'm teaching him HTML."

"No fever?" She dumped the bags in the galley kitchen and came over to the computer center, which consisted of the dinette table and the Portacrib. Gabe was waving his arms excitedly, and in a second she was holding him, cheek to cheek, her eyes closed. "He's nice and cool."

"I hope that fever thing hasn't retreated to the cell cytoplasm level where it's just waiting to break out again," Kenny said.

"I hate it when you say things like that. Do you even know what you're talking about? Because I sure don't."

"Sorry." Here he went, irritating her again, when he was merely interested in sharing some intriguing tidbits of knowledge he had picked up in his browsing. He was a Renaissance man in a time when many talents were useless and one miserly, focused ability got you what you wanted.

"That was a higher temperature than ever three days ago," she said. Gabe echoed that thought with a wail. "I was scared."

"I thought medicine was a science," Kenny said. "Why can't the doctor look at him and figure out what is wrong?"

"You haven't been around very many sick people, have you?"

"Did they give him antibiotics? Just in case?"

"No. Because he had no sign of an infection and if it's a virus, that wouldn't help. C'mon, Gabe, back into the Portacrib, Mommy's right here putting stuff away. See?" She dropped her head back and rolled her shoulders, and Kenny watched, helplessly admiring the hollow below her clavicle and the swelling skin below.

"Lipton's. I'll put some water on and you can go nuts. I bought myself a pint of vodka and Rose's lime juice. You ever have a gimlet?"

"I'm not much of a drinker."

"You can try one out, if you want. Anyway, he says babies get these ambiguous fevers often," she went on. "Some of them even have seizures. As long as you catch it before the fever is too high, it's no big deal."

"Gabe's seizure was no big deal?"

"He seemed to think it wasn't. They're common in infancy, he said." She looked unconvinced. "I couldn't tell if he just said that to make me feel better, either."

She finished putting the food in the tiny cupboard and poured spring water into Nina's saucepan on the stove and said, "Damn. I was thinking as I drove up the dirt road, it's just us and the buzzards out here. This can't go on much longer. I need a decent place to live, some land where I can . . . I need for this kid to get a thorough workup. I don't care what that doctor says, this just doesn't feel right to me."

How tricky, to give life to another human being and then to have so little control over his survival. The water boiled and Jessie made tea and fixed herself a big vodka gimlet. The slow descent of the sun had begun again in the stillness of the late afternoon. Dry cool air, windless, amplified their words. Jessie let Gabe crawl around in front of the trailer and sat on the steps with Kenny.

Jessie drank the gimlet down pretty fast and her cheeks got flushed. "It's nice to see you relaxing," Kenny said.

"Don't kid yourself. I can get it back together in a half second."

"I didn't mean that."

"You know, this whole jackpot thing—I'm not really expecting to collect. I just want Gabe to be safe and healthy. But, you know, that first moment when you said, 'You hit!' and I could see it on the machine, the three banks. For just that moment—oh, the feeling was—I felt this enormous burden on my shoulders. I had never noticed it before, but now I felt it, because now I could imagine it going away. It hasn't been easy."

"I can't imagine what it would be like to lose your whole family," Kenny said.

"I thought the Marine Corps would be my home. I lost that. And I lost Dan. After so many losses something happened here"—she put her fist to her chest—"and I wanted to give up. But then Gabe came and I had to keep fighting."

"You kept me alive. I would be dead if not for you."

"Don't talk stupid."

"It's true."

She frowned. "I get tired of your bull, Kenny. Is this your way of making a pass?"

"I'm going to fry that sausage you brought. And get the rice going." He went inside the screen door and started banging around the pots, a comforting activity for him. "And I'm going to tell you a story. A true story. About me."

He told it to her, all of it, about the restaurant and his father and the company, the people he had to lay off, the bad decisions, the money he'd lost. It was easier to be moving around, setting the table, checking pots so he wouldn't have to look at her. She never interrupted once. She just sat out there on the steps, watching Gabe, frowning.

When he was through, so was their paper-plate dinner. Gabe went back to the Portacrib and they pushed aside the laptop.

"You have to make it right with your parents," Jessie said.

"I either come to them with the money you're giving me, or I don't know."

"You're not going to kill yourself now, are you? After seeing how quickly your life can change?"

He decided to keep her guessing, maybe worrying about him for a stolen second here and there, in between the long runs through the desert, two hundred sit-ups, and caring for Gabe. "Hasn't changed yet. How are the carrots?"

"Too chewy."

"Gabe ate all his carrots. Bioflavonoids are important. You don't eat well."

"As opposed to you, who eats all the time."

"But usually nutritiously."

"Your parents must be really worried about you."

"Yeah."

Jessie washed the dishes. Kenny drank his tea, saying, "I have to go up the hill."

"Not a good plan."

"I'll be careful."

"Must be important. Considering everything. So go. I'll be okay. No TV, no company except my aunt's rifle."

"You could read. I have a really good book in my pack over there. It's by William Gibson. You know him?"

"No."

"Visionary stuff. Futuristic."

"Kenny, we don't have the same interests. I read how-to and gardening books when I have time, which I never do."

She didn't understand yet that that was the intriguing part. The simple perfection of the two of them together escaped her. She was passionate physicality; he embodied the obsessed mental realm. They were complements, two halves that, combined, made a fascinating whole, and separate, existed only as fragments. Chemistry is all that matters, he wanted to say to her, but she would have taken it wrong and gotten mad and he wanted to leave her in a good mood. He put on his jacket. "Bye-bye, Gabe. Jessie, you'll lock up tight?"

"What do you think? Can't this wait until morning? Where are you going?"

"The Horizon."

"Not to gamble."

"No fear," he said. "I've got about thirty bucks Nina loaned me and I plan to use that for gas and food until our mega money pours through the door."

"When do we expect you back?"

"After, I might make another stop."

"Oh?"

"To see my family."

"Yeah, do that. You'll feel better. You'll be fine. Go on and take care of your business."

"Anyway, I'm not sure when I'll be back. I may have to stay until morning." Suddenly he saw Charlie Kemp's face again and thought, What am I doing? Would she and Gabe really be safe?

He clumped down the trailer steps and went toward the Lexus, debating with himself.

"Wait," she called, disappearing inside.

Lounging against the hood of the car, he let himself indulge in a brief fantasy in which he went back inside and everything was different, Jessie really became Joya, submissive to his every whim. A long, romantic desert night.

She came back with a ham sandwich. The offering wasn't quite as good as his fantasy, but he smiled.

"I know you'll get hungry later," she said.

"Thanks," he said, taking a bite. Ah, his favorite spicy mustard.

She had remembered.

The drive took longer than he could ever have imagined, but he made it by seven-thirty, prime gambling time. He found Amanda Lewis in the change booth by the dollar slots. He stood in line at the counter, astonished at the number of people that found gambling so infernally fascinating. When he got up to her window, he asked for five dollars in quarters.

"That all?" she said.

Was she supposed to say things like that? Make a man feel like some small-time loser?

"For now," he said, resisting mightily the impulse to toss the whole thirty and make a big show about it. He tipped her a buck. "Uh," he said.

"Yes?" She gave him her nice smile.

He had been the last in the line, and right now, he remained last, so he felt he had some time to come up with something catchy. If only he could think what to say. There was something so hard about direct confrontation. Women, excepting Jessie, who didn't give a damn about him—yet—often responded so awkwardly to his awkwardness.

"Oh, it's you!" she said. "Hey, aren't you married to that woman, what was her name—the woman that won the monster pot?"

"But—how would you know that? You left," he said.

"My friend—the guy that was with me—he was interested in all that commotion, so we went back. We were only three rows down from you. Wow," she said, looking hard at him. "You're rich now, aren't you?"

"Yeah, filthy rich." He nursed a brief vision of what it would be like if he really could experience even fifteen minutes of filthy richness.

"Buy me a drink?" she said. "I'm done with the shift as of"—she peered down the aisle, and along came her replacement—"now. I want to know all about what people like you do when you hit big like that. I mean, did you tie one on?" Closing her window with a clatter she came rolling out, this time using her own steam to move the wheels of her chair. As she got closer he saw that she was laughing. "Oh, I forgot," he said. "You already had."

Her dark hair streamed down the back of her chair, and Kenny followed her, trying to remember how to flirt.

She steered up a ramp to a cocktail lounge overlooking the action on the floor. "Bourbon and soda, if you please. Or tell you what. I'll buy, since I invited you." She held her hand out and shook his. She had a good grip.

"Why are you here, anyway?" she asked him a few minutes later, taking a sip of bourbon. "You've got enough money now to blow this town. Or are you one of those guys, whatchamacallem, a compulsive gambler?"

"Not at all," Kenny said.

"Well, then."

"I came to talk to you," he said, all plans to be devious completely abandoned in the face of her merry candor.

"Why? You want to talk to me? You want to know what it's like to be in a wheelchair? You one of those freaks?"

"Don't be touchy. I want to know," Kenny said, "whether you know Charlie Kemp."

"Charlie who?"

"Kemp." Kenny described him for her. "Oh, yeah," she said. "The man on the stool next to you."

"You remember him."

"No. Just that he was on the stool there. You were between us. Why do you care, anyway?"

"I need to find out about him."

She shrugged. "Can't help. Never saw him before in my life." As far as Kenny could tell, she told the truth. She seemed relaxed but curious. "Why?"

"Come on. I saw you talk to him."

"You never."

"Then maybe it was your friend. I can't remember. Somebody said something."

"What's the matter? Why are you quizzing me about this stuff?"

"I'm not just asking out of idle curiosity. Kemp—he threatened some people." He didn't mention that Kemp's days of threatening people were over.

"Who?"

"What difference does it make, who?" he said, exasperated.

"I bet he's threatening your wife. She got the jackpot. He wants some of it, right? It is such a bitch being rich." She drew lines in the moisture on her glass with a pretty, pink-tipped finger, her face resentful. Some people have all the luck, her face said, but not me.

"Listen. Kemp's dead. He was murdered three days after the jackpot."

"That's weird." Her shoulders slumped and she got a sad and hurt look, and he got an idea how hard it was for her to keep that cheerful expression all the time.

"Amanda? She's not rich. She's had a rough time. She hasn't seen a dime of the jackpot. It's all tied up. She may never get it. I'm afraid. Someone tried to hurt us too. I thought it might be Kemp, but now I don't know. Do you know a man named Atchison Potter?"

"Never heard of him. I don't want to talk about this anymore." She put on that look of gaiety, flushed, smiled, gathered herself to herself. Kenny tried to go with her mood.

A three-person band climbed up onto a small stage next to the bar and began setting up. Amanda studied them. "The token thin blonde," she said. "The token tall hunk. The token hairy brown man. Same old thing. No doubt they're talented, too, and destined to shoot beyond this lowly start into superstardom. I'd like to see a band with some hideous people."

"With blue skin," Kenny said, getting into it. "Tokens of nothing. No possibility of being stereotyped."

"Exactly."

"Then, to completely shatter our expectations, they need to play like shit."

She laughed hard.

Kenny thought, Well, a long trip for nothing. "Could I talk to your friend?" he said, not hoping for much.

"He's not from around here. He was just visiting."

"From where?"

"Transylvania, I think he said. Just kidding. Pennsylvania."

"You know how to tell a liar?" Kenny said. "They get this wavering in the eyes. It's called nystagmus."

"I've heard of that. Cops look in your eyes to see if you're drunk."

"Amanda, I am no good at this. I'm doing this all wrong. I think you're lying about your friend. So I'm just going to ask. Are you?"

She had nice eyes, large, not much mascara. "No."

"Nystagmus city," Kenny said, and she laughed again.

"I like you. You were nice to me that night. You wanted to talk to me, didn't you? But I was with someone, I had to go. You know, when we heard the commotion and came back—I was watching your wife, and there was something bothering her a lot. And she hardly seemed to know you existed. I don't know—I picture you with a different type." Just then, the band broke into a rowdy, bottleneck blues version of Fred MacDowell's "You Got to Move." Amanda stopped what she was saying and clapped her hand against the table, keeping the beat. "I just love that song!" she shouted. "I take back every rude thing I said about this band."

"What type is my type?" Kenny asked her. "Who in this world is my type?"

But Amanda was singing along with the band. She had a nice voice, too. Kenny found himself relaxing along with her.

When the band left the stage, Amanda said, "I have to get home."

"Does your friend live with you?" Kenny said, feeling, to heck with politeness. I mean, there were all kinds of friends, and he was running out of time.

"Don't you wish you knew," the little flirt said. She patted his cheek and rolled off into the night, her long skirt melting into the blackness. Kenny escorted her out the door. She waved and said good night to several people on the way out. Outside, in front of the Horizon, she motioned to him to bend in closer to her, then gave him a peck on the cheek.

She smelled like lemongrass and honey.

Not that he let the innocent aura stop him from sneaking over to his car and following her progress across the parking lot to her special van.

She scooted up to the side of the van, pulled the handle on the door, and slid it back. Mechanical sounds inside were followed by a lift lowering itself slowly to the ground. She rolled on, up, and into the van. After the lift rose up, disappearing behind her, the sliding door closed.

She drove herself, Kenny thought, then kicked himself for being surprised. She held a job, she gambled, she drove with hand controls. He knew people could do that, he just hadn't given it any thought before. She was like anyone else, and like anyone else, she lied. She had deflected every question about her friend, and he just didn't believe her.

Watching her maneuver the van out onto the street, he considered what she had said. Not enough.

He followed close on the tail of the red van, wondering if her friend the biker was really a friend. He imagined a scenario: he probably was a real biker, and she had been riding on the back of his motorcycle when she had had this accident that cost her the use of her legs. She was the type with a good heart, who would forgive the stinker for doing something so horrendous to her, but the friend, eaten up with guilt, spent all his time off from the repair shop trying to make it up to her, even though he never could.

Kenny did wonder what had caused Amanda's paralysis, but after that crack suggesting he might be some kind of wheelchair freak, he had permanently lost the nerve to ask.

She cut off Lake Tahoe Boulevard at Al Tahoe, swinging into a right turn onto Pioneer Trail. Up here in the mountains, there were no streetlights. A soft summer drizzle made the headlights of oncoming cars shimmer in Kenny's windshield, but the night was his cover. She drove at a cautious speed, so he had no trouble following her. After Elks Club Drive, she made a left, then he followed her through a few dizzying turns until she parked in the driveway of a dark cabin on a street called Chippewa. She ended up close to the house. When she stopped, the lights went on in the van. He watched her work the lift again and roll slowly toward a back porch that had been equipped with a temporary-looking wooden ramp.

She went inside the cabin.

Kenny parked nearby, watching as the lights went on, room by room, and she moved through, presumably making herself at home. The ramp did not look permanent, but then nothing old did in Tahoe. The wood cabins rotted, burned, and fell just like the trees eventually. They were never built with posterity in mind, and lay lightly upon the land. They were simple abodes of the forest, as Kenny's family house was.

He started thinking about his family, and what Jessie had said. He couldn't hide forever. If he waited the full ten days before getting in touch, they would have the police out looking for him. What on earth would he say to them? He had landed in a situation that was complicated and frightening, and he wanted them kept out of it. If only he had the money right now. He would go over to the Five Happinesses—he checked his watch—they would still be there, mopping floors and washing pans—and hand over the check to his father with a promise to make up the interest and small losses.

Some of Amanda's windows did not have curtains or blinds, Kenny noticed disapprovingly. Here was another feature of proud old Tahoe cabins. With nothing but the animals and forest to witness them, people felt private. Pulling his jacket off the back seat and putting it on, Kenny got out of the car, feeling bad and good at the same time. He didn't want to peep. He just wanted to see, he told himself.

But before he could get closer to the house, another car drove up, parking directly in front of the cabin. This car looked out of place in rustic, windswept Tahoe. This car rated an immaculate, air-filtered garage with only the odd genteel Sunday outing to sully its low mileage. A warm gold color, the car was small, pointed and dynamic as an arrow, and low to the ground. It irradiated the small street with its glow. A Porsche Boxster. Whew.

A man with a goatee and baseball cap got out, slamming the door, without a care in the world, his ponytail flying. The boyfriend. What should he do? Wait and watch, he decided.

That car was far from the world of Harley. Odd.

Kenny waited until Amanda's friend had knocked and been admitted into Amanda's cabin. He then moved as slowly as he could across the side yard until he could see directly into the living room. And oh, joy. The window was open. He could hear them inside.

The friend had his back to Kenny, however, so he could only see the accusation on Amanda's face.

"You did say something to him," Amanda said hotly. "I remember. And now he's dead. Why did you bring me to Prize's that night? You were so nice, so sweet. I really thought it was for me. But it wasn't for me, was it?"

Repeat what you just said, Kenny said in his mind. Speak up! But his thoughts fell on deaf ears or else Amanda's friend had decided his leather jacket was not enough to cut the chill in her voice, because the next thing that happened was that the window slammed down right next to him. Kenny nearly fell over in fright.

Their voices lowered to a murmur. Kenny wished he had a glass so he could press it to the window and hear what they were saying, but, thwarted in that, he followed the action on Amanda's face.

She got madder and madder. Shouts emerged along with the tramping of boots moving around the room. Then the man walked right up to Amanda. Standing in front of her, he shouted directly into her face.

Well, most people would be able to get up and get out of his way, but how could she, trapped like that in her wheelchair? Should he interfere? Kenny worried, watching her, but the next thing she did answered his question. Picking up an orange glass-shaded Tiffany-style lamp, she leaned back, took aim, and hurled it.

"Get out!" Kenny heard the words, as loud as the shattering glass shade.

The man had managed to sidestep the lamp, but no doubt she had finally convinced him that it was time to go after all. He moved toward the front door.

Kenny crouched down lower, suddenly aware of the light pouring through the living room window directly on him. He would get out of the way, but there wasn't time, so he cowered low and hoped for the best. He could see the porch clearly from where he was, which wasn't good. That meant the man could see him, too.

But he appeared too angry for reconnaissance. He stood glowering, facing the living-room door until it slammed shut in his face.

As soon as he left, Kenny knocked on Amanda's door. He was furious with himself. Once again, he had forgotten to read the license plate on the car. Too interested in the man. He wasn't a professional. He wasn't sure what he was doing here, except that he felt drawn to Amanda.

"I told you to take off!"

"It's me, Kenny."

Silence. The door opened a crack. "Kenny?"

"I followed you here."

"I guess you did."

"Everything okay?"

She looked rattled, and giggled. "There's glass all over in here, which I now realize is going to be a pain in the butt to sweep up without help."

"I'll do it," he said.

"Okay." She let him inside. "I really liked that lamp."

He found a broom in a closet in the kitchen and set right to work. "Is that guy really your friend?"

"You already asked me that."

"How about an answer?"

"I don't owe you anything. Unless you want that measly buck tip back from earlier or to collect on the bourbon."

"Come on, Amanda . . ."

"Put the glass in a brown paper bag before you dump it in the plastic, will you? There are some under the kitchen sink."

"Amanda . . ."

"Then I think you better go."

He finished cleaning up. He looked at her to see if she seemed more mellow now that the floor was clean, and decided from the expression on her face that she was not. He walked toward the door.

"It's really too bad," she said suddenly.

"What?"

"You were after something. You wouldn't believe how people treat me now that I'm in this chair. Men. I don't think I've been asked out for so much as a glass of wine in months. And then if they do somehow breach the weirdness barrier, after the novelty wears off, after they figure out my limitations really do mean I can't ski or dance or run marathons, or whatever the hell they absolutely have to do on weekends, they ditch. I'm alone again, with my cat to pet and only my friend to check up on me." She laughed painfully. "I'm hanging with the wrong crowd."

As if hearing itself mentioned, a white cat jumped on her lap, settling in. She petted it. "People are no damn good." Then she smiled. "You've just messed up my life, Kenny."

"He wouldn't hurt you?"

"Him? He's the one who crashed the car. He owes me. He'll always owe me."

"I do like you, Amanda. It's just that I love somebody."

"That's a strange way to put it. You mean your wife?"

"My wife."

"Well, I'm not alone either. My friend—he needs me, and I need him. It'll be okay."

"What did he say to Kemp that night?"

"I don't remember." Her face sagged into fatigue. "Go away, will you?"

"I'm afraid for you."

"Just go away."

16

PAUL WAS SICK AND TIRED of her shenanigans. She was acting up. She was running wild. She was damn confusing.

To say nothing about her lawyering.

He wasn't sure he'd sleep with her if she begged him at this point. She had no idea what she was doing to his head, pouring so many conflicting flavors into his mental cocktail.

He brought himself back to the feminine face in front of him. This elegant controlled face with a plumeria blossom tucked behind her ear belonged to the clerk of the Honolulu District Circuit Court, the Honorable Philip Otaru presiding. A flowered umbrella and Korean wall art in the back office beyond betrayed no hint of Judge Otaru's whereabouts.

"I was just in your courtroom," Paul said. "Through for the day, right?" The clerk's name was Betty Watanabe. Betty Watanabe, he thought, be nice to me.

"Oh? When were you there?"

"Two hours ago. But the judge was busy."

"Of course he is busy. He doesn't talk about his cases, either. So maybe you should rethink waiting around. It won't do you any good."

"But I only have one question." That got her. She had to ask, and Paul thought for a moment before he said anything. "I have to ask him, Why did he grant a default judgment for eight million dollars against a girl who never even knew she was being sued?"

"Who are you?" Philip Otaru came around the door, behind which he had evidently been listening. He said again in a more polite tone, "Who are you?"

Paul gave him a card, but not right away. First he pulled out his Italian wallet. Out of that he pulled a silver card case. A card came out of that to be inspected first by Paul for crinkles and dirt, before being handed ceremoniously to the judge. Otaru examined it carefully, holding it back from his face.

He needed bifocals, Paul thought. Vanity, thy name is man.

Small droplets of sweat had beaded up on Otaru's nose, but the pattern was so neat and even, it looked like he had sprayed it with water. He was Asian-American, Japanese-American from his name, tall and aloha-shirted like everybody else, and sweating even in these air-conditioned environs. The Honolulu humidity suddenly rolled through Paul, sending sweat trickling down his back, his armpits, and his forehead.

Otaru was watching him. "It's good to sweat," he said. "It's an adaptation to heat, a cooling mechanism." Paul wanted to ask Otaru if it was hot hiding behind his door, but there appeared to be a chance, however minuscule, that he would get along with him, so he kept his mouth shut. Otaru beckoned Paul in. Before he went inside Paul said to Betty, "Thanks for your time."

She kept her head and her eyelashes down. She wasn't available. No ring, so . . . he indulged his imagination, inventing the usual banal fling with the married boss but then discarding the thought. She acted too intelligent for that.

As soon as the door closed, Otaru said, "I'm waiting." He didn't sit down or offer Paul a chair. Although the office wasn't sumptuous, a couple of bright upholstered chairs and a small antique table in the corner added character. A large window framed lush coconut palms and floating cumuli in a stupendous view.

Paul went to one of the chairs and stretched out. "Tired feet," he said, smiling.

"I am still waiting."

Paul explained what was going on in the Tahoe court. When he was finished, Otaru just said, "So?"

"Why did you grant this judgment here in Hawaii after eighteen minutes of testimony and no appearance by Jessie Potter?"

"You'd be surprised how much justice can be dispensed in eighteen minutes," Otaru said.

"How can anyone prove a negligent homicide in eighteen minutes? I'm curious."

"Prepared attorneys, and the defendant doesn't come to court."

"She wasn't in the state and didn't know about the lawsuit."

"She waited too long to protest that. She sat on her rights."

"What would you do if I could show you that the plaintiff knew she wasn't in the state when he published notice of the lawsuit in the Hawaii papers?"

Otaru drummed his fingers on the desk. "Nothing," he said. "I am a judge. I react, I do not initiate. The cases come to me. There is no motion to reopen before me in this case. There can be no such motion, because the judgment so far as this state is concerned is final. Ms. Reilly should talk to a Hawaii lawyer about this, not me. Mr. Potter's lawyer, as I recall, was Ruth Anzai. Well respected here."

"I appreciate your taking the time," Paul said. "I really do. Ms. Reilly is a funny one. She tells me to go to the source. To the main man. It's not proper sometimes, but she gets frustrated."

"She shouldn't be a lawyer, then. Patience is the biggest virtue of a lawyer."

"Maybe here in Hawaii. In California, it's the ability to cut through the b.s.," Paul said. "On that note, do you mind telling me if you knew Mr. Potter socially before you heard this case?"

"Yes. I mind."

The judge came to rest in front of Paul, his arms folded across the cotton of his shirt. He appeared annoyed, but Paul was uncertain. There might be some cultural difference in play. Or possibly the humidity was affecting Paul's ability to read thoughts.

"Judge Otaru," he asked. "Did you and Mr. Potter share any business interests?"

"So that's it."

He was definitely annoyed.

"Not all it," Paul said. "Just some of it."

"Kindly inform your boss, Ms. Reilly, that attacking me isn't going to do her or you any good. I find you extremely discourteous and I have no comment on any case which has come before me. That is my policy."

"And it's usually my policy not to quibble, but it seems to me you already broke rule number one by making comments about the case."

"I do not comment on cases! Now, do you leave peacefully or do I call the bailiff?"

"Tell me more about you and Potter. Golfers? The Honolulu Club? The Academy of Arts Board of Directors? I understand you have a lot in common."

Otaru picked up his phone and hit a single button.

"We're about the same age," Paul said. "Remember Rosemary Woods? The eighteen minutes of silence on the tape? Long time ago, I know."

"So?" Otaru looked toward the door.

"She was loyal to Nixon, but look what it got her: public infamy. She became a laughingstock." He folded his arms to match Otaru. "No one respected her."

"I am not Potter's lackey. I resent that comparison, and Ms. Reilly would do well to stay out of my courtroom." The bailiff came in, saw Paul, put his hand to his holster.

"Get him out of here," Otaru said.

For the next few minutes a happy Paul enjoyed a brisk walk with the bailiff that ended outside the front doors of the building. Otaru had many connections to Potter. Otaru hadn't wanted to lie, so he had simply had him thrown out on general grounds that Paul was a jerk. He hadn't said yes, he hadn't said no. Paul didn't need telepathy to hear a rousing yes behind the wish-wash. Nina would like that.

In addition, Paul had scored a complete copy of the *Potter v. Potter* file on the way out, heavy in a white and blue cardboard box. He had ordered it and was told it was ready just as the bailiff was encouraging a speedier pace past the clerk's office. "I already paid for that," Paul protested, and got his file.

Paul walked until he got to a place called Thomas Square, shaded by a many-ribbed banyan tree. By now, rush hour had its grip on the street leading up to the freeway. But this Hawaiian scene did not resemble any traffic jam in his recent memory, spent squandering precious minutes of his life locked between homicidal commuters. Here, the drivers sat patiently, and the sounds of slack-key guitar drifted past from somebody's radio station. Quite a few of the men didn't seem to be wearing shirts. Maybe they ripped them off as soon as they left work. People were smiling. Even rush hour had a happy-go-lucky flavor here. Paul found a bench, pulled out his cell phone, and tapped in a number.

"Leeward Investigations."

"Lenny? It's Paul. Are you ready to write this down?"

"Ready."

"I need a thorough background check on Judge Philip Otaru. Business dealings primarily. There are probably some corporations with no assets and highly fictitious names involved. Does he need money? Any connections with a Honolulu man named Atchison Potter?"

"Oh, everybody knows Mr. Potter. Okay, by when?"

"Day after tomorrow? That's when I fly out."

"I'll tell you on the way to the airport. That's all you want?"

"Could you find me a Hawaii lawyer who is good on state court civil procedure to look at some case files for me? Have him or her call me tonight at the Outrigger? A day's work, but time is of the essence. The day is tomorrow. A thousand bucks is all I've got to work with."

"No problem. My wife will be perfect. She works for one of the big firms here, Carlsmith Ball, in the litigation department, but she's currently out on maternity leave with our first. She'd love to call in her mother to baby-sit and get out of the house for a day."

"Sounds good. Thanks, Lenny."

"You want to get a drink after work at Duke's?"

"Sure. Where's that?"

"On the beach, man. Diamondhead side of the Shorebird. Go out on the beach by your hotel and walk left. Ask anybody. Look for the happy people."

Paul went back to the Outrigger, took a cool shower, combed his hair, and put on a fresh aloha shirt. He was in Rome, but besides that he'd always liked aloha shirts. This one was decorated with a subtle combination of ochre, chartreuse, hot pink, and orange surfboards.

Then he went out to the beach past the rock jetty where a couple of dozen rapt tourists faced a sun sinking like a tangerine-hued hibiscus bloom into the green ocean. Two catamarans were putting in, their colored sails surrounded by flaming sky. The hotels had lit their tiki torches, and here came the moon from behind a fluffy pink cloud.

It was too much, this profligate beauty, the warm smell of flowers, the velvet sky, and the laughing girls still in their swim gear parading past him. Too seductive. One must not submit, or one would not return with one's heart all in one piece.

Duke's was so jammed Paul was amazed to see that Lenny had managed to save him a place at a tiny table. Lenny even had a frosty beer waiting for him. Duke's was part pickup bar, part safe-for-the-tourists beachfront bar, open to whatever breezes might enter. Lenny had been talking to the girl at the next table, but he winked and turned away as Paul came up.

"I talked to my wife," Lenny said. "She's calling you later." He sucked through a straw a margarita with an umbrella in it. Paul put his head up close to Lenny to hear over the riot of festive patrons. "I started checking on Otaru's clubs and business affairs. He and Atchison Potter go way back, but it's all social, not business, so I don't have anything hard to give you there. I don't think you can knock the case out with a fraud charge against Otaru. He's straight-up."

"Potter's his buddy, you say," Paul said. "In California, they watch the social dealings."

"I'm not saying Otaru didn't give Potter all the courtesies. But the

justice system is more Asian-style here. Courtesy, handshakes, golf, dinner, gets things done."

"That's all okay-fine," Paul said. "Except that the little guy isn't part
of that loop."

"True, but I hear California has gone so far the other way that it's a
war zone in the courts. You ready for another?"

"Yeah, sure, I'll have one more. Bring it on."

"You don't have to drive tonight," Lenny said, spreading a smile
over a broad face that wore smiles easily. "You can just lurch back to the
hotel."

"I'll try to stay coherent so I can talk to your wife later."

"Here's to Buck's." They drank, ruminatively. All around Paul ex-
quisite-looking girls partied in outrageous getups that showed their
navels. Paul felt exhilarated, like he was Steve McGarrett, a big hero of
his youth.

"Was this place here in the early seventies?" he asked Lenny.

"This place has been here since I was a kid. I spent my adolescence
here and I'll probably die here."

"I can see Steve McGarrett sitting here relaxing after a hard day being a TV cop on *Hawaii Five-0*," Paul said.

"Oh, yeah, he used to come here. He died not too long ago. Jack
Lord. Lived in Kahala."

"Book 'em, Danno," Paul said, or shouted, because it was getting
louder and he could barely hear Lenny.

Lenny drank some more, then said, "You remember at the opening,
first there's the Wave—"

"I have a theory about the Wave. Did you ever notice that Steve
McGarrett's famous lock of hair that fell down on his forehead—that it
was an exact replica of the Wave?"

"Huh. It *is* like a wave, and it's falling down over his forehead."

"And it never crashes."

"It blows in the breeze, though."

"So why the Wave and the Wave?" Paul asked again.

"To show his connection with the ocean," Lenny said.

Paul was struck with this. "That's pretty good," he said.

"He's a child of the islands. He's part of it, see, so he has the support
of the gods—you know, Lono and Pele and them. He has spiritual and
moral authority."

"You're good, Lenny."

"Thanks." Lenny took a swig.

They went on to argue about whether Martina Hingis was good-
looking or not, and after a while they went over to the Shorebird and

cooked their own meat on a grill big enough for a couple of dozen customers. Paul got pretty loaded. He felt as if he had dropped twenty
years and reverted to a college kid in flip-flops, it was great, and he finally left Lenny and staggered a few long feet to the Outrigger elevators.
It was four A.M. Hawaii time, but it was only one A.M. California time,
so no big deal.

He tossed in the too-firm hotel bed, wondering whether attacking
this judge so frontally had been the wise choice. He pictured Miss
Watanabe's glistening eyes and thick shining black hair, and he wondered again if the judge was getting any. And then he thought some
more about that opening sequence on *Hawaii Five-0,* with the lithe hula
dancer in a grass skirt and a lei encircling her long sleek hair, dancing,
shaking it, then stopped suddenly by the camera, stopped in an erotic
pose, with her hips cocked and her brown waist creased—how that soft
crease in the smooth flesh had riveted him to his set when he was
twelve or thirteen.

He thought of Nina and felt the familiar exasperation and pain. He
wasn't sure if he wanted to try anymore.

Next day, not too early, after making sure that Lenny's wife was
hard at work over at the courthouse and downing a raw egg in Tabasco
and tomato juice, Paul went to see Dr. Justin Jun, who had treated Dan
Potter.

Jun's office was in one of the towers near Queen Emma Hospital,
just off Lusitana and the Pali Highway. The exterior of the building was
impressive, even for high-rise Honolulu, with entry pillars stretching
like elegant silver candlesticks toward the sky, but inside the twelfth-
floor reception area the walls were dun, partitions poked out here and
there, and the magazines deserved rejection by the Salvation Army. Jun
probably never even saw this room with its intimidating frosted window, and probably didn't care what it looked like. The doctor was, Paul
decided after cataloging the detritus, a neglectful bachelor in his private
life, overworked, young, and abrupt with his patients.

The nurse beckoned Paul in. They walked down a depressing dun
hall under fluorescent light and turned in to a gray cubby full of files,
where Paul shook hands with the doc and sat down. Jun appeared very
young and very wary, but then all docs have good reason to be wary;
they're waiting to get sued, no matter how good they are.

After they finished talking about the islands and the weather and
Paul's flight, Jun seemed more relaxed. Paul saw no point in shilly-
shallying around. He started in on Jessie Potter and the case in Tahoe.

Jun nodded all the way through Paul's story. Puffs under his eyes indicated he'd just finished a long shift, although it was only 8:15 in the morning. When Paul finished, he held up a finger and went out, returning a second later with a couple of orange cans of soda.

They popped the tops.

"This is embarrassing for me. I want Jessie Potter to know her husband's father subpoenaed my records. I never met him. Then I was subpoenaed."

"They pay you as a treating doctor when you testified?"

"No, they paid expert witness fees. That's usual here in Hawaii. There's a greater emphasis on courtesy than on the mainland. They could have paid me less."

"So you didn't have a problem being subpoenaed for this trial?"

"Oh, I did, I did. I called Mr. Potter's lawyer and tried to talk him out of it. But he said I wouldn't be the principal witness. He said the evidence was overwhelming and all he wanted me to do was authenticate the records and confirm that I had not been able to diagnose any problem."

"But you were the principal witness," Paul said.

"I figured that out afterward. I am truly sorry. I couldn't believe he got that judgment. Whether that girl did something to her husband—I wouldn't know, and I would doubt it. She came in with him both times and she seemed concerned."

"Mind running through it with me?" Paul said.

"No. I have the file right here. They were still married and she can have the files if she wants. No confidentiality problem. I made copies." He passed them to Paul, and Paul decided he was an all right guy.

"I'm a gastroenterologist," the doctor said. "He came to see me the first time for an attack of severe abdominal pain that lasted about forty-eight hours. I examined him and took a blood sample and stool sample, had him X-rayed, and gave him a prescription for an analgesic. He was in a lot of pain. There was local abdominal tenderness. I thought about appendicitis, but the pain wasn't in the right upper quadrant. I thought about peritonitis, but there weren't any obvious signs of an infection. A strangulated hernia, twisted bowel, cancer—I thought about all these and many more. I wanted to put him in the hospital but he said no, he had had a couple of attacks like this before and it would be over by the next day. He called the next day and said he felt fine. The lab tests all came back negative, except for a slight elevation in inflammatory parameters. WBC, ESR, CRP, and fibrinogen . . ."

"Which meant?"

"It's a general indicator that some sort of inflammatory process was occurring. But I couldn't pin it down, especially with the speed of the recovery. He came back in a week later and even those tests were normal."

"It says here in the court file that you checked for poisoning," Paul said. "Anything about the wife make you suspicious?"

"Not at all. I liked her. But it could have been inadvertent, who knows—I had a series of lab tests done and nothing turned up, not even pakalolo. . . ."

"What's that?"

"Marijuana. Pretty usual for young guys, but he was a straight-up citizen at least as far as his ingestion habits. I liked him too. He wasn't exaggerating, I don't think. Anyway, we didn't find anything—"

"But you said in your testimony that poisoning was as good a guess as any."

"I didn't say it like that. The lawyer was very persistent. Like, 'It could have been poison, right? You couldn't rule that out?' Well, how could I? There are too many poisons in this world and they don't all show up on lab tests."

"What about the second attack?" Paul said.

"Same as the first, same abdominal pain, same forty-eight hours. Very peculiar. I tested him up, down, and sideways. There was nothing objectively wrong with him except that slight inflammation."

"Stress? Mental illness?"

"That's where you go when you can't figure it out, but I never had time. He knew it would go away by itself, and he knew I couldn't treat it, so he wouldn't go into the hospital. He refused further testing. Six weeks later he was dead."

"Well, the fact that he had already had at least two attacks of acute pain before the day he drowned would seem to confirm Jessie Potter's story," Paul said.

"But we had no diagnosis. The lawyer insinuated to the judge that she must have been doing something to Dan Potter. She made it sound suspicious, like she was setting up a murder. I didn't like the way she questioned me."

"You said a few minutes ago that you were embarrassed," Paul said.

"Well, if she had been there with a lawyer my testimony would have seemed quite different. I wanted to be objective but this lawyer turned what I said into other things. She could cut me off when I tried to explain, and she never asked me the right questions. And she wouldn't let me volunteer anything. It was very frustrating."

"Volunteer? Like what?"

"Well, like—like the fact that my notes contain a very significant statement that supports Mrs. Potter. It just never came out. This default hearing business is very unfair."

"I'd like to hear more," Paul said. "Even though it may be too late."

"Right here. See? I even underlined it—'Attack came on suddenly, in less than five minutes pain severe.' "

Paul leaned back and thought about that. "Shows he could have got into trouble fast," he said.

"Right. The judge seemed to think he would have had plenty of time to talk to her, to turn back for the shore, to do something. But I think what she told the police could be true. Dan Potter was fine one minute, then he was writhing in pain. That's what he did in my office. Maybe he fell over and couldn't stay afloat. It's possible."

"But you never got to tell the judge that."

"It was the way the lawyer asked the questions."

"If you were looking at Dan Potter today, knowing what you know now, what would you do for him?" Paul asked.

"I don't know. I still don't have the slightest idea what could have been wrong with him. I hate to say it, my patients wouldn't want to hear this, but rather often I don't have a clue. Some transient disturbance occurs in the body, and it rights itself. I sometimes just try to stay out of the way. I talked to several colleagues about this here in Honolulu. They had never come across anything like it."

"Send him to another specialist?"

"There simply weren't any test results to work with."

"Okay," Paul said. He got up.

"I could file another declaration for you expressing my doubts that she killed him—I was very uncomfortable with that trial."

"I may be back in touch. Thanks, Doc. I'm gonna pass all this on."

Paul left frustrated. What had killed Jessie's husband? Sandy had called Hawaii for the coroner's reports and so on, but nobody except Judge Otaru had ever come to any conclusion.

Walking out to the shady parking lot with his haul of files, Paul noticed a whole fence of flaming pink bougainvillea. The parking lot of the tower was bordered by this fantastic sight and Paul went over to look at it. Where the fence had broken down, on the other side, dwarfed by the skyscraper, he saw a ramshackle bungalow with peeling green paint, a front veranda, and a front yard rioting with flowers, including many flowers Paul had never seen before. But he recognized the mango tree and the banana palms, the green bamboo in the corner, the red ginger and the jasmine looped over the door. A little old Asian lady came out, carrying a shopping bag. She went down the steps slowly and opened her umbrella and started down the street.

Honolulu was like that, full of exotic contrasts. The sun made everything beautiful and at night the moon did the same. All seemed benevolent, in balance, even the meth heads and bar girls part of the golden whole.

He decided to can his next city appointment. The morning was too sensational.

He took the H1 freeway to the H3 just past the airport, and went over the skyway through the jungly mountains, through the tunnels and onto the Windward side of the island. Several hundred feet up, he was still coming down the mountain, and he could see a quarter of the island, Kaneohe Bay with Coconut Island basking in the sun, the golf course, and the cliffs over toward the north shore. With all that condensed geography, he was surprised to find himself pulling into the public beach at Chinaman's Hat less than forty minutes after leaving Jun's office.

Dan Potter had died out there.

Across the long expanse of yellow sand, the ocean looked overflowing, as if it might spill over and cover all the land any minute. But it was as calm as Tahoe today, just a different color entirely. Pale jade. And then there was the island, close enough to touch, it seemed, tall and pointy and brown and about a half mile offshore. Chinaman's Hat.

Shoes off. After taking the field glasses and camera out of the glove compartment, he rolled up his pants legs. Pearly clouds scudded across a lurid blue sky. Walking across the warm sand onto the sun-splotched beach Paul felt tension leach out in a rush, the same feeling that happened when he got poison oak rash and attacked it with a shower of hot water. His body let loose.

Two kayaks were just setting out from the beach, a boy and a girl in each kayak. Paul sat down under a coconut palm and took some photos for Nina. Wiggling his bare toes in the sand, he watched them, thinking of Nina, remembering that she had come to Oahu with another man.

The girls climbed into the back benches and the boys pushed the kayaks out and pulled themselves in in a practiced way that showed they did this a lot. In seconds, all four were paddling smoothly, the double paddles synchronous between the partners in each boat.

They got smaller fast. The water wasn't glass at all. Currents and choppy waves impeded their progress. The trades gusted. Chinaman's Hat was no pushover, at least in this kind of weather. A current of air seemed to flow between the shore and the island, stirring up the waves and making the kayakers work hard. He saw whitecaps.

He imagined Jessie and Dan out there, the boy clutching at his stomach, trying to stand up, falling, the girl jumping in after him.

The kayakers pulled up on an invisible beach on the island way out there in the ocean. The landing didn't go smoothly and one kayak went over but in a minute they had recovered and brought the kayaks in and out of Paul's sight even with the field glasses. If they climbed up the central cone, which was rocky and barren, he would see them again. Meantime, he stretched out luxuriously in the sand under the riffling palms. Warmth flowed through him, and, in the natural way of things, he fell asleep.

When he woke, bathed in sweat and nibbled by tiny red ants, he looked around. A weekday in summer on a superb beach, and there was hardly anyone around.

A witness would have saved Jessie so much trouble.

He stripped his pants down to blue shorts. His shirt went next, down to bare skin. Making a bundle out of his clothing, he hid everything well out of sight under a bush.

He ran in and dove and came up tossing his head and blowing water out of his nose.

It wasn't solving the case, but then again, the case might not be solvable.

17

CURIOSITY DROVE KENNY PAST HIS family's restaurant. The desperate hopeless feeling grabbed him again as he watched the lights dim in the Inn of the Five Happinesses. They would be going home, bringing something from the restaurant for a midnight snack.

Even now, his stomach ached when he realized how low to the ground he had sunk. Why couldn't he be the son his parents deserved? He was a bad fit in the real world, hopeless at the restaurant, skating by on the fringes in human relationships. . . . His father had been right calling him a malcontent.

He had been so sure he had finally found his place in Silicon Valley. There, under the sunny skies of Santa Clara and San Mateo counties, Linux rebels welcomed him with stimulating technobabble, and the jeans-and-dress-shirt trailblazers rousted him out of bed for power eggs at Buck's in Woodside or smoky chai at Konditorei in Portola Valley. He had fit in. Everyone needed to feel purposeful, and Kenny's purpose had seemed so clear, so beautiful, so twenty-first century.

How strange! He hadn't even thought about the City of Gold for days!

Pulling over beside a heavy bush, he parked his car near a two-story cabin with a wide yard on both sides. He felt very tired.

Locking the car door, he slipped around past the garage and shimmied up the tree to his old bedroom. Good. The window, as it had been for all the years of his childhood, was cracked open for air. In defiance of his father's basic distrust of anything that moved except for his family, his mother held on to certain naive truths, such as the one, so often disproved by the teenaged version of Kenny, that said a window on the second story was not accessible. She always wanted Kenny's window open, because it caught the evening breezes.

Flopping rather noisily onto the floor beyond the window, he looked around his room with a melancholy sense of the time that had passed. In the dark, he saw shadowy forms, but not familiar ones. A treadmill and Exercycle now took the place of his bed.

He set the nylon bag which held his computer down on the floor in one corner. Creeping into the hallway, he gathered up a sheet, pillow, and blanket in the closet and dragged them to an open space on the floor. Lulled by the creaking of the tree branch against his house, the same one that had scared him as a boy, he fell asleep.

"Who's there!" Kenny's father shouted.

Dressed in sweat shorts and a loose T-shirt, Kenny's father was standing in the doorway to Kenny's room, morning sun pouring down the hallway behind him, coffee mug spilling coffee in one hand, newspaper in the other.

"Hi, Dad."

"Tan-Kwo?" He peered into the face of his son. Setting his now half-full mug into a plastic holder on the treadmill and newspaper on a nearby table, he stood over Kenny and ruffled his head. "Hey, son! Good golly Miss Molly! What a shock!"

Kenny scrambled out from under the covers, looking for a rag to wipe up the spilled coffee. Finding nothing handy, he used his shirt. "Son, you better watch your step," he answered, wanting to please and no longer needing to pick rock 'n' roll bones with his father's taste. His dad was a big Jerry Lee Lewis fan.

"Your mother will kill you," his father said.

"For showing up without calling? For being out of touch? I'm sorry, Dad, I . . ."

"For using that expensive shirt to wipe up coffee. Well, go see her. She'll make you some breakfast."

"Wait, Dad. Actually, I wanted to talk to you."

"Before you have tea? You're pretty grouchy before that. I haven't forgotten."

"I'm fine. Really. There's just something I have to say to you, and it's hard."

"Okay. Shoot."

"But—I can see you were about to exercise."

"This sounds more important." He seemed to understand that Kenny needed him to go ahead. He had always seemed to read Kenny's mind, which was why Kenny hadn't been home for several months. Nodding, his father got onto the Exercycle and began pumping away. "Now, what's this about? Why do we have to talk before breakfast?"

Kenny opened his mouth, fully intending to tell him everything. He had the story worked out in his mind, even some of the words. He would pull no punches. He would not attempt in any way to present himself in a positive light. This story of loss and failure was all his, his alone. There would be no blaming of business rivals or the stock market.

"Made a killing, eh?" his father said, chuckling. "Wanted to tell us all about it?" He was already starting to sweat. The machine whirred as he pedaled. He sure wasn't reading Kenny's mind this time.

"I just—blew into town for a quick visit," Kenny said. "What's for breakfast? I'm starving."

The rattling of the cycle ceased. "You said you wanted to talk to me about something, son."

"Just wondering if you'd mind if I plug my computer into your phone line for a while this morning after breakfast."

His father's head tipped to one side. "It sounded urgent."

"You know how urgent I am about breakfast."

"You don't fool me, son."

"Really, Dad. I just want to do a little—um—financial research. Something I thought of last night."

His father looked unconvinced, but let the subject drop. He looked at the bedding on the floor and asked, "How did you get in?"

"Colleen." His sister's name popped out by long-entrenched habit. He and Colleen had always colluded on backing up each other's alibis. "I threw a rock at her window." He prayed that she had been home last night.

His father's face opened into a wide smile. "Well, it's good to see you. Are you home for long?"

"Just for today, this trip."

"Ah. Too bad."

"But I'll be back next week." He hoped he would.

"How's the City of Gold, Tan-Kwo? How's this earthshaking computer-rattling dynamo of modern thought going?"

"Still shakin'."

"And rattlin' and rollin'." His smile restored, his father waved him downstairs. "Try some of my special muffins. Keep your strength up," he said, starting up the Exercycle again.

"I'll die first," Kenny whispered, already having sampled his father's flaxseed lumps.

His mother was out taking her morning constitutional, so Kenny and Colleen made rice and poached eggs for breakfast, surprising her when she came through the door, her face screwed up in joy at seeing him. When their father came down to join them, after a disapproving glance at their choice of foods, he ate hurriedly, tossing back another cup of coffee. He munched a heavy black muffin, adding sound effects as he chewed, so that they would all regret the glorious enzymes they were missing. The family left after breakfast, leaving Kenny on his own, but not before Colleen extracted a discreet promise that Kenny would pay big for her silence about his arrival through the window.

He sat down at the dining-room table and put his head in his hands. His cowardice disgusted him. But he couldn't do it to his father, watch the handsome old face crumble, face his mother's tears.

He would pretend for a while longer. He plugged his computer into the phone jack, logged on to the Net, and went back to his research.

He found "A Slot Mechanic Tells All," scrolled through the page, selected a few items to save, and studied "Mega-winning tip number three":

"If you are worried that the guy who sat down on the stool you just left and won got 'your' jackpot, rest easy. The random number generator is moving constantly, faster than you can swing that handle down or punch that button, picking different combinations and wildly creating patterns. This happens even when the machine is not being played! The rhythm of your play is not like anyone else's rhythm, so it will hit different at different moments, depending on who is playing. So move on and don't worry that someone's gonna break into your dance—you've got just as much chance as the next guy of snagging the next big beauty.

"Smart gamblers stay away from the slots. Two-thirds of all casino profits come from slots. The odds are stacked heavily against you."

He logged off, feeling such advice arose out of those polyglot unreliables, myth, fact, belief, and anecdote. He couldn't reach any reliable conclusions. He thought of accessing the City of Gold site. He used to sit for hours, scrolling around and flying from place to place, inhabiting his dream.

But not today. He realized that all he really wanted to do was get back to the trailer. He would swipe some spices from his mother's kitchen and make pineapple chicken and walnut prawns for Jessie's dinner.

18

Marine Corps Base, Kaneohe, island of Oahu, Hawaii. A long curving road along the bay led to the guardhouse. Paul was given a map and waved in.

The girl, or woman, or better still the Marine, lived at #203 Company B Barracks. Marine Corps Specialist Grade 2 Bonita Banks answered the door. She was African-American. Hawaii's ethnicities were so intermixed and so diverse that Paul was starting to see himself as locals here must see him—as a pasty-faced Caucasian, just another minority.

"Jessie called me last night. Come in." A few plants dangled in the window, but nothing could disguise the military-issue furniture.

"Iced tea or orange juice?" Her small-chinned, oval face contrasted with a sturdy body clothed in camouflage fatigues. Her hair was severely controlled into a small bun at the back of her head, and her lips bore traces of sunscreen. Paul noted tangerine toenail polish on her bare feet and felt relief. Not that he was uncomfortable just because she was a Marine. Certainly not.

"Whatever you're having."

"How is Jessie?" She poured two drinks, handing him one. "She sounded unsettled. Things haven't gotten any better, I guess. Running away's a bum's solution, that's what I told her. You can't escape yourself or your problems that way."

"She's got troubles. She told you about them?"

"Yeah. But what could be worse than last year? She lost her husband and her military career, all she ever wanted. 'Course, she still has . . ." She stopped.

"What?" Paul's eyes had gone back to her toes.

"Yeah. I'm a woman, all right."

"I'm aware," Paul said.

She seemed to like the way he said that and curled her toes like a happy cat to prove it.

"How long have you known Jessie?"

"The whole time she was in the Corps. We went through boot camp together. Jessie and I had both been jocks in high school. Runners. Somehow Jessie managed to get together some money for boxing lessons, too. We played tennis after our duty shifts. She was my best friend out here. Outsiders, you know?"

"Outsiders?"

"Wrong minority groups for this place."

"There are right ones?"

"Oh, yes indeed. Hawaiian, of course. Portuguese, anything Asian or Pacific Islander. She could get away with looking kind of Hawaiian when she was out of uniform, that was cool, even if her hair was so short. But not me. When this tour is over, I'm headin' back to Atlanta."

"So she felt out of place?"

"There are more Natives than you might think on this rock. She loved it here. She didn't let it bother her. Even her racist father-in-law, she tried to be nice to him again and again. He never said anything but she knew. And I met him once. You could feel it like you feel the sun burning your skin here in August."

"Amazing he could live here at all, if that was his attitude."

"He was one messed-up rich *haole*."

"It must have affected her marriage."

"Jessie thought, you know, keep trying. He'll come around. I could have told her. Then this thing with Dan came down. She put up with the backbiting and the rumors for a long time. But then she told me one day that fella broke into her apartment and left her a nasty little present. Her tour was just ending, and she changed her mind about reenlisting and she booked. I didn't hear from her again until last night."

"How did she explain that?"

"She said she was sorry and she had good reason."

"Did you believe what she said? That Atchison Potter broke in?"

"I believed her. I told her, 'Go to the police.' But she wouldn't. I said, 'Why not?' But you can't make that girl talk if she doesn't want to."

"What exactly was her work at the base?"

"Started out learning to be a communications specialist, but she transferred out and went into landscape maintenance. She did a good job, got along good with the guys. They knew she was taken and they let her alone."

"Hard to believe," Paul said. "She's attractive."

"No, no, she didn't step out on Dan."

"She use computers in her work?"

"Everybody does. She was always coming up with systems, spreadsheets, all that. Native Hawaiian plants to replace invading species, designs for the pathways." She laughed, lowering the lids over her brown eyes. When she raised them up again, her eyes sparkled. "Not that anyone took a bit of notice. Which gravel is more aesthetic and practical, questions like that only Jessie cared about.

"But that's not really why you're here, is it? You want to know, did she kill him."

"That's right."

"No. She had no reason to. She didn't care about the money. She was in love. Let me tell you something. I was with her right after Dan drowned, down at the beach and later right here in this room. You never heard such carryin' on. This girl grieved."

Paul put on his dubious look. "Come on," he said. "Everybody cares about money. Husbands and wives—they have problems. I've been married a few times. I ought to know."

"Well, I haven't, but in this case, I know better. They were always talking about the future, how she'd reenlist and he'd finish his degrees and get a teaching job at UH." Bonita had been leaning against the chair. Now she sat down in it, straight backed, hands on her knees, vigilant but not hostile. Paul felt appreciative to have someone like her protecting his shores.

"What did you think of him? Dan?"

"Oh, he was a honey. Mature for his age. Not a kid, no sir. His grilled ahi was the best. What are you looking for? That he beat her? He was gentle with her. A shame he went the way he did."

"You're very direct, Bonita. I appreciate that."

"Thank you. I intend to be."

"When did you meet Dan's father? Atchison Potter?"

"Only after Dan died. After the funeral. He came up to Jessie and me and he said, get this, 'You won't get a cent.' I was proud of her. She looked him in the eye, and said, 'I forgive you for that, Mr. Potter.' But he got on her case after that. He talked to Sergeant Irwyn and told him something, I don't know what. Next thing that happened, we walked into the lunchroom and one of the men made a remark and the other guys laughed, not funny laughs, you know what I'm saying? And then—I already told you—she tell you what he did once he got in?"

"Yeah, she did. What I can't understand," Paul said. "What I can't get—why is he so sure she killed his son?"

"From the start he never liked her. I told you. He was so proud of Dan. He didn't want his precious boy marrying an Indian. You might think I'm saying this because I'm a person of color myself and maybe oversensitive. I'm not. He hated her because of her race. Now this was interesting, because Dan was dark for a *haole* boy. And so was Mr. Potter. That's how it works. Somebody probably called him a name when he was a kid and he felt bad. So he got this hateful pride at being a *haole*. See? You registering that?"

"I think so," Paul said.

"Here's something even more bizarre, now I've got you going on the race thing. All right. Often in Hawaii, people are proud *not* to be *haole*. If you're born here with the bad luck to be Caucasian, you try to marry a Filipina, a *hapa*—mixed race—an AJA, a Portuguese-background person, or best of all, a Hawaiian. So your kids will be real locals."

"You're making my head spin," Paul said.

"So it was a strange attitude." She laughed again. "I have this theory that he was afraid his mama strayed. You know."

Paul remembered something Nina had told him. "He was adopted," he said.

Bonita nodded, shook her head. "Ooh, that fool," she said. "What a hypocrite. He was in a masquerade. If he couldn't really be *haole* I suppose he thought he could at least make sure the grandkids came close."

Outside the open door, a Marine was mowing the square of crabgrass and it smelled and looked like Kansas, like Wheaties and church and the mall. With a coconut palm waving in the background.

"Did you ever see Dan when he was sick?"

"Oh, yeah. The second time, Jessie said. I went to their place to pick her up for tennis and she said he was in the bedroom. He had bad stomach flu or something. I could hear him in there groaning."

"Do you Marines learn about poisons—biochemical agents and so on? Did Jessie have access . . ."

Well, he had to ask.

The eyelids half lowered and her head bent forward to put what was left showing of her eyes in a direct line with his. "You just blew it bad, baby. I thought you had some sense."

"I need an answer, though," Paul said, standing his ground. "If the other side hears about it and we don't—you see?"

She considered the argument and restored her head to a less confrontational position. "We had a course in biochemical agents. Anthrax, that kind of stuff. She didn't poison him, though."

Paul smiled. "Just had to ask. Don't worry." He would do the worrying.

"You and the police and Potter's lawyer. All nice and then you spring the same old b.s. questions. I only put up with you today because Jessie asked me to. Don't be sending anybody else. You register that?"

"I had to ask," Paul repeated.

"Yeah, you did. I don't have to like it."

He had promised to buy lunch for Dan Potter's best friend, a UH grad student named Byron Eppley. He took his time driving back over the Pali, stopping to linger at the lookout and catch the view back toward the Windward side. In the distance, he could just make out Chinaman's Hat before the mountains came down to the sea and cut off the rest of the view toward the North Shore. Droplets of rain dashed against his face on the windy cliff. Just as he made it back to the car, the heavens dumped buckets.

But fifteen minutes later as he turned onto University Avenue toward Manoa Valley, the sun shone again, opposite a sky-spanning rainbow. The kids on the street hadn't even bothered to take shelter. A girl in front of the Varsity Theater smiled, drying her hair with her T-shirt, not caring that she was showing more than she probably should of her toned brown stomach. Three Asian girls sat together at a table in front of the Greek Restaurant, wiggling their tiny feet in black wedgies, backpacks piled at their feet. Paul smiled. They smiled back.

Eppley waited at a small table inside, positioned with an ideal view out the window toward the girls.

They shook hands and ordered from the proprietor. Eppley had chosen the place, probably because it was close to home for him. When the beer came, Eppley ducked his head shyly and asked what this was all about, and Paul gave him the truth, that he was trying to help Dan Potter's wife. He talked about the legal maneuvers going on in Tahoe but Eppley wasn't picking up much of it.

He was of indeterminate ethnicity—it wasn't normally the first thing Paul would have noticed but Hawaii was getting to him—a thick, black-haired, substantial customer, wearing cheap eyeglasses and the usual baggy shorts. The T-shirt said, "Bruddah Iz," and showed a picture of an even more substantial customer with a sweet expression, swathed in leis and holding a ukulele. Eppley's hand jiggled when he picked up his glass. Paul thought, We're on to something.

"I suppose you want to know—uh, if I can get Jessie off the hook. I can't."

"Okay," Paul said. The moussaka came. Paul was hungry. He dove into it.

"That's it?" Eppley said. He stopped eating and pushed his chair back an inch, as if freeing himself up for flight.

"What are you so antsy about?" Paul said. The lamb flavor was right there and it wasn't too greasy. Here Paul was eating Greek food in Hawaii. Go figure.

"She probably thinks—maybe she thinks I did what I did because I believed the stories or something."

Astonished, Paul grabbed his napkin and wiped his mouth until he had adjusted his expression to expressionless.

"Jessie told you, didn't she? It makes me look bad, I know."

"She told me," Paul said gravely.

"I was under a lot of stress. The thesis. I'm going for a Ph.D. in Applied Linguistics. UH is world class in the field, in case you didn't know."

"That's why it happened?" Paul said, running alongside, making an encouraging remark.

"And I admit it, I needed the money badly. Tuition. I'm not a rich kid like Dan was."

Now Paul could hardly wait. He poked around in the moussaka as if there might be a gold piece in there, trying to look neutral so Eppley could project whatever he needed to project on him.

"Oh, hell. I'm ashamed. I won't make excuses."

Enough with the mea culpas! Paul squeezed his napkin, nodding knowingly. "Get it off your chest," he said. Nudge, nudge.

"Maybe it's not too late. The sonofabitch shouldn't be able to steamroll her out of that money. Who would have thought she'd ever get any? I thought, He'll get his judgment, his revenge paper. He'll be happy. He'll never get anything from her because she's never going to have much, she's not the type. Know why he did it? Other than general malice."

Paul shook his head, too excited now even to make a pretense of eating.

Eppley spread his hands. "To keep her from making any claim on his money. Dan had a trust account. He thought she might try to take it. So, see, if he had a big judgment against her, it would be no use her trying to get it. He would just take it back. That's how I worked it out, anyway. He sure didn't seem to need the money. I guess he had plenty of his own."

"You mean the father."

"Mr. Potter. Jessie had just taken off and I was getting ready to drop out of UH, because I couldn't pay the tuition. It was only a couple thousand but I didn't have it. I have five younger brothers and two sisters. I couldn't go to my parents. I'm Tongan, by the way."

"Bully for you," Paul said.

"What?"

"So how were you getting along before that?"

"Waiting tables at Cafe Sistina on South King. It's this place with frescoes all over the walls. Mr. Potter came in one night with a man in a suit and asked for me to be his waiter."

"When was all this?"

"About four months after Dan died. Here's what happened. Mr. Potter introduced himself. I told him how sorry I was about Dan. He said he knew I was Dan's friend and in the same department at UH and saw him most days. I was kind of taken aback at how much he knew about me."

Paul pushed away his plate. The girls picked up their packs, meandering off in the direction of the UH campus, displaying not one trace of cellulite although their shorts were scandalous.

"So Mr. Potter said, 'You never saw him sick those last months, did you?' I started to say, But I did. Because, see, Dan told me one day in class that he had missed two days of school the week before. He was sick as a dog with some kind of stomach pain and he thought it might be appendicitis. But Potter wouldn't let me finish. He said"—and Eppley put his hand to his mouth and leaned toward Paul— "'I know your circumstances, Byron. I want to help you today, because you were Dan's friend. I'm going to leave you a tip that'll help.'"

"How much?"

"Five thousand, cash, in hundreds. He had it ready in an envelope. Well, I'd never seen so much money in my life. I just looked at it. Then I said—okay, this is the bad part, yeah?—I said, 'Okay, what do I have to do for it?' And you know the rest."

"Outline it for me."

"I had to testify in that court case he brought against Jessie. Swear Dan never was sick, never looked sick, never talked about being sick. The judge was taking notes and never even looked at me. The entire case was over in five minutes. I was surprised Jessie wasn't there—that was what I had worried about the most—but I knew she'd find out somehow. I paid my tuition but I couldn't sleep for weeks. I felt like a Hotel Street hooker."

"Hmm. So what now?"

"What do you mean, what now? What do I have to do?"

"Maybe sign some papers. Maybe take a trip. Maybe nothing."

"Just keep the university out of it. Nobody in my family ever got even a college degree. I want to teach. Can you do that?"

"No deals this time, Byron," Paul said. "You have to be straight no matter what or the contempt you feel for yourself is going to make you want to hurt yourself. Drink, do drugs, do anything to forget. You're lucky I came along to give you one more chance to get your self-respect back."

Byron took in this speech. He nodded and stretched like he was feeling better. Then his shoulders hunched again and he said, "Potter might do something to me. He ran Jessie out of town."

"We'll keep him busy. We'll do our best."

"What if he tells my professor?"

"At least you won't be turning tricks anymore."

"I don't know. Now I'm starting to . . ."

"Don't worry. You won't forget." Paul showed him the small tape recorder he had kept running in his lap.

"Shit." But his voice held resignation.

They left the restaurant and walked back to the parking area out back called Puck's Alley, where there was a Thai restaurant, a cafe, and Revolution Books with a small group of earnest revolutionaries standing around in the sunshine smoking and chatting and sticking "Refuse and Resist" stickers on their bumpers.

Paul drove Eppley through the maze of palmy streets to the Italian cafe where he worked. As he got out, Eppley said, "Was it a boy or a girl?"

"Huh?"

"The baby. Jessie and Dan's baby. She told me she was pregnant the last time I saw her. That's one reason I felt so bad about what I did."

Baby? Paul hadn't heard about any kid. Had she miscarried? Better not field this one.

"I'll be getting back to you." He handed his card over through the driver's window.

"Tell her this. I never said one word about her being pregnant to Potter. Not one. He didn't deserve to know."

"I'll tell her." Go and sin no more, my son, Paul thought as Eppley went to the door and inside. His stomach was flopping around. He was either very excited or the moussaka was going to give him a bad night tonight.

19

"WHAT HAPPENED TO YOU?" SANDY said the next day as Nina staggered into the office with briefcases in both hands. Nina hadn't had time even to take a shower this morning, she'd gotten up so late, and her hair had been secured with one of those plastic grabbers that only added to the general dishevelment.

"Little-known fact," Nina said. "If Deputy Kimura approves of you, you can get a key into the building so you can go to the law library at all hours. Only thing is, Bob was alone again last night. However."

"However what?"

"I have been talking to myself, Sandy."

"Uh oh."

"I have come to realize something about this Potter case, Sandy. It crystallizes a lot of things about law in this country that I have been slowly and painfully learning."

"Such as?"

"The near-impossibility of beating a guy who is bigger than you. It's a cliché that the system is stacked against the little guy, but nobody seems to be able to do a thing about it. There are too many fronts. But in this case the display of power is naked. And why has the display appeared without its clothes? Because they are in a hurry, Sandy. They don't have time to cover things up properly. Paul flew in about an hour ago. He'll be here at ten. I talked to him briefly while he was waiting for his flight out of Honolulu."

"And?"

"And we are going on the warpath. We are going to fight."

"How?"

"Simple. All it takes is a complete disregard for prudence and custom and what is expected. We are up against real power, the Potters and the big business interests. They have attacked and we have circled our wagons, but there are too many of them."

"If only the Western had never been invented," Sandy muttered. "What else can we do?"

"We attack back. Take our single-action rifles, go out in the middle of the night, surprise them."

Sandy moved her lower lip in and out, in and out, the Washoe version of Nero Wolfe.

"I'm tired of running from these jerks," Nina said. "Defending. Reacting. Trying to cut losses." She marched into her office and dumped the briefcases on her desk, then came back out, hands on her hips.

"We've gotten too used to it, Sandy," she said. "In a sense, we play along with it. We're supposed to be groveling for a settlement right now. Well, I'm not going to do it."

"Then what are you going to do?" But Nina's tirade was over, because just then Alex and his mother came in. Nina had forgotten about this appointment.

The boy looked very white, very tired. He walked with difficulty, stooped like an old man. His mother smiled painfully at Nina as they slowly entered her office.

"Good going, honey," his mother said to Alex, holding one arm, steering him. "That's the way." Her forced cheerfulness appeared somewhat out of line with the circumstances, but then Nina had no idea what appropriate behavior under such circumstances should be.

"I want to add something to my will," Alex said when he was settled.

"Sure. What you want is called a codicil," Nina said.

"Okay."

"No problem," Nina said, waiting while he slowly withdrew a slip of paper from his pocket.

"I actually don't want him to do this," the mother said with a tortured smile, sounding just short of desperate, her real feelings already starting to crack through her brittle pose.

Nina read the crumpled slip of paper. Alex wanted to give his body to Stanford University Medical School for use in medical research.

His mother dropped the fake smile entirely. "He can't do this. I want a place to go," she said. "To be with him. Where I can bring flowers."

"I want to do some good," Alex said firmly. "Maybe some other kid can have a chance. I read about this on the Internet. I called the school. They said I'm over eighteen, I can do it." Looking at his pinched, exhausted face, Nina saw that he had made up his mind. The mother gave Nina a pleading look, and Nina saw that she was hoping Nina could change it.

"Alex, could you just give us a minute?" Nina said.

"Sure."

He walked out slowly, waving off his mother's offer of help, shutting the door. His mother turned agonized eyes to Nina. "I can't keep any part of him?" she cried. "It's not right. It's cruel. I deserve to have him buried. I deserve to have a headstone. They'll carve him up and he'll disappear."

"He wants to do something good for others," Nina said. "He wants to leave his mark. He's such a fine kid. I have nothing but admiration for him."

"But what about me? I'll have nothing but memories!"

"That's all any of us get."

"You're as cruel as he is. I can't believe you won't help me. We've talked about our sons—you would let your son do this?"

"It's a way of fighting on," Nina said. "Not letting the disease win. He has so little control. This he can control. It's a disposition of property, a special gift to the world."

"Please. Help me. Talk to him. I've already lost his father. I need this one thing. Don't I deserve it?"

"Oh, yes. Yes, you deserve it. You deserve so much more. You deserve a healthy child, grandchildren. You deserve to be happy. It isn't fair. You look around you and wonder how come it wasn't the family next door, why it had to be yours."

"Yes."

"You need support yourself. You're in pain, too."

"Yes!" She clenched her fists, held them to her head, squeezed her eyes shut. Tears rolled down her cheeks.

"I am going to get you some support." Nina touched her arm gently. "Okay?"

She didn't answer. She was weeping without making any sound. Nina imagined her at home in her bedroom, Alex not far away in his room, and this courteous silent weeping going on in the house, because she didn't want to disturb him. And at breakfast, the smiley face. She needed help, and fast.

Nina got on the phone and called Matt's wife, Andrea, at the women's shelter. While Andrea spoke with Alex's mother, Nina went outside and sat with Alex.

When his mother came out into the reception area, she had a yellow phone slip in her hand with some numbers on it. She held a hand out to Nina. She had recovered the matter-of-fact overlay. "Thanks for your help," she said. "Andrea's given me someone to call. She was very understanding."

"Should I make the changes Alex wants?" Nina asked.

"No." She put her hand on her son's shoulder. "We need to talk some more. I don't think he understands what he's doing."

"Mom. I've decided."

"No."

"It's my body. I'm going to do it."

"I said no!" The door closed behind them.

"Now what?" Sandy said. "Poor things."

"I don't know," Nina said.

"He's your client, he's an adult, he asked you to do it."

"I know. It's going to be hard for him to come here again to sign it too. I guess I'll wait for a phone call and run it out to him."

"What if he dies before he can get his mother's agreement?"

"Then he dies."

"What's that supposed to mean?"

"It means I couldn't do it to her today."

Paul had driven straight from the airport. His board shorts and the shirt with the grass shacks, banished from their tropical setting, clashed severely with the office decor. "Aloha, my fine feathered friends," he said. He placed a box of chocolate-covered macadamia nuts on Sandy's desk.

"Tweet, tweet," said Sandy. "You're gonna make Joseph jealous, giving me presents." She put her thumb to the turboball and began to whirl and click.

"How are you, Sandy?"

"Busy. Good trip?"

"Excellent. I can't sit another minute, Nina. Can we walk?"

They left Sandy plying her word processor and went down to the street to the open land where the Truckee marsh trail began. As they crossed the small bridge over the trout stream, Paul took Nina's hand as though he felt how disturbed she was. Alex's mother's agony had affected her deeply. The quiet scene ahead, of bikers and a grassy meadow surrounded by mountains, seemed sad and transient. But it would always be there, and maybe the boy would achieve some kind of immortality, too.

"Where'd you go?" Paul said. "Wherever it was, I can't follow you. Come back."

"Sorry." She came back into focus.

"Ready for the quickie report? I typed it up on my laptop on the plane and I'll pass it on with the case file and the other documents when we get back."

"Good news? I'd like that."

"I'm gonna give you the broad outline first. That judgment is attackable. Potter intimidated the doctor and bribed another of his witnesses, Byron Eppley. Jessie's story checks out. There was something wrong with her husband, though nobody seems to know just what. Potter spread rumors that if he was sick, it was because she poisoned him. There's no evidence of that. And he did persecute her."

Nina didn't change her pace. "He lost it, Paul," she said. "His son died, and he had so much power that when he couldn't accept it as an act of God, he made Jessie a scapegoat and set out to destroy her. Too bad she couldn't fight it in Hawaii. I could countersue Potter for harassment even now, but then the burden of proof would shift to Jessie. What else did the doctor say?"

"He witnessed the kid in severe pain. But there's a problem. He never did figure out what was wrong with him. I mean, he doesn't even have a working theory."

She stopped to look at a daisy thriving in the shadow of a bush. "Then we don't have enough to prove what happened to Dan Potter."

"No, I'd say I can't produce that. Still, with the witness tampering, we have some very good stuff."

"I'll study it. What about Judge Otaru? Anything there?"

"Not enough," Paul said briefly.

"And the procedural review? Did you find a Hawaii lawyer?"

"Yeah, and this lady produced a ten-page report which says in essence that every 't' was crossed twice and every 'i' had dots upon dots. The notice and publication were impeccable."

"Too bad. But I can't wait to read your report on Eppley and Dr. Jun. What about Bonita Banks? What did she have to say?"

"That Jessie's telling the truth."

Nina nodded. They had crossed the meadow and come to the deserted beach. The sun beat down. The lake stretched before them, endless, detached from human cares, powerful, protected by its mountains.

"It's brooding," Paul said. "You get the feeling things move in it at night. Coelacanths, other ancient animals. What about the jackpot front? Did Kenny come up with anything?"

"He's such a classic M.I.T. boy. I called him last night and he's been living on the Web, floating around and reading the legal cases and news-papers and financial reports and exposés by disgruntled employees. Hard to say what we have here."

"Yeah?" He strode along the beach beside her, taking one step for her two. "Explain."

"Well, the word 'random' doesn't seem to have the same definition in Regulation 14 in Nevada as it has in the dictionary. Kenny's still working on it. Marlis Djina, who is a Nevada attorney, sent me the applicable regulations from the State Gaming Control Board. I'm reading them. It's like studying Sanskrit, but between Kenny and Marlis I'm going to figure out what Global Gaming is up to."

"Is the Greed Machine one of the slots with these microchips?"

"I asked Kenny to find that out. He says he never met a microchip he couldn't make friends with."

"I'll never gamble again."

"That's what they all say."

"No, really. I've been investing my nickels in European high-growth stocks."

Nina smiled faintly. "How much have you lost?"

"Oh, about forty percent of my nickels seem to have disappeared, but at least I'm not gambling." They stopped and turned again to the lake, watching the gulls waddle across the wet sand. From this small promontory no buildings could be seen. They were alone.

Nina was still disturbed. She realized that she felt guilty about Alex. It was the same feeling she had experienced when her husband died nine months before—guilt at being a survivor, a lucky one. Yet, even while she revisited these painful feelings, she could feel something new in herself, a brightening, a flowing of an old energy, a reconnecting. I'm getting better, she thought, I'm like someone convalescing from a long illness. It was happening in jerks and starts, in awkward movements she kept making back toward life.

So a person could recover. She hadn't believed it. She had gone to work, gone for walks, slept, ate—but she had been numb inside. She looked at Paul, emptying sand out of his shoe.

"Let's go back," she said. As they turned back toward the path, she went back to the thorny problem of Global Gaming.

"They may claim the jackpot was rigged somehow," she said. "Then it will be assumed the cheater was Jessie."

"Well, who else could it be?"

"Think about it," Nina said.

Paul walked on for a while, mulling this over. Then he said, "And so we look again at Kemp. He thought the money should be his."

"It's hard to believe, but imagine that Kemp had rigged the machine and then left, as we know he did, just before it hit."

"I don't believe that. He wouldn't leave the machine at the crucial moment."

"Well, he's dead," Nina said, pushing a branch out of the way as they came back to the bridge. "Maybe he screwed up."

"I hope not. Because that would mean the killer cares about Jessie and her jackpot too. A black knight could be out there, who we know nothing about."

"I'm so glad Jessie and Kenny are tucked away safely. It gives me the creeps even to think it. Can you stay for a few more days? Follow this murder investigation? And try to figure out what Global Gaming wants to surprise us with?"

"I'll get right on it," Paul said. "As soon as I get some clean clothes and a nap."

"You're staying at Caesars?"

"Where else?"

They had come to a place in the trail where water from last night's rain had made a pothole filled with mud. They stopped again and Paul took Nina's arm.

At Paul's car out in the parking lot, he took the bag of files out and followed her into the office and set it in the only corner that had any room left, where it leaned heavily against the fig tree.

"I'll see you later," Nina said. "Thanks for everything."

At the door, Paul turned and said, "Oh . . . one more thing, but I don't know what to make of it. Dan Potter's friend says that Jessie was pregnant when she left the islands. I don't . . ."

Nina dropped into her chair. "Oh, boy," she said.

"Nina?"

"So that's what she's been hiding from Potter. She had a baby! And Kenny's been lying about it, too."

"Why not tell you?"

"Potter will want that child. She's afraid."

"Potter doesn't have to find out."

"He'll find out." She took her keys out of the glass bowl on her desk. "I'm going to go out and see for myself. Otherwise she'll just keep lying."

"Want me to go, too?"

"No. I don't want to scare her. I am so sick of clients that lie, Paul. I'm so disappointed. But—I just can't blame her."

"I don't like that there's a kid involved."

"I know what you mean. It turns games into—something else."

"When can I see you?"

"Maybe tomorrow night. Call me at home after work."

She gassed up the Bronco at Kingsbury Grade and coasted down the mountain to the Carson Valley. First thick forest dotted with blooming golden aster gave way to scrub, then the desert sage and tumbleweed appeared. The heat built. She drank water, listened to KTHO on the radio until it faded out, and drove fast down the flat highway that stretched across the valley, past Minden and Gardnerville and the Washoe settlement, sleepy places on a weekday. A half hour farther out, way out where the settlements were all gone, she came to the unmarked turn onto the dirt road which led to her place.

As she bumped along she felt the usual sense of relief at leaving it all behind. The desert displayed its beauty without its heat, since she was blasting the AC with the windows open, a treeless vista for many miles butting up against the distant black mountain range, the rock formations smoothed by millennia of winds, the deep-cut arroyos left after old rains. She glimpsed a snake sunning itself by the side of the road.

Arriving in a cloud of dust that would certainly alert Kenny and Jessie, she opened the screen and gave the door a whack. Kenny opened up. He had tied a rag around his head to keep the sweat off his brow, his glasses were slipping down, and his shirtlessness revealed that he would never lack for a spare if he had a flat. He looked astonished.

"I could have been anybody," Nina said. "But you opened right up."

"I saw it was you. See, I drilled a hole in your door."

It was neatly done, and she could use it after they left. She went back to the car, pulled some cold sodas and sandwiches she had bought at the 7-Eleven in Gardnerville from a plastic cooler in the back seat, and brought them inside. A laptop humming on the table, a fan facing Kenny's chair, the couch piled with pillows and sheets—it was Kenny's new home. Nina saw that the door to the bedroom, the only other room, was closed. She called, "Jessie?" and started that way, but Kenny caught her arm.

"She's gone."

"Where?"

"She had to go to Gardnerville."

"When will she be back?"

"I'm not sure."

"You're lying to me, Kenny."

"She's in Gardnerville," he said stubbornly. "What's going on?"

"With the baby? Is it a boy or a girl?"

Kenny sat down on the couch. He took his glasses off and blew lengthily and noisily on the lenses.

"Kenny?"

"Please do not press me on this point," he said.

"I'll talk to her. I'll take the flak. You'll still get the money."

"The money! What's the money got to do with it? It's just that she's very very touchy and we're just starting to get along." Sweat had gathered on his nose and a gob of it chose this moment to drop off. "I don't know what you're talking about."

"I can't believe you'd lie to my face, no matter how madly in love you are."

"Oh, man. Don't tell her what you just said, okay, Nina? I can't—that is, I won't—I'm very sorry, Nina."

"Me too. Give her a message. Tell her to get another lawyer. Tell her you don't get through trouble like this holding out on your lawyer."

"You wouldn't really walk out on her, would you?"

Nina turned and went back out the door and trotted to the truck. For a minute, she was afraid Kenny wouldn't follow her.

But he ran after her.

"Wait! It's not that she doesn't trust you. Couldn't you—check with her on this? Tomorrow or something?"

Nina set her dark glasses on her face. "She can call Sandy tomorrow. I'll make sure she has some good referrals." She was intentionally cold, a blast of ice in the heat.

"She won't want another lawyer!"

Nina turned the key and the Bronco revved harsh and loud.

"She's at the Carson Valley Medical Center."

"Why?"

He struggled with himself. She observed the fight with interest. "The baby's sick," he said finally.

Nina nodded, rubbing her hand across her mouth. So it was true.

"Is it a boy or a girl?"

"A boy. His name is Gabe."

"How old?"

"Nine months, I think."

"What's wrong with him?"

"A virus, maybe? He had a fever of a hundred and four again this morning and she couldn't get it down. He keeps getting sick."

"Where is the center?"

• • •

Carson Valley Medical Center was just off the highway. Nina mistook it at first for offices.

"Hi, Jessie."

Slumped in a metal-armed chair in the dim yellow-lit waiting room, sleeping maybe, Jessie jerked up, instantly alert. "Kenny told you." She balled her fist.

"Calm down. I already knew most of it."

"Why are you here?"

"To see him. Gabe. He's the heart of this case, isn't he?"

"He has nothing to do with it."

"He's why you couldn't take the flak and left Hawaii. He's why you wouldn't give your name. He's why you perjured yourself to Riesner. He's what really needs protecting here, not the money. But you didn't trust me to protect him."

Jessie stood up and the light from a lamp cast the planes of her face into contrast. In her shorts and sandals she looked very young, but her eyes showed anger. She came over and got in Nina's face, saying, "Leave my kid out of this. Hear?"

Two years in the Marine Corps had created those hard eyes.

"I don't have that luxury. You think Riesner won't figure this out, if he hasn't already? A birth certificate is public record."

"He doesn't know to look for one. And there isn't one. I had Gabe in Dresslerville, in the Washoe colony. The birth wasn't reported."

"You going to hide him his whole life?" Jessie's eyes darted toward the door, where the nurse had just come out. She gave Jessie a smile, saying, "I thought you were going to take a nap."

When she gave up waiting for an answer and left, they got back to it.

"What's the matter with him?" Nina said.

"They're giving him tests. He cries a lot. Fever."

"Is it serious?"

"I don't know! His temperature has stabilized. He had a seizure."

"Why can't they bring it down?"

"I keep asking them that. They don't know. They think it might be some sort of relapsing fever that you can get from a tick in the western states. Several people came down with it in Las Vegas recently. But they can't find any bite marks, and I keep him close by. I don't think I could have missed a tick." Guilt and worry sounded in her voice.

"You stayed here last night?"

"Of course."

"What about your safety?"

"Screw my safety!"

Nina stopped, stepped back. Jessie's fists had balled again. She thought, Why, this girl is going to knock me flat. Taking the hard line with her was clearly not working.

Nobody said anything for a minute, so Nina said, "At ease."

Jessie breathed hard, getting control of herself. "Okay," she said finally. "Now you know I have a baby, a sick baby, and I'm sure you've figured out the reason I have to protect him. Now what?"

"I want to meet him, of course. And I want to help you protect him."

"Gabe is Atchison Potter's grandson. He could—he would claim I'm an unfit mother—that judgment of his—that stinking lawsuit—it's like he's psychic—a lawyer told me he could try to get custody. . . ."

"We won't let that happen. We'll fight him. We'll fight him together."

In a cool, dark room humming with silver equipment, Jessie's baby slept, twitching now and then, puckering his lips as if dreaming of the bottle.

Dark and plentiful hair gleamed on his head. Lavish eyelashes brushed his cheek. Gabe was a strapping, chubby fellow.

His forehead shone with fever.

"Hi, there, Gabe," Nina said in a low voice. Jessie put her hand on his forehead very gently, but he woke up. Groggy eyes opened and the baby reached his round arms up toward his mother.

20

UP IN NINA'S ATTIC BEDROOM, through a break in the curtain, Paul could see a light, but downstairs, the living-room lights were low. He knocked three times, hard, and was met with nervous deep woofs by Hitchcock. A moment later, the door opened and Bob stood there.

"Hey," Paul said.

"Hey," said Bob, smiling. He had his hands in his pockets and watched while Hitchcock jumped and battered Paul's legs for a while.

Paul considered giving the boy a lecture about opening the door without checking to see who was out there, but he was actually glad to see this sign that some of the bad dreams and daytime fears he had suffered from in recent months had been put to rest. "Your mom home? She called. Asked me to stop by."

"No."

When he had nothing to add to that, Paul said, "Uh, do you know when she'll be home?"

"Not really." Bob's head swiveled back toward the living room.

"Did I catch you in the middle of something?"

"Want to come in?" Bob asked. "Because I'm right in the middle of *Funk Lords of Wu Tang*."

Paul followed him inside. Bob rushed over to the video player and pushed stop.

"You a movie hound these days?"

"This is for the bad movie club at school this fall. I've got to preview a bunch of things."

"See if they're bad enough."

"Right." Bob plopped down on the couch, took a mess of chips from a bowl on the table, brought them halfway to his lips, and stopped. "Want some?" He waved the handful at Paul.

"No, thanks."

He chomped a few. "Mom's over at Uncle Matt's and Aunt Andrea's. She said she wanted to go in the hot tub, but lots of times she goes over there and they just talk."

"Why didn't you go?"

"Too boring," he said. "Troy is visiting his real dad. Oops. Mom gets so p.o.'d when I say that. She says Matt's his real dad. He raised him."

"Really." Paul had never heard much about Bob's cousin's biological father except that he visited occasionally.

"He wanted to see Troy. What could Aunt Andrea do? She made him go."

"Where?"

"He took him to that little amusement park near Mom's office," Bob said, his voice dripping with disgust. "That place was great when I was like four years old. He's way too old. Troy's twelve!"

Paul thought he heard just a hint of jealousy in Bob's voice. A father had arrived in his cousin's life, as one had not so very long ago into Bob's. Well, they were all so modern, weren't they? Fathers here, fathers there, or more commonly, fathers not there . . . "How about your dad?"

"What about him? He's making a new CD in Frankfurt."

"But how's he doing?"

Bob gave him a look which said, Why oh why do adults ask such things, but he answered with forbearance. "Fine."

"Planning a visit again soon?"

"I'm always planning a visit. The problem is getting my mom to let me go."

"Talked to him lately?"

"He called last night." Bob looked at the blank television screen, then back at Paul. "So . . ." he said. "What can I do for you?" He peered out from under thick, dark eyebrows that brought up his eyes and shocked Paul with their familiarity. Well, of course. He had his mother's eyes. And his mother's cutthroat attitudes, it seemed.

"I think I'll just mosey on over to Matt's and say hi to everybody," Paul said. "Would you mind calling over there and warning them that I'm on my way?"

"No problem," Bob said, picking up the remote control and holding a hovering finger over the Play button. "Mind shutting the door behind you?"

"You bolt it," Paul said. "And make the rounds and lock your windows and doors."

"Why?"

"Because that's what the man of the house does. Keeps it safe."

Matt answered the door and let Paul inside. They could hear laughter in the other room.

"Isn't that Andrea?" Paul asked. "What's so funny?"

"Hey, Paul," Matt said. "Good to see you. How was Hawaii? You've got such superb timing. I was just getting myself a beer."

Paul followed Matt, wondering at his good humor.

"So. Hawaii," Matt said.

"I was only there a few days."

"Andrea always says that's where she wants to go when she dies. Paradise on earth, right?"

Paul thought about that. "Not at all," he said. "It's no fantasy. I've been there before on vacation, but this time I talked to some local people. It's a real place, real people. You know, I was a minority-group member there."

"And how'd you like that?"

"I liked it a lot. All the pressure was off."

"I don't get that."

Paul shrugged. "I don't know. It's hard to explain, but your roots— they're not ashamed of them. They care about their roots. Somebody asked me if my ancestors came from Amsterdam, because of my name. Nobody in California would ever ask me that. You're not supposed to talk about ethnic background."

"So? Did they come from Amsterdam?"

"They came from Rotterdam, and Lyons, and London," Paul said. He laughed. "I'm a mutt. So how's it going with you?"

Matt closed the door. "Come into the kitchen. It's less noisy." A large square table in the middle of the room was covered with a red-and-white cloth, and in the middle sat a ceramic pot of even redder geraniums. Paul took a seat at the table. Matt reached into the refrigerator and pulled out two Heinekens. He didn't need to ask Paul what he'd like to drink anymore. They had known each other for a long time, played a few games of chess in the backyard, and survived a few unpleasant brushes with the wrong side of the law.

Years before, before he left the Monterey Bay area, Matt had fought a battle with drugs and won. Paul knew how hard that battle had been. He knew Matt to be a good family man and a help to his sister, whether she asked or not. He respected Matt, and Paul didn't respect most people.

They drank in companionable silence. Matt was in an unusually good mood. He kept checking Paul out as if Paul was supposed to say something. After a few minutes of this, he said, "I don't mean to be begging for something I don't deserve, but don't you have anything to say?"

"About what? Troy's father? But I don't know him."

"I guess Nina told Bob not to tell you."

"Tell me what?"

Matt slammed his bottle down on the table. "I'm going to be a father again! Damn, Paul! It's almost the best night of my life, that's all!"

"Holy shit, Matt!" Paul stood up, grabbed his hand, and pumped away. "Congratulations! It is really great news!"

Matt nodded for a while, then stuck his head into the cupboard, hunting out some pretzels. "Andrea always wanted another child. I adopted Troy and we were so happy to have Brianna. I can't believe my good luck."

"So you're both happy. How about the kids?"

"Thrilled to be a big sister and big brother."

Andrea and Nina came into the kitchen. Paul jumped up again to hug and congratulate Andrea. She sat down across from Paul, wiping a nose as red as her hair. "I'll have tea. With honey," she said. "Hold the whiskey for about six months, okay?" Andrea leaned back in her chair. Paul couldn't see anything special about her stomach except the careful way she laid her hands on it.

"How about a pretzel?" Nina asked.

"Either that, or maybe I should never eat again?" said Andrea. "I forgot how bad feeling good can feel."

Matt sat down beside her. "Queasy, huh?"

"I already have formed an opinion about this child of ours, Matt," Andrea said. "She's developing sea legs, when she doesn't even have legs yet."

"You mean 'he,' don't you?"

"We shall see what we shall see."

"Fortunately," Nina said. "You already have both."

"No preference, right," said Matt.

"But he'd prefer a boy," Andrea said.

"Not so! Just so she can drive a tow truck in winter."

"You've already got her grown up and employed, Matt. She doesn't even have the manual dexterity to operate a rattle yet. Or even fingers, for that matter."

They teased each other for a few minutes.

Nina, who had been fiddling with things on the stove, stood nearby watching and smiling. In another of her shifty moods, she was now acting shy, not meeting Paul's eyes, which were conveying his message loud and clear. When the pot whistled, she poured tea and honey in a mug, then handed it to Andrea, who gulped it down. Nina sipped tea. Paul finished his beer.

"You ever thought of having kids, Paul?" Matt asked, moving his chair next to his wife's and putting an arm around her.

"I'm not married at the moment," he said. "Not that that stops a lot of people these days, but I'm old-fashioned that way."

"You're what, forty? You must think about it. . . ."

"Yeah, Paul," Andrea said. "Do like Matt. Plan for one to take over the family business. She could grow up to be a detective just like her daddy."

"Ha, ha," said Paul, getting up. "Like I said, there's the small question of a mother for this imaginary being to settle first."

"So you'd have kids if you could?" Matt asked.

Paul felt Nina's curiosity emanating from across the table. "Can this man be trusted with the government of others? Perhaps history will answer this question, as Jefferson, his words adjusted to the situation and butchered, once said."

"In other words, you decline to state. I find that telling," said Matt.

Paul said, "I'm sorry to have to drink and run, but I've got to get going. Nina, could I talk to you?"

She followed him to the front door.

"You promised to call me, and you didn't," Paul said. "So I came looking for you."

Those downcast eyes again. "Oh. I thought it was the Potter case that brought you."

"I don't have anything to report about the Potter case right now. I'm not here on business. I am here for you. Are you coming back to Caesars with me or not?"

She wouldn't look at him. "I'm not sure," she said.

"Then let me decide for you."

"All right."

"Where's your jacket?" He put it around her shoulders, squeezing them, letting her know that he would take care of her. "Go get in the Mustang." She turned without a word and did as he'd asked. He went back to the kitchen and said, "We have to get going."

"We, huh?" said Matt.

"See you guys later," Andrea said.

"It's great news. It really is. So long."

• • •

Nina still seemed wound up when they arrived, and Paul didn't want that, so he suggested they warm up with a drink. "Shake off the cold," he said. She liked the idea. They stopped off in the downstairs bar.

Paul ordered his second beer of the night, and Nina had a Jack Daniel's on the rocks, a good sign. He lifted his glass. "'Shoulder the sky, my lass, and drink your ale.'"

She smiled and made a face as the bourbon went down. "Who said that?"

"A. E. Housman."

"I would have said Dylan Thomas. Singing in his chains like the sea. A sea of ale."

"Keep your voice down," Paul said. "You want people to think you're a pointy-headed intellectual?"

"You started it."

"Hey. Isn't that your guy over there?" He pointed inconspicuously across the bar.

"You're right," Nina said. "It's Atchison Potter, in town for his court appearance. All alone."

"The worse for wear," Paul said. "Too much travel or too much alcohol, maybe."

"Maybe," Nina said, studying the man. "He looks ill."

"And you're thinking that might be helpful in court somehow."

"Can't help myself. He may not even make it to court."

Potter didn't notice them. He drew a fiver out of his wallet, laid it on the counter, and got up wearily.

"Almost makes me feel sorry for him," Nina said. "But not quite."

They finished their drinks, talking little.

"I forgot how much I need this."

"You mean, how much you need me."

She smiled up at him. "We've been through so much together, haven't we, Paul?"

"Let's leave it at, you need me. And Nina, I need you."

They had the elevator to themselves. By the time they made it inside the door of Paul's room, they had their outer layers off and within moments, the rest fell to the floor.

"Have I ever told you you're breathtaking?" Paul said, steering her gently toward the bed.

Still her body seemed coiled tight. She was holding back. This, he could fix. This time, she would not hold back. This time, he would crack through that layer of control and find his way to the tender woman he knew lived deep inside her.

He took his time, kissing her lips until she moaned and her thighs until she was quivering. He ran his hands along the liquid curves of her body, feeling her ripening under his fingers.

"Just wait there," he said, letting his hand run down her shoulder to her hand. He let go and lit a candle in red glass he had placed next to the bed.

"You knew I would tag along," she said, her eyes still closed.

"I hoped. I never know with you." And his hand was back on her leg, traveling up, reaching for her. "I do love you, Nina." He loved the sound of her name on his lips. "Nina," he said. "My Nina."

She had turned onto her side, and her back was to him. He massaged her back softly. He stroked her hair and lay down behind her, spoon-style, inhaling the perfume of her hair.

Then, "Nina?"

She was shaking.

"Are you cold? Here, let me pull up the covers." As he did that, gently pushing her onto her back and over farther on the bed, he saw her face. "Hey," he said. "What's this?" He sat up, holding her face in his hands. "Why are you crying?"

"I don't know!" Anger leaked into her sobs. "I'm sorry!"

"Is this about Andrea? Babies?"

She cried hard. "No!"

"What, then? Help me," he said.

"It—it feels like good-bye."

"To Collier? Or me?"

He pulled her head onto his shoulder. She had never shared these feelings with him. She must know it would be painful for him to hear.

"I had it. Just for an instant. R-real love. He was such a good man."

"And I'm not. I'm not a good man. That's the problem, isn't it?"

"You'd d-do anything," she said. This pierced Paul's heart like a hot needle.

"Don't idealize him," Paul said. "Don't make him the measure of all other men. He wouldn't want you to turn him into a plaster saint."

"It's not about him!"

"It shouldn't be. It should be about us. Listen, maybe you're with me for the wrong reasons tonight." He was stroking her back, trying to relax her. "That doesn't matter. Let me show you—I'll make everything right."

"It'll never be right again."

"That's not true," Paul said. He took her in his arms and tasted the salt on her cheeks. "You're coming back. You're recovering. I can tell."

"I died with him," she sobbed.

"No. No, honey. Part of you, maybe, but the rest of you wants to be happy again. Let me make you happy."

"I'm s-sorry."

"There, there." He patted her as if he could soothe her with the gentle motion of his fingers and join the fragments of her shattered emotions together. "Settle down."

She couldn't settle down, and gradually Paul realized that she was still stuck in a vision that didn't include him. With her good man.

Bitterly, he thought, I'll never live up to it. I'll never earn her love. She came to me out of gratitude, not because she really wanted me.

He covered her up and went over to sit in the chair by the window. It seemed to him that he had never felt so low. He was still sitting there, sound asleep, when Nina got up softly, blew her nose in the bathroom, got dressed, and left.

The next morning, she drove Bob to the meeting place of an Audubon Society hike, and arrived at her office ready to plow through whatever was in her way. She was angry, at herself, maybe. She felt guilty about Paul, frightened about the emotional explosion. But law practice does not accommodate personal emotion. She put the feelings aside because she had to.

"Someone to see you," Sandy greeted her. "He's waiting in the conference room." Sandy examined her puffy eyes but said nothing. The door to the conference room was closed.

"Who is it?"

"Thomas Munzinger, Global Gaming."

"Really."

"I got him coffee."

"Thanks. Did he say what he wanted?"

"Just marched in and said he needed to see you."

"Nice little office," said Munzinger.

Nina hadn't seen him since jackpot night at the casino. His look to-day confirmed her earlier guess that he was an outdoorsman. He wore a plaid shirt and old blue jeans over dusty leather boots, and looked younger and less impressive than she remembered.

Even so, she noted in the primitive female part of her mind that

Thomas Munzinger was an attractive man. He had lowering eyebrows and an intent way of looking at her that would stir up a woman.

"Don't mind my clothes," he said, noticing her attention, "but I came right over here this morning as soon as I could. I have a few acres in the foothills on the Nevada side, and had some things to take care of this morning. Haven't had time to change."

She took one of the chairs. The blinds on the window facing the boulevard were still down against the stark morning sun and the room seemed shadowy. "What can I do for you, Mr. Munzinger?"

"Well, I'd like to talk to you. And I'm going to need to talk to Mrs. Leung. I'd like to get her address from you today."

Nina folded her hands. "What did you want to talk about?"

"Global Gaming is the largest manufacturer of gaming devices in the world, Mrs. Reilly. Our reputation has always been of the highest. We're happy to pay out jackpots when they legitimately occur—it's great P.R. But there's also a constant struggle to prevent fraud."

"Fraud," Nina said carefully.

"You ever heard of Dennis Nikrasch?"

"I don't think so." Was this someone Kenny had mentioned?

"Las Vegas man. Went down in 1986 for cheating the slots, and was accused again in 1998. Ten million dollars in the first case, and six in the next one. I helped figure things out in that case. It's a gift, like being able to heal a horse by whispering to it."

"Can you do that?"

"No. Movie stars do that. I confine my talent to riding a fast horse and keeping the wins clean." He laughed, but the eyes still smoldered with something held back.

"How in the world did someone manage to steal that much from slot machines before anyone noticed?"

"Oh, he was smart. I consider myself smarter, of course. But the way it worked was, he tampered with the machines, set 'em up to hit, then got several confederates, friends and family, to collect the wins. Took a while for us and the Gaming Control Board to catch on."

"How did he tamper with the machines?"

"He wasn't the only one involved. There were several people doing these things. They used keys, wires, magnets, even some computer rig to jog bogus jackpots. Ever heard of a monkey's paw?"

"What's that?"

"People put a tiny flashlight on the tip of a piece of wire about eight inches long. When you slip it up the chute, it's supposed to confuse the machine's sensor. That prevents the machine from counting the coins on a win. Can increase jackpots by a factor of ten. That was just one of the things they tried."

Nina decided to get right to it. "I understand it's in your company's interest to ensure that Jessie Potter's jackpot is legitimate. I mean, nobody wants to pay on a bad win, right?"

"Including Prize's. You know Steve Rossmoor?"

She knew Steve Rossmoor pretty darned well. He was the CEO at Prize's. His current wife had been her first murder client. "Yes."

"Guy's got one big fault."

"What's that, Mr. Munzinger?"

"He listens to me. And I told him, there's something wrong. I called a meeting. You know the group. Andy Doig, Gary Gray, John Jovanic from Prize's. Ully Miller from the Gaming Control Board. Yesterday. We agreed that I ought to talk to your client, unofficially."

Nina said, still watching her words, "What makes you think there's something wrong with the jackpot? Have you found some evidence of tampering?"

"No. The chip checks out. That particular Greed Machine has been taken out of service while we think about things, though."

"So?"

"There was a man on the stool just before your client sat down. Made a stink when he got back and saw she had won. One of Prize's security people talked to him while they were in the process of kicking him off the casino floor right after the win. Got the name. Charlie Kemp. Kemp claimed the jackpot belonged to him."

"Anybody would. It was bad luck."

"Have you talked to Kemp?"

"Uh, well, yes, I did have a brief conversation with him a few days ago. He said essentially the same thing to me."

"He told the Prize's guard that it was all set up for him. And I quote."

Nina stopped breathing. "What? Are you sure?"

"That's how the guard remembers it. And now he's dead."

Nina said, "But my information is that Kemp was a hard liver. He left a trail of broken promises wherever he went. He was a transient, a boozer, a user, and a gambler. He had just been fired from a job in LA for smoking marijuana on the job. Obviously, he had enemies. Why blame the machine?"

"The time factor. It suggests a scenario to me I have surely seen before. A killing by a confederate. I'll be honest with you. Ully and John think Kemp was just blowing hot air. But I don't agree. Don't know why. Just got the old gut to go by." He patted his lean stomach.

"Mr. Munzinger, I promise you, if you try to obstruct my client's legitimate win, we will give you the fight of your life." She stood up and opened the door. He stood up in response. "You said yourself there's no evidence of tampering on that machine."

"It would help if I could talk to your client. Satisfy myself that she didn't know Kemp. All I want is her address. A few minutes of her time."

"That's not convenient. She's going into a stressful court hearing in a few days, as you know. She's resting."

"You're leaving me with a bad feeling," Munzinger said. "We might even intervene in that court proceeding, hold that money up from both parties."

"Not without the support of the Gaming Control Board and Prize's," Nina said. "You'd never go to court. And if you did, you'd lose, because you don't have any evidence. So don't try to bluff me."

Munzinger looked down and gave the floor a rueful smile. "You won't let me talk to her?"

"Sorry."

"You're making a mistake. I'll have to draw my own conclusions."

"Not so fast," Donna said. "You know I don't like going too fast."

Red, who already felt like they were crawling, slowed the boat down to a slither. He moved in closer to the beach so that he could get a better view of the sunbathers near Zephyr Cove at the state beach. The glitter of sun on miles of smooth yellow sand made his eyes hurt. He fumbled around for his sunglasses and put them on. "Did you bring food?"

"Sandwiches and cake. I picked them up at the Raley's."

"Nothing fresh?"

"The potato salad looked real good."

"Probably a month old." He looked at it with distaste.

"Why do you care?" she asked curiously. "You never eat anymore, Red. You're getting so skinny."

"It's your cooking."

She sighed. "Maybe it was a mistake, coming out here. I don't think you're enjoying yourself at all."

"Aren't you?"

"C'mon. Let's have some cake. Maybe a full stomach will keep you from jumping out of your skin every time I say a word. Pull in over there." She pointed to a deserted stretch of beach.

He flung the wheel to the right and pulled the boat up to the beach as close as he could without scraping the bottom off, turned off the motor, and threw down the anchor. Donna held the food bags high as she waded into shore. He brought the cooler. Whiskey to soften the edges. Every knob of bone on his body hurt. Possibly he'd been overdoing the pills. He vowed to slow down just as soon as all this was over. As soon as he had the jackpot in hand, as soon as he had removed—another obstruction.

The Leungs had disappeared. He had only seen them in court, surrounded by people. He couldn't find them in the Indian colony or anywhere else. They were obviously hiding, since Kemp had scared them. And if he couldn't find them, he couldn't get the husband.

The kidnapping idea was dead. Jessie was tied up in court for a couple of weeks and couldn't pay him off anyway. Good thing Kemp had blown it. He'd learned from Potter's lawyer that Leung hardly knew the girl. The marriage was a sham. He didn't care what that scam might be. He would have plenty of time to brace young Jessie later, after the court decision.

The problem of Kenny Leung remained. Red had to go to the hearings and he was scared shitless that the husband would come up to him and point a finger in his face and say, You were there, you said something to Kemp. That would be the end of the dream. He really needed to get rid of him, and he would first chance he had.

But now there was the other problem.

His clueless wife spread a blanket on the sand and laid out food. He sat beside her, but couldn't stay still. She had no idea what was going on, no idea what he was going through. He was getting thin? Fuck that shit. He was getting more alive by the minute. He was fighting for his dream against any and all adversaries.

Donna handed him a turkey sandwich. "Eat," she said.

He took a bite of dry dust and coughed. He twisted open the pint bottle and swallowed.

Tasted like alcohol, plain alcohol, no flavor. Something was happening to his taste buds.

"Don't forget me," Donna said, taking the bottle. She took a sip. "You know, I've been meaning to thank you for how good you've been to Amanda. I'm going to see her for lunch tomorrow, catch up on things."

He drank, staring out at the wide blue lake, thinking, Oh, I doubt that very much. Amanda was his problem of the day.

She had been quite a gal when they'd first met, five years before, a real life of the party. He'd even thought he was in love with her. They'd had a safe fling. Amanda was a very clean girl who understood about showering before and after and keeping her bathroom disinfected. He never felt like he had to worry that Amanda would tell Donna. Not her style. She was a good girl.

Then, the accident. A one-car accident, on Kingsbury Grade up by the lake on a snowy night. He had been driving. Just one passenger, spinal injury.

Donna stuck by him, believed the story he told her. Donna loved him.

Amanda forgave him. He told himself he felt sorry for her, but the truth was, he didn't want to lose her. He needed a friend, and besides Donna, he had nobody else. So he took care of her, gave her money, helped her out. She was Red's friend and she knew about his outfit. She'd gamble with him.

She'd been window-dressing on the night Kemp blew the jackpot. All fine, until she heard about Kemp. She had surprised him there. He'd never even thought about her figuring it out. The problem was, she knew him too well. He'd even offered her a share of the winnings, but she had drawn her own line at Kemp's murder. She didn't understand. She had thrown him out.

She would betray him, later if not sooner. He didn't want to do it, but her suspicious attitude had come along and taken the decision out of his hands. After all the secrets he had told her—she really knew him.

After all he had done for her, which was considerable! She had no right! She was going to take that wheelchair that he had bought, go down the ramp he had built from the rented house he helped pay for, get into that van which he had helped her lease, and go to the cops. Traitor!

Well, she had brought this on herself. He should have finished it that night, not left this issue lingering around, keeping him up at night. Another ghost to follow him while he paced the floor trying to figure out how to get his hands on his money.

He would try to make it clean and quick. She shouldn't suffer. He liked her. Maybe he even loved her. He would miss her a lot.

He still had the gun he had stolen from that investigator of Nina Reilly's. Not traceable to him, if it came to that.

He would make it look like a hit. She worked with money at The Horizon. The cops would have a thousand theories.

Satisfied that he had a plan, he took a few deep breaths. His heart was racing and he felt like he was going to scream if he had to stay here much longer. But Donna hadn't had much attention lately.

He wouldn't survive if she left him too. He could not be alone. So he was trying hard today, even though he felt like his eyeballs were about to pop out of his head.

Donna put a hand on his bare arm and squeezed.

"It's deserted here, honey. No one around." She looked at him meaningfully.

She wanted to get laid. Of course she did. She hadn't been laid in a couple of months.

The quicker she got laid, the quicker they got the hell off the beach. The quicker he got to his business of the day. Plus, it would keep Donna happy. Soon he would be able to fill up the IRA again, to pay off the bills, take her on a trip. She'd shut up for good about the gambling.

Could he do it, that was the question. He hadn't been interested lately.

He pulled his pants down and rolled over on top of her. Her eyes fluttered and she spread her legs and gave him a moan.

One thing about taking speed, if you start up about two hours after you popped, you could go all afternoon. Maybe never come.

He concentrated. Not too fast. Crawling, the way she liked it. Like those waves coming into shore, one after another, just touching the sand here and climbing right on top, smothering it there . . .

Happy anniversary, Donna.

After returning the rental boat at the marina, wondering just how long his credit would continue to be good on the card he had used, he dropped his smiling wife off at the house. She wasn't going to make any scenes for a few days. While she waved from the doorway, he drove away, fortifying himself with a couple more pills and more whiskey, a combination he'd tinkered with until he had created the right brew of confidence, energy, and coolheadedness.

He opened the bottle between his legs and drank again, putting his foot down hard on the gas.

This time in the afternoon, Amanda usually worked. However, he knew for a fact, right before her shift started she usually took a spin down to the lake to enjoy the summer sunshine. He had been with her a few times on these jaunts, but why think about that now?

He spotted her parked on Wildwood Avenue at Beach Road, where she could get the best view without the hassle of leaving her van. She had her head leaned back against the headrest, her eyes half closed. She was dreaming.

For a moment, he wondered what her dreams were. He'd never asked.

He cruised Lake Tahoe Boulevard a couple of times before all the necessary elements came together, all the time operating at fever pitch, his hands on the steering wheel moving constantly, roaming for the best spot, his eyes on the alert for a policeman, the gun loaded and ready on the seat beside him.

The moment came like a gentle breeze over the lake, and it was like something he remembered from movies, freeze-frame, everything stopped for an instant while one character continued to move forward through the frozen scene, gun in hand.

Amanda, silhouetted by the twinkling azure lake behind her, eyes closed, caught totally off guard.

No traffic, no cops. He unrolled his window. Hers was higher but it was open and he could manage.

Boom, boom, you're dead.

She slumped in the car seat and began to slide down.

Sad.

He sped away.

21

"KENNY? WHY AREN'T YOU READY?" Jessie came out of the tiny back bedroom of the trailer dressed in a skirt and blouse, carrying Gabe. "We have to leave right now for Nina's office and drop Gabe off with Sandy, or we'll be late for court. Who was on the phone?"

"I'm not going." Kenny sat in the dining nook which was also his bedroom, his fingers playing over the keys of the laptop.

"Are you kidding? This is it! What's the matter?"

"Nina called. She has some work I have to do. You tell me how it goes."

"What are you doing?" She set Gabe in the Portacrib and leaned over the table. Kenny wouldn't let himself be distracted. He was on a mission.

"Amanda Lewis is dead," he said. "Nina just heard, I confirmed it half an hour ago on the Tahoe Police Department internal Web site. Last night. Shot in her car at Tahoe. Like Charlie Kemp. It didn't make the morning *Tahoe Mirror*."

Jessie sat down beside him. "Shot," she said. He didn't look at her.

"I'm going to figure out who did this," he said. "It has to be the jackpot. Kemp was on my right. Amanda was on my left."

"What about us?" Jessie said.

"They tried," Kenny said. "They lost track of us. For now. You have to be very careful to stay with people at all times. Make sure no one follows you back."

"But—what about Gabe?"

"Gabe?"

"Would they try to hurt him?"

"I don't know. I don't understand. But I am going to understand it. Leave Gabe here."

"No. I want him close to me. Sandy won't let anyone hurt him."

"Okay. I'll concentrate a lot better anyway."

"Kenny, you don't sound like yourself."

"I liked Amanda. I was worried about her. I think I should have done better when I talked to her."

"Nina thought you did very well."

"No. Amanda didn't tell me who the biker is, and now I have to find him myself. I feel responsible."

Jessie touched his back. She said, "All right, buddy, get him."

Kenny nodded, his eyes on the monitor.

"This is the time and place set for the Motion to Vacate a Judgment entered in California based upon a Money Judgment issued by the State of Hawaii on November twelve, 2000."

Judge Simeon Amagosian spoke these words in a calm strong voice. Even in the lurid yellow light of Courtroom Two, he exuded healthy outdoor vitality, as if he'd ridden to court on horseback that morning. Amagosian had really changed in the past year. Nina had heard he was on a health kick. The notoriously intemperate outbreaks of rage had become fewer, and even his formerly purple complexion could now be kindly described as ruddy rather than florid. Nina had heard he was spending more time out on his land and less in court, shifting his focus as he edged toward retirement.

He looked up from the paperwork in front of him and his eye again rested on Jessie's face. Nina thought, He's curious about her. He didn't usually look at the parties at all, as if afraid he would be prejudiced inadvertently by some quirk of the person. He did sneak one quick peek at Nina's legs and new shoes. Some things never changed.

Jeff Riesner, at the plaintiff's table with Atchison Potter, was smiling as though Potter had just told him a funny joke. If Amagosian had just cantered in, Riesner seemed to have just flown there on the Concorde. He was immaculate, his balding spot carefully stranded over, his nails manicured, his—did he pluck his eyebrows? The area between the brows seemed to have lost something.

Or so Nina thought, meanly. As for Mr. Potter, he was hunched in his seat like a blue-jawed Eastern European refugee on a ship bound for Ellis Island—okay, also mean. She was in a mean mood today.

Mutual glares were exchanged. The high road had been abandoned the moment they entered court.

Jessie wore a starched white blouse and a straight brown skirt which set off her caramel coloring and short jet hair. She looked straight ahead. Gabe had just gone through another bout of his fever and Nina knew she would rather be with him. Sandy was watching him at the office today, the Portacrib right by her desk, so Jessie could run over there at the lunch break.

She had just come in, breathless, as court was going into session, and asked Nina and Paul about Amanda Lewis.

"They don't have the gun on this one either," Paul whispered while Amagosian was still opening his files.

"It must be a coincidence! Just because she was sitting by Kenny for a few minutes—she was murdered? Is that what you think?"

"I just heard," Paul whispered back to Jessie. "I'll find out everything I can today and report to Nina. You can talk to her later."

Nina touched his arm and he fell silent.

Paul sat to Nina's right, farthest away from Riesner's table. He had met both Byron Eppley and Dr. Jun when their connecting flight came into Reno the night before. Nina had been prepping them since seven A.M. They were both waiting outside, both supportive, both hanging in there. The question was whether Amagosian would allow them to take the stand at all. This hearing was unexplored territory for Nina. There was relatively little law on challenging final judgments which had been filed in another state.

Paul reached his hand over under the table and squeezed Nina's hand. Nina glanced over her shoulder and saw that the gesture had been noticed by the group of men seated behind the bar. Old friends by now—Thomas Munzinger, thin-lipped, riding the range for Global Gaming; Ully Miller, frowning, looking around as if expecting to discover the other people already in court all hid slot machine jimmies in their pockets; John Jovanic, standing with Deputy Kimura; two lawyers trailing Munzinger, trolling for trouble; a lawyer from the bank. And Barbet Schroeder of the *Tahoe Mirror,* with several more reporters.

Riesner and Nina stood up and stated their appearances. Amagosian said to Riesner, "Let's see. This court granted a *pendente lite* order of attachment of funds from a Global Gaming check, deposited into a trust account in the name of Nina Reilly, Attorney at Law, at California Republic Bank. Those funds still frozen? No trouble there?"

They both nodded. "Today we have a contested hearing before the monies can actually be seized by a Writ of Execution. Am I in the ballpark?"

More nods.

Amagosian said to Riesner, "Okay. You want the Writ of

Execution, Counsel. It's your ball." Nina sat down and wrote the date on her legal pad.

She had a lot on her mind, and one major complicating factor: she was under strict orders not to let Potter find out about Gabe.

Riesner began by introducing into evidence a flurry of certified pleadings from Hawaii: the Judgment, the original complaint for wrongful death, the notices of publication, and the other papers which would firmly establish that all technical requirements had been met. When he asked that the Hawaii pleadings be accepted into evidence, Nina said, "No objection, Your Honor. In fact, we could save some time by adding the only written exhibit I have from the Hawaii court case."

"Which is?"

"A certified transcript of the testimony taken at the Default Hearing."

"All right," Riesner said, standing up and putting his hands up as if they were in a fight, which they were, "let's get right to it. I have an objection to the transcript. This is a final judgment, Judge. That has to mean something, even with all the erosion of every legal rule I can think of lately. That's why the United States Constitution gives full force and credit to the legal decisions of other states. A final judgment means it can't be reopened on the testimony for this court to reweigh the evidence. The only question legitimately before us is whether the judgment is void because of some gross procedural error."

"Not true, Your Honor," Nina said. "The moment Mr. Potter decided to try to get a California court to enforce this shoddy piece of legal work, he made the judgment reviewable. Section 1710.40 of the California Code of Civil Procedure provides that such a judgment may be vacated upon any ground which would be a defense to an action in California. This court has the discretion to correct a manifest injustice today by vacating this judgment."

"A discretion that is rarely used," Riesner said. "And for good reason. The loser in a court case can dance all over the country and try venue-shopping forever unless the Constitution is followed. The only discretion this court has is to remedy a gross error by the other court. There's no error at all here, Judge. As you can see, the pleadings are perfectly in order. She wants to open it all up again, Judge, take testimony all day and all night, as if a judge hadn't already gone through this."

Nina said, "Again, not true. The Hawaii court didn't have a full opportunity to hear the issues. The defendant, my client, had no chance to appear—"

"The proper notice by publication appears to have been given, however," Amagosian said. "The law isn't omnipotent. We have to set some practical limits, or a defendant can avoid all responsibility simply by running off somewhere where she can't be found."

"That's exactly what she tried to do, Judge—" Riesner said.

"Just a moment," Nina said, very firmly. "I'm not saying that the notice was improperly given. I'm saying that because there was no actual notice, Mr. Potter was able to subvert the processes of the court and obtain a fraudulent judgment."

Words have power, and these were very powerful words. Amagosian stopped shuffling the papers and stared at her. Riesner just stood there, absorbing this all-barrels attack. Somebody in back said, "Whew!"

Riesner found his voice. He turned to the court reporter and said furiously, "Did you get that? Did you get that?" When she nodded, Riesner said to Amagosian, "I respectfully request that the court note for the record that this scurrilous attack on my client accuses him of a criminal act as well as moral turpitude. It's beyond outrageous. Counsel can't seem to muzzle herself. I hold Counsel personally responsible for that statement. I—I am giving notice that I intend to pursue this slander and—"

Nina interrupted in as dry and measured a tone as she could muster, "Well, let's see if I can back that scurrilous statement up. I only request limited testimony, Your Honor. Mr. Potter himself, and two witnesses who have voluntarily flown in from Hawaii in order to correct what they see as—"

"Stop right there," Riesner said. "Now she's going to moralize and twist and try to prejudice the court. I request that Counsel be held in contempt of court for the way she is subverting the court's process."

Amagosian stroked his chin, then answered, "Well, that doesn't seem quite called for yet. And I believe I'm the one who decides whether a lawyer in my courtroom is in contempt, Counsel."

Riesner huffed and said, "It's only the start. She hasn't even gotten going."

"So you object to any testimony whatsoever being taken?" Amagosian said. "Have you received timely notice that Counsel intended to call witnesses at this hearing?"

"It's absurd to reopen the Judgment! The court shouldn't reweigh the evidence!"

"But one of these witnesses, it is claimed, will testify that he was bribed, which means bought and paid for, Counsel, by your client. And the other, it is claimed, wants to change his testimony appreciably. And don't presume to tell me what this court should or shouldn't do."

"I apologize, Your Honor. That wasn't my intent."

"You may be assured, Mr. Riesner, that if these claims are not borne out by the sworn testimony of these witnesses, this court will consider the Declarations filed by Ms. Reilly on behalf of her client as perjury," Amagosian said. These last words were spoken in Nina's direction, and her throat went dry. If Byron Eppley and Dr. Jun, who were waiting out in the hall right now, changed their minds or got their minds changed, she was probably going to go to jail for contempt that very night.

Should have packed an overnight bag. She had made a serious allegation and she sure hoped she could substantiate it.

"I'm going to allow a limited review of the underlying judgment based on these specific allegations," Amagosian said. "The transcript of the evidence taken in the Hawaii trial is hereby admitted along with the legal pleadings previously marked. I'm going to allow the three witnesses you requested, Ms. Reilly. Mr. Riesner, you will have the opportunity to rebut with independent testimony.

"Now. Having said that, I am also going to find at this time that the judgment creditor, Mr. Potter, has made a *prima facie* case that the judgment is valid and enforceable. Therefore, unless the presumption of validity is overcome by some very clear and convincing evidence of fraud, Ms. Reilly, the judgment will stand."

"I understand, Your Honor." The burden was on her. The stone had to be rolled uphill. Fair enough.

"I call Mr. Byron Eppley to the stand," she said, and Deputy Kimura went outside to bring him in.

Eppley didn't look good. The hair growing halfway down his neck looked unkempt. He overflowed from the witness chair. He wore a wrinkled black T-shirt, and Paul hadn't been able to talk him out of sandals so well-worn they had taken on the shape of his foot. He looked around the courtroom, blinking, and when his eyes fell on Atchison Potter, who surely should patent that look of burning malice, he recoiled visibly.

"Good morning, Mr. Eppley," Nina said.

Eppley mumbled something.

"Please be sure to speak up so the reporter can hear you," Nina said.

"Good morning."

"You are here voluntarily today? You have not been subpoenaed?"
"Yes. No."

"You are not being paid for your testimony today in any way?"

"Well, you paid for the plane ticket. And the room at the Royal Valhalla last night. The breakfast was included, I guess."

"Other than direct travel expenses, did you receive any other payment from me or anyone associated with this trip?"

"No."

"All right. You knew Daniel Potter in Hawaii?"

"Yes. We roomed together before he got married. We were close friends, in the same department at UH."

"How often did you see him in the months prior to his death on February seven last year?"

"Pretty much every day once the Christmas break ended."

"Were you acquainted during that time with Atchison Potter, Dan Potter's father?"

"No. Never met him, though Dan talked about him."

Avoiding that territory, which could inspire a blitz of hearsay objections, Nina went on, "Did you meet Mr. Potter after Dan Potter's death?"

"Well, I saw him at the funeral. Then one more time, at the place where I worked in Honolulu. He came in with another man and ate dinner at a table where I was the waiter."

"How soon was this after Dan Potter's death?"

"I can't remember exactly. Several months, maybe four or so. I had heard from Jessie that . . ."

"Never mind what you heard. Mr. Potter was sitting at one of your tables?"

"Yeah. He ordered the chicken Caesar salad. No wine. Then   en he was finished, he stopped me as I was clearing the plates and said he wanted to talk to me for a minute. We weren't very busy. I said sure. He introduced himself and I thought I should have known, because he looked a lot like Dan."

"Then what happened?"

"Well, I said I felt lousy about Dan's de—passing, and how smart he was and a good friend. And Mr. Potter was nodding and looking sad. We talked about what a good guy Dan was. Then Mr. Potter says, 'By the way, you never saw Dan sick during his last months, did you?' And he said it in this sort of new tone that made me wonder what—"

"Objection. Speculation."

"Sustained. Strike the last sentence."

"So he asked you if you ever saw Dan sick—"

"Objection. Misstates the testimony."

"Withdrawn. What did you answer, if anything, to that question?"

"I started to say—"

"Objection. Nonresponsive. It doesn't matter what he started to say, unless he said it."

"Sustained. What did you answer?" Amagosian said, looking up from his notes.

"Well, I didn't get a chance to say anything."

"Nothing?"

"Not right then. He holds up a finger and he says, uh, 'I know your circumstances, Byron, and I'm going to help you because you were Danny's friend. I'm going to leave you a tip that'll help.'"

"He kept you from responding to his question?" Nina asked.

"He held up his finger. Like this." Byron held up a finger and everybody looked at it. Big deal, Riesner's expression said. It didn't look like Byron had been menaced or threatened by that finger. Nina was getting more uneasy with each answer.

"And did you understand that the tip he was going to leave was a quid pro quo for—"

"Objection," Riesner said. "His understanding of the words spoken is irrelevant. The point is, what were the words."

"It goes to his state of mind," Nina said. "When he accepted the tip."

"His state of mind is irrelevant," Riesner said.

"I'll sustain the objection," Amagosian said. It was a blow. Byron had never actually opened his mouth and told Atchison Potter flatly that his son had, in fact, been sick. Nina had prepped him so she knew this.

"So he gave you this tip?"

"He was sitting right at the table and he handed me this envelope full of bills."

"How much was this tip?"

"Five thousand dollars cash."

Nina paused. There were whispers behind her. The implication was clear, but implications weren't going to get Jessie out of this judgment.

"Were you accustomed to receiving such large tips?"

"Twenty dollars was the biggest tip I had ever gotten."

"So the amount of the tip was entirely out of proportion to the services you had rendered as a waiter?"

"Definitely."

"What if anything did you say upon receiving this large sum of money?"

"Well, I looked at him and I said, 'Okay, what do I have to do for it?'"

"Did he respond?"

"He smiled and said, 'We'll be in touch.' Then they left."

"Was he subsequently in touch?"

"Not him specifically. One of his lawyers came over one night and handed me a subpoena to testify in the court case against Jessie. He said, 'Now, as I understand it, you never saw Dan Potter sick. He never looked sick, never talked about being sick. Is that correct?' "

"And did you subsequently testify exactly that at the court trial?"

"Yes. I'm ashamed to say I did." He looked directly at Jessie as he said this.

"And was that testimony truthful?"

"No."

"Speak up, Mr. Eppley," Nina said.

"No. I lied. The truth is that Dan really was sick. About two weeks before he died he told me one day in class that he was really sick and missed two days of school the week before. He thought he had appendicitis or something, and he had to go to the doctor. He told me it was the second time this had happened to him and the pain was excruciating."

"And did you tell the judge in Hawaii any of this?"

"No. I knew what I was supposed to say." Nina glanced at Riesner, who was smiling incredulously. It's going to be a rough cross-exam, she thought.

And it was. Riesner got up and adjusted his lapels.

"Let's start with the dinner," he said. "Mr. Potter and his associate sat down at one of your tables and Mr. Potter identified himself and you talked about his son, Dan. Correct so far?"

"Yes."

"Mr. Potter said he knew your circumstances and he was going to help you because you were Dan's friend. Right?" Nina was checking her notes. That was exactly what Potter had said, so she couldn't object.

"That's right."

"Did he help you?"

"Well, he gave me five thousand dollars."

"Was that helpful to you?"

"Very. I needed it for tuition fees."

"Did he say anything along the lines of 'This money is a bribe for you to lie in court'?"

"No. But I knew he wanted something from me."

"And how did you know that?"

"Because I said, 'What do I have to do for it?' And he said I'd be hearing from him."

"So?"

"Well, I heard from him. I heard from his lawyer. I heard what I was supposed to testify."

"Really. You heard what you were supposed to testify. The lawyer asked you if it was correct that you had no information that Dan Potter was ever sick—"

"Objection. Misstates the testimony," Nina said.

The testimony was read back. Atchison Potter's lawyer had been very careful to phrase the information in the form of a question.

Riesner barked, "And you lied to that lawyer, didn't you!"

"A lie I knew he wanted to hear."

"Move to strike that last remark! Speculation!" Riesner shouted.

"Sustained," Amagosian said.

"You told him Dan Potter was never sick?"

"Yes."

"That was a lie?"

"Yes."

"All right. And then you repeated that lie in court? You perjured yourself?"

"I did. I'm very sorry I did."

"But Atchison Potter never asked you to lie?"

"Not in so many words. C'mon, I knew. . . ."

"You've told us everything he said?"

"Yes."

"How do you feel about Mr. Potter today, as we sit here in court?"

"I despise him," Eppley said. "And I despise myself for getting mixed up in this."

"You took his money but you despise him for trying to help you," Riesner said as if to himself, shaking his head wonderingly.

"No editorial comments are necessary, Counsel," Amagosian said.

"Sorry, Judge. It's just—I'm afraid I was carried away with indignation. . . ."

"Move on, Counsel."

"What did you do with the money, exactly?" Riesner said. "Did you deposit it in a bank account?"

"N-no."

"Well, what did you do with it?"

"Kept it at home."

"Let's see, how much was your tuition for that semester?"

"Two thousand five hundred."

"Did you pay it with that money?"

"Yes."

"Did you pay with a check?"

"No. I paid a friend back some money I owed him and then I borrowed from him again. He wrote the check."

"You paid your friend in cash?"

"Yes."

"And how do we know that?" Riesner said. "How do we know any of this crazy story is true? How do we know you ever received any money from my client?"

"That's why he paid cash," Eppley said. "So it wouldn't be traceable."

"Sure. And that's why you can't show us a deposit slip, any record at all, to prove independently that you ever received this money?"

"There was another man there with him," Eppley said stubbornly. Nina did the squirm thing.

"So, he's here no doubt to prove your story since you acknowledge you're a liar? What's his name?"

"I haven't got a clue."

"What did you do with the rest of the money?"

"I spent it. On living expenses."

"Paid for things in cash?"

"Right." Eppley's head was hanging low.

"You're not exactly a solid citizen, Mr. Eppley, are you? Excuse me, got carried away, withdraw that question. Your family is from Tonga?"

"Yes."

"You *are* a citizen, by the way? A U.S. citizen?"

"Yes." Eppley gripped the witness stand and Nina thought, Oh, no.

"In fact, you've just committed some more perjury, haven't you?"

Eppley said nothing.

"You're not a citizen, but you claimed you were when you applied to the University of Hawaii, didn't you?" Riesner picked up a pile of official-looking papers. He passed some copies over to Nina and gave copies to the clerk and said, "Mark for identification."

And then he gave the marked exhibit to Byron Eppley and forced him to admit that he had lied about his citizenship to get into the Applied Linguistics program at UH. Paul had his head in his hands. Obviously Eppley hadn't mentioned this to him.

He hadn't told Nina this either. She had asked him whether there was anything in his circumstances that could hurt him.

Eppley was a liar and his testimony was useless. And Riesner knew it. As a hound releases the mangled bird at the foot of his master, Riesner deposited Eppley, limp and half dead, in front of Amagosian.

Amagosian said to his reporter and the clerk, "Have the district attorney's office look at this witness's testimony over the lunch hour. I want a decision as to whether perjury charges should be brought against him before he leaves California. I want a copy of the testimony forwarded to the Circuit Court in Honolulu that originally heard this case. And I want a copy sent to the registrar's office of the University of Hawaii. Ms. Reilly."

"Yes, Your Honor?"

"I hold you responsible for keeping that witness here in town until a decision has been made whether to arrest him."

"I will do what I can, Your Honor."

"You have his return ticket?"

"Yes."

"Don't let him have it." He looked at his watch. "We will take the morning break at this time."

They all rose as he disappeared behind his private door. Eppley, dismissed, got up and left the courtroom, not looking at anyone.

"I'll tear him apart," Paul fumed in Nina's ear.

"Shh."

Riesner chose this moment to walk over to Nina and say, "Gotcha, you little bitch," in a low voice. Paul grabbed him by his expensive lapels and pulled him close. Riesner let out a half-strangled chuckle. A flash memorialized them as a camera went off. Then Deputy Kimura appeared at Paul's side, hand on his holster.

Paul let Riesner go. Riesner turned his back and went back to collect his client, dusting off his lapels. Laughing all the way, ha, ha, ha.

22

"CALL DR. JUSTIN JUN."

Today Dan Potter's doctor looked like a man who could stand up to some pressure, unlike Eppley, who had squished like a banana under a tank tread. Sporting a tailored suit, polished shoes, and an assured walk, he took on power and weight.

But Dr. Jun had a lot less on Atchison Potter. Eppley had been bribed. Jun had merely been subjected to a legal technique common to witnesses in default hearings: he had been distorted. His testimony alone wouldn't overturn the judgment.

Eppley had been a stinging blow. Nina felt herself flinch as she mentally relived the savagery attending his demolition. The little guy often didn't win, because often his witnesses were not impressive. Poor people seldom made it to adulthood without having at least one brush with the law that made them look like flakes or worse on cross-examination.

Mel Akers, her old boss back in San Francisco, used to say that poor people made poor witnesses. "Of course they do," he would say in his soft controlled voice. "They have had poor educations, poor stability, poor pay. Worst of all, they've been involved with bureaucracies all their lives. The bureaucracies hound them as much as help them, and they document everything."

So what if Eppley had lied to UH? Who knew what bureaucratic obstacles had stymied his family when they tried to become citizens? He wanted a graduate degree. He lived in Hawaii. He couldn't attend college without lying, so he lied. He accepted a bribe, yes, but he was trying to make that right.

Nina wasn't angry at him, but she was angry.

She admitted it to herself. She wanted to win partly because she wanted to beat Riesner. It was personal. But angry lawyers make mistakes. She would have to be careful. Paul, sitting at her right again, rubbing a fist with his other hand, was angry too and wasn't always careful. This worried her.

She took Jun through his education and experience as a gastroenterologist. Jun's parents had come from Seoul before Jun was born. They had died soon after, but they had left Jun with an extended family who took good care of him. Jun had gone to Notre Dame.

First she established the approach that had been made to Jun by Potter's Hawaii lawyer: that he was tangential; that the unspecified evidence that Jessie had caused her husband's death was overwhelming; that he would be paid a high fee as an expert witness.

Then she took him through the two visits Dan Potter had made to him, the young man's symptoms, and the tests he had run. Jun made it plain that he had observed Dan Potter in severe pain on two occasions.

"Now. With reference to the questions and your answers on page 34, commencing at line 13 of the trial transcript." Jun read through the sequence from the Hawaii proceeding. Judge Amagosian and Riesner were also reading from their copies.

Nina quoted, " 'Question by Ms. Anzai: Well, it sounds like you performed every test you could think of on this young man, didn't you?' "

" 'Answer by Dr. Jun: No. I performed the tests that I felt would be most likely to reveal the problem.' "

" 'Question: And all you found was this slight elevation in inflammatory parameters, as you put it?' "

" 'Answer: Correct.' "

" 'Question: But you say that this young man was in severe pain! Severe, right?' "

" 'Answer: I would characterize it as severe. And I do not believe he was malingering.' "

" 'Question: And how do you explain, based on your education and experience and personal observations and all the tests you ran, how he could be in severe pain but have nothing wrong with him?' "

" 'Answer: I'm not saying he had nothing wrong with him. I'm saying that I couldn't find out what the problem was.' "

" 'Question: Did you test him for arsenic poisoning?' "

" 'Answer: There was no—' "

" 'Ms. Anzai: Nonresponsive, Judge.' "

" 'Judge Otaru: Answer the question as it has been put to you.' "

" 'Answer: No. I didn't.' "

" 'Question: Did you test him for exposure to any type of poison?' "

" 'Answer: No, but—' "

" 'Ms. Anzai: Answer yes or no.' "

" 'Answer: No.' "

" 'Question: It could have been poison, right?' "

" 'Answer: Anything is possible.' "

" 'Question: You couldn't rule out poison? You didn't test for poison?' "

" 'Answer: No. I wasn't looking for that. I—' "

" 'Question: His wife could have been slowly poisoning him for weeks, so he would be sick, so she could concoct this story later, after she did away with him?' "

" 'Answer: As I said, anything is in the realm of possibility. Although I feel that—' "

" 'Question: So since you don't have a clue what was wrong with this young man, poison is as good a guess as any, correct?' "

" '(Witness shrugs).' "

" 'Judge Otaru: You have to speak audibly for the record.' "

" 'Question: Well? Yes or no?' "

" 'Answer: Yes.' "

Nina stopped and waited until she had Amagosian's full attention. "Was this testimony true and correct?"

"No. It was not the full truth. I was prevented from answering fully. I was not asked questions that would have brought forth the full truth. I was forced to answer with a yes or a no even when the answer would be misleading unless I could explain it."

Nina watched Riesner stand up, smoothing his hair back. "I move to strike all the, quote, testimony, end quote, of this witness," he said. "I have listened in fascinated horror as Ms. Reilly walked tediously through a replay of a trial which is now over. Perhaps, I thought, this witness too will confess to some egregious action which reflects more on him than on the trial. But we do not have a confession of perjury this time. We have absolutely nothing. The full truth did not come out? Really. The witness was prejudiced in favor of the defendant but could not indulge his prejudice because the defendant did not decide to show up at all. That is his complaint. It is a pseudo-complaint. He was examined and gave testimony. Now it is far too late to whine about being kept close to the point."

"Well, Counsel?" Amagosian asked Nina. "The witness is not changing his testimony, although I suppose he wants to embellish it. I'm not inclined to allow that at this late date."

"For him to take this last possible opportunity to bring forth the truth has nothing to do with embellishment, Your Honor," Nina said. "We're here to find the truth, aren't we? In Hawaii, no opposing counsel appeared in court to object to the leading questions, the repeated and calculated interruption of the witness, the limiting of the witness to yes or no answers. An obvious miscarriage of justice was the result. Surely this court can spend a few minutes more hearing what this witness would have testified if given a fair opportunity to do so."

Amagosian sighed. "Keep it brief," he said. Nina gave him a heartfelt smile and he looked disapprovingly back to his paperwork.

Jun sat quite calmly throughout this exchange, his files and the trial transcript exhibit spread in front of him.

"Dr. Jun," Nina said, "what in the testimony that was just read back to the court was misleading or false?"

"Objected to as vague, leading, overbroad, and generally of the kitchen-sink strategy for which Counsel is becoming infamous," Riesner said, yawning.

"Overruled," Amagosian said before Nina could open her mouth. "It's as good a question as any. Let's hear what the doctor was trying to say. Well, Doctor?"

"I can answer the question?" Jun said. Nina nodded, and he said, "All right. What I was trying to explain to the judge in that proceeding was that if there had been any poison such as arsenic in Dan Potter's body, it would have been found as a result of the autopsy, which was very thorough. The lawyer had to know there were no such findings."

Riesner's voice rose again. "Pure, unadulterated hearsay," he said.

"Sustained," Amagosian said, as he had to, since Jun was trying to report on an autopsy someone else had done. Nevertheless, Nina could see she had piqued his interest, and was heartened.

"What else?" Nina said, and Riesner groaned. Paul tensed and seemed about to get up, and Nina elbowed him as invisibly as possible. "Don't you dare," she whispered, and he subsided.

"I'll take that as an objection," Amagosian said to Riesner. "And I will overrule it. Go on, Doctor."

"I found no basis for any belief that the young man had been poisoned. I regret if that implication was taken from my testimony."

"Go on," Nina said, having realized that these were the magic words, that Amagosian just wanted Jun to spit it out.

"The main thing which I wish to clarify is that the young man, Dan Potter, advised me that he had suffered at least two attacks of severe abdominal pain. The pain came on in less than five minutes in both instances."

"Would you say at this time that the death was consistent or inconsistent with a sudden attack of severe abdominal pain which caused the young man to fall from his kayak and drown?"

"Entirely consistent," Jun said, rapping it out. He had flown all the way from Hawaii to say that. He looked at Jessie and gave her a short nod. Riesner was objecting, but Amagosian said, "Let's just leave that in the record for what it's worth, Counsel. Ms. Reilly. Anything further?"

Jun had made his point. "No, Your Honor."

"You may cross-examine."

But Riesner, ever wily, said, "No cross, Judge," knowing that Jun would spring at any further chance to help Jessie. Jun left the stand. With a whisper to Nina, Paul followed him out of the court. He had promised to get Jun back to the Reno airport. Byron Eppley would be sticking around.

The judge called a recess for lunch. Nina fled before Riesner could hassle her some more. Out in the parking lot bees buzzed the flowering bushes, and a warm breeze brushed through her hair. A dozen bicyclists dressed in their spidery spandex whizzed by.

She was tossing her briefcase onto the seat when she heard Amagosian say, "Ms. Reilly?"

"Judge?" She was alarmed. They weren't supposed to discuss the case at all. What could he want?

"Nice day," Amagosian said. He was much smaller close up, older, and his face seemed kinder too.

"Sure is."

"I was wondering, nothing to do with the case of course, but your client bears a remarkable resemblance to a man I once knew. Actually worked for me for some years as a foreman on my ranch. Just wondering if she could be a relation."

"I don't know," Nina said. "All I really know is that she is a Washoe."

"Oh, then it can't be."

"Why not?" Nina said.

"Well, this man was Armenian. There are so few of us in this area." He nodded and got into his car.

She met Paul and Dr. Jun at Sato's. Paul was driving Jun to Reno to catch a flight and they had to hurry, so they had wisely started without her. "Sorry," she said. "Amagosian caught me in the parking lot. Then I had to stop for gas."

"What did Amagosian want?" Paul said. He looked quite handsome

in his blue court suit, but the hula-girl tie detracted from the otherwise
sedate impression.

"Oh, just to chat. He thought Jessie looked like this Armenian who
used to work for him. I told him she's a Washoe and took off."

"I'll never think about ethnic heritage the same again after this visit
to Hawaii," Paul said. "Pride in your roots, but people of different back-
grounds intermarrying at the same time. Not that there aren't still problems, but they're on the right track."

"It's history, I think," Jun said. "The first American generation
sometimes doesn't want to think about the old country. It's the grandchildren who realize they've been left rootless in this world. I can't
speak a word of Korean, but I'm going to study it someday."

"Maybe I'll put the O back on the Reilly name someday," Nina
said. "It got lost when the boat landed." Her sushi came and she poured
soy sauce onto her ginger and wasabi, then picked up a piece with her
chopsticks and dunked it in before putting it in her mouth. "Manna,"
she said.

Paul looked at his watch. "Well, we better haul if we're going to
make the flight. You sure you don't need me later?"

"I'll be fine." If only it were true. She hadn't made the clear and
convincing case she had thought she would. Atchison Potter was the
only witness she had left, and he was a lawyer. "Potter's all we have left.
We'll finish this afternoon."

"He looks quite a bit better today." Paul turned to Dr. Jun and said,
"He had jet lag or something when we saw him a few nights ago."

Dr. Jun said, "Well, he looked fine today." He got up with Paul.
"Well, *a hui ho*," he told Nina. "It means, See you soon. Let me know
how it comes out."

"Of course." She shook Jun's hand.

"Be careful," Paul said. "I'll get back as soon as I can." He jingled
his keys.

She watched Paul and her witness get into Paul's Mustang and drive
off and ate some more California roll.

Amanda Lewis—Kenny had gone to see her. Had he somehow pre-
cipitated her murder? Had she been killed with a Glock? Could Kenny
be involved? Could Jessie?

She still had an hour, since Amagosian had some intervening matter,
so she decided to stop by the office.

In the parking lot of the Starlake Building, she was stunned to see
Riesner's Jag taking up two spots. She ran down the hall, remembering

that Sandy was watching the baby, that Jessie was probably there. As she got closer she heard the unmistakable deep voice of Sandy telling somebody to leave.

The door was open. Inside, an apocalyptic scene which struck Nina dumb—Jessie holding the baby at her shoulder, backed against the wall, her face hard and set; Sandy, standing protectively in front of her, arms folded, feet apart; Riesner, tall and imposing, sitting on Sandy's desk with an expression of triumph and glee.

And his stocky client, the blue-jawed Mr. Atchison Potter, in Sandy's face, eyes bulging, seeming about to burst from his jacket, hands up as though the next step would be to try to strangle Sandy, which would not be a good plan.

At her entrance, they all turned to her, Jessie with relief, Riesner with a smile, Potter with a snarl.

"Well, well, well," Riesner said. "Get Shorty."

"What's going on?"

"Oh, a little matter of a grandchild. You really are unbelievable," Riesner said.

"Let's all calm down. Let's talk about this," Nina said.

"I want to hold Dan's son," Potter said. "She won't even let me touch him."

"Let's go in the conference room. Sandy, you watch the baby out here."

"Oh, no. I don't leave the baby," Potter said. "Not until I hold him."

"Then get out of my office. Take your pick."

"I'm not leaving, I said. Not leaving him. I want to hold him. She won't even tell me his name."

"I'll take the baby into the conference room," Jessie said. "As long as you and Sandy stay with us."

"Don't worry," Nina said.

It was crowded in there. Atchison sat across the table from Jessie, still unable to see Gabe's face. Gabe, oblivious to all the commotion, seemed to be having a postprandial snooze.

Atchison was laboring under great emotion. He didn't seem angry anymore, but studied the blue blanket and the fluffy hair with an intensity they could all feel. Sandy closed the door and stood there like a bouncer, feet apart and arms folded.

"Now," Nina said. "What brought you here?"

"He did," Potter said, pointing at the baby.

Riesner said, "A friend at the Tahoe Valley Medical Clinic happened to mention young Jessie had been in for a checkup for her baby.

My friend was just curious about our big slot winner. She happened to be around when the baby was brought in last week. Judging from this child's age, I'd say it's Dan Potter's child. Is it, Mrs. Potter?"

"Wait, Jessie," Nina said.

"Yes, he's Dan's child." Jessie spoke directly to Potter.

"Jessie!"

"And you'll never get him." Hate shone in her eyes. "You're evil and you're trying to destroy me. Well, if you do . . ."

Potter said thickly, "What? You'll destroy him? Like you did my son? Oh, no, you won't. You're an unfit mother. You're a killer. You won't have him much longer."

"Be quiet, now, Atchison," Riesner said. "I know you had to say that. But don't say anything else, all right?" He laid a warning hand on Potter's shoulder. Potter looked at him and seemed to realize he could hurt himself if he went on. He sat back in the chair, still watching Riesner.

"I have called Child Protective Services," Riesner said to Nina. "I'm sure you don't mind."

"You're wasting your time."

"You know what this young lady is going to do? The minute we turn our backs, she's going to flee this jurisdiction with that child. You heard her. She won't even let Mr. Potter touch his own grandson. We need immediate protective custody."

"He's trying to take Gabe!" Jessie cried out. "Nina! You promised me!"

"Look," Nina said. "Let's work something out. Let's not have the baby torn from his mother, not that you will necessarily get your wish, Mr. Potter—"

"That's not my wish," Potter said. "My wish is to hold my grandson. And to prevent her from spiriting him away."

"She did kill the baby's father," Riesner said. "As you may have noticed, we have a judgment to that effect. And she does tend to flee when things don't go her way."

"How long ago did you make that call?"

"—Jeff?" Riesner said. "My name, remember?"

"Well?"

"About ten minutes ago."

"Let's work something out," Nina repeated. She was afraid that she and Jessie would not get out of there with Gabe. She was trying to think. Jessie obviously had full custody; she was Gabe's mother.

Jessie hadn't even registered Gabe's birth. Gabe didn't exist legally.

A chill swept over Nina. Paul had predicted that this would not end well.

"What did you have in mind?" Riesner said. He was smiling again. Jerk!

"You folks leave, Jessie promises to stay here in this county, and we finish the hearing."

"How about, we have the baby taken into protective custody until you lose the hearing, we make sure young Jessie here gets a perjury charge for lying to me at the Examination, and both Jessie and Mr. Potter have visitation rights to the child in the interim."

Jessie got up, holding the baby, her face determined. "I'm leaving," she said. Nina said nothing. She was at a loss. Atchison Potter got up too, knocking his chair back against the wall, and said, "No, you're not."

"If you touch her, it's a battery, Mr. Potter. You will be prosecuted and it will strongly affect any possibility of access to this child," Nina said. She was standing, too. They were all standing.

"Don't give my client advice," Riesner said, his face ugly. But he, too, didn't seem to know what to do. The law didn't seem to have much guidance to offer for this emotional situation. Jessie edged toward the door, but Sandy didn't move.

"Jessie," she said. "Don't run."

"I have to. Let me go."

"He'll find you. Make your stand here, with your friends."

"Don't make me push you away, Sandy. Please. Get out of the way."

Potter made a move. Sandy stepped aside and Jessie rushed for the door.

"Wait!" Potter yelled. Jessie stopped, her hand on the door, still out of his range.

Potter yelped, "Just let me hold him, and we'll cancel the call!"

"Listen to him, Jessie! Wait!" Nina said.

"Just let me hold him!"

"Why should I?"

"Please!" Potter said. "He's Dan's little boy!"

She turned slowly, her hand still on the knob. "And you won't try to take him from me?"

"Not this way," Potter said.

"You're just trying to keep me here until they come," Jessie said. "It's a trick. Right, Nina?"

"Will you cancel the call if Mr. Potter is permitted to hold the child?" Nina asked Riesner.

"She'll run right after," Riesner said. "That's the risk, Atchison."

"Swear to me that you will stay here," Potter said to Jessie. "I don't mean like in court. I mean, swear it to me, before God."

"And you will leave us alone?"

"Until the hearing is over."

She looked at Nina, hesitating. Nina nodded slightly.

"I swear," she said. "Before God."

"Call them," Nina said. Riesner took out his phone and pressed the redial button. He asked for a particular name. He put his hand over the phone and said, "Have her give that baby to Mr. Potter. Right now."

Nina said, "Jessie?"

"Five minutes," Jessie said. "That's it."

"Alone," Potter said.

"No!"

"All right. Not alone. All right."

Jessie looked at Riesner. "Just a second," he said into the phone.

Jessie went over to Potter and handed him the bundle and stepped back. Gabe woke up. They all waited for him to start wailing at finding himself in a stranger's arms.

But Gabe started playing with Potter's blue silk tie. Potter held him very carefully.

Riesner began speaking into the phone, saying there had been a misunderstanding, no intervention was requested at this time.

Potter clutched the baby to his chest. His eyes were pressed shut. His hand rubbed the baby's back, moved to his hair, smoothed it. His hand was shaking, tender. Jessie watched, an agonized expression on her face. Nina was biting her nails again. She noticed what she was doing and put her hand in her pocket.

"His name is Gabe," Jessie said.

Gabe let out a little fart.

Sandy said, "Remember, you gotta hold him the whole five minutes."

23

WHAT A LUNCH IT HAD been, with bedlam barely suppressed in her office. And now she was back in court at her table, studiously ignoring Riesner, still trying not to think about the shootings, planning her next move.

Hmm. Time to put sweet old Gramps on the stand and expose him as a racist, possibly homicidal, verdict-buyer.

Possibly she should adjust that strategy. Possibly she could bring Gramps and Mom and Baby together. Gramps would put away his suspicions and Jessie would forgive him his persecutions and . . .

She stole a quick look at Jessie, who, as she had throughout the hearing, stared stonily ahead. Put the right hat on her and she could guard Arafat's tent. She did not exactly appear willing to back down.

Atchison Potter's voice held a new determination as he said, "I do," and took the stand. Finding a new family member seemed to have galvanized him. Nina took a swift trip through Riesner's mind. If she were his attorney, what would she tell Potter?

That getting the money away from Jessie would leave her helpless. That siccing a private detective on her right away would keep her in view. That Potter should bide his time and ride through the rest of the hearing because he was probably going to win it.

No strategy adjustment appeared necessary. She had to try to convince Amagosian to throw out the judgment.

"Good afternoon, Mr. Potter."

He gave a distant nod. Nina thought, Dive on in, the water's cold but it won't be getting any warmer.

"At what point after your son's death did you become convinced

238 PERRI O'SHAUGHNESSY

that his wife had caused his death?" she asked him. That made the courtroom sit up straight.

"Immediately. My son was an excellent swimmer and boater. The story never made any sense to me."

"Did you convey your suspicions to the police?"

"Repeatedly. They were incompetent. They were afraid to proceed. I was told that the district attorney's office did not determine it had enough evidence to proceed."

"Did your son ever complain to you of suffering any illness in the last months of his life?"

"Never. Never said a word."

"How often did you speak to him during that time?"

"Well, not very often. He was very busy."

"How many times?"

"I don't remember."

"Did you speak to him at all?"

"I don't recall."

"In fact, you and your son were not on speaking terms during the last months of his life, isn't that correct?"

"We were having some family difficulties."

"What family difficulties?"

Riesner ascendant. "Objection. How close Mr. Potter was to his son at that time is totally irrelevant to the issues in this hearing. We have a judgment. Should it be enforced? What has that got to do with this line of questioning?"

"This lawsuit was brought in bad faith, out of personal animosity, Your Honor. I am going to demonstrate that in a moment," Nina said.

Amagosian said, "Unfortunately, personal animosity is often a factor inspiring a lawsuit. It doesn't invalidate a resultant judgment."

"But the bad faith extends all the way from the initiation of the lawsuit through the trial. I am introducing this important background material so that the court can understand this gentleman's subsequent actions," Nina said.

"Keep it brief, please. I'll allow it."

"What family difficulties?" Nina said again.

"I didn't approve of my son's marriage."

"To Jessie Potter? The judgment debtor?"

"Yes."

"Why?"

"I didn't like her or trust her. She was not my idea of a good wife. A Marine! An outsider. Of course, like many parents, I had hoped my son would marry into a local family."

"A family of Caucasian ancestry?" Riesner stayed in his chair. Evidently he felt that Potter could handle this.

"Not at all," Potter said. "I wouldn't care if she was a green Martian, so long as she had grown up in Hawaii."

"Isn't it true that your main objection was that Mrs. Potter was of Native American ancestry?"

"No," Potter said, looking shocked, like Nina had said a bad word. Nina was getting nowhere with this, so she switched to a new subject.

"Prior to bringing the lawsuit, did you urge the local authorities to arrest Mrs. Potter for killing your son?"

"Yes, I did," Potter said. "Dan spent his life in those waters. He had kayaked thousands of times without mishap. I knew she was lying about what happened out there. She had something to do with his death. My son had a trust fund, and she didn't have two nickels to rub together."

"Has she made a claim on the trust-fund money?" Nina said.

"No, only because she knows what would happen if she did."

"You would stop her? By any means possible?"

"Yes. Of course. By any legal means possible."

"In fact, by obtaining this judgment, you ensured that she would not be able to make any claim on the trust fund, didn't you? If she did, you would come in with this colossal judgment and take the trust fund away from her, am I correct?"

"That would be one course of action." He didn't seem ashamed of it, either.

"In fact, Dan Potter's estate is still in probate, isn't it?"

"Yes. These things take time."

"Especially since you are fighting the executor bank, which indicated it would distribute the trust-fund monies to Mrs. Potter?"

"Yes. She will not be rewarded for my son's death."

"If she doesn't get the trust fund, who does, Mr. Potter?"

"Well, it came from my father. It would revert to the sole surviving member of the family."

"You?"

"Yes. Of course, everything has changed now that I have learned that I have a grandson, who Mrs. Potter took from Hawaii and has been cruelly hiding from me."

A stir in the back. Amagosian stopped writing and gave Potter his full attention. "You say Mrs. Potter has a child?"

"I was holding him half an hour ago. She admitted he was Dan's child. She hid him from me."

Amagosian thought about this. "Then," he said, "you seem to be in a rather different position, Mr. Potter. Your grandchild will be affected by the result of this writ."

Riesner stood up and said, "I have discussed these new developments with my client. Nothing has changed. We are requesting to enforce the judgment."

"Still, an informal settlement conference might be in order. I would be willing to make time for that tomorrow morning," Amagosian said.

"There is nothing to settle. The judgment is either going to be executed or it isn't," Riesner said. "A settlement conference will achieve nothing at this time."

"Well, I thought I'd make the offer," Amagosian said to Potter. "It's your grandchild."

"There is nothing to settle," Potter said, parroting Riesner.

"You may continue," Amagosian said to Nina. His look said, I tried. She appreciated that, but even full-bore sympathy wasn't going to make her feel better if he had to enforce the judgment.

"Now, then," she said to Potter. "At the time you sued Mrs. Potter, you knew she had left Hawaii, did you not?"

"I had no idea."

"You had hounded her out of the Marines, had you not?"

"Certainly not. My understanding is that she chose not to reenlist."

"After you spoke to her commanding officer? Accused her of murder? Spread rumors on the base?"

"I did speak to her commanding officer at a function we both attended. That is all."

"You accused her of murder at that time?"

"I told him my suspicions."

"You also spoke to her landlord and told *him* of your suspicions, did you not?"

"Yes. We attended high school together. Honolulu is not an anonymous city. We're all friendly and try to get along. I thought he should know what he was harboring."

"And as a result she was evicted from her home?" Nina waited a beat for Riesner to object, but he didn't bother. Potter was doing fine.

"I don't have the slightest idea about that," Potter said. "I assume she left town to hide her pregnancy from me."

Nina lost her temper. "Did you try to attack my client and her husband a few weeks ago in Markleeville?" she said very sharply.

Potter stared at her, as if he had never heard anything so idiotic in his life. Then he burst out laughing. Riesner joined in.

The whole courtroom started to laugh.

"Ha, ha. I—I think Counsel might need a break," Riesner said. Amagosian looked astonished, but at least he had not laughed.

"You have evidence of this?" he said to Nina.

"Somebody attacked my client's husband, tried to run him down with a car, and was stalking him and my client," Nina said stubbornly.

"Just a moment. What evidence do you have that Mr. Potter might have had anything to do with that?" Amagosian said, stopping her cold.

"The whole pattern of events." Nina stopped. She had let herself get angry and fallen into a thicket.

Riesner was smiling broadly, like she'd made a joke.

"That's all the evidence you have?"

"No direct evidence, Your Honor. But given Mr. Potter's—"

"Oh, no. Don't say another word. I'm going to direct you to move on from this line of questioning, Counsel."

She had miscalculated. She had lost a lot of credibility.

But it had happened, according to Jessie and Kenny. She wrote it off and went on. But she was afraid she had taken a bad hit. She felt her case hemorrhaging along with her credibility.

"All right. You spoke with Mr. Byron Eppley at the Cafe Sistina not long before you filed the lawsuit?"

"Yes. He had been Dan's friend."

"You paid him five thousand dollars cash on that occasion?"

"Absolutely. I knew what a hard time he was having paying his university tuition. I wanted to help him, in Dan's memory."

"Come on, Mr. Potter. You made sure before you paid him that he was going to go along with your version of events at the trial, didn't you?"

"Objection. Misstates the previous testimony. Leading. Badgering, really. Vague. Incompetent." Riesner had thrown that last word in for the fun of it. He was having a wonderful time.

Before Nina could open her mouth, Amagosian said, "Sustained."

"But, Your Honor—"

"Sus-tained. I have heard Mr. Eppley's testimony. We do not need to rehash it at this time."

"Very well, Your Honor." She paused, her chest heaving. They were beating her. She bit her lip. Riesner could see she was in trouble. So could Jessie.

"And Dr. Jun, your other witness in this eighteen-minute trial—"

"Objection. The trial was not eighteen minutes. Written evidence was introduced. A trial brief was submitted. Opening and closing statements were made."

"I'm just pointing out that the taking of the evidence lasted eighteen minutes," Nina said.

"Your point?" Amagosian said, though he seemed to have figured her point out pretty well and already dismissed it.

"My point is that it wasn't enough time for the trial judge to hear such a complicated matter as how a man died," Nina said. "Dr. Jun has testified that his testimony was twisted. Mr. Eppley has testified that he lied. They were the only two witnesses, besides the documents—"

"Which were quite sufficient, standing on their own, to support the Judgment," Riesner put in.

Amagosian said, "We have Dr. Jun's testimony. What is your question to this witness?" Nina didn't like the way he was looking at her.

She said quickly to Potter, "You paid Dr. Jun as an expert witness, didn't you? Instead of as a treating physician, which is what he actually was?"

"Objection," Riesner said, a real hound of the Baskervilles, baying behind her. "We will stipulate that Dr. Jun was paid as an expert witness. Dr. Jun rendered an opinion as an expert regarding various matters in connection with the so-called treatment of the nonexistent disorder Daniel Potter allegedly suffered from."

"Well, which is it?" Nina said to Potter. "Was it a nonexistent illness? Or was it poison? Make up your mind."

"Objection! I ask that Counsel be admonished."

"Counsel," Amagosian said, "I am going to be charitable. I am going to take an early afternoon break. Collect yourself, or you will wish you had."

She went out to the hall. Jessie said not a word but went straight to the phone. Barbet Schroeder, trotting alongside Nina and no doubt dreaming up a juicy headline for the *Tahoe Mirror,* said, "So you're saying that Potter was stalking your client?"

"No comment, Barbet."

"He tried to run Mr. Leung down, you said."

"No comment." Nina ducked into the bathroom.

But there was to be no mercy. Barbet followed her in. "What's this about a grandchild?" she said from the other stall. "Is Potter going to try to get custody?"

"No comment! Maybe when the hearing is over! But only if you stop now!"

"Okay, okay. Stress gettin' to you, kid?"

Nina said nothing. Waiting until she heard Barbet wash her hands and exit, she came out and furiously brushed her hair in front of the mirror.

Dr. Jun waited for her outside.

He rushed up, Paul on his heels. "I hope I'm not too late!" he said. "Is Mr. Potter still being examined?"

"Yes, but—what in the world are you doing here, Dr. Jun? You're supposed to be in the mid-Pacific by now!"

"It was something you said at the lunch," Jun said.

"Me? Paul, what's going on?"

"I took him to the airport but he wouldn't get out of the car. He said he had to get to a computer right away, so we went to this funky Internet cafe right by the airport and he went online. And he sat there for two solid hours," Paul said. "Missed the flight. Won't tell me what it's all about."

"I've figured this out," Jun said. "The illness. I think I know what happened to Dan."

Nina looked at her watch. They still had five minutes. "Come on," she said, and propelled them outside into the balmy afternoon, out behind the courthouse into the trees.

"It's the Armenian connection," Jun said. "And Paul told me about the sick baby on the way to Reno." The words tumbled out of his mouth. "You said the judge thought Jessie looked like an Armenian. Is she? I have to know. It's essential."

"But she's Washoe! I explained that. . . ."

"Please. Just ask her." Paul was already trotting back in to look for Jessie.

"It's a genetic illness," Jun went on. "What about Mr. Potter? How is he doing?"

Nina thought back and remembered how Potter had looked at the bar at Caesars. "He did look sick when I saw him recently. But maybe he was just having a bad night."

"Because it's a series of acute episodes," Jun said. "Three generations. In Hawaii, of all places. It's a small world."

"But what is it? What have you learned?"

Paul came running back with Jessie. "What?" she cried, breathless.

Dr. Jun said, "Do you have any Armenian ancestry?"

And Jessie laughed. "That's what you wanted to ask me so bad?" She caught her breath. "How did you know? My father was Armenian."

Jun's mouth fell open. An expression of wonder and joy came into his eyes. "Okay. Let me think," he said. They all stood around, befuddled, while he did that.

"The baby," he said. "Fever attacks? How many?"

"Four, so far."

"How long do they last? About two days?"

"Y-yes. What has Gabe got to do with this?"

"Mr. Potter," Jun said. "What is his ethnicity?"

"Well, he's *haole*—well, he was adopted."

"What is his ethnicity? What was Dan's ethnicity? His mother?"

"Dan's mother—she was Caucasian," Jessie said. "I mean Northern European."

"Then it has to be Mr. Potter. Adopted! What do you know about his birth parents?"

"N-nothing!" Jessie cried. "I'm sorry! He never said anything about it to me!"

Nina looked at her watch. "We have to go back in right away. I mean right now."

"Let me sit with you," Jun said. "You have to ask him some questions. You have to find out about his birth parents."

"But why?"

"I'll tell you. After the questions." He started away, but Nina took him by the arm.

"Dr. Jun," she said. "Can I trust you?"

The young doctor swallowed and said, "I think I am right. Please. Let's go find out."

By the time Nina got back to her table, Atchison Potter had taken the stand again. Dr. Jun sat right behind her, leaning over toward her. Nina passed him her legal pad and a pen.

"I remind you that you are still under oath," Amagosian told Potter, who nodded and crossed his legs. A walk in the park.

Jun passed her the pad. On it he had written in capital letters POTTER SICK?

"Mr. Potter, how are you feeling today?"

Potter looked at Riesner, who shrugged. "Fine," he said.

"Do you suffer from any sort of chronic or intermittent illness?"

"Objection. Irrelevant, immaterial. And—it almost goes without saying, doesn't it?—incompetent."

"Uh, it goes to the witness's ability to perceive the events spoken of," Nina said. She was hoping to skate by with that, since she wasn't sure what it went to at all.

"What events? What's she talking about? When he talked to Eppley? If so, the question has to be whether he was ill on that day."

"Reframe the question," Amagosian said.

"Certainly, Your Honor." Jun's yellow sheet of paper said RECURRENT FEVER. "Do you suffer from attacks of recurrent fever?"

"Objection. I must reiterate. What is she talking about?"

Amagosian put down his head and seemed to meditate for a moment. Then he said, "Sustained."

NO! MUST FIND OUT!

"May I be permitted to argue the objection before the court rules on the objection?" Nina said, although Amagosian had in fact just ruled on it.

Amagosian scratched his white head, said, "Go ahead, though I don't think you're going to get anywhere, since Mr. Potter's general health is irrelevant to the issues in this hearing."

Several tortured moments went by. You've got to find a way in! Nina told herself. All the years of training, all the bitter experience, all came down to this—she couldn't figure out how to get this question in. Pretending to drop her file, she said, "A moment, Your Honor." As she knelt to the floor to retrieve it she saw Riesner's boots at the table on the right. They were made of some kind of snakeskin. Wasn't that just perfect! While her guts reacted unfavorably to his footwear, her mind zipped through the rules of admissible evidence. Had to be relevant to an issue in this hearing. What issue? Bribery? Fraud? Procedural defectiveness?

No. The question wasn't relevant to any of that. She straightened up and tucked her hair behind her ear. Her eyes caught Jessie, with her ramrod posture and the look of suffering under the steel.

The issue was—the issue was—

The issue was, did Jessie kill her husband. Of course!

"This question goes to the ultimate fact issue in this case, Your Honor," Nina blurted, stumbling over the words. "Whether there was a wrongful death. Whether my client had something to do with the death of her husband."

"I am all ears, Counsel." But he said this wearily, because what she was saying sounded bizarre. She knew it. They all knew it.

CONGENITAL ILLNESS DIFFERENT SYMPTOMS!

"My client maintains, has maintained all along, and would have testified at the trial, that her husband suffered an acute attack of illness that caused him to fall out of the kayak and drown," she said. "It is our contention that Mr. Potter may suffer from the same illness, although the symptomology may be different."

"So?"

"So, we may be able to finally identify the illness if I can just ask a few more questions along these lines."

"Invasion of privacy," Riesner said, ticking it off on his fingers. "Speculation. Beyond the bounds of any issue introduced in the trial. Vague. Immaterial. Off we go on another one of her inadequately financed flights into outer space, Your Honor."

"The objection is sustained," Amagosian said.

She had lost that battle. She put her hand to the mouth that had just been muzzled.

Another sheet of yellow paper. ETHNICITY! ADOPTED!

She almost burst out in bitter laughter. Didn't Jun get it—if she couldn't ask about Potter's health, how in hell was she going to get away with asking about his ethnicity?

"C'mon, Nina," Paul said in a low voice.

"Next question, Counsel."

"All right. Now, Mr. Potter, you were adopted as a child, is that correct?"

"Your Honor, this has gone far enough. I ask for sanctions against Counsel. She's wasting our time with her incompetent questioning. What is she trying to imply? That my client is somehow a lesser human being because he may have been adopted? I move to strike the question."

"The question shall be stricken. The objection is sustained. Next question." Amagosian's patience was strained, never a good thing.

Nina inhaled. Exhaled. "What is your ethnic background?" she asked Potter.

An indignant buzz of voices behind her. "Sanctions! Sanctions!" Riesner bayed. Potter sat back in his chair, an incredulous grin stuck on his face.

"Counsel, what is the meaning of this outrageous question?" Amagosian asked. She had to get this one through.

She thought for a minute, then said, "Ethnicity does matter, Your Honor. It matters in many ways, including in the world of medicine. And it matters legally in this case. My questions are crucial to showing what happened to Dan Potter, Your Honor. There is no other way to ask them. A miscarriage of justice will result if I cannot ask this question and have it answered." She pulled out her one-eyed Jack. "Just as my client's ethnicity, which is half-Armenian and half-Washoe, is crucial in this case."

A beat. "Half-Armenian?" Amagosian said. "Really?"

"Her father was of Armenian heritage," Nina said. "From Alpine

County. Her maiden name was Kiyan." The whole courtroom took a look at Jessie with her cockeyed ethnic background, Amagosian, the Armenian-American, first and foremost. Nina had drawn him in and in spite of Riesner's asking in what way this amounted to a hill of beans in the background, even Riesner seemed curious to know how she could dig her way out of this one.

Amagosian said, "Kiyan. Really. I will allow some latitude, but I hope you know what you are doing."

"Thank you. Thank you very much, Your Honor. What is your ethnicity, Mr. Potter?"

Potter looked at Riesner, who shrugged again. "I really resent having to answer such a personal question," he said.

"What is your ethnicity?" Nina repeated.

"Well, I'm . . . I was adopted. My birth parents, I was told, were from North Africa."

NOT GOOD ENOUGH. ETHNICITY.

"I didn't ask where they were from. I asked your ethnic background."

"They were Jews. All right? Sephardic Jews." A pained expression crossed his face, and Nina thought, And I bet his adoptive parents gave him hell for it. So they had been anti-Semitic. Suddenly he came into focus. Yes. His heritage was there in his face. His treatment of Jessie was beginning to make sense. As Jessie had said, he had suffered from his adoptive parents' prejudice growing up, but he had internalized it, becoming prejudiced himself.

"Those people—the birth parents—they died in Algeria. My adopted parents were traveling there. They had false papers prepared and got me out of there. I was a baby. I don't remember any of it. There aren't even any pictures. Anyway, I don't think of those people as my parents. My mother didn't wish to discuss them."

Nina turned to Jun. The doc was practically panting in excitement. With a twist of his slender wrist, he scrawled on the pad. He showed it to her.

JACKPOT!   BUT—RECURRENT   ILLNESS—FEVER! PLEASE!

"Your Honor, the court has kindly permitted me the latitude to ask the last question, and the answer will be linked up to the factual issue in a moment. But I must ask the court to reconsider one more question I asked before, which is also crucial in this inquiry. I must know if Mr. Potter has a recurrent illness involving fever."

But she didn't have to wait. Potter answered before Amagosian could open his mouth.

"Over the last six months," Potter said. "High fever. Very debilitating, but seems to resolve on its own."

Jun was tugging at her arm. She looked down.

MEGAJACKPOT!

"What is it?" she whispered to him urgently. He wrote it down for her.

FAMILIAL MEDITERRANEAN FEVER. UNKNOWN IN HAWAII.

"Has your illness been diagnosed, Mr. Potter?"

"That's one question too many," Riesner said. "Move that this entire line of questioning be stricken."

"I'm undergoing tests," Potter said.

"Wait until this objection is ruled upon, sir," Amagosian said to Potter, but too late.

"But what is this all about?" Potter said, a plaintive note entering his voice.

Nina said, "Your Honor, I would like to recall Dr. Jun to the stand at this time."

"What about this witness here?"

"I will excuse this witness."

"Then, unless the rules of court have been completely overturned, it is my turn to cross-examine," Riesner said. "Or have we all gone through the looking glass?"

"In the interests of making our proof in an orderly fashion, may we just have Dr. Jun on the stand for ten minutes out of order?" Nina said. "He has to catch a plane." Maybe not right away, but they didn't have to know that.

Riesner started to say something, but Amagosian held up his hand. "Let us continue this line of questioning for ten more minutes," he said. "I admit I am not fully aware of what Counsel is getting at, but I have the impression that something important is going on. I am going to allow Dr. Jun to take the stand out of order."

Riesner sat down, turned sideways in disgust, stretched out his legs, and crossed his snakeskin boots.

"Mr. Potter, you are excused for the moment, but you are still under oath," Amagosian said. Potter returned to the counsel table, sitting down beside Riesner.

"I will recall Dr. Justin Jun to the stand," Nina said.

Jun rushed up to the witness box and was called back down to be sworn in again. He breathed hard and ran his tongue over his lips.

"Dr. Jun. You have heard Mr. Potter's testimony? Regarding his ethnicity and his illness?"

"Oh, yes."

"You previously testified that you treated and tested Dan Potter before his death for an unspecified medical disorder?"

"Yes."

"And has Atchison Potter's testimony caused you in any way to wish to revise your previous testimony?"

"Yes!" They all waited, but Jun just leaned forward, eyes now wide, aflame.

"So what—"

Jun said very rapidly, "I have a diagnosis for Dan Potter's illness. I have been through his medical files, all the test results, again. I consulted with a gastroenterologist in Reno this afternoon. And now all this is confirmed by Mr. Potter's testimony. It is amazing, absolutely amazing."

"What is?"

"Mr. Potter most likely has it too. It is called Familial Mediterranean Fever, or FMF. It is a congenital illness, usually passed through a recessive gene. Both parents generally have to have the gene but not always. It is found among Arabs, in Turkey, Greece, among other places. And among Sephardic Jews. Oh, yes. I also read a number of research papers on the Internet this afternoon. But I didn't recognize it before, when Dan Potter came in to see me. He didn't have the cardinal sign of the illness, a recurrent high fever. . . ."

Jessie gasped behind Nina, but Nina couldn't turn around, she had to keep Jun on his roll.

"Then how do you now diagnose it as FMF?" she said.

"Because only three-quarters of patients get the fever," he said. "As with Mr. Potter there, symptoms can vary. Acute abdominal pain is the next most common presenting factor. I shouldn't say common. This disease is well known in Israel and Turkey, for instance, but in Hawaii it is practically unknown. Still, I might have caught it if I had known Dan was a descendant of Sephardic Jews. I said it is a recessive gene, but there are exceptions. There are reports of it passing with only one parent known to be carrying the gene."

"Speak more slowly," Amagosian interrupted. "I'm having trouble following."

"I am sorry, Your Honor, but I am so—so elated to finally know what happened to my patient."

"Objection!" came from the next table.

Amagosian said, "The court will disregard that last statement. Now then, Dr. Jun. This illness. You are making this diagnosis rather late, more than a year after the young man's death."

"I practice medicine in Hawaii. I am well acquainted with genetic illnesses of Portuguese, Hawaiians, Vietnamese, Pacific Islanders, Japanese, Chinese. . . ."

"But there are not that many Sephardic Jews in Hawaii. As there are not many Armenians in Alpine County, where I live," Amagosian said.

"Precisely. The test results match perfectly what I would expect. And Dan's symptoms. The severe pain. The recovery after about forty-eight hours."

"I don't understand. This young man's illness came on in his early twenties?"

"Yes. This illness can come on at almost any time in a person's life. So Mr. Potter here has had a late onset."

Amagosian sat back in his chair and nodded for Nina to proceed. She asked, "Could an attack cause such debility that a person would fall out of a small boat? Could it cause such severe pain that the person wouldn't know what he was doing?"

"Oh, yes. Some FMF patients have suffered from psychiatric problems. The fear of developing another attack was so strong, the fear of the pain. Some have actually committed suicide. That is how severe the pain may be."

Nina heard a sob.

"A moment, Your Honor," Nina said, and went to Jessie. Jessie pushed her away, face distorted with horror. "Gabe," she cried. "He has it. Oh, God, my baby."

Nina, shocked, turned back to Jun.

"Could this illness have been passed on to Dan's son?" she said. "Based on what you currently know, Dr. Jun?" She knew Potter wouldn't let Riesner object to that one.

"Didn't I mention it? One out of seven Armenians carry the gene. It's a small world. Sephardic Jewish genes meet Armenian genes in Hawaii. The baby has the symptoms and the test results, and now, the heritage. I'm going to write it up as soon as I get back."

"You are sure about this?"

"Reasonably sure. Recurrent high fever, ethnic background, vague test results except for the elevated ESR. The illness strikes infants as well. Early onset in the baby's case. Usually more severe when it starts early." He sounded cruelly clinical. Jessie continued to cry. She sounded heartbroken.

Shaken out of his reverie of scientific discovery, Jun fixed his eyes on her and focused.

"Oh. Please. No need to cry," he said to Jessie. Atchison Potter's mouth was set slightly shut as if to limit his ingestion of these dreadful ramifications.

"Dr. Jun . . ." Nina said. But she couldn't think of anything else to ask him. A Pandora's box had opened and pain and uncertainty had flown out. Jun waited for her to finish, but she couldn't. She was thinking about Gabe, growing up, dreading the attacks, going through hell. . . .

And then, out of the box of horrors, a sunny little face emerged, as hope, true to the legend, flitted out of the box. Jun smiled. He said, "But you see, now that we know what it is, we're all set. There's a new treatment for FMF. Prevents the attacks. Very effective."

"What?" Nina said, beyond all other words.

"Colchicine. Gout medicine. Very effective. Just discovered in the eighties. The baby may never have another attack. And Mr. Potter? See your doctor for the prescription right away."

Four-thirty. Amagosian had adjourned court for the day and summoned them to his chambers for a heart-to-heart settlement talk. Parties only, so Paul and Dr. Jun were waiting in Paul's Mustang out in the courthouse lot.

Amagosian looked much more comfortable behind his desk with its folk art and solid old furniture he must have installed himself. In front of him were arrayed Jessie, Nina, Riesner, and Potter.

"No reporter here," he said. "Just us folks. No rules of evidence. Now, then. I feel that events have taken a turn. First of all, we have this baby. We have this family situation. Secondly, we have a pretty good idea that Mrs. Potter's story about the boat may be true."

"It doesn't prove a thing," Riesner said.

"I have to agree with that, Jeff. It's not proof that Dan Potter did get sick on that boat on that particular day. No, we don't have this thing nailed down. But a number of facts have sure come together. There's a sort of moral certainty creeping around here, isn't there? Does your client still think Mrs. Potter poisoned her husband?"

"He stands by the Judgment and he wants it enforced," Riesner said, not even looking at Potter.

"You have talked it over with him?" Amagosian said.

"He has not talked it over with me," Potter said. "I—I'm not sure—"

"Ah. Well. Here's what I propose. Jeff, you and your client go out and discuss this for a few minutes. See if there's any change in your position. See if anything can be done."

"Nothing's going to change," Riesner said.

"I would like to talk with my attorney," Potter said. Riesner shook his head sharply, his eyes on the floor. But he had no choice in the matter, so he got up. The two men went outside.

When they were gone, Amagosian said, "How old is the baby?"

"Nine months. Almost ten months now." Jessie's voice was almost inaudible.

"Gabe, eh? Gabriel, that's a good Armenian name," Amagosian said, smiling. "Good choice. So your father was from Alpine County?"

"Yes. He was a ranch hand." Amagosian nodded, smiling. "He and my mother were both killed in a car wreck when I was six," Jessie added.

"I'm very sorry to hear that. I remember your father. You should come to one of our association meetings. The fourth Friday of each month. Good food, music, sometimes a little dancing. Speeches on topics of interest to the Armenian community. I'm going to suggest a talk on this illness. FMF."

"I never had anything to do with my father's side," Jessie said.

"Never too late. Eh?" Nina watched them talking. Now she had the feeling that Jessie's face was moving into focus. The smoothness of her skin, the shape of her features, a cast of the eyes—she and Amagosian were cousins in one of the families of man.

The talk moved on to the weather. Nina was aware that Amagosian was not asking her to try to dream up some sort of compromise with Riesner. It was obvious what he wanted. He wanted Potter to drop the request for the Writ of Execution, so that he, Amagosian, would not have to make the decision. Like any good judge, if there was a fair way to resolve the situation that wouldn't lay all the responsibility on him, he favored it. He probably didn't feel that he had substance enough to overturn the judgment.

Too agitated to chat, Nina dropped out of the conversation, wondering if Potter was a bigger man than she had thought.

The conference between attorney and client took a full eighteen minutes, as long as the original trial had taken. The two men came back in, Riesner in front. The arch of his eyebrow told Nina they were sunk.

"I have discussed all of this with my client as you requested, Judge," Riesner said. "My client wishes to pursue this matter. We do not intend to change our position at this time."

Jessie closed her eyes, as though she just couldn't manage to keep them open anymore.

"Are you certain about this?" Amagosian said, speaking directly to Potter.

"I—I'm certain," Potter said. But he didn't seem certain. It crossed Nina's mind that Potter had wanted to settle but Riesner had talked him out of it. Why? Why would Riesner do that? Because of her? Could this be some kind of macho game? If so, Potter was being ill-served. Nina said, "Counsel, let's talk. Briefly."

Out they went into one of the jury rooms. Nina remembered this room. It had been bugged during deliberations in the Markov trial. A juror had died in this room. Nothing had changed. Brown microwave oven, conference table, yellowish light. The door closed as she set her briefcase on the table and she thought, Uh oh. Mistake.

"I know we're tired, Jeff. . . ."

"*Now* you remember my name."

"I hope this has nothing to do with the problems between us."

Riesner pursed his lips.

It was agony, being polite to him. "This isn't about us, Jeff," she added.

"Actually, it isn't," Riesner said, sidling up to her, violating her personal space. "It would mean a lot to your client if I persuaded Atchison to get out and go home, wouldn't it?"

The hair rose on her arms and she stepped back. His left eyebrow had lifted, and he wore the leering smirk on his hatchet face that always suggested to her he was mentally undressing her. Repulsed, Nina spoke without her usual prudence. "Don't even think about coming on to me, Jeff. If you touch me, I'll yell so loud I'll rupture your eardrums. And then I'll sue you."

Riesner moved away. "God forbid, you bitch," he said.

Nina tried again. "Look. This is business. You can't be sure Amagosian is going to rule in your client's favor."

"You want to give us half the money? Split it?"

Nina swallowed. This might be the best way out. "I would be willing to discuss it with my client."

"Well, sadly, I wouldn't be willing to discuss it with mine. I don't care what the fuck he thinks he wants. I call the shots. And there's not going to be a settlement. Amagosian's enjoying your little medical mystery but when it comes time to rule you are going to lose. And I'm going to take forty percent of the settlement on contingency. I think I'll buy another speedboat. A really fast one. I'll take my wife on a cruise. I know. We'll cruise the Mediterranean! Thanks for bringing that to mind!"

"You know what?"

"Fuck you. I know that much. You and your multiethnic bullshit."

"You're not a lawyer," Nina said.

"Yeah? Well, I passed the bar long before you, pip-squeak."

"You're a con artist. I haven't seen you practice law in two years. You just con your way through everything. You ought to be thrown out of town. You and all your shell corporations."

"What? What did you say?" His face had gone green.

"And I'm tired of you trying to intimidate me. You don't scare me."

Uh oh. Catching her hands, Riesner said, "You're all alone in here with me, you know. Your meatball boyfriend isn't here to protect you."

"Let me go."

"In the ass," Riesner said. "That's where I'm going to have you." They were actually struggling physically, it had come to that, and Nina was no match for him. She jerked a hand loose, snaked it into her briefcase, and pulled out her brand-new tiny canister of pepper spray. And gave him a short spritz right in the center of his forehead.

"Aaughhh!" Riesner put his hands over his face, tore open the door, and ran out.

Nina straightened her jacket, patted her hair, tucked the can away, and went back to Amagosian's chambers.

"Any luck?" he said.

"I'm afraid not," she said. "Mr. Riesner had to leave. A hot situation. He apologized for not being able to come back."

"Too bad," Amagosian said. "Well, let's finish up tomorrow morning. Eight-thirty. You'll let Jeff's office know?"

"Certainly," Nina said.

24

RED, WEARING HIS SUIT, FRESH out of the bizarre court hearing, was
having a drink after court, mulling it all over in his mind.

He had seen Riesner running to the water fountain downstairs and
had followed him and watched as the lawyer tossed water onto his face
for about five minutes, snuffling and cursing. He had waited patiently
until Riesner had calmed down somewhat and sat down on a bench, all
without saying one word to Red. Red had sat down beside him.

"Mace?" he said. "Tear gas? Pepper spray? I used to work security.
Women carried that stuff and I saw several men with redder eyes than
you rinsing their faces in the bathrooms in my time. Don't worry, the
worst is over. Who did it?"

Riesner didn't answer. He was still rubbing his eyes.

"Don't trust me, eh? I could make a guess, but I'll leave you your
secret. Well, what now? They adjourned until tomorrow. What happens
tomorrow?"

A hollow voice. "I can't talk right now."

"Pull yourself together. You want her to see you like this?"

The tall lawyer had covered his face with his handkerchief. "I'm
leaving as soon as I can see to drive," he said from behind the handkerchief.

"Can't blame you for that. And your Writ of Execution's down the
toilet, it seems. What with it turning out that the son was sick after all.
Strange twist of fate."

"Do you mind?" Riesner said.

"Sure, I'll go. But tell me first, like I said, what happens tomorrow?
Your client going to bow out?"

For a few seconds all he could hear was Riesner sniffing behind the handkerchief. Then Riesner said, "No, he's not going to bow out. He's going to keep going. He's going to get that money."

"Yeah? What's your fee?"

"That's none of your business."

Red said, "Potter's going to keep after her? How long is this all going to take?"

"I don't care if it takes forever," Riesner said.

"In-fucking-furiating," Red told the video poker machine embedded in the bar in front of him. A pair of tens. He had lost his dollar.

Potter could have ended the whole thing today, but he wasn't going to butt out. He could win and go back to Hawaii, forever out of Red's reach. He could tie the money up forever. Red had been unbelievably patient about all this, waiting for the legal process to take its course, rooting for the girl because she was the better shakedown.

But he was starting to realize that these things went on and on. He couldn't wait a few more months or a few more years for her to get his money. This was worse than trying to figure out who Florida had voted for for President.

He couldn't wait a few more days. He couldn't wait another fucking minute. The craving to gamble came up naked and ravening inside of him. Nobody and nothing was more important than getting his stake. He would not be denied. Yeah. "I will not be denied," he said out loud.

"Right on, my brother," said the bartender. "You want another one?"

"One more."

Think. Think. Wait a minute! He couldn't kill Potter! The girl might get the blame, she was the one with the motive. Then the money would get all tied up someplace else.

More court. More lawyers.

Tears of frustration came to his eyes. Was this the end? All he needed was his money. Now Potter was trying to steal it. It was Red's score, nobody else's!

But these people kept getting in his way, one after the other, popping up like ducks in a shooting gallery!

He heard the ringer go off on the floor over there, screams of joy. It went on and on. A big score.

It hurt so bad, to be impeded like this. To be told "no," when it was the only thing that felt good in the whole world. He was jumping out of his fucking skin. If he could make Potter go away, all that would be left was the girl. Potter had had his chance today. He could have dropped the case and looked like a loving grandpa. It would have been the right thing to do. He was a lawyer himself, why didn't he use his own judgment instead of relying on that prick Riesner?

The bartender slapped the shot down in front of him. Red barely had the cash to cover it. He looked at the glass before he chugged it down and there was a trace of lipstick on the lip. He'd almost drunk out of it! Furious, he set it back down. He felt like shit. Like a loser. He wiped his fingers on the napkin and got up to leave. . . .

And over there on the casino floor he caught a glimpse of Nina Reilly marching along, tight skirt and a silk blouse, very sexy girl, and here came young Jessie the Washoe-Armenian Marine—good grief—who was the center of all this, striding along behind her. And a big middle-aged Native American woman by her side, holding a baby. And the blond detective, van Wagoner. And the Korean doc, and then the Chinese pseudo-husband hove into view. It was a fucking U.N. parade!

He slid off the barstool and threw down just enough for the drink and followed them, not really thinking about what he was going to do, just interested. Maybe Kenny Leung would veer off and go somewhere, leave the crowd he was always with, go somewhere so that Red could get at him.

Leung. The loose end. He hadn't shown any sign of recognition when he'd seen Red, dressed in business clothes, during the first court appearance, and Leung hadn't shown up for this last hearing at all. But the danger from him was now worse, because now Amanda was dead, and Red was linked to her. Leung could still put it together. The Glock was out in the trunk.

Staying behind them in the crowd, he saw them get in the line for the buffet. They were going to eat dinner like ordinary people, chat and spoon chocolate mousse into their mouths like the world wasn't crashing around Red.

Then, suddenly, he understood the gift that fate had brought him. He couldn't get Kenny Leung tonight, but he could take out the next duck in the gallery.

He felt a thrill run through him, that thrill like forces in the universe were aligning just for his benefit. Lady Luck was pushing her way through the clouds and shining on him again. His luck had turned.

He looked at his watch. Six-forty-five.

He could take care of the whole thing while they were eating dinner. Easy.

And young Jessie would have her alibi.

. . .

He knew Potter was staying at Caesars. He had followed him there the night before. He knew where the man liked to park, on a side street up a few blocks from the hotel. Who knew why he avoided the big lot behind, but it worked for Red.

On his way through the casino, he picked up a plastic cup, filling it with a few quarters from his pocket, studiously avoiding the cameras he knew about and anyone familiar. Then he hauled, catching up with Potter at the elevator.

"Hey there, how you doing," he said. "Strange day in court today." They had chatted a couple of times with Riesner hovering in the background just before court.

"Very draining. I didn't know you were staying here," Potter said. He looked surprised, but not suspicious.

"Long drive back and forth from Reno." Potter nodded. "Even brought the wife," Red went on, smiling.

While they waited together for the elevator to arrive, he rattled his empty coin holder until Potter said something sympathetic.

"Oh, no. You misunderstand," Red said. "I cashed in. Tonight definitely qualifies as one of my best nights ever." Not yours, though, even if you don't know it yet. Really, everything made him want to laugh all of a sudden, and the effort of restraining his chuckles made him shake.

They started in on the topic of gambling. Potter didn't think much of it, he declared. "The stock market's always been my game."

"Same thing on a bigger scale," Red said.

"I never thought about it that way."

"Oh, sure. Same principle applies, what I call the uncertainty factor." Brring. They were going up.

Potter looked vaguely curious. "And what's that?"

"Well, people buy stocks when they're uncertain. They sell when they're uncertain. When the market's way up, they're happy and they don't buy or sell. No action, loss of faith. So down it goes."

"You've read up on the topic, I see. But what's that got to do with gambling?"

"Gamblers are uncertainty junkies, just like investors. They like the drama. The part where investors get happy and sit on their money? That doesn't last long with a gambler. They crave the thrill too much. They go back in the game, winning and losing. Mostly losing." He laughed. "Now, me," he said quickly as the car began to slow, "I'm a variation on the type, the type that doesn't miss the excitement of losing. I only play to win."

"Everybody plays to win."

"Everybody else loses. I win."

Potter smiled. "You and every other gambler with a foolproof method."

Red shrugged. "Believe it or not."

Potter stepped out of the elevator, holding his hand in the door to keep the doors from closing. "Okay, I'll bite. What's your game?"

Red laughed. "Well, it's not something I tell everyone, but I don't mind if you want to try to pry it out of me over a drink. Forget about your troubles in court today. We won't even talk about that. You can give me some tips on investing my winnings. . . ."

"I don't think I can offer a similar assurance of winning in that case. But I'd like a drink. And you're right, I don't want to talk about today."

Red forced a chuckle. "Okay, then. Drop by my room. . . . Hmm, no. My wife's taking a nap in there. Tell you what, I'll meet you out front. I'll walk you to a place only the locals know about. Busy, good drinks, not far. Your treat."

Potter checked his watch. "Give me five minutes. I'll meet you out front."

Elated, Red punched the button and the doors closed. He was thinking, I'm on the big roll now. A big one.

Like drinking good whiskey. Like screwing his pretty wife on a beach. It was so easy to tie just the right fly to reel in a fellow gambler. Potter didn't really expect to hear that Red knew just the way to win at gambling. He thought he'd amuse himself at Red's expense, have a hearty laugh back in his room later. Maybe one percent of him hoped for a useful tip, the unregenerate gambler percent. And then, setting up to meet in a public place, it sounded so innocent, even if it also fit Red's purposes, which were far from innocent.

Red got off at the fourteenth floor, one above Potter's, and then hurried down the stairway, taking the steps two at a time. He checked the gun, which was fully loaded, screwed the silencer onto it, and stuck it back into the shopping bag he carried. Then he popped a couple uppers.

"Some things I've been thinking about," Atchison Potter said as they left the building. "Although I don't have much time for it, I have done some reading on gambling. If you bet a hundred an hour on roulette, just to use an example, in the long run you will lose five bucks an hour. In the short run, you might be way up, or way down. I'm talking about commitment here. You stay committed, you lose. Now, that's not been true with the stock market. Until lately, anyway."

He was a talker. Good. That way, Red could concentrate on what he needed to do. It was too quiet out here. He wanted witnesses and he wanted this done fast, before the lawyer and her clients finished their meal.

"You ever play roulette?" Potter asked.

"My all-time favorite game," Red said, scanning the street. For some reason, things were quiet this evening. Shit. "But I work up to it, play some blackjack first, usually. I love the silver ball, that sound it makes while the wheel is spinning, when you're thinking, hoping, no, maybe you're convinced this time is it, you're going to win. For me, it always comes down to Red. Red, Three, Odd. What do you bet, or don't you play?"

"I bet a few on the wheel last night. My son's birthday. My age. The usual."

"How'd you do?"

"I won't say I always won, but I agree, roulette has satisfactions that go beyond winning. It's so tantalizing. When you put your chips down on a number, you know the odds are poor and you don't care. You're betting this time is the charm. That's the allure. It feels so good."

Ah. Potter was a gambler, all right.

"Yes," Red said. "It's a noble game. I read a column once," he said. "A guy called roulette the perfect game for someone who wants to meet destiny face-to-face."

"And you've got a foolproof method," Potter said.

"Yes, I do," Red answered. "Hmm. I just had a thought." He stopped walking.

"What?"

"There's a big-screen TV at a place down the street about a mile. We could watch a game while we talk." He nodded toward the casino across the street. "My car's out back. About seven miles from here," he joked. "Mind a walk?"

"No need. Mine's right here," Potter said, pointing up the street.

"Excellent." He followed Potter to a white Toyota Corolla rental car and got in, feeling rage rise up in him when Potter took his time getting settled behind the wheel. Time was short. He needed to get this thing done. "Make a right at the corner."

"About blackjack," Potter said. "Basic strategy, that what you use? Because I know all that."

"Oh, no. Much more sophisticated than that. My wife's uncle taught me the cards. A real pro. A professional gambler."

"I read some books on it, but they didn't do me any good." Potter fingered his jaw. "I need a shave. I'm a twice-a-day man, like Nixon."

"I lost a bundle over the years playing blackjack," Red said. "People who write those books, you know, how to win? I read them all. And you know what I decided? I decided, you can't win. I decided the bastards writing the books know full well you can't win. Probably they're all shills for the gaming industry," he said. "Wouldn't surprise me. Park here, okay?"

"I thought you said you had a surefire method of winning, not losing," Potter said, pulling over to the curb.

"I win with slots."

"Impossible."

"No, it isn't," Red said calmly. "And now, I'm going to reveal my secret. There's only one way to win," he said. "You cheat. Rig it to favor you instead of the house."

He reached into his shopping bag while Potter was busy parking and pulled on his gloves. Potter had his eyes where they belonged, on the car in front. Wouldn't want to scrape the shiny paint on the rental car! Forces aligned, shifted, watched over him. . . . He waited for just the right moment, then pulled out the Glock and shot.

But the gun didn't fire. The safety was on—

Potter screamed something, reaching for the gun, struggling with him. The car bammed into the parked car in front, still in gear. Red felt his neck spasm and fear cut through him.

Potter lunged for the door but Red dragged him back and got an arm around his neck, the other hand reaching around blindly for the Glock, come on come on, and he felt the cold steel and within an instant, he had the safety off and the gun pointed at Potter's head.

He let go of Potter. Potter fell against the door. If it had been open, he would have fallen to the pavement and escaped.

But the door held. Potter scrabbled at the handle and Red took aim and shot twice.

Potter gave one final lurch. Both arms flailed out as the bullet entered his brain, and one arm knocked Red's hand.

The gun flew into the back seat.

Potter fell forward and now the horn was blasting. Red tried pulling him off so that he would have a second to hunt for the Glock, but it was too late. The street had suddenly accumulated quite a crowd, and they were all coming his way.

He lunged from the car, pulling the bloody gloves off and stuffing them back in the shopping bag, melting into a crowd of gamblers across the street while a throng piled around the white Corolla.

25

"BARBECUED STEAK, BAKED POTATOES, FRESH green beans with roasted pine nuts, Caesar salad."

"Perfect. I'm glad we didn't stay for the buffet." Paul sprawled in a butterfly chair on the deck right outside the open kitchen door of Nina's house, field binoculars in his hand.

"Actually, I'm hoping you'll do the grilling. I got the coals going before I dropped Bob at Taylor's house."

"Oh ho. It was a setup." For a few more moments he scanned the yard through the binoculars. "I know there's a woodpecker out there. I'm going to nab that sucker."

A flurry of tapping got him out of his chair. "Well, look at that. You've got yourself a three-toed woodpecker visiting this evening."

Nina took a turn looking through the glasses, seeing close-up a black, sharp-beaked bird with a yellow head pecking at a red fir in her backyard. "I didn't know you knew anything about birds."

"Doesn't take much learning to count toes," Paul said. He positioned himself at the barbecue and wrapped a dish towel around his shorts. The steaks sizzled as he dropped them onto the grill.

"So here we are," he said.

"Uh huh."

A chirping started up in the backyard. They allowed the summer evening to wash over them. Lying on the chaise longue with her legs drawn up, Nina felt a sense of great satisfaction. The trees darkened and the clouds faded as the streetlights on Kulow came on. She put the binoculars down and sat on the bench by the table watching Paul cook, sipping a margarita.

"Doc Jun didn't seem to mind having to stay over," Paul said, his back to her.

"What a day. He was great. He came through, but not in a way I ever would have imagined. Poor Dan Potter. I imagine Dr. Jun will always regret not making the diagnosis. I really think Mr. Potter was in shock. You should have seen him with the baby! What a scene!"

"What amazes me is that Amagosian gave Dr. Jun the hint."

"I know! I know! Amazing! To think three generations of the family might have the illness, and no one knew it! Jessie was so frightened. Then to learn there's a treatment!"

"But Potter's still not going to let it go?"

"All he has to do—all Riesner has to do—is file a request to lift the levy on the money, allow the Entry of Judgment to be vacated. But he won't do it, Paul. And Mr. Potter is taking his advice."

"Did you talk to Riesner about it?"

"I had to. To see if some of it was his personal animosity."

"And?"

"He likes me even less now," Nina said.

"So it's not over."

"No. And the good old boys who run Nevada are lurking around in the background too. I'd like to know what they're thinking."

"You sound like you still have plenty of energy. After today, I think I'd be upstairs in bed—"

"With a wet washcloth on my forehead?" Nina said. "Sandy's expression. No. I'm not going to fade out. I've got the momentum now and I'm going to keep it. I told you, I'm changing my style. Going on the attack and staying there."

He brought the steak to the picnic table and she brought out the rest of their dinner. They sat across from each other, yellow candles puddling golden pools of light. She poured two glasses of cold white wine, and they clinked their glasses.

"To summer nights," said Nina.

"Summer nights."

Nina ate slowly, enjoying the meal and Paul's company. He ate with such gusto. He did it like he did everything else, fully absorbed in the moment, every lift of the fork direct and no-nonsense. He looked very good right now, his blond hair a little long at the moment, relaxed.

She was so lonely. And he had done so much for her. She didn't feel the usual pressure from him tonight, and that scared her. She had gotten used to being desired. But she didn't feel Paul's desire now. Was he just tired? Or had he made a decision about them?

So go with the flow.

She intended to let nature take its course. No fancy footwork, no candles—well, maybe one—no sexy underwear tonight. She hadn't organized another seduction scene, she'd been busy practicing law all day and he would understand. Clean sheets and good intentions were the best she could do.

Maybe she would never accept Paul. She needed to find out about that. This was a way to find out. But she knew one thing. No more mourning. She had to stop mourning.

She set the dishes in the sink.

He came in from the deck, carrying the barbecue tongs, and she said, "Paul?"

"Mmm-hmm?"

"Let's turn off the lights and lock up and go upstairs." She waited for a response, but Paul just slipped the tongs into the soapy water as if he hadn't heard her.

"Let's try again," she said. "No more weeping. I promise." She went up to him and put her arms around his neck. "Please," she said. "Give me another chance."

Paul's body didn't react. He reached his hands up and took her arms away. "I don't think you're ready."

She buried her face in his shirt, breathed in his smell.

"It's obvious you don't want me."

She cupped his face in her hands and looked him in the eye. "I can't tell," she said. "Try me. It won't be like last time."

"Don't do this to me," he said. "Stop torturing me." But he let her take his hand and lead him upstairs.

She began to undress and he watched her. When she was down to her panties, she climbed into bed. Hitchcock had followed them in. He sat by the door, his head cocked, trying to decide if he should circle on his rug and lie down to sleep.

Paul still stood in the dusk, uncertain. She could see that he wasn't sure he wanted to come to her.

"I can't live up to him," he said. He reached down and petted Hitchcock. "You know, I think we better not."

"Oh, God, Paul," Nina said. "We're this close to losing each other. Don't give up. Please. Get in bed with me." Paul came slowly to the bed. He sat down, not looking at her. Nina stroked his back, ran her hand through his hair.

He lay down beside her, and she kept rubbing him, his temples, his jawline. His eyes were closed. He was letting her lead, and this was the right way. She nuzzled at his neck. His hand came up and gently, lightly, he traced her lips with his finger.

"You sure this time?" he whispered. "You sure, Nina? Because I can't take any more pushing and pulling."

A sharp knock came at the front door downstairs.

Another knock. Louder.

"There is no way we're going to answer that. No way. It's not Bob," Paul said in a bleak voice, opening his eyes. "You said he was safe at Taylor's."

"We won't answer," she whispered.

Three impatient knocks on the door, and a loud voice. "Police. Anybody home?"

"My clothes," Nina said. She jumped out of the bed and rushed around the room. "Never mind. I'll find something. You answer."

Swearing, Paul was already up, pulling himself back together. She ran her hand over the hair she had rumpled and sent him out the door and down the stairs. He cursed every step of the way.

"If it isn't Sergeant Cheney," Paul said.

Sergeant Cheney pulled up on the waistband of his pants, adjusting the gun at his side, his big brown face impassive. "Hello, Paul. Long time no see. Is this a bad time?"

Paul crossed his arms. "You could say that. So, is this something that can wait? 'Cause, as one old pal to another, I'd sure appreciate that."

"Can't wait," Cheney said, shaking his head. "Won't wait. Gonna invite me in?"

Nina arrived at the door, demurely dressed in a striped shirt and jeans. "What's this about?" she asked. She motioned to Paul and they stepped out onto the porch with Cheney. She closed her door firmly behind her. No warrant, no entry, that was her motto.

"Little matter of a gun," Cheney said. "You know a fellow named Kenny Leung?"

"Uh oh," Paul said. "You finally found Kenny's gun, and not in a good place."

"At the scene of a homicide."

Nina and Paul looked at each other. "Amanda Lewis?" Nina said.

Sergeant Cheney reached a big paw into the pocket of his shirt and pulled out a tiny spiral notebook. He flipped through it. "Man by the name of Atchison Potter. A visitor from Oahu in Hawaii. At six oh eight. This evening. Shot at close range in his rental car just past Caesars, with a nine-millimeter Glock. Recovered at the scene."

"Potter?" Nina's mouth was hanging open. What was happening? Nina thought immediately of Charlie Kemp. Shot. And Amanda Lewis.

Also shot. With the Glock? All connected to the jackpot. All connected to Kenny and Jessie.

She could see Potter holding Gabe just a few hours before. He might have come around. He hadn't deserved to die like that, no matter what he had put Jessie through.

She thought wildly, Paul didn't get here until seven-thirty or later. Her eyes went to him, unguarded, and she was afraid he saw what she was thinking. She held the door tightly. Cheney shifted from foot to foot.

"Are you really going to make me stand out here on the porch and talk to you? Don't you worry about the neighbors?"

"Yes," Nina said, "and no, I'm not worried about my neighbors. I'm sorry, Sergeant. It's just my policy not to let police inside my home unless there's a very good reason or a warrant."

"There's good reason," Cheney said. Paul and Nina had worked with him before. The relationship had been friendly, but Nina was feeling a difference now,

Cheney went on, "The gun was registered to Leung's father, who owns a local restaurant called the Inn of Five Happinesses. His father admitted loaning the gun to Leung months ago. Leung said he wanted to do some target shooting for relaxation. Apparently, that's a big activity on weekends in Silicon Valley." Cheney shook his head. "Nothing like firing off a gun to make you feel real calm. Anyway, Mr. Leung helped me find his son. They had a phone number for Kenny Leung logged on their caller ID. Called him up, and he answered. One thing that did come up was that Mr. Ken Leung had surrendered his gun to a Mr. van Wagoner a couple of weeks ago. Is that a fact?"

"Paul, wait," Nina said. "You don't have to say anything."

"Let's get this cleared up. He gave me the gun."

"Well, grab your jacket. I need a couple hours out of your life."

"Am I under suspicion?"

"I'll wait in my car." He held up his hand, fingers open. "Five minutes," he said. He went out to the street where the cruiser was waiting.

"I'm not a suspect, or Cheney wouldn't have turned his back on me and wouldn't be waiting in the cruiser," Paul said as they went back into the living room. "Where's my wallet?" He finished dressing rapidly.

"I'll come too."

"I don't need a lawyer. I'll learn as much as I tell."

"Don't implicate Jessie," Nina said. Paul laughed curtly.

"Always on the lookout for the client," he said.

"Kemp, Amanda Lewis, Potter—I don't know who is next on this death list. Maybe it's Jessie and Kenny."

"Maybe one of them is the shooter."

"No. I don't believe that. It's much more likely that they're in danger. Paul, Cheney's going to want to know where Jessie and Kenny are. He's going to insist on interviewing them."

"Should I refuse?"

"No. No. He'll arrest you. But—tell him I'll produce them both tomorrow morning at his office instead. See if he'll go along. If not, do what you have to do."

"Will do." At the door he stopped and turned to her. His eyes looked puzzled, hurt. "It wasn't going to work, up there in your bedroom."

"It was just bad luck." But she didn't run to him. Bad luck, and they had lost. They both knew it.

The South Lake Tahoe police station was in the same courthouse complex where Paul had spent the day. Cheney escorted Paul through the buzz-through door, past the curious stares of two or three officers on duty, into his office, which bore a photograph of his pretty young wife and not much else other than two chairs, beige, and stacks of paper and file boxes.

Paul felt very different than he had felt the last time he had been here. A delicate balance between cops had been upset. Now Cheney sat on the high side of the seesaw, and Paul sat down in the dirt with the dirty people. He had a desperate urge to defend himself, and a consciousness of the strangeness of his position.

After all, he had done nothing wrong. Not in this case, anyway.

"Storage," Cheney said, noticing his glance. "My pending files. No case is ever dead for me until I solve it."

"I remember. The girls who disappeared in winter." A few years before, Cheney had allowed Paul to examine some old files that eventually led to the solution of a serial murder case. That had been back when Paul's days as a homicide detective in San Francisco still felt fresh, and being fired from that job still felt okay, as if the rebellion and insubordination he could not help were somehow symbols of something weightier than immaturity.

"Yeah, that's right. You were helpful with that, and I appreciated it. Well, for every one solved, there's another one waiting in these boxes. I keep 'em handy. Never know when insight or inspiration might strike."

"You're looking fitter than when I last saw you."

"Oh, yeah, that's my wife. She's got me on the Omega Three plan. Certain kind of eggs only, grain-fed, some special hormones. Black bread for toast. A Mediterranean emphasis. She's twenty years younger than me, you know. I got to run to keep up with her. I just turned fifty-four, and she says she wants me to live to ninety, but let me tell you, I do sneak out for the occasional cheeseburger."

"Otherwise, why live?" Paul asked.

"Now, about the Glock. Okay to tape this?"

Paul told the tape recorder that it was fine, and they went through the preliminaries.

"I did take Kenny Leung's weapon. He brought it into Nina Reilly's law offices, and I didn't feel it was an appropriate accessory."

Cheney pulled out a notebook. "When was this?"

Paul gave him the rundown on Kenny's 9-millimeter, when he took it, when he saw it last, trying to keep out privileged information. But he had to explain about the marriage. It was damned embarrassing. It made them all sound like con men. Cheney listened to the whole story, blinking, writing down occasional notes.

"You put it in the right-hand pocket of your jacket. You wore that jacket the rest of the night. Took it off when you got home, and no more gun."

"That's right."

"Ms. Reilly, Kenny Leung, and Jessie Potter knew you had it. Saw you put it in that pocket."

"A pro might have been able to tell I was carrying from the weight and the outline," Paul said. "I brushed against a dozen or more people walking across the casino floor when we went back for the check. I stood around for an hour in the banquet room waiting for the check to be handed over."

That led to a whole lot of talk, as Paul patiently went through what he knew about the legal dispute between Atchison and Jessie Potter. He asked for water.

"So Jeff Riesner's his lawyer." Cheney sighed when he came back with a paper cup. "All I needed."

"Have fun."

"You talk to Jessie Potter about the gun?"

"Why pick on her?"

"She sat next to you in the car."

"I asked her later and she said she didn't take it."

"Hmm. Let's get some addresses and phone numbers."

Cheney didn't accept Nina's offer to have Jessie and Kenny go to his office. He wanted to know where they were right that moment, and when Paul realized Cheney would arrest him if he didn't give the information, he described the location of Nina's property. That blew the desert trailer for Kenny and Jessie. It wouldn't be safe for them any longer, when the address went into the reports and onto the radio waves. It got later. Paul yawned. If he returned to Nina's bed now, she would be sleeping a sleep she really needed, since she had to go back next door tomorrow to deal with some more hell breaking loose. He wasn't going to make it back tonight. What was it, an unlucky star?

"You do believe me about the gun, don't you?"

"I don't disbelieve you," Cheney said. "You're an ex-cop. You know the story."

"Well, don't waste your time pursuing that line. I didn't use Leung's gun to kill Potter. It was stolen." He knew he sounded defensive. He wondered how many people had sat across from Cheney over the years feeling the same way, innocent and yet guilty. Shaky, not because the police had caught them in a crime, but simply because now they were in the official sight. All the dead, forgotten corpses in their pasts were going to reanimate and crawl to the surface, or in Paul's case, be dug up and reassembled, since he had left the body of the man he had killed nearly eight months before in more than one piece.

Taking a deep breath he hoped was not visible to Cheney, he reminded himself about all the good reasons for that man to die. As a result of an action he still considered righteous, now, and forevermore, he belonged in a new place, on the wrong side of the law, when all his life had been about seeing justice done.

Wasn't life surprising.

"How about a rundown on your activities from, say"—Cheney consulted his notes—"six-thirty this evening."

He concentrated on facts. So soothing. "I left the courthouse with Nina Reilly around five-thirty. We met several other people at the main Caesars entrance and went together to the Caesars buffet. I'd say we got into line at just about six-forty-five."

"Do you happen to know where Jessie Potter was at this time?"

"With the group."

Cheney scratched out a note.

"How long were you there?"

"The line at the buffet didn't suit me. The place was mobbed and it didn't look like we'd be seated until the next morning."

"You didn't stay for the buffet."

"No. I left after about five minutes to go upstairs and have a shower and change. Nina and I agreed to meet at her place for dinner instead. You already know this, if you've talked to Kenny Leung on the phone."

"He did mention you left."

"And that Jessie Potter stayed?"

"That's what he claims."

"Until when?"

Cheney didn't need to consult his notes. "After eight o'clock."

"And the shooting took place when?"

"Seven-twenty."

"So they're covered. They were in the group. Nina decided to leave at the same time. She picked up her son from summer camp, drove him over to his friend's, visited for a while, and went home." Thank God, Nina had also been with people the whole time. "We met at her house about eight-thirty. At dusk."

"So, how long would you say you were up in your room?"

"Seven to about eight-fifteen. No alibi, but I don't have a motive either. Lucky for me."

"But you were the last person known to be in possession of the weapon."

"Right," said Paul, intensely disliking this turn in the conversation. Why hadn't he stayed to eat with the others? Would his life from here on out be a series of disrupted sexual encounters with Nina that had him ready to explode, all mixed up with invitations from the police? Was it possible that during the course of his investigation of Atchison Potter's murder, the simple fact that Paul did not have an alibi would cause Sergeant Chency to look further into past events and relationships . . . and wonder what had become of a certain person no one seemed able to find? Cheney was persistent enough. Paul believed that. He wished he didn't.

"And then you did what?"

"Drove straight to Nina's place."

He'd like to get his hands on that soft-bellied Kenny right about now, give him a poke in that pudgy flesh for getting him into this.

"Where's your own gun?" Cheney was saying.

"In a locked case in the locked trunk of my car. Sergeant, forget about me. Let's talk about a shooting in Minden a couple of weeks ago, and the shooting at Regan Beach last week. My guess is you're going to find that the Glock was the gun used in all the shootings. It's the same guy."

Cheney set his paper and pen down. He leaned forward and said, "Been withholding evidence, Paul?"

"No. I'm just one step ahead of you in making some connections. I think we're looking for a biker, a biker who has been seen driving a gold Porsche Boxster."

"A high-income biker," Cheney said.

Paul found himself spilling his guts to Cheney. He told him about the lineup at the Greed Machines the night of the jackpot—not the lineup of the three banks, but the human lineup. Amanda Lewis and her biker friend. Kenny. Charlie Kemp. He described the biker as Kenny had described him to Paul, and Cheney got excited and went out of the room and made some calls to Nevada. Then he told Cheney about Kenny being attacked and stalked. They talked about Atchison Potter's lawsuit.

Midnight came and went. Paul was hoarse.

"I knew it was a good idea to drag your ass down here, the minute I heard your name pop up," Cheney said, clicking off the tape recorder at last.

"What happens now?"

"Well, I'm gonna share something with you, Paul. We have at least one witness to the Potter shooting who says she saw the shooter. She's working up a description with our artist as we speak."

Paul's heart beat faster. "What did she see?"

"She said he wore a baseball cap and she couldn't see his face too well, but he had a goatee and a ponytail."

"It's him."

"Yeah. So, to answer your question, now we pick up the biker."

26

If Nina was beat at court the next morning, if she had gotten up at dawn to get on the phone with Paul and Jessie and Kenny and Cheney, Jeff Riesner nevertheless took the prize for most frazzled of all. Still red-eyed and sniffly from the pepper spray, he looked positively grief-stricken. True, Atchison Potter's death was a calamity for him. She might not like Riesner, but she knew how it felt to have a client murdered.

And then there was his case, which had evaporated with Potter's death. Potter's need for vengeance had animated it in the first place. Now what remained were ashes.

Or so she hoped. She had done some legal research at seven A.M. in an arcane area of the law called survival of actions. She was trying to find out what could happen next, legally. It wasn't easy. The cause of action for wrongful death suits did die when the plaintiff died, but in this case Potter had obtained a judgment. Could the case somehow continue, with the money, assuming the judgment was executed, going into Potter's estate to be probated along with his other assets?

Which brought up questions she couldn't answer yet, such as whether Potter had a will and who he had left his money to. And the fact that he had a grandson who might be a pretermitted heir with a claim on Potter's estate. She had even tried to call Ruth Anzai, the lawyer who had won the judgment for Potter in Hawaii, forgetting it was the middle of the night there. All she had gotten was a recording.

There was only one good thing in this whole mess: they couldn't even think about nailing Jessie or Kenny for this, because the time of Potter's death was known, and they had been eating dinner at the

Caesars buffet in full view of hundreds of people. It was a monster break.

Cheney wanted to see Kenny and Jessie as soon as the court session was over. He was taking no chances. There he sat in the audience, solid, sleepy-looking. Outside the courtroom door a portable metal detector had been set up, manned by two uniformed police officers.

And then there was Paul. He sat right beside her, but a gulf had opened between them. The case had beaten them somehow. It had interfered with Paul and her.

They weren't going to make it. She didn't have time to care right now.

She looked around at all the reporters jamming the back rows. Flashbulbs went off. Deputy Kimura had called in a second bailiff to control the crowd, and the doors were long shut. She had had to duck in through the jury door instead of the main door.

Matt had called the office just before she left. He had heard about Potter. She had felt the old accusation in his voice. He couldn't help it, but whenever violence came anywhere near her, he took it as a personal threat against his family. He had told her that she ought to get out of law entirely, and it had hurt even though she knew he would calm down later.

"All rise." Amagosian appeared on the bench in his black robes. His face was stern. He didn't like commotions, maybe because he was so excitable himself.

He took a look at the crowd, which was still rustling papers and closing briefcases and finishing sentences, and he said, glaring at all of them, "This is a continuation from yesterday of the hearing in *Potter v. Potter*. If there is any disturbance from any person, that person will immediately be evicted from this court."

Quiet spread over the room. Amagosian looked at Riesner, who was on his feet.

"Your statement for the record, Counsel," he said. He looked at the stenographer.

"Atchison Potter, the judgment creditor in this action, was shot to death in the casino district just after seven o'clock last night, Your Honor," Riesner said. "He was shot in the temple and was dead at the scene when the ambulance arrived, murdered by an unknown assailant. The police are investigating."

"For the record, I have spoken with Sergeant Cheney of the Lake Tahoe police department, and I can confirm these statements myself," Amagosian said. "The court wishes to express its condolences to Mr. Potter's family. The court wishes to express its regret that this man should have left his home and come here to our town and lost his life here. It is a sad moment for this court."

"He will be missed," Riesner said. He bowed his head. They all bowed their heads. It was sad, and wrong. Yesterday, Nina had thought Potter had been very shaken by Dr. Jun's testimony. He might have somehow made up with Jessie. She bowed her head, unable to see clearly through the tangle of family and heartache.

After a moment or two, Amagosian said, "I suppose the question we face is how to proceed with this hearing. Mr. Potter was actually testifying yesterday, and due for cross-examination today. We can't complete the hearing, obviously. Which doesn't even address the larger issue, which is whether the action can proceed at this time. Counsel, will you please address these questions. The court is aware that you have had little time to prepare."

"I have spent the whole night thinking about these things, Judge," Riesner said. "It is the first time I have lost a client." He sounded pretty broken up. Nina felt softened by this show of humanity. She had a motion to dismiss the writ proceeding prepared, but she didn't want to have to use it. Maybe Riesner would gracefully let the case go. She kept her papers inside her briefcase, along with the pepper spray. It must have stung very badly, and she appreciated that he hadn't made a stink about it. Maybe he understood that he had asked for it. Maybe he was biding his time.

Anyway, the problem was, what now?

Riesner said, "What hurts the most, Judge, was that Mr. Potter felt very strongly about all this. I know he would have wanted to finish this matter, to get a resolution. Those were the last words I heard from him, in fact, to finish it."

"What do you suggest, Counsel?"

"Let's finish it. I will waive any cross-examination and waive further argument, and submit the issue for decision."

"Just a moment," Nina said, getting up. "I hope we are going to be consulted on this. First of all, it is we who called for this hearing to object to issuance of the Writ of Execution. It seems to me that there is no way to finish this hearing without the participation and assent of the judgment-debtor."

"Finish it and submit it for decision, Your Honor," Riesner insisted.

"For what purpose?" Nina said. "I don't understand."

"The money should go into Mr. Potter's estate."

"But the only heir I am aware of is the little boy, Gabe Potter. The matter is moot, Your Honor. Gabe Potter will receive the benefit of the money either way. We are in a gray area of the law. Let us be sensible and close this chapter in Gabe's life."

"Not so fast. There is at least one other claimant to the estate, Judge," Riesner said. "I have a copy of a valid contract which inures to the heirs, assigns, and estate of Mr. Potter in the event of his death. The amount is just a little more than three million dollars."

That amount sounded familiar to Nina. She tried to remember where she had heard it before.

"Let me see that," Amagosian said. Riesner handed him a copy of several sheets of paper, then, with a suspicious flourish, gave Nina a copy too.

"Oh, no," she said, reading it. "I don't think so."

"As Counsel is attempting to point out, my law firm is the primary creditor with a claim against the estate. Our agreement with Mr. Potter was that in the event that this proceeding concluded with a favorable outcome for Mr. Potter, he would pay to this firm forty percent of the monies currently under lien."

Nina said, "Well, now we see the reason for the crocodile tears and the attempt to keep this hearing going. But even if Mr. Riesner's firm is entitled to such a fee, the law provides for a contingency like this. He can bill the hours at his usual hourly rate and simply collect from the other assets of Mr. Potter's estate."

"And I might consider doing that," Riesner said. "If he had any other assets. Unfortunately, Mr. Potter left only debts."

A buzz of astonishment enveloped the room, and Amagosian said sharply, "Quiet! Quiet!" He banged down the gavel. When he could be heard again, he said, "You say this is the only potential asset you could collect any fees from?"

"That is correct. Mr. Potter suffered major reverses in the stock market recently. Apple Computers, I believe he said was the problem."

"Your Honor," Nina said, "I move to set aside the levy on funds awarded to Jessie Potter presently held in California Republic Bank. I move to dismiss the request for issuance of the Writ of Execution. I have prepared a short motion, but due to the swiftness of events, I could not prepare points and authorities."

She served Riesner with the papers and passed a copy to the judge's clerk.

"I will not agree to that," Riesner said. "I move to substitute in my firm, Caplan, Stamp, Powell, and Riesner, as the party of record in place of Atchison Potter. I have prepared that motion, but I also did not have time to prepare supporting points and authorities." He passed over some pleadings to Nina.

Amagosian looked at the new pile of papers on his desk. He seemed angry and confused. He didn't know what to do either.

"Your Honor, if I may . . ." Nina started, but he stopped her with a glare as impervious as Lucite.

"I am going to continue this entire matter for two days," he said. "We are going to have to determine whether Mr. Riesner's firm can step in here. I will need points and authorities from both sides." There was a deflated sigh from the audience. The show would continue. Amagosian went on with the details, setting dates, setting a new hearing time. Nina made herself get it all down.

Court adjourned. She packed up her briefcase and said to Jessie and Paul, "Meet you at the police station. Sergeant Cheney said to come as soon as the hearing was over."

John Jovanic came up to her. He was sweating in the hot courtroom and his big burly body didn't fit the expensive suit.

"Congratulations," he said. "I like your style. I'd like to talk to you about getting you to handle some of our legal work at Prize's."

"I'm not licensed in Nevada."

"Weren't you working on the Kiss My Foot campaign?"

"Marlis Djina is the attorney of record on that."

"Well, anyway, maybe we could give you a boost somewhere."

"In return for what?"

"I could be in touch on that."

"You sound just like Atchison Potter when he tried to buy Byron Eppley, Mr. Jovanic. Haven't we had enough of that?"

Jovanic just laughed. "Fine," he said. "Didn't think you'd be interested."

As she was leaving, she looked over at the row of Nevada casino people who had become regulars at the hearing. They were standing together. Jovanic was explaining something in that good-humored way of his. Ully Miller, the Gaming Control Board inspector, was deep in thought. Thomas Munzinger was looking at his watch like he couldn't wait to get out of there. Andy Doig, his red hair flaming even in the dull light, and the two lawyers were listening to Jovanic. Gary Gray, the slots supervisor at Prize's, was just leaving the courtroom, tearing off his red bow tie as he flung open the door.

They'd all be in meetings for the rest of the day, figuring out the P.R. angles, the legal strategies, the money impact of Potter's death. That was what they did. They went to work, sat in meetings, went home to their families. They were ordinary people, caught, as she was, in an extraordinary situation. No baseball caps here, she thought, at least that's not the kind of trouble they cause.

27

"Look at the telephone messages," Sandy said as Nina came in after lunch, Paul, Kenny, and Jessie behind her. "It's a callback. You people wait out here a minute."

Nina flopped into the chair behind the desk, slipped off her shoes, and picked up the pile of messages. On top was the one from Alex's mother Sandy had wanted her to see.

"Alex is gone. Funeral Saturday at 11, St. John Vianney Episcopal Church," said the note.

Just like that. The pale, smart teenager had left this earth. Nina took it hard. The words of the message blurred in front of her.

So many losses! Where were they, the ones who left early?

Alex's mother answered the phone. "At noon," she said. "I was there with him. His soccer coach was there, his best friend, his aunt and uncle, his grandfather. He was very comfortable. No pain at all. He had been unconscious for two days."

Nina shivered. It had just happened. Alex's mother had just been brushed by the chilling wind.

"Don't be sad," Alex's mother said. "We were prepared. Alex left gently. It's all right. Don't cry."

"He—was such a—great kid."

"I just wanted to thank you. For showing me that Alex had a right to decide what came after. The medical school already has his body. He wanted to make his mark. I'm willing to take the chance with him— that it'll do some good."

"That's wonderful. It's what he wanted."

"We worked it out at home. It wasn't the sort of thing you work out in a law office."

"It must be so hard for you."

"I'm going to volunteer for the Leukemia Society and follow the research. Alex never had a chance to have children. But, you see, his cells—his living DNA—may save other children someday."

"I'm so sorry," Nina said.

"Thank you for caring so much, Nina. I'll see you Saturday. We're celebrating his wonderful life. Don't wear black."

"What hit you?" Paul said, coming in and closing the door. Nina was wiping her eyes with the tissue she kept for clients.

"Alex. He died." She went to him and let herself be held. For some time they stood there while she let the tears fall onto his shoulder.

"You should go home," he said. "It's bringing back some memories."

"No. I'll be all right now." Awkwardly, she moved away from him. "Too much to do. Let's get Kenny and Jessie in here."

Kenny was lugging his laptop, no case, just the black Mac Powerbook. He would be one of the first people to have computer implants, Nina imagined. His eyes were bloodshot. He had slept in his clothes, if he had slept. They all looked ten years older. Stress, the murders, the court battles, the interview with Cheney today—and Jessie had just started Gabe on colchicine that morning.

"All right," Nina said. "You've been carrying that thing close to your chest all morning like it has the Mona Lisa inside it. What is this information you weren't ready to talk to Sergeant Cheney about?"

"Kemp definitely knew," Kenny said, plopping down in a chair and booting up.

"He knew the jackpot would hit?" Paul asked.

"That's right."

"You're sure of this?"

"If I had the access Kemp's co-conspirator must have had to some crucial information, I could do it myself."

"You mean the hypothetical insider you've been talking about?"

"That's him. He has to exist. Kemp couldn't pull this off without the insider."

"Are we all thinking the same thing?" Nina said. "That the biker is the insider?"

"As soon as you do find him, we can kiss the money good-bye,"

Jessie said. "Kenny doesn't seem to care about that. Gabe's medical care, Kenny's debts, your legal fee, Nina." Jessie's voice broke. "Everything."

"Oh, I'm very mindful of that," Kenny said, looking surprised. He took his glasses off and rubbed them on his sleeve. "And I would never do anything to hurt you, Jessie. You should be mindful of that, too. But the law, that's Nina's department. I'm sure she'll figure out some legal way to keep the money, because you didn't do anything wrong."

"Kenny, who rigged the machine doesn't matter. If it was rigged, Jessie won't get the money," Nina said. "I can tell you Nevada law is quite clear on that."

"But it wasn't rigged," Kenny said.

"It wasn't?" Jessie said, frantic. "Was it or wasn't it? If I wasn't dying to hear the end of this story I would kick you right out of here into your City of Gold to rot and play with imaginary dollies for the rest of your life, Ken Leung!"

Kenny chuckled. "I've discovered something so interesting," he said. "Real life. I don't need the City anymore."

That fist of hers went up, clenched tight. "Then tell us! Go on, spoil it!"

Kenny put up a fist to match hers. Then, slowly, tenderly, he opened his hand and wrapped his fingers around hers. He gave her a re-assuring smile.

Nobody moved while the gesture registered with Jessie. Startled but clearly moved, she relaxed her hand slowly, pulling it away gently and settling it into her lap. She tipped her head up to study Kenny, and then down again to study her hand.

"To return to the point," Paul said, clearing his throat. "What makes you say the machine wasn't rigged, Kenny? You just told us Kemp knew the jackpot was coming. How could he know it, if he didn't rig it?"

"This," Kenny said, holding up some printed pages. "I got the first clue straight out of an online local paper called the *Nevada Appeal*. According to a story on gaming from several years ago, some of the slots are programmed so that the random number generators are not actually random, but cyclical."

"Cyclical? What do you mean?" Paul asked.

"They run through the same long series of plays over and over again. I mean, we are talking about thousands and thousands of numbers. But not random. Cyclical."

"But that's illegal!" Nina said.

Kenny shook his head. "Here's a copy I printed out of the article.

Nevada Appeal, September 24, 1997. The reporter's name was Geoff Dornan." He handed the papers to Nina.

She read with growing fascination, while in the room around her Jessie curled and uncurled fingers around the arm of her chair, Kenny booted up and tapped on his laptop, and Paul coughed, each trying to give her time, each feigning patience. She passed the story on to Paul, who read it with pained attention. While she waited, she leaned over to see that Kenny was reviewing local news articles on gambling he had downloaded from tahoe.com on his computer.

"It's legal," Kenny said, looking up. "Like it's legal to set slot machines so they give a seventy-five-percent return. Or the way it's legal to program sevens so they line up a lot more often than randomly on the line above or the line below, to keep the sucker playing. Your department, Nina. You figure the legal part out.

"Now, this long series of numbers is generated from a source code that is kept under lock and key at Global Gaming. The security level has to be high. But if you had the source code and a laptop computer, you could go around to certain slot machines and find where they are in the sequence. Say, the sequence was twenty percent through its cycle. You wouldn't bother with that one, because there are other variables like the one they call the action—the number of times the button gets pushed, or the handle gets pulled, per hour. With so many numbers to go, you couldn't really predict when the machine would hit.

"But let's say you keep checking a lot of machines, and finally you find one that's ninety-five or ninety-eight percent through the cycle. You can look at average action figures, if you're an insider, and you can predict within, say, an hour or so when that machine will hit the big one."

"But that would mean that Global Gaming is rigging its own machines to control the payoffs," Nina said slowly.

"Right," Paul said grimly, "to be sure they don't have to make too many big payouts in any one year."

"But—wouldn't something so important be picked up by the big newspaper chains? Gannett? Hearst?" Nina asked.

"Hear the thuds?" Paul said. "That's us losing chunks of naiveté."

"So an insider took advantage of knowledge about a machine that was already legally rigged at the factory," Nina said, thinking hard. "That's what you're suggesting?"

"Right. Kemp told me he had already lost three thousand dollars in that machine. He had been there a while. He may have been starting to doubt what his boss told him, or he just had to hit the head. Many a man has been undone by his bladder." Kenny smiled triumphantly. "Am I good or am I good?"

"Then," Paul said, "the insider works at Global Gaming."

"Munzinger must have access to all the codes," Nina said. "Or it's one of the people he supervises."

"I don't know who has the access," Kenny said. "Maybe the operations people at the casinos. I doubt it, though. Maybe the Nevada Gaming Control Board. They oversee Global Gaming's operations."

"Why did Atchison Potter have to die, though?" Paul said. "I can see that this insider goes after Kemp. Some kind of falling-out among thieves. And if our insider is the man in the goatee, he was with Amanda Lewis right before the jackpot hit. Maybe she knew too much. Or more likely, she heard Kemp was killed and decided to bail or speak up. He couldn't afford that, and so he killed her. My money's on the man with the goatee for Charlie Kemp and Amanda Lewis."

"Which is a problem," Kenny admitted. "I hacked into Global Gaming's Human Resources files and found a directory with employee pictures. I can tell you, he wasn't in the group. I also checked the Gaming Control Board and Prize's."

"Then this whole thing falls apart," Paul said. "Unless he was wearing a disguise. I mean, people only do that in old British mysteries. Sherlock Holmes."

"It's not so outrageous, Paul," Nina said. "The man in the goatee wanted to see the hit happen, but he couldn't show up in a casino looking like himself if he works in the business. He might be recognized. Remember Al Otis?" She turned to Kenny and Jessie and explained, "I had a case when I first came to Tahoe which involved a card-counter named Al Otis who wore disguises into the casinos so he wouldn't be recognized and thrown out."

"Okay, maybe it's a disguise," Paul said. "But I repeat. Why did Atchison Potter have to die? Why kill him?"

"I can't imagine," Kenny said.

"Could our insider with the goatee," Nina said, "now this is going to sound far-fetched, but bear with me, could he be nuts enough to still be trying to get his hands on the jackpot money?" Confusion crowded out other thoughts. "But how would killing Potter help him do that?"

"Potter was holding the money hostage in court. Kill Potter, and the only remaining obstacle is Jessie," Paul said.

They all looked at Jessie.

"But then I've got the money. I'm hardly going to hand it over to someone," Jessie said, scowling.

"Remember, we're talking about someone we think has killed

three people," Paul said. "And tried to kill Kenny. I don't think he expects you to hand over the money. I don't think he's counting on that at all."

"You mean he would wait until I had the jackpot and then kill me? I'm not walking around with that kind of money on me."

"He might extort it," Nina said. "Threaten you or your family. Demand a ransom."

"For Gabe?" Agitated, Jessie leaned forward. "Don't even suggest such a thing!"

"You know what?" Paul said. "I don't think we can predict what this guy is planning, because there's a spontaneous quality behind these murders. Like the guy is making up his mind five minutes before he does it. But he does it execution-style. He's not getting pleasure out of it. He's coldly eliminating people. My take on this guy is—he's very narrow, very focused. Obsessed. He wants the jackpot money. He thinks the money is his. And by God, he's going to get it and nobody stays alive standing in his way. Unless . . ."

"Unless what, Paul," Nina asked.

"Unless Jessie is involved. Potter's death works to her advantage, no doubt about it. How about it, Jessie? Own any baseball hats?" Paul was half-kidding, but only half.

Jessie had fallen into a funk. She didn't lift her head or speak.

"Did you take the gun, Jessie?" Paul said. "If you did, tell us now and we'll try to help you. But by God, if you don't tell Nina now and you kept the gun, you'll have me to deal with."

Nina took a breath and held it.

Jessie got up and went to the window. She put her hand down flat on the windowsill and ran it along the paint. "I didn't take the gun," she said.

"Jessie, is there anything you want to talk to me about privately?" Nina asked the pensive figure at the window

Jessie turned around. "No," she said. "And the hell with you people if you don't believe me. Forget the jackpot. You know what? I'm going home to my baby." Slipping swiftly past Paul's chair, she went out the door, leaving the other three to their doubts and discomfort.

"Now see what you've done," Kenny said, eyes stuck on the doorway. "Everything was going along fine."

"What *I've* done?" Paul said. "This was your great hypothetical scheme."

"Paul," Nina said, "you are a fine detective. But now and then you throw out such an enormous blooper that I can only listen in awe."

"What's that supposed to mean?"

"You forgot that Jessie was eating dinner at Caesars with Kenny, not to mention Gabe and Dr. Jun, during the Potter shooting."

"Jesus," Paul said. "I did forget." He laughed, relieved.

"Three murders. The man in the goatee is still out there. He doesn't have his money. Not yet."

"Jessie!" Kenny came to life. "I don't think she should be alone with that guy out there. I've got to catch her." He slammed the lid of his computer shut and scuttled out the door.

"So much for science," Nina said. "He did have a lot to say before he rushed out. I think we're on the right track."

"He's more confident with Jessie. He's in love with her, isn't he?" Paul said.

"Sure looks like it."

"What does she feel for him?"

"She trusts him and I think she's impressed with his intelligence after all. But they don't have much in common."

"Neither do we."

"That doesn't stop us," Nina said. "Does it?"

"I don't know, Nina. Does it?"

"I don't know either."

"Stalemate. After this is over, I want something from you," Paul said.

"What?"

"A gift."

"Anything special?"

"Time. Undivided. Uncontested."

Paul didn't wait for her answer. He went out to rustle up some fresh coffee. While he was gone, Nina leaned back and put her feet up, scattering her messages, closing her eyes.

She imagined the scene in the casino just before Jessie sat down on the stool. Kemp playing to Kenny's right. Amanda Lewis on his left. The goateed man handing her money and finally wheeling her away. If only she could go back to that night, that moment, watch the people playing the Greed Machine, watch the forces set in motion, see it all. . . .

A thought came. "Oh, for Pete's sake," she said out loud. She sat up and smiled.

"Paul," she said when he returned, bearing two dripping mugs, "I've been thinking."

"Again? I turn my back on you for one second and you're up to your old tricks."

"No, listen, now. We need to figure out who the man in the goatee is. If he's Munzinger, we've got to get him stopped. And I've got an idea about that—about that man in the goatee. You know how we were saying he went into Prize's in disguise so that they wouldn't recognize him? Well, there's another good reason he might wear a disguise."

"Oh?" he said, baffled.

"And I think I know how we can get a look at the killer. Now, wouldn't that be handy?"

"How?"

"I'll tell you on the way," Nina said, pulling her cell phone out of the clutter on her desk and stowing it in her pocket.

Kenny found Jessie in the parking lot, rearranging boxes in the trunk of her car. "I'm getting so tired of not having a permanent residence. I hope this is all over soon," she said.

At that moment, Paul and Nina left the building. They waved, but hurried into Nina's Bronco and drove off.

"They know you didn't do it," Kenny told Jessie. "He apologized."

"They're like some old couple that does crossword puzzles together. Why don't they just get married?"

"They're not so old."

"Come on, he's at least forty. The way they're always finding a way to touch each other—what's holding them back?"

"I guess life can get pretty complicated by then."

"It's complicated now. I just had to get out of there. All this law stuff. I hate it."

"I'm glad you didn't leave without me," Kenny said. "You shouldn't be out here alone."

"I have a temper, don't I?"

"Yes."

"I'm a rough character."

"It's you. You're fiery. It's beautiful."

"You are so half-baked." She shoved a box to the back of the trunk. "You don't know how to censor yourself. You just blurt things out like a kid."

"Why shouldn't I tell you how I feel? When I lie awake at night dreaming of you, not the City, thinking of you and me and Gabe. Happy."

"Stop!"

"Do you have to leave right away?"

"You need a ride?"

"Yeah. I'd like to come back with you. I'll just be a minute. Lock up inside the car while I'm gone." He handed her the laptop.

"Don't be such a mother hen." But she slid into the driver's seat.

"Okay."

Kenny trotted back into the Starlake Building with his gym bag and into the bathroom at the end of the hall. On the way back to Jessie, he paused in the hallway and studied the black-and-white photographs of old Tahoe lining the walls, trying to steady his ragged breathing. He wanted her; he wanted to be with her, and he would run through fire for her if that's what it took. How would his mother advise him? "Don't scare her," she would say. "Go slow."

Jessie was watching the sky from inside the car. Kenny looked all around. Nobody. Afternoon clouds gathered behind the mountains.

"Last night," she said, "I saw Dan in my dream. I talked to him."

"What did he say?"

"He warned me about cold winds." She smiled. "I guess he noticed I'm not in Hawaii anymore."

He didn't want her thinking about Dan anymore. He wanted her absorbed with him, and he had a plan to make it happen, starting right now.

Jessie went on, "I'm satisfied. All I really cared about was showing everyone that I didn't kill Dan. And then Gabe got sick. I thought—I thought I might lose him too. But now, I'm sorry about Mr. Potter, but I just want to move on. I don't really care about the money. I can do the rest of what I want to do myself."

"Gabe's going to be big and healthy. He'll be an athlete like you."

"Yeah, I think he will. I said I don't care about the money. That was selfish. I do care about the money, 'cause I'd like you to get your share."

Kenny, staggered, thought, She cares about me. She does.

"Speaking of which, you changed your clothes. You don't look like yourself in those shorts."

He looked down. "My mother always says my knees are bony and my father says my legs are bowed. That's how they show their love for me."

"By criticizing?"

"By pointing out minor flaws. It serves two purposes. It keeps them humble, not having a perfect child, and keeps the gods from noticing how great I am so they won't swoop down and take me back. It's traditional behavior. Took me a long time to figure out what was going on. I thought they really cared about my knobby knees. You'll be amazed when you meet them. They sound like they hate me when they talk about me to other people. Actually it's the opposite. They dote on me."

"When I first met you, I thought—well, never mind."

"No. Come on. What did you think?"

"Well, I thought you were a boring little nerd." She laughed. "Sorry."

"I've been called worse. Actually, I am a boring little nerd. Where I went to school, it's practically a badge of honor. What do you think of me now?"

"I think—you have very knobby knees."

They both laughed.

"So why are you dressed like that?" Jessie asked.

"To go running."

"Is that why you wanted me to wait?"

"I wondered if you would come along, pace me to the lake? It's flat here and cooler than in the desert. You have a few more minutes, don't you?"

"When did you, master of all things mental, suddenly jump up and become a runner?" she asked.

"Because I want to be more than what I am. For you. I've never run before. Today's my first day," he admitted.

"Okay." Opening the back door of the car, she grabbed a sweatshirt and cinched it around her waist, then slung the rifle case across her back and slid a few bullets into her pocket. "It'll be just like being back in the Corps," she said. "Except the weapon's lighter. I'll teach you a really stupid song to keep you going. We'll be careful. Quick, before the rain comes."

28

RED COUNTED ON THE FACT that Donna always took off her wedding rings when she took a shower, leaving the single-carat diamond and the gold band on the brass tray on her bureau.

He could hear her in the bathroom right now, running the shower. She thought they were going to bed. She was, but he wasn't. He looked at the rings.

Their rings, really. He would borrow them, that's all. She'd have them back safe and sound the next day.

He stuck the rings into his pants pocket. If he didn't leave some kind of note, she might call the police. But what could he say?

He took a pen off the tray and found an old birthday card of Donna's on the bureau. On the back he wrote: Had to go out. Had to borrow rings. Don't worry.

What the fuck else was there to say? They would be back in her drawer by the end of the night, or they wouldn't and she'd pack up and—he'd win, that was all there was to it. He changed into his outfit in the garage so that he wouldn't disturb Donna, picking a spot near the back door where the floor remained relatively sanitary. Then he pushed the Harley outside and down the driveway until it was far enough away to start up. Nice house, only two years old, cathedral ceilings, grassy yard from Donna watering it all day. Three payments behind, just like the car.

He did the math as he got onto the Reno freeway. Ten thousand just to hang on. He had to hold out until the case went somewhere. A few days, max. The woman lawyer would figure out something, kick Riesner in the teeth.

He just couldn't believe how that smirking fool had stepped up in court to hold up the money the minute Potter went down. A shooting gallery! But he had dropped the gun in Potter's car, and, looking back, he was starting to realize that he had blown away three people.

This couldn't go on forever.

He had really thought whacking Potter would finally free up the money for Jessie. She was his horse, and he was helping her come in first. He sometimes imagined himself telling her everything he had done to help her win the case. But he could tell she was like all the rest—conventional, forehead-deep in the usual sanctimonious shit. She was just his horse, she didn't have to like it.

Now that the bourgeoisie were all safely tucked away in their subdivisions, eating healthy and watching TV, traffic was light on South Virginia. He pulled in on the outskirts of the gambling district to a place that stayed open until midnight. He pawned the wedding set.

Three hundred dollars! It was a pathetic stake, he knew that. But he was gripped by an overwhelming feeling that tonight was the night when it would all come together for him. He had done everything he could do to align the stars properly, that was for sure.

On the anonymous floor at the Reno Hilton, lots of kiddies who had stayed up late were hanging around the video arcade as he came in adjusting the goatee. The tables were hopping. For a few minutes he sauntered around, his excitement gearing up to racing speed, while he located the five-dollar minimum tables and previewed the dealers. He always went for the women because they were slower and just dealt the cards. Male dealers were full of themselves and possessive about the tables. Their egos spread out all over and made it hard for Red to catch the evanescent feeling that told him when to take a chance and bet big.

Tonight would be big. He felt luck sparking around him like electricity.

He sat down at first base at one of the tables and played a few hands, taking it easy, watching the girl shuffle her two decks, watching the old lady at his right cut the cards very deftly. She was at least seventy and by the looks of her had spent most of those years with a deck in hand. A young couple sat next to her, the boy making sure the girl didn't make any mistakes. Not a bad group.

Filled with pleasurable anticipation, heart thudding, he started slow with a five-dollar chip. The dealer handed him a ten and an eight and he stayed. Not a great hand, but that wasn't the question. The question was, how hot was she?

She pulled a hard seventeen and that was that. He stacked up the two chips and waited. Two jacks. Would she make twenty-one?

She busted. The golden feeling gathered around Red, pulsing. The whole table won. This was the night! But he stayed cool. Back to a single chip, still testing the cosmic flow.

She busted again to the sixteen he had decided not to draw to. That was it. He stacked up five chips, and she busted again. She was so stone cold she could keep ice cubes in her mouth. And she didn't seem to mind, she looked happy that the customers were winning. He liked that. He hoped she still had plenty of time on her shift.

Playing like that for half an hour, he won more often than not, and he stayed cool. When she clapped her hands and spread them so the cameras above could see they were empty and said good luck, Red took a break and counted up. He was up five hundred fifty and still hot. Feeling expansive, he passed her ten bucks before she left, basking in her smile and the "Thank you, sir" she gave him in return.

Roulette time. He had told Potter the truth. He loved roulette the best, though the wheel could be cruel and he knew the odds were bad. But it was so alluring, the silver ball spinning its way counter to the wheel, the people leaning forward to stack their chips, the croupier saying the phrases that had been said just that way for hundreds of years— he felt like James Bond, and the thought came into his head to bet it all on Three.

No!

A thrill burned through him like flames and his heart thumped but his fingers on the chips felt cool. He laid down his routine first bet, one five-dollar chip each on Red and Three and Odd. He forced himself to sit quietly, like he didn't care, like it was all for fun. The ball jumped in and out of the number notches . . . settled. Three!

Amazing!

He raked it in, thinking thirty-five to one made a hundred seventy-five for one five-dollar bet plus a few bucks extra for Red and Odd, licking his lower lip, wishing he had bet more, thinking, I am so hot right now, what now? How far could he go?

Then, in a kind of terror, he thought, How long? How long would it last? He needed ten thousand, then he definitely would walk out . . . he saw himself getting back onto his motorcycle with his wallet stuffed with hundreds, back to the pawnshop and stop at the Safeway on South Virginia, open all night. They would carry roses. . . .

He thought, I'm coming to the end of the line. But what line? What end? How far could he push all this?

He made a side bet with himself. Hit ten thousand tonight, and he wouldn't kill Riesner. He would forget about his jackpot, pay some bills, and cool it. Hear that, Lady Luck?

Let the silver ball decide.

With the wheel already spinning, he set down five chips on the Three, five chips on Red, five on Odd. The threesome next to him spread their dollars all over the board, diffusing the luck all over. He felt that terror-thrill, the sense of someone watching over him, deciding if he was worthy.

The ball dropped into the slot at Twenty. Black. Even.

Okay, let that be a lesson.

His hands trembling slightly, he set another five on Three and Red and Odd. You had to be consistent and go with the hunch and go big.

Twenty-four! All his chips were raked in.

He looked at his stash. He still had money. He was being tested, but he would show them what real gambling was.

He put ten on each. Three. Red. Odd.

"Two," the croupier called out. Reeling, Red saw all his chips on the board raked away again. It couldn't be! He couldn't turn cold that fast! He would force it. That was the only way. Bring it back, dare it to dissipate. He looked around him, suspicious, wondering if somebody was draining off his luck.

No, they were all losing. Ten dollars on Three, Red, Odd. He fucking lost again.

Three, Red, Odd. The wheel spun. He couldn't breathe. Terror gripped him.

He lost.

Furious, he threw chips out onto the board. Three, Red, Odd!

The ball dropped into Double Zero. Double Zero! The ball never dropped into that! Every chip on the board was raked away.

Sweat broke out all over him and he ripped off the jacket. "Get out of my way," he hissed to the woman standing next to him, her fat arm pressing against his shoulder. She jumped back at the sound of his voice, because he had become terrible. He was more angry than he had ever been in his life. Fate was going to take him to the ultimate place, where he had to risk it all.

"Take a break, buddy," said the red-faced man on his right. "The wheel's not going your way."

"Shut up or I'll shut you up," Red said. He could hardly remember the great mood he had just been in. He was in a battle with Fate now, and he had to stay on her, had to ride her all the way.

Looking at his chips, he expelled a sharp breath. The croupier set the silver ball in motion, saying, "Place your bets."

All the rest of it on Three, Red, Odd! All or nothing! Red would come through! It always had!

It was a courageous, magnificent gesture, bound to bring Fate back so he could mount her again, and his eyes focused with painful intensity on the ball whirling around like the thoughts in his brain. Around and around it goes, and where it stops . . .

The ball circled, spiraled downward.

But what if—he could lose everything! Red suddenly reached out and grabbed his chips, hasty fingers in his kid gloves making piles on Two, Black, Even.

"No more bets."

He was half fainting, holding the table to stay upright.

It bounced into the Two.

And bounced out.

"No!" Red yelled at it. But it bounced on, into the Fifteen, into the Thirty-two, and back around, like Hell was on its silver heels.

Past the Two. Into the Three.

And stuck there.

Red froze, stopped breathing.

"Three," the croupier said. "Red, Odd."

"It can't be! It's fixed!" Red said. The croupier looked at his assistant and they both looked at Red. Red saw that he was attracting attention. He couldn't attract attention. In a low voice he said, "Somebody nudged the table."

"Do you wish to make a complaint, sir?"

The bastard must have knocked against it somehow, seeing all of Red's heart and soul laid out on the table on Two. He would know how to do it. He had cheated Red out of his money and the bastard knew it. The croupier stood there, hand in the air, his eyebrow tipped into an inquiring look, the picture of polite courtesy, just waiting to see if Red would have the balls to call him on it.

Red got up. Pushing his way through the people watching, he ran down the red-carpeted aisles, outside into the night.

Rain splattered his clothes. He had lost it all. Every nickel. All!

He had to get some more money. He couldn't go home now. He hadn't been able to hold on, to ride her, because he hadn't had enough of a stake. It wasn't his fault. The ball was landing on Three right now, while he stood in the rain, impotent, drops streaming down his face which was screwed up like a boy who has just been told he can't have something that he wants very, very much.

Lost and lonely. Lost and lonely. Lost and lonely.

He sat down on the bike. Set the helmet on his head, fastened the strap. His hands gripped the handlebars. Where to?

He started the Harley up and soon realized he was heading out of town toward Tahoe. He didn't want to think anymore. He just let himself ride. Up he went into the dark Sierra, screeching around the curves, rain shooting around him and nobody on the road.

Something has to give! he thought. My money! He saw it, his millions, his intelligence behind that jackpot, and now another duck popping up with a long smirking face. Jeffrey Riesner. Red didn't know where he lived, but they had talked a few times at court and there was one thing he did know.

Riesner played poker at Prize's.

He had to go looking for him. He could get lucky again. Then Jessie, his long lean beautiful horse, would nose past all the others and he would ride Jessie to the finish, he would ride her hard and let her feel the whip and take his winnings and he would be the winner. The winner, never the loser—

Never the loser and never lonely. Never!

29

NINA MADE THE CALL AS they negotiated clots of traffic on the last block before Prize's. Cars in the opposite lane beamed headlights in their eyes as they passed, primed for the night's slick roads. For her second, lengthier call, she checked on Bob, who had already eaten and was playing African drum songs but had a lot to tell her about nevertheless. Most of what he said buried itself in the musical din.

She punched End. "Steve Rossmoor says that he'll have things ready when we arrive. He didn't want to do it, but we got lucky. Michelle was there. She insisted he help." She felt the twinge of a smile pulling her lips.

"Lucky us, with friends in such high places."

"One day I'll know everybody in this town," she said, taking a curve with one hand. Paul took the phone out of her other hand so that she could put both hands on the wheel. Traffic moved with funereal slowness through the dampening winds. She felt time pressing on her. A black knight was out there in the rain, a murderer.

"Everybody, including Jeff Riesner, unhappy ex-clients and assorted foes," Paul said. "And you'll have to have a book to keep the favors you owe even with the favors owed you. All part of living in a small town."

"I don't see things that way. Tahoe isn't a small town, anyway. Not with millions of tourists coming through every year."

She parked in the lot behind Prize's and zipped past the clanging bells and smoky metal smells of the casino, taking the elevator up to the penthouse, where Rossmoor had his offices.

Steve Rossmoor opened the door himself. Tanned, as always, slimmer than Nina remembered, he wore a spiffy gray suit only a shade darker than the texturally complicated, single-hued decor. She remembered Paul saying he came from East Coast money. He sure looked it. Dressy California style at this hour for businessmen would be tieless, a business shirt over clean jeans. "Sorry to bother you so late. Is Michelle still here?"

"She apologized for missing you. Said she'd give you a call soon."

"I'd like that."

"It's good to see you both again," he said. "Although, as I told Paul on the last occasion, it seems like bad news for me and my business every time I hear from either one of you. Maybe we can play tennis next time. Innocent fun for a change, eh?"

They walked into the suite and got the polite pleasantries out of the way quickly, admiring the drizzling view out of floor-to-ceiling windows.

"John Jovanic is keeping me posted on the court hearings. He knows you're here. He advised me not to show you these."

"Did he say why not?"

"You're not a friend of the casinos. But I can't see the harm in letting you see the tapes," Rossmoor said, "as long as they remain here in my office. I do have to insist on knowing why you want to see them so badly."

He gestured, and they sank into gray chenille chairs that faced a flat-screen hanging on the wall.

Rossmoor walked over to a glossy cherry cabinet and opened it. He held up three small cassettes.

"Three?" Paul asked.

"Only one is really excellent. The other two are less useful. The floor is extensively covered by cameras. Does that surprise you?"

"No," Paul said. "Makes sense."

"Your client chose a seat that is blocked somewhat by a pillar, making some of our other coverage ineffective. We're now looking at relocating that bank of machines. If, in fact, someone was trying to hide, that would be a good spot, considering the alternatives in that room.

"Of course, we had these jackpot tapes right at hand. The Nevada Gaming Control Board has copies, and so does Global Gaming. The people in both organizations and the police have already reviewed them and found nothing particularly enlightening, unless it is that our server was possibly overgenerous with the Buds that night when it came to a certain young Asian man."

Nina was disappointed. If neither the Gaming Control Board nor

Global Gaming had recognized the goateed man, how in the world could they?

"It's a long story," Paul said. "The abbreviated version is, we want to see someone who was standing near Nina's client right before she won the jackpot."

"Ah. You're interested in Charlie Kemp. But he left the stool before she arrived, as I recall. Some possible connection to his death?"

"Maybe. But it's not Kemp we want to see."

"No?"

"The man accompanying the girl in the wheelchair. That's who we need to look at."

"Why?"

Paul looked at Nina, who nodded slightly, then back at Rossmoor. "We have reason to believe he may be involved in Kemp's murder, among other things."

"Really," Rossmoor said. "Why do you think that?"

Paul gave him the severely edited version of their ruminations, leaving out their speculations about how the jackpot had been predicted.

"If you believe the jackpot was manipulated somehow, isn't that going to pose a problem for your client, Nina?"

Nina pitched in at this point, making her explanations without telling him much. A killer was out there, possibly planning another murder, that was what mattered right now, not the jackpot, not anything else. She explained that she didn't want to get into her legal strategy at this point, and didn't really expect grand results from viewing the tapes. She was operating on instinct.

Rossmoor shrugged and slid in the first tape. Nina opened a small notebook in her lap and got out a pen.

They watched all three tapes until Rossmoor was reduced to an ordinary, exhausted businessman snoring away in his chair, the shadows on his shaved cheeks suddenly darker, his silk tie askew. A dozen times, they ran back the sequence where the man in the leather jacket came up behind Amanda Lewis, the moment he pointed a finger at Kemp and said a short phrase. Although the tapes did have an audio track, the background noise of the casino made voices unintelligible.

"You were right," Paul said afterward to Nina. "Our man in the goatee was definitely avoiding being filmed. He moved with his back to the cameras more than would be normal without knowledge of the location of each and every one. What did you think?" They arrived back at the Bronco, wet and cold in the open lot. He unlocked Nina's door, then the driver's side, and got in.

"Disappointing." She scooted closer to him. "I only cared about one thing. I expected to recognize him."

"But you didn't."

"No. Did you notice anything?"

"No. Good try, though. Where to?" Paul asked.

She frowned. "Head back to the office, I guess." She smacked her hand down on the seat beside her. "I know you must be tired of hearing me say it, but will this guy go after Jessie or not?"

"I did notice one thing," Paul said. "Right about when he was straightening Amanda's sweater on the back of her chair."

"What?"

"His hands. Twitching as he watched the others play. Like he was just bustin' to get his hands on those machines."

"What about when he left Amanda and hit the machine two rows away? He lost hundreds in those couple of minutes. I stopped counting at two fifty."

"Yeah. He poured the money away, and he got angry about it. Remember? Holy shit, Nina."

"What?"

"Our man is a compulsive gambler."

"Keep going."

"His job that night was to keep an eye on Kemp. He shouldn't have let the guy out of his sight. Never! But he did! He wheeled her away just before Kemp got up!"

"Yes, I saw that."

"He rushed over to the machine where he had just lost the money and started playing it again. He was totally blind to what was happening with Kemp. He was completely wrapped up in that machine. Our man's got a problem, Nina. He literally couldn't help himself. He couldn't pull himself away, not even to ensure the biggest hit of his life."

"Kemp lost the jackpot. He must have been beyond anger," she said. "Anger at himself as well as Kemp. If he'd controlled his habit, stayed there and watched Kemp—"

"He wouldn't have blamed himself. He would have felt that he was a victim."

"So he started shooting whoever—whoever what, Paul? Whoever was keeping him from the money? I can understand Kemp, but not Amanda Lewis."

"But she knew he knew Kemp," Paul said. "Kenny heard him say something to Kemp. She heard it too."

"So he tried to kill Kenny. And he shot her."

"But not Jessie," Paul said. "No, she's under the protection of the gods. He's got some idea that as soon as she gets the money, it'll be his."

"He identifies with her. Or, no, Paul, it's more as if she belongs to him, because she holds the money. But how would he—"

"Get it from her? I doubt he thinks that far ahead," Paul said. "He sees an obstacle and he shoots it. He sees another obstacle, and—"

"But how could he have that gun!"

Paul shook his head, slammed his hand on the wheel. "Took it from my goddamn pocket that night. Touched me. Stole from me."

A creepy feeling came over Nina. "Paul, something happened today. I figured, and the killer must have figured too, that the money would now be freed up for Jessie. But a new—a new obstacle has appeared."

"I'm not following."

"We've had another change of fortunes. In the case. The money is still tied up. And our killer isn't much good at waiting around for the law to sort things out."

Paul said, "No. Not—tell me it isn't so. The killer won't go after . . ."

"He's in the way," Nina said.

"You really think so?"

"He's on the payline. He put himself there today."

"I can't believe it."

"We have to warn him."

"We could just go put our feet up. Would the legal profession really miss him?"

"At least we have to tell Cheney!"

"Let's not do it and say we did."

"Come on!"

Red pulled the Harley right up to the back door of Prize's and parked. They wouldn't ticket his bike tonight in this rain, the lazy bums. They would be taking it easy in some heated room somewhere, not out here worrying about a few stray vehicles. Hell, Prize's ought to be happy for the business on a night like this. They ought to be encouraging his business. Anyway, he didn't need long for what he had to do. Just lure Jeffrey Fucking Riesner outside into the night and kill him.

His long ride up into the mountains had changed his mood. He had ridden fast and taken chances. There was one moment there when, at fantastic speed, he had cut in front of a semi. The truck swerved, closely avoiding a jackknife, and Red had skidded so close to a cliff edge he had previewed a dark glimpse into the void to come, but luck was with him after all. He had survived to win another game.

So now he was experiencing a resurgence of the old confidence, flooded by the same rush of pleasure he felt when he was swept along on a winning streak. Whatever faint glimmerings of conscience he had he pushed back behind the much more brightly shining thought of the money to come. He could still pull this thing off, get the money, make it up to Donna. Really, it was so simple, it amazed him. In twenty minutes, hell, half that maybe, it would all be over.

Then the girl would roll over like a pussycat. She had a baby, he now knew, and no mother would risk losing her child over mere money.

He pushed the door to the casino open, breathed the heady mix of smoke, sweat, and metal, and stepped in, thinking he would stop first to wash the ride off his hands before replacing his leather gloves. He wanted to do this in an orderly fashion. He wanted to be prepared.

"Have we done our duty?" Paul said as they rushed along the slick black road away from the South Tahoe police station.

"Cheney said he'd call Riesner's house and have a talk with him," Nina said. "I think he understands." Her cell phone rang. "Hello?"

"I can't reach him," Cheney said. "His wife and kid were home and said he'd gone out, but she didn't know where. Any idea where he might be?"

"I sure don't hang out with him," Nina said. Then she remembered something Michelle Rossmoor had told her once. "He plays poker," she said. "I think he has a regular place but I can't remember where."

"I asked the wife if he might be out and about in the casino district," Cheney said. "Where else would a man be on a night like this? But she mumbled something about work. I called his private number at his office. He's not there."

"If I think of the place, I'll let you know," Nina said. She pushed closed the phone and looked at Paul, who was driving, appraisingly.

"Don't start. We've done more than enough," Paul said, eyes on the road.

"Cheney's not going to check from casino to casino for him," she said. "But it wouldn't take long. An hour or so. The district is small and compact. Caesars, Prize's, the Horizon, Bill's, the Lakeside, Harvey's, and Harrah's."

"It wouldn't be Bill's or the Lakeside," Paul said. "No good poker games there. Too small. Tell me again why we should ransack the casinos for him."

"Don't ask me," Nina said. "I can't stand him."

"Charlie Kemp. Amanda Lewis. Atchison Potter," Paul said. "Are we thinking straight here?"

"Sergeant Cheney seemed to think we weren't complete idiots."

"Who is it?" Paul said. "Munzinger? He stayed close to me that night. Jovanic gave me a bear hug at one point. That guy is a jolly green menace. Ully Miller, he was working the whole room. Andy Doig, I talked to him for half an hour in the corner, both of us trying to keep our eyelids open. Gary Gray. I don't remember much about him. He's—gray. It could have been any of them."

Nina grabbed his arm. "Pull over. I have to think. I remember something on the video that's coming back as we talk about these guys. Remember the biker, he's playing his slot machine on the video, pushing the buttons. And he's still wearing his gloves."

"Yeah. Which incidentally is screwing up the investigation, because he seems to wear them on his shooting sprees too."

"He wore gloves that night," Nina said. "The night of the jackpot. I shook hands with a man wearing gloves. But I was tired. Watch the road!"

"Think!"

"There were so many people. Do you remember anything like that?"

"I was staying in the background. I didn't get to all of them."

Nina clutched her head. "Which one? God, Paul, I can't remember!"

"It was Doig. Short, red-haired, he reaches out his hand—"

"No. He had a strong grip. I thought, He's compensating because he's not tall."

"Okay. It was Gray. He faded out of the woodwork and never said a thing."

"No. No, not Gray. It was Jovanic—"

"Jovanic?"

"—or, wait, it was Jovanic or Munzinger or maybe Miller. They came up in a group. It was one of them! Soft kid gloves that felt like skin."

"Which one? Take your time, take it easy. We're stopped. Here. Breathe deep a few times. Just sit still."

They sat in the bus lane on the bright casino strip, cars whipping by to Paul's left. She was still holding her head as if she could wrench the information out.

"Jovanic, or Munzinger, or Miller," she repeated. "One of them, but I just can't remember!"

"It's okay. Let's go looking for all of them."

30

PAUL SAID, AS THEY SAT in traffic, "We're just guessing."

"Right."

Maybe Riesner's in no danger. Maybe we ought to head straight back to my hotel room and forget about chasing around this forest of casinos."

"Look, we'll just find him and call Cheney. Let the police do what they are good at. We don't have to do anything except make sure he's safe for the moment."

Paul breathed deeply. "Okay, then. Let's get out the white horses and make like heroes, even though it's the last role I want to be playing tonight." A pause while he drove expertly around a fender-bender only to get stuck behind a long red light.

"Do you know why they use fruit and bars on the slots?" he said while they waited.

"No."

"Because in the olden days, paying money out was illegal. The bars were for gum. The cherries stood for fruit. And that was the payout."

"And back then, they didn't have all that sophisticated technology, and the reels hit randomly, too," Nina said.

"The past is always greener," Paul said, roaring forward as the light changed to favor them. "Back then they stuck wires up the pay slots, or played phony quarters."

"I swear I will never play another slot after this," Nina said.

"How much do you want to bet?"

She picked up the phone once again.

"Are you calling Cheney again?" Paul asked.

"No," she said, then, into the phone, "Sandy?"

"Whozzat," said Sandy's muffled voice.

"I'm sorry if I woke you, but I need help. I got to thinking about Jeff Riesner . . ."

"You do need help." The phone clattered and Nina imagined Sandy sitting up in bed. She wondered what Sandy's nightgown looked like.

"I remember hearing he plays poker," she said.

"Typical loser mentality."

"I wonder if maybe you know where."

"Yeah, I know where."

"Well, where?"

"It's after ten o'clock. Joseph works hard all day, and we were sound asleep. But you woke us up to find out where that man plays cards?"

"I have my reasons."

"No doubt," Sandy said, waiting to hear them.

Nina gave her the condensed version.

"Let me get this straight. You found someone willing to spare us the misery of his existence and you want to interfere? I'm still asleep. In a nightmare."

"You know we have to do something, Sandy."

"Bad idea. Bad, bad idea."

"Where does he play, Sandy? You have to tell me."

The phone went dead.

Nina called back. "Please don't kid around on this, Sandy."

"Kid!" Her voice was outraged. "I told you! I never kid!"

A murmur in the background. Nina waited, listening intently but unable to make out what was being said.

"That was Joseph," Sandy said. "He says I gotta tell you, that I can't mess around with his life just because that man should never have been born."

"Joseph's right. We don't have any right to judge Riesner."

Paul, listening, stifled a chuckle. Nina wagged a finger at him. Sandy snorted.

"Joseph says that man will answer to a higher justice, can you believe that? I say let's start with a whip to his rear end and move up from that point."

"Sandy, where does Riesner play poker?"

"I don't want to tell you."

"But you will. So tell me. Get back to sleep."

"Prize's. Oh, I'm gonna live to regret this. We both will."

"Kiss your husband for me, okay?" Nina said. "He's a good guy."

"Good or gullible?" Sandy said. "The jury's out."

Nina tapped the phone again. "Busy," she said, trying again.

"Who are you calling now?"

"Cheney. Let the police handle this."

But Cheney was out. She left a message on his voice mail and snapped the phone into her belt holder. "Okay, Paul, back to Prize's. Cheney won't be gone long, and he knows where we are going. We'll call again the minute we spot Riesner."

"This is stupid," Paul said. "Talk about going in circles. I want a drink."

"Pull in right there," Nina said, pointing at a space close to the back door. "Now, park and be good. You'll get your drink eventually."

"Thanks a bunch."

They walked from the parking lot straight through double glass doors into the casino. All around bells sounded, alarms, sirens, announcements, warnings.

Paul said, "The tintinnabulation of the bells. What a tale of bankruptcy their clamorous sound foretells."

Nina did not really expect to find Riesner but she had to make the effort. What she wouldn't give to shuffle guilt out of her life permanently. Tonight must be her punishment for something, for the pepper spray, perhaps: having to try to keep Jeff Riesner alive to try another case.

They checked the tables in the main casino but didn't see him or any other familiar faces, goateed or otherwise. "It's a short walk from here to a nightcap in my room," Paul said as they wandered around. "That's all you'll be allowed to wear. A nightcap."

"I'll have to take a taxi home."

Paul gave the main gaming room one last survey. "He's not here."

At Nina's request and against Paul's protests, they circuited the room twice more before landing back in the same spot.

"We should be thorough," Nina said.

"Maybe he isn't even playing tonight! Maybe he's hiking Tallac in the moonlight! Maybe he's pondering his sins in the chapel at the Hilton!"

"I really think he's here somewhere." She didn't want to say it, but she could feel Riesner and she could feel danger. The ringing bells were sounding warnings all around for her, and her nerves jangled in response.

"Let's go. We've wasted enough attention on him. We've done everything we could to find the bastard. Now he's on his own."

"Maybe there are special rooms for high rollers. I wouldn't know, never having been one."

"You know, Henry Miller once said that real antagonism is based on love. You think that's true?"

"Henry Miller made impressive bloopers now and then, too. I do not love Jeff Riesner. Are you nuts?"

"Then why are we doing this, Nina?"

She understood his perplexity but she couldn't explain. She couldn't bear the blight of another death. "Just a few more minutes."

He stood with his arms crossed, leaning against a corner slot machine.

"Let's just check for special rooms." She pulled on him. "Please. I don't want to face him alone."

He didn't budge.

"I need you."

His arms unfolded slowly and stretched. "Oh, you shameless devil woman."

Rather than begin by opening a hundred random doors on the main floor, they called Rossmoor's office. Steve was out, but an assistant was happy to tell them where to go to drop a few thousand bucks. The room was on the southeastern side of the building up five steps and through a set of unmarked doors. Five or six men perched at each table. Plenty of spectators surrounded them, wives, girlfriends, wannabe gamblers.

Nina saw him first, then Paul.

In casual Armani for a change, his sleek slacks falling into ironed pleats, Jeffrey Riesner sat at three o'clock from the dealer. A glance revealed a man having a good time, but a more incisive examination of his face and bearing told Nina that he was losing. He was unhappy. He was, if the short stack of chips left in front of him was any indication, about to be cleaned out.

"Let me talk to him," Nina said, watching Paul's temple throb at the sight of Riesner. "He doesn't seem to be in any immediate danger, and there's quite a crowd here. I'll just tell him what's going on and we can leave."

"I'll call Cheney and tell him we found him. Riesner's not going to listen to you."

"Good."

She came within five feet of Riesner before he noticed her. Knocking back a clear drink, he motioned for another, before turning slightly on his stool to say softly, "Get the fuck away from me, you unlucky bitch."

"I have to talk with you."

He turned back to his cards, laying three down for the dealer to re-place. He studied his new hand.

"It'll just take a minute."

He pushed a stack of red chips into the center, then a stack of white, and a small stack of blue. He ran his fingers through his hair, mussing the immaculate styling.

"Do you think I would come here if it wasn't an emergency?" Nina asked.

"Four kings," said the man across from Riesner, spreading his cards for all to see.

"Fuck," Riesner muttered.

"Listen," Nina started.

"Get the hell out of my face!" he cried, slamming his cards face-down on the table, whirling around to look at her. Indifferent to the as-tonished stares his shout generated, he tossed a few last chips at the dealer and stood up to leave.

Nina looked around for Paul, who had temporarily disappeared, maybe gone to find a pay phone, she realized, touching the cell phone on her belt. He didn't always carry his.

Riesner pushed past her violently, and made his way rapidly toward the exit.

"Wait!" she said, following him through the doors into the main part of the casino. But he was tall, with far longer legs, and was already yards ahead of her.

"Wait!" she shouted, but a jackpot hit somewhere, and the bells clanged. He went through the outside doors.

She ran after him.

What was this? Red thought, following his prey and the woman lawyer fast enough to stay close without being noticed. A tagalong. A complication.

He had patiently watched Jeff Riesner lose money steadily for al-most an hour. By his accounts, the lawyer had lost a sizable amount, possibly more than a few thousand, and he was a poor sport, who was playing the wrong game. His emotions showed in every thick twitch of the muscles on his neck. But he was an attorney, a mighty successful one from the looks of his clothing. He had had his chance to lose big, and win big. Now it was Red's turn.

Fortunately, some clown in bicycle gear was jumping up and down in excitement over a hit, a measly two thousand bucks, Red noted in passing swiftly through the main casino. Not even enough to buy Donna another one-carat ring. Her ring had originally cost him seven thousand. Jesus, for all the commotion, you would think he'd won a million! Some people had no sense of proportion. But the ringing and excitement had dual effects, preparing Red for what was to come by pumping up his heartbeat, and disguising his race through the casino to the parking lot.

He had his hand in his pocket on Donna's sharpest kitchen knife. Without a gun, he was forced to rely on primitive means, but he knew where to cut to make death come quick and to keep the blood off him.

If Jessie's lawyer got in the way, she'd go down also. A pity. Scenes of mayhem were not his bag in any way, but this might be his only chance in the foreseeable future to take Riesner down. He simply couldn't wait any longer.

Riesner had just stepped outside when Nina caught up to him. She was out of breath, panting, and so mad at him she couldn't see straight.

She punched him on the arm. "Listen to me, you idiot! There's a man who may be trying to kill you! I'm warning you . . ."

But Riesner had fixed on the slight blow to his arm. His hand flew out, grabbing her by the forearm.

"Ow," Nina said. "Let go!"

"What's this really about?" he asked. "Huh? Are you here to finish our unfinished business? Maybe now's the time to conduct it."

He clamped a hand on her breast. "No bag along, huh? No hidden weapons."

"Pay attention, you idiot—!" She looked up.

Crazy eyes under a baseball cap—a leather jacket—too small to be Jovanic—

But Riesner had glazed eyes only for her, all his fury wrapped up in that look.

"Look out!" she screamed. Using all her strength, she twisted her arm out of his grasp and pushed the astonished Riesner back into the casino.

Red couldn't believe it. He had thrown away his chance by being overeager, an amateur's error! He should have waited until they had gotten farther into the parking lot. . . .

Nina Reilly had recognized him. He was almost sure of it. That instant when she saw him had caused him to falter, and that hesitation had cost him the moment. Any doubt about what had to happen to her vaporized. She had to die. The smart thing would be to fade away into the dark forest of automobiles in the parking lot. He could lie in wait. But he was tired of waiting, primed perfectly with pills and alcohol to a lusty peak. A feeling washed over him. Compulsion, pulling him as strongly as the moon pulled the tides. He couldn't quit now. He was on the verge of the biggest jackpot of his life. He couldn't stop. He couldn't let go.

He could still win this. He was taking a big risk but he didn't care.

The key was speed. First Riesner, then the woman. Wham, bam, thank you ma'am, then exit. Like it was before, when he had killed Amanda and Potter, before the witnesses even registered what they saw. And what would they see? An alter ego, a phantom in a baseball cap and goatee. Plenty to talk about in his clothes and disguise, but not a thing to mark who he really was, not a thing.

Removing his gloves, he wiped his hands against his jeans and replaced them. He hurried up to the casino doors. He felt his fingers reach automatically out for the handle.

Just inside the doors, Riesner tried to shake Nina off him. "Are you crazy? You're assaulting me." He waved at the witnesses that were turning their eyes toward the two people raising such a ruckus in the doorway.

"We have to find the security police. Right now!" Nina said, pulling him.

He pushed her. She fell back against the wall.

Through blurry eyes, she saw him again, the man with the baseball cap, not running away into the darkness at all, but coming back through the double doors into the casino behind Riesner. Something glinted in his hand. Striking out with the speed of a snake, he reached out and grabbed Riesner's thinning hair and jerked his head back, so Nina could see his wide terrified eyes. The hand with the knife came up—

And Paul's hand, like a flat knife itself, cut upward. The man's arm flew up and he seemed to mount into the air, holding tight to the knife. Something small and white fell out of his pocket and skidded across the floor. Paul threw him onto the ground and stepped on his arm, which made the man emit a short scream of his own. Paul ground his shoe into the man's arm like he was stubbing out a cigarette, slowly and methodically, and the knife fell. The baseball cap rolled to a stop on the floor.

Paul bent down, pulled him up, and came up behind him in one seamless action. "Security!" he commanded, but the first two sturdy uniforms that materialized beside him were city police, followed closely by Sergeant Cheney.

Riesner had fallen onto the ground, where he lay with his cheek nestled into the garish pattern of the red carpet. He raised his head and put a hand on his neck. When he took it away, he stared at the blood and his eyes widened.

He saw Nina.

"You!" he said. "I'll have you arrested. . . ." But hands were pulling at him, pointing at the man with his hands behind his back, groaning. His jacket was still zipped up and he wore jeans and Nikes. His face was pale and something was wrong with his goatee. Paul had torn his goatee almost off, but there was no bleeding. The man's mouth opened in another groan and Nina saw the gap in the front teeth, the gap which she knew well.

She bent down and gingerly picked up the white container Ully Miller had dropped. Another weapon? Small, plastic—

Dental floss.

31

IF YOU DON'T LIKE SOMEBODY, but they do you a good turn, and you're a normal person, you tend to look upon them more softly. And if you don't like somebody, but you do them a good turn, same thing: You have a positive stake in this person.

But this is not the psychology of lawyers. In the psychology of lawyers, you have been one-upped in the former case, and you have kicked butt in the latter case. In neither situation does one party like the other party any better.

So it was that Jeff Riesner's first words to Nina at the meeting in her conference room that Friday were "Still in this dump, I see." He was resplendent in a shiny gray suit, no sign of the incident in the casino two days before except a Band-Aid on the left side of his neck where Ully Miller—or Ulrich Miller, as they called him in the papers—had begun to cut his throat.

As he pulled out one of the office chairs, which, true, were from Office Depot, on sale, guaranteed stackable, and sat gingerly down, Nina's impulse was to pour her hot double espresso over his head. But that would have been a waste of good espresso.

Was Riesner humiliated at being saved by Paul? No doubt. He hadn't thanked Paul yet, and he probably never would. Right now, Paul was on the road, driving back to the central Coast, to pick up the threads in Carmel.

He was gone. She couldn't think about that right now.

She snapped back into her focus on Riesner. Would he rather have been gutted like a snapper, murdered in full view of dozens of people?

Maybe so. At least he wouldn't be sitting here today, summoned by

Nina, who, having pepper-sprayed and mortified him, had called a meeting of casino officials that he could not avoid.

His unsurprising public reaction to all these latest events was to affect unruffled aplomb. His personal reaction had lodged like Ully Miller's knife somewhere between his corrupt black heart and slimy soul. He would not forget or forgive her for any of it, that she knew for sure.

John Jovanic laughed about something into his cell phone. Prince Hatfield, an ex-Nevada state senator, member of the Nevada Gaming Control Board, and Ully Miller's boss, sat next to him, trying to get comfortable in one chair when it would have taken two to hold his girth. And Thomas Munzinger, Global Gaming's vice president, he of the Marlboro Man face and the cowboy hat, was at the far end of the table. He was waiting.

"John," Riesner said, shaking hands across the crowded table. "Mr. Hatfield. Hello, Thomas."

Munzinger nodded, not a pleasant nod.

The second hand of the wall clock jigged past the twelve, signifying that it was ten A.M. exactly, and Munzinger said, "Let's get started." Jovanic murmured something and hung up. Nina sipped her coffee and wondered if she could carry it off. A year before, she would have been tongue-tied with anxiety, but she had changed. The men in the room seemed to sense this. Riesner was watching her uneasily.

"Gentlemen," she said, "thank you for coming. But where are your attorneys?"

"We've talked to our attorneys and decided to leave them behind today. We can handle this," said Jovanic.

Nina shrugged. "I won't take up much of your valuable time this morning. I have a press conference at eleven."

"And that's what this is all about," Munzinger said softly.

"Yes. I will be frank. I think you have a problem, and I think I have a solution.

"Your problem is that I am about to go on national television and discuss how Ulrich Miller knew the Greed Machine was going to hit. I am going to be asked about the random number generators, about the sevens on top of the line and below the line but hardly ever on the line, about the house percentages being carefully set in a nonrandom fashion, about the big spenders who can slip in their club cards and change the odds. And of course, about the nonrandom nature of the microchip in the high-jackpot slot machines.

"I am likely to be asked just how important slot machines are to the state of Nevada, and I will of course answer truthfully that slots are

Nevada's biggest industry. And I will be compelled to point out that in the case of this particular jackpot, all Mr. Miller did was predict the jackpot, not tamper with it. In other words, all he did was take advantage of the way the machine was already legally rigged by Global Gaming."

"That statement is actionable," John Jovanic began. He looked at Munzinger, who gave one short shake of his head. Jovanic sat back.

Munzinger said, "At the very least, he stole proprietary information from us to win a jackpot. That is illegal. Therefore the jackpot is void."

"I thought you would say that," Nina said. "In fact, let me try to state your position. It is that you are going to wait for Judge Amagosian to rule on the Writ of Execution, and then you are going to step in and void the jackpot if Jessie Potter wins the case. So she won't get the money anyway, at least without a formidable fight in court."

"There is still Mr. Riesner," Munzinger said. "He might win."

"There is still my fee," Riesner said at the same time. "Forty percent of the jackpot. That was the contingency agreement with Atchison Potter. I have a notarized retainer agreement."

"No doubt. Let's say Judge Amagosian decides in your favor. If you billed at a fair rate of, say, $200 per hour, your fee would be somewhere around ten thousand dollars. Of course, I'm being generous with that estimate. So if you win, Mr. Riesner, what happens to the jackpot? You're hoping that at the end you will be awarded almost three million dollars, and the rest will go to pay off Mr. Potter's margin calls. But the end will be a long way away for you."

"I have a contract," Riesner repeated to the whole table. He turned to Munzinger. "I practically got killed by your buddy Miller. He killed my client. I have suffered a lot of trauma. I am going to collect."

Munzinger ignored him. He said to Nina, "What is your proposition?"

"Simple," Nina said. "You gentlemen persuade Mr. Riesner to drop his claim, which will end the writ hearing and allow Mrs. Potter to take the jackpot. Sign a waiver of all claims against Mrs. Potter for the jackpot. After all, she is an innocent third party. Nobody is suggesting she had anything to do with Miller."

"And what do we get out of this mess?" Munzinger said.

"I'll have to cancel out of the press conference due to other commitments," Nina said. "And so will Kenny Leung, Mrs. Potter, and my staff. We will sign an agreement not to discuss this settlement of your potential claim against Mrs. Potter. At all. Including, of course, the microchip information."

"Most of what you plan to say is already public knowledge, available to anyone who reads the newspaper. And we can tie you up for a very long time, and probably get a gag order," Munzinger said.

"That's right," Riesner said. "Let's get real. My firm and the Gaming Control Board and Global Gaming—you are gonna get smashed so hard you'll wish you never took the bar."

"Maybe. But you may be surprised at the fight we'll put up. I'm betting we will win down the line," Nina said. "That's the alternative, and we'll beat you the hard way if it takes ten years, and we will get Mr. Riesner's fee knocked down to something reasonable, and I will ask for my attorney's fees ten years down the line. Meantime, the information about the slot machines will appear as major news all over the place, not just in the local papers, even if you get a gag order, leaked by persons unknown and unfindable by you. Bet on it."

"That boy, Kenny Leung, he's the smartest kid I've ever seen when it comes to computers," Prince Hatfield said thoughtfully. "I don't know if we ever would have known how Miller did it if you hadn't brought him to us yesterday. What's going on with Miller, Mrs. Reilly?"

"He's still being held at the Douglas County jail while the Nevada D.A. drafts up the murder charges," Nina said. "I wouldn't be surprised if he tries for an insanity defense."

"May we have a few minutes?" Munzinger said.

"We don't need a few minutes," Riesner said.

"Quiet, Jeff," Munzinger said.

"Of course." Nina got up. "Oh, one other thing," she said. "Part of any settlement among us. You gentlemen know Marlis Djina, the attorney who has been working with the Nevada Empowered Women's Project?"

John Jovanic said, "The Kiss My Foot campaign. The lawyer."

"That's right. You also agree to a one-inch-heel maximum for shoes for the cocktail waitresses at Prize's. No higher, unless the waitress wants it higher. The rest of the casinos that haven't already will fall in line."

She glided out. In the outer office Sandy was pretending to do some word processing. She straightened up and waggled an eyebrow. Nina put her finger to her lips. Then she went over to the wall and put her ear to it. It was cheap, paper-thin Sheetrock, not thick insulated paneling like the expensive office walls of Riesner and Munzinger.

She could hear perfectly.

Sandy couldn't stand it. She tiptoed over, as well as a person of her substance could tiptoe, and put her ear to the wall too.

"She's a menace," Riesner was telling the rest. "We need to teach her a lesson. She's lying. She couldn't hold on six months. I have a friend at her bank, and I happen to know she hasn't got squat for a bank account. She couldn't bankroll lunch at a deli."

Nina's eyes narrowed and she gritted her teeth. Sandy put a hand on her arm.

"The publicity could bring in federal regulators," Munzinger said. "They don't mind looking the other way as long as it stays quiet, but she's got CNN, Fox News, coming over here in half an hour. I heard 20/20 wants to do a story."

"No," a masculine voice said in horrified tones.

"It's all legal," Riesner went on. "20/20 already did a story, you remember, couple of years ago. And nobody cared. Why all the panic? It's all been legitimized in your own state supreme court, by your A.G.'s office. You're not gonna panic, are you? You think anybody's gonna care about this story? You think you're gonna lose one dollar of business? Think again. I've seen Reilly herself down there at Prize's tossing in the quarters, and she'll be there again come Saturday night."

"Maybe if you adjusted your fees some, Jeff, we could get her to cover them as part of the settlement," someone said. "My boss wants this over, and he told me not to take her to the wall. His wife was a client of hers. He has a soft spot." It was John Jovanic, so he must be talking about Steve Rossmoor, the manager of Prize's.

Ah. Thank you, Steve, Nina thought. So she did have a friend in the castle.

"Not gonna happen," Riesner said.

"You have the hots for this little gal, don't you, Jeff?" said a rumbling voice that could only belong to Prince Hatfield. "Makes you stubborn. Can't let her whup your ass. Will you take fifty thousand?"

"No!"

"And the continued association of Global Gaming with your partners for our business needs?" Munzinger said.

"Oh. Now I see it. You're gonna sacrifice me. The fatted calf—"

"Pretty lean at the moment," Prince Hatfield said. Nina and Sandy heard the jolly laughs in the background. "Fifty is better than nothing."

"You're making a big mistake," Riesner said. "You give her this, she's gonna think she can do anything in this town. You'll see her again. She'll sting you every time if you don't deal with her now."

"Float like a butterfly, sting like a bee," someone said. More laughter.

"What about the cocktail waitresses, John?" Prince Hatfield said. "The heel height for the cocktail servers?"

"You think it's a deal-breaker?" John Jovanic said. " 'Cuz if it's not legs, it's got to be tits, no offense to you ass men." More chuckles all around. Both Sandy and Nina gritted their teeth.

"I think we have about twenty minutes to get this contained," somebody said.

"Well," Jovanic said, "the club owners of the Northern Nevada Gambling Association have been discussing this at great length. And we already decided to let the girls lower the shoe height."

"Yeah? We're all gettin' pussy-whipped today," somebody said.

Jovanic said, "Uh huh. We're going to give 'em the low heels, but we're gonna lower the bustiers by an inch. All new costumes." Nina was pretty sure she was hearing some high fives in the conference room amid the general hilarity. "An inch for an inch," Jovanic said, all choked up with laughter.

"Okay, so we're all set," Prince Hatfield said.

"No way," Riesner said. "I haven't agreed to anything."

"Shut up, Jeff. Or we reduce your take to twenty thousand," Thomas Munzinger said. "Okay? We all set?" Murmurs of approbation. Nina and Sandy tiptoed quickly to the front of the office and Sandy slid into her seat. Nina looked over Sandy's shoulder at what Sandy was writing.

"@#%KJHCV:<?\," was all Sandy's neat letterhead paper said. The door opened. Nina assumed a face of extreme gravity.

"Please."

She followed the arm wave into the roomful of men, who seemed to her now like a bunch of the boys in high school she remembered. She sat down and folded her hands.

"In the interests of all of us getting back to work, we are going to accept your proposal," Thomas Munzinger said.

"Good move," Nina said.

"One caveat."

"Yes?"

"Mr. Riesner has indicated his willingness to reduce his fee to one hundred thousand dollars as his part in settling this matter. Now, that's very fair. Of course, the money would have to come from Mrs. Potter's winnings."

"Sorry," Nina said. "No deal."

"Seven million dollars and you're kicking about a hundred grand?" Prince Hatfield said.

"Not one dime out of my client's money for this asshole," Nina said.

They looked at each other. Riesner was, well, she thought, there was only one way to describe it.

Riesner was bullshit.

Jovanic looked to Munzinger. Munzinger looked to Prince Hatfield.

"Okay," Prince Hatfield said. "We'll cover his fee."

"I'll prepare the waiver and the settlement agreement," Nina said. "The documents will be faxed to you tomorrow." She stood up. "Thank you, gentlemen and Mr. Riesner," she said, and John Jovanic gave a hearty laugh.

"It's been a pleasure," he said.

The men filed out, shaking hands, except for Riesner, who gave an inarticulate growl and rushed out the door without talking to anybody.

They were gone. "Cancel the press conference, Sandy," Nina said. "The American public doesn't want to hear this anyway."

Sandy looked at her, a glint in the obsidian eyes.

"Well?" Nina said.

"I always said you had potential," Sandy said. "There were doubters, but I always thought you'd get good eventually."

"And I was good today," Nina said.

"Yeah, you were. You finally got good." The corner of her lip rose slightly.

"We've got court in the afternoon. We're going to get this case dismissed, so let's eat early, Sandy. I'm buying, and I'm thinking Mexican."

"You're always thinking Mexican." But she got up and picked up her purse and Nina grabbed her wallet. They walked across the street to the Mexican restaurant and Nina had a margarita. And she thought about all the misery of practicing law, but then she thought about the scene in her conference room that had just occurred, and it felt like this:

She had never had so much fun in her entire life. And she wasn't going to quit, because she had been made for this.

32

KENNY ASKED JESSIE TO COME with him to meet his parents.

"I don't want to meet them like this," she said in the car on the way over. "Can't we wait for a better time?"

There's no better time. The lunch crowd will be gone. They close for an hour about now to rest before the dinner rush. And don't worry." He patted her thigh. "They'll love you, I promise."

They parked close to the restaurant.

"Pink and red," Jessie said. "Bright."

"My mother's idea to attract the eye. Some people in the neighborhood think it's tacky, but Mom's right. No chance this business will recede tastefully into the forest."

A "closed" sign hung in the window. He used a key.

Waving at his sister, who was clearing some tables, he sat Jessie down at a large, curved red leatherette booth. Colleen came over to introduce herself, set cups around, and poured tea. A few minutes later, following further introductions, Kenny's parents were seated beside them, his father's face long, his mother's slightly alarmed.

"Where's Tan-Mo?" Kenny asked.

"Gone back to school. Oh," his father said nervously. "We need to speak to you about that, son."

"You need your money."

His parents glanced at Jessie. They looked deeply embarrassed.

"Don't worry. Jessie knows everything, all about how generous you've been. And I came here to pay you back today, with interest."

His parents beamed.

He told them almost all that had happened. The story took shape in his own mind as he told it to them, and as he spoke, leaving out the Glock but thinking about it, he saw that he had been about to kill himself over a fantasy. He stopped and bowed his head. But Jessie was there, and his family. He straightened up and went on.

Matt and his family waited at the dock, Matt bobbing in his new speedboat, the motor running. Troy and Brianna ran up to Bob, saying, "You're late!"

"My mom," Bob said. "She was busy."

It was the morning of the last day of July, full sun, the air thin and pure, the water calm, the mountains ringing the lake all blue. Overhead, lake gulls wheeled and dipped.

Andrea helped Nina sling the picnic basket into the boat. Nina took Matt's hand and got in, and the kids jumped in and sat in back where they could take the full force of the wind. Andrea was about to cast off the line when a big black pickup roared into the Ski Run Marina lot and stopped, the motor still running. Jessie Potter was driving. Kenny Leung was in the passenger seat. He held up a small face in the open window, grinning toothlessly. Gabe.

"I wanted to give you the key to the trailer," Jessie said, running up. "Glad I caught you." She passed over the keys and Nina stuck them in her pocket.

"Nice truck," Matt said. "I'm jealous."

"You like it? A Ford One-Fifty. Bought it yesterday. I'm going to use it in my gardening business." She grinned. "It's what I always wanted. Somehow, compared to trying to do something new and brilliant like Kenny did, or going back to college, it seemed like a tiny dream to start my own landscape design and contracting business. But Kenny and I talked, and he's right about something. It's all about taking risks, and dreaming dreams and making them real and to hell with logic! Kenny and I have so much to do. He's going to set up a Web site for me, a place where my clients can see their own properties come to life in 3-D. Right now, we're going to Reno to buy tools and some computer stuff."

"That's great," Nina said. "So, uh, how's it going with Kenny?"

"We're looking for a place to live. Has to be around Reno. There's some nice country out past Sparks along the river."

"You and Kenny?" Nina said.

Her healthy brown cheeks colored. "Me and Kenny." She nodded. "That's right. We're shooting for a real wedding someday. Soon, if Kenny gets his way, but we'll see. I promise, you'll be invited if that ever comes off. Meanwhile, we went and saw his parents last week, and he paid them back. Next week, he's cleaning out his condo in Mountain View."

"Congratulations," Andrea said. Jessie looked so strong and beautiful in her blue-striped shirt and tan shorts and hiking boots, and Kenny was hanging out the window now, helping the baby wave.

"Oh, and you probably don't know it yet." She was breathless with news and radiating happiness. "Kenny got a call yesterday. He went to talk to some people while I was out buying the truck. He lined up a great job working with computers in Reno. Isn't that great? Starts next week."

"Wonderful," Nina said.

"We owe it all to you," Jessie said. "The money's the smallest part of it. You gave me my integrity back and saved Gabe's life, maybe. This is for you." It was a small white box with a green ribbon around it. "Come on, the motor's running, open it!" Jessie cried, laughing. Nina pried off the ribbon and opened the lid. Inside under fluffy cotton was a thin gold chain. A golden charm dangled from it. Nina held it away from the sun, trying to get a good look at the charm.

"Why, it's a slot machine!" Andrea said. It was about an inch square, with a minuscule handle. Nina touched the handle with the tip of her finger and it clicked down. The reels moved and three gold stars popped up. A tiny bell jingled.

"It's a scream," Andrea said. "Look at this, kids!"

"It always comes up stars. You always win. It's for good luck," Jessie said.

"I love it," Nina said. Andrea helped her put it around her neck.

"Well, gotta go. Hope you're going to get a few days off. Coming!" she called to Gabe, who was starting to holler. She said, "Bye!" and ran back to the truck.

"Cast off, Andrea," Matt said. "Sit down, Nina."

"Just a second. Kenny! Hey!"

Kenny leaned back out the window.

"Good luck in your new job!"

"Thanks! Prince Hatfield said to say hello!" They were shouting to be heard over the motor.

"Who?"

"Prince Hatfield!"

"From the Gaming Control Board? When did you see him?"

"Yesterday! He's my new boss!"

Nina cupped an ear. She had sat down and Matt was moving slowly out.

"My new boss!" Kenny yelled, but it was faint on the wind. "I'm taking Miller's job!" He waved and the truck left.

"Uh oh, shoot," Nina said, dropping Jessie's gift box. The small carton disassembled. Below the cotton that had held the charm snuggled a folded piece of paper. "What's this?" She unfolded it.

A great big bonus check from Jessie. "For everything, with my thanks," said the memo line.

"Jackpot," Andrea said, peering over her shoulder at the amount. "Nina, I'm so glad for you! You are going to keep it?"

Nina put the check into her jacket pocket and zipped it tightly. "I certainly will, at least until Sandy gets her hands on it. Oh, Andrea! I can finally give Sandy a bonus."

Ahead of them, water and wind. Matt pulled back on the throttle and they roared out. Hitchcock dove to the floor and seemed to put his paws over his ears. Nina made sure she held his leash tight.

"Maybe she'll take a vacation," Andrea yelled over the engine. "Which you might find very restful!"

Nina pulled down her hat and hunkered down with the dog, laughing helplessly.

Clouds lay docile behind the mountains surrounded in blue as they cruised all the way across Lake Tahoe. The lake was so transparent Nina felt she could see a hundred feet down. At King's Beach they dropped anchor and laid out blankets on the beach for a picnic. Matt and the kids went for a walk and Andrea went looking for birds to photograph. Nina pulled off her shirt and lay back in the sun, falling promptly into a doze. All the events of the past weeks rose around her like sand castles, the endless jackpot night, Atchison Potter holding the baby in her office, Dr. Jun's testimony, the attack on Riesner at the casino, eavesdropping on the boys in the conference room . . .

She was sound asleep when Andrea tapped her shoulder and said, "Wake up, sleepyhead, time to go."

Bob sat up front with Matt on the way back so Matt could show him how to drive the boat. He took the wheel as they got closer to the shore and treated them to some fast water.

Nina watched Bob from the seat behind. His hair had grown out from the last buzz cut and it streamed in the wind. He wore sunglasses and kept his hands on the wheel, talking with Matt as they went.

She thought of Alex, and Alex's mother. Brave people.

I'm so lucky. So lucky to be here today with people I love, she thought.

They got in about five and tied up.

"Good work, lieutenant," Matt told Bob, giving him a soft sock on the chin. They gathered up the gear and Nina stashed the basket on the floor in the back of the Bronco.

"Come on over later if you want," Andrea called from their car. "It's Jet Li night around the old DVD."

"Can't," Nina said. "We're taking off. We'll be back in a few days. Or so."

Andrea came over to the Bronco and her practiced eye took in the backpacks in the back seat, the thermos, and the extra jackets.

"You're taking a vacation?" she said. "How'd you talk her into it, Bob?"

"It was her idea," Bob said, wiping sand off his feet with a towel.

"Let's roll," Nina said. Hitchcock jumped in and Bob climbed aboard and shut the passenger door. Andrea's eyebrows were up around her hairline.

"Where . . ." she began.

"I'll call," Nina said. She reversed, backed up, and bumped out of the lot, leaving Andrea staring after them.

"Mom?" They had just passed Echo Summit.

"Uh huh. Don't eat all those peanut butter crackers. You'll be hungry later."

"You sure this is a good idea?"

"I don't know, Bob."

"How long before we get there?"

"About five and a half hours."

"I guess this means you love him."

"No, it doesn't, honey."

"Well, what does it mean, that we're going to Carmel where Paul lives?"

"I don't know for sure," Nina said. "All I know is it's good to be alive."

Bob lowered the window to let his hand catch the breeze.

They rolled down the mountain, away from Tahoe.

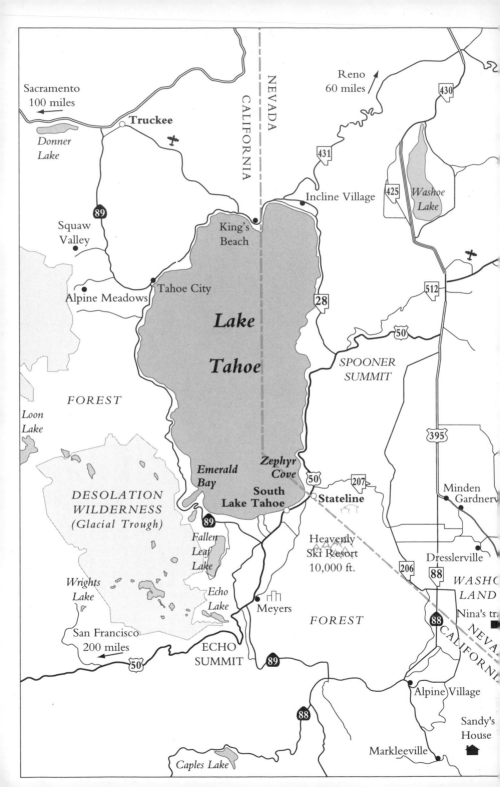